RIDERS OF
THE STORM

RIDERS OF THE STORM

Stratification #2

Julie E. Czerneda

DAW BOOKS, INC.

DONALD A. WOLLHEIM, FOUNDER

375 Hudson Street, New York, NY 10014

ELIZABETH R. WOLLHEIM
SHEILA E. GILBERT
PUBLISHERS

http://www.dawbooks.com

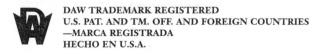

DAW TRADEMARK REGISTERED
U.S. PAT. AND TM. OFF. AND FOREIGN COUNTRIES
—MARCA REGISTRADA
HECHO EN U.S.A.

PRINTED IN THE U.S.A.

To Sheila E. Gilbert

There are people you can't imagine your life without, even though you'd never imagined them part of your life years ago. After all, what would a Canadian biologist and a New York editor have in common?

More than you'd think.

Certainly more than I thought, twenty-two years ago (oh, yes) when I sent out my first novel and began that dream. Sheila Gilbert, after all, of DAW, publisher of my favorite books. If our paths ever crossed, I hoped not to gibber like an idiot.

Fourteen years ago, we did speak. On the phone. Which she answered. Herself. Nothing's more terrifying on a cold call, believe me. The brain slides off the desk and lands with a splot. There was gibber. Eventually, as we worked by phone, fax, and e-mail, I became immune. Okay, no. I'd freeze at her name like a deer in the headlights.

I was on my second novel for Sheila when we met in the flesh. Huge hotel lobby, mass of intimidatingly famous sorts, and there she was, smiling at me. I couldn't believe my eyes. You see, I'd worked for years with a tiny, mind-like-a-steel-trap editor who knew everyone and everything in her field, had the work output of thirty normal beings, yet was incredibly gracious and easygoing in person. Sheila? Multiply all that.

I knew then I had a friend on my side, and there was nothing to fear but the writing itself. As I've aimed higher and wider with each book, Sheila believes in me before I do. If I soar a little too wide, I can trust her to swat.

What we have in common? A love of family, of the absurd and wonderful, of big ideas. Our labors together are marked by visits and long conversations, puzzles and DAW Dinners™, and by friendship. Sheila's part of my life.

Wasn't she always?

Acknowledgments

An even dozen!!! How fun is that? By such a number does a career continue, and I have many people who've helped both career and this book happen.

My thanks to the never-say-it-can't-be-done folks at DAW for the gorgeous presentation of this book. I'd like to thank Elizabeth Glover for her design and to mention, with hugs, Joshua Starr for his patience and helpfulness throughout. Luis Royo went the distance for this cover and, as always, it's exactly right. Thank you very much.

Several individuals, through their generosity at charity auctions and other functions, supplied names for characters in this book. I hope you enjoy! (There was no maiming.) My thanks to Cindy Raskin, Howard Slapcoff, Karina Sumner-Smith, and Kelly Scoffield.

These people kindly read manuscript for me: Timothy Bowie, Jana Paniccia, Jihane Billacois, Janet E. Chase, Ruth Stuart, and Shannan Palma. Suffice to say, the finished product is far better for their input. Thank you!

I've had wonderful hosts over the past year and would like to thank the concoms of Ad Astra, Eeriecon, and Polaris for their hospitality and support. My thanks to Donna Young of the Wright Center and all those who attended her marvelous educator's workshop in California. My special thanks to the many involved with LTUE, especially Charlie, Steve, Aleta, Zina, and Josh, for not only a great convention, but for saving me from that northern snowstorm.

My tenth anniversary contained special celebrations: a fabulous launch at Bakka-Phoenix Books (Toronto), a Science Alumni of Honor Award from the University of Waterloo ably hosted by Bonnie Fretz and Sharon McFarlanel, and the best-ever launch party/reception thrown by DAW at World Fantasy for myself and Kristen Britain. Good times!

Which reminds me. I'd like to acknowledge all those Newsgroup Friends who, aided and abetted by it's-never-enough Jana and whatever-you-need Roger, recorded a DVD of congratulations for that party. Yes, it makes me cry every single time. Fiends, the lot of you.

As our son reminds me, I need to write my Baker's Dozen novel next. Best get back to work.

Thank you!

Prelude

AN OUD DIED.
As was normal for its kind, this death took place somewhere dark, moist, and warm, where its naked remains would
decay to nourish those above. It was alone, also normal, for Oud
avoided those ill or wounded or otherwise infirm, even when
dying themselves. There were dwellers in the tunnels to take care
of any unable to reach a useful deathbed on their own. Nothing
would be wasted. All would be reshaped. It had always been thus
among Oud.

An Oud died. What was not normal for its kind was that it had
crawled and humped to its final resting place with ventral pouches
stuffed with treasures, instead of empty as was proper. Treasures
which were not Oud. For this Oud had touched the unknown and
Forbidden, sought answers only to find questions. Before the end,
it had learned certain truths about its world.

In death, it would keep them.

Chapter 1

ARYL SARC LAY AWAKE, disturbed by her cousin's weeping. Soft, the sound. Weary.

Without hope.

Not that Seru Parth was any different from the rest of Yena's exiles. Despair. Grief. Dread of this unfamiliar landscape. All were kept private behind the mind's shield; any needful tears hidden by truenight and a blanket's cover. None wished to burden the others, though they shared the same past and pain. Exiled by their own Clan, who themselves faced a chancy future. Forced to seek a new place to live, to survive on their own. No wonder some wept.

But all truenight?

Soft. Weary. Without hope.

Aryl abandoned the effort to sleep and sat up. She hugged her share of their blanket, careful not to pull it from her cousin, and gazed helplessly at the bump lying beside her. Seru had lost parents as well as home.

Hadn't they all?

She shivered. Each firstnight, as the sun left them, darkness moved up the mountain ridges like a swarm of shadow, consuming not only light but warmth. Their tiny fire gave the reassurance of a glow but never enough heat, not for twenty-three exhausted Om'ray. The Chosen and families huddled together, sleeping in their clothes and sharing blankets, always cold. Her nose, Aryl was sure, was permanently numb. Was it almost firstlight?

Unlike the others, Seru's weeping had only started last truenight. A few moments, a hiccup, then peace. This?

"Seru," Aryl whispered as quietly as possible. The bump didn't move. The sound of weeping didn't stop. She lowered her shields and *reached* ever-so-gently to let her inner sense seek the other's mind. *Cousin* . . . she began to send, then stopped, realizing what she felt.

No wonder Seru didn't respond. She was fast asleep.

With a sigh, Aryl laid down, pressing her forearm over her ear. Whatever dream troubled the other's rest was none of her business. They all needed sleep.

There were troubles enough ahead.

Could the exiles take to the air, their route would be a straight line over the mountain ridges that crested one after the other, each higher and more jagged than its predecessor. Sunlight flowed across bare rock, carving harsh, angled shadows that changed shape throughout the day. Clouds caught on the most distant ridge, as if its summit crushed the sky. A fitting end to the world, in Aryl's estimation, except that the world inconveniently extended beyond. Vyna and Rayna. Two more chances to find a home among their kind. And they couldn't fly.

Vyna was unknown. Its Om'ray could be *felt*, of course; they all knew exactly where it was. But could they get there? No one could recall a Vyna unChosen arriving on Passage, implying a barrier too difficult for Om'ray to cross isolated Vyna from the rest of Cersi.

Rayna was their best hope. It was also the nearest Clan to them, the lure of its hundreds of Om'ray like the warmth of the sun on cold cheeks. It wasn't right, for Om'ray to be separated. Aryl took comfort in every step closer.

Though there were, she thought wryly, a great many steps to go. To reach Rayna meant this too-slow march around the lowest reaches of the mountains. Part of the time, they walked across shadowed valleys. At others, they would top a rise and be able to gaze down toward Amna and Yena, see the broad, glittering darkness that severed the two: the Lay Swamp, here open to the sky. Herds of what Aryl guessed to be osst moved through its bent vegetation. Sometimes their deep grunts carried up on the night breeze, making her shudder. They belonged to the Tikitik. Not friends to Om'ray. Not friends at all.

The solid footing close to the mountains was the only choice. There was a road of sorts, winding with the ridges, if the word applied to an uneven trail free of worrisome boulders. The exiles took it, since it went the way they needed to go. Easier walking, maybe. Monotonous, definitely.

Aryl kept a worried eye on her cousin throughout the morning. During their daily march, Seru stayed back in the latter half of their group, seeming content with the Uruus family. She entertained their precocious daughter Ziba—surely a valuable service to all. Once in a while, the two burst into giggles, startling smiles from those nearby. Aryl might have dreamed the endless weeping.

She yawned. No. Hadn't slept enough to dream.

"Something wrong?"

Enris Mendolar, the only one of their company not of Yena, matched his pace to hers. Being a Tuana flatlander, he wasn't as light-footed or quick as the rest; being bigger than any, he could—and did—carry the heaviest pack with ease. Hardly older than she, he'd earned respect from all. Enris had risked his life to save them; his knowledge of similar landscapes helped guide them now. Dark hair, dark eyes, a powerful mind full of secrets. He laughed when she least expected it.

A stranger, by Om'ray terms. An eligible unChosen, as yet more interested in puzzles than any Chooser. Poor Seru had learned not to cast longing looks his way across the evening fire.

A friend to whom Aryl could speak her mind without fear. She looked up with a small frown. "Wrong? Tell me what isn't." She gestured to the ridge that loomed beside them. "Rocks that hunt." Another to the dome of sky above, still strange to the younger Yena. "No shelter." She finished by patting the rope wound around her flat stomach. "Should I mention food?"

That laugh, deep and amused. "Please don't. I'm fading away."

She didn't point out that there was more flesh on his bones than on any Yena. It was, she knew, not the Tuana's fault. They'd been the ones living with starvation. She couldn't remember the last time she'd eaten her fill without thought to the next day. The Grona had given the Yena a feast—she hadn't been the only one to tuck excess in her pockets. "We've Grona bread," she reminded Enris.

They'd left Grona Clan with high spirits, full if not of hope, then the determination to find some. Before leaving, the other exiles had filled packs with supplies, Grona obliged to be generous to those on Passage, even if these were the most unlikely travelers. After three days on this road, Aryl knew she wasn't the only one to put away most of her ration. This terrain was barren; a barrier to life, she decided, rather than home for it. The grove was a distant line of lush green within the Lay, tempting their eyes.

It wasn't safe. By day, Tikitik would be watching for them. By truenight?

Truenight in the mountains might be cold but, away from the rock hunters, it was safe. The same could never be said of the canopy. The towering groves of rastis and nekis were home to myriad forms of life, most, in Aryl's experience, fond of Om'ray flesh, while the black waters of the Lay held the swarms that climbed by truenight to hunt. To be caught away from light by those was to be eaten before you died.

"We aren't thirsty," Enris commented.

Aryl grimaced, her feet damp from crossing the last mountain torrent. More strangeness. Where did it come from, without rain? Why was the water numbingly cold no matter if the day warmed? The Tuana's thick boots at last made sense. Haxel, being no fool, had obtained a similar pair before leaving Grona, as had a few of the others. Her own departure had been more abrupt. Remembering turned her grimace into a real frown.

"Do you feel it? There are Grona away from their village."

"Fields," Enris said mildly. "Grains and other crops to reap. They aren't following us."

"They" being Bern and his Chosen, the Adept Oran di Caraat. The two were why the exiles were again without a home. Oran had wanted Aryl's ability to access the *other place*, to move through its darkness at will. A new Talent, barely under her control, not ready to be shared. A Talent fraught with danger to the user, let alone all Om'ray.

For Cersi, this world, was held in peace by the Agreement. What was, should remain. Change, significant and sudden, in Tikitik, Oud, or Om'ray, would break that Agreement. The consequence? Aryl was quite sure Oran di Caraat didn't worry about that, safe in her stony village.

She did. So did those with her.

"I could find out."

A sharp look. Enris knew what she meant. Aryl had the Talent to *reach* and learn identity. It took Power. "Too risky." He scuffed the toe of his boot, raising a puff of dust. "See?"

She dutifully stared down at the road. "See what?"

Haxel Vendan glanced over her shoulder. "Oud. Their machines crush the small stones to powder."

"Exactly," Enris said with a nod to the First Scout. "This is their road, not Om'ray. No recent tread marks, maybe, but—" he shrugged, the motion letting him adjust the pack on his shoulders. "It's not worth the risk. Trust me. Unless necessary, don't use Power where they might be close."

By close, he meant under their feet. Oud tunneled. Aryl wasn't sure what a tunnel would be like; she was sure she didn't want to find out. Nor was she anxious to find out for herself what he meant by "risk," though others among the exiles had also heard of this peculiarity of Oud, that a few had minds that interfered—painfully—with an Om'ray's natural ability if used.

Having joined their conversation, Haxel paused to let them catch up. They moved through this unfamiliar territory with their strongest members to the fore and rear. The First Scout and Syb sud Uruus led the way, with Aryl and Enris next. Rorn sud Vendan, Haxel's Chosen, came last with the Kessa'ats, Veca and Tilip, as well as Ael sud Sarc. The four eldest, the children, and pregnant Juo Vendan stayed in the midst with the others.

Their only Looker, Weth Teerac, had left a tenth earlier, at firstlight. What her Talent could find out of place in a land none of them had seen before, no one knew. But it was a precaution, of sorts, against being surprised.

"Good advice," the First Scout asserted. "Besides, the Grona walk like him. We'd hear those big feet long before being in sight."

Enris chuckled, not denying it. Even in the same kind of boots, Yena were a great deal quieter.

"Besides," continued the scout, her wicked grin twisting the scar that ran from cheek to eyebrow, "who'd follow us? One of their unChosen lusting for our Seru? Hah! Bunch of diggers. Not one looked worth feeding. She's a Parth. She can wait for better." This with a meaningful glance at Enris, who smiled. Haxel laughed, then lengthened her stride to rejoin Syb at the front.

The Tuana raised one eyebrow. "Should I be flattered or insulted?"

Aryl ignored him. The other problem with this too-flat road was time to think—too much of it. "Oran could have told all of Grona by now."

"She could," Enris agreed. "But she won't. I know her kind.

They don't share secrets—not when there's some advantage. Relax, Aryl."

She tightened her shields, her cheeks growing warm despite the chill breeze that fingered its way past her hood. Enris didn't mean her. It didn't change anything. She hadn't shared her secret, hadn't explained to the others why she'd fled Grona with only the clothes she wore, without a word to anyone.

She must. She would. When the time was right. Each 'night, they crowded together, exhausted and worn, staring at a fire smaller than two fists. Yena nerves twitched to the darkness; children whimpered. She couldn't bring herself to add to their burden.

Only Enris knew the whole truth. He'd left it for her to decide when and what to share. He'd told her people Bern and Oran had made it impossible for her to stay in Grona. The other exiles had followed without hesitation. She owed him for that. She owed them all.

She would find them shelter and food, make them safe.

Then find a way to tell them all this was her fault.

Aryl removed her boots and turned them upside down. Water gushed out, then settled into a steady drip. The stone underfoot was warm, for once; the sun high overhead. No biters or flitters. They were, as far as she could tell, the only living things in this desolate place. Unless she counted the occasional wispy clump of dried vegetation, none of it more than ankle-high.

She wasn't the only one dealing with the aftermath of their latest crossing. The mountain river had been shallow, but so white with froth there'd been no telling where best to step. Or not step. Enris, who professed to love the noisy, annoying streams, had managed to soak his feet this time as well. Aryl lowered her head to grin.

Some of the exiles took advantage of the respite to lay wet clothing out to dry. They'd learned the hard way how quickly it chilled the skin beneath. On that thought, Aryl untied her leg wraps and squeezed them to merely damp, then spread the gauze strips over a dark flat rock. Bare, her shins and ankles showed the cost of a moment's carelessness: the pink of new scars showed where her flesh had fed the swarm. No swarm here.

She grabbed a pair of small stones, then stared at them, her skin crawling.

There were other threats.

Feeling the fool, Aryl flattened her palms to give each stone a chance to move, if it was so inclined.

Being ordinary matter, they did nothing of the kind.

She used them to weigh down her wraps, in case the breeze kicked up. Better safe than supper, she consoled herself. She'd shared her memories of the rock hunters with Haxel and the others. The Grona spoke of them, too, but claimed the bizarre creatures stayed to uncivilized slopes, where they could hide among the real thing. Camouflage was their only weapon; they moved too slowly to catch living prey. So Grona believed.

Grona believed truenight was safe, too.

Aryl decided she wasn't wrong to be wary of loose rock.

After consideration, she kept on her longest coat. The hem might drip, but the sun wasn't that warm.

Beside her, Chaun sud Teerac slowly straightened to look into the distance, a smile lighting his face. She followed his gaze and saw a figure appear at the rise of the next hill. It would be Weth, his Chosen.

Who was walking toward them. Quickly.

All the exiles rose to their feet, clothing forgotten. "What's brought her back?" Haxel said for all, and strode off to meet their guide, collecting Ael and Syb—and their longknives— with a look.

"She's found it, hasn't she?" Seru came to stand close to Aryl, arms wrapped around her middle. Her hood was down and hair escaped its net, black strands playing against her too-pale cheeks, catching on the cracks of her lips. They all suffered in the dry cold air, soaked feet and legs notwithstanding. "I knew it would be soon."

"What are you talking about?" Remembering how her cousin had wept in her sleep, Aryl gentled her tone. "Found what?"

Seru's green eyes were huge and unfocused. "Where they died."

Who? For an instant, Aryl couldn't answer, her mind racing through possibilities. There had been Yena unChosen sent on Passage. A couple had taken this route. She didn't know if they'd survived it.

Or had Seru talked to Grona Om'ray, heard of a misadventure of that Clan? Or . . . "Who?" she asked, staring at her cousin. "Who died?"

"Sona." Quick and certain, Seru hesitated then, licked her lower lip before taking it between her teeth. "It's a name," she said at last, looking directly at Aryl. "Of something. I don't know what. I don't know how I know, Aryl. I don't!"

"Sona" meant nothing to Aryl. What did was the stricken look on her cousin's face. "It's all right, Seru," she soothed, mystified. "You've been having bad dreams. That's probably what it was. A dream."

"No." Seru's chin trembled. "We're getting closer with every step, Aryl. Closer to where they died! All of them died!! It's dangerous here! We have to turn around. You have to believe me!"

They had an audience; there was no avoiding it. The other exiles granted them a semblance of privacy by a sudden interest in drying boots and clothes. Enris, who sat near enough to hear every word, gave Seru a pitying look before turning away.

She noticed. Her small frame straightened within its burden of heavy Grona clothing, and she blinked as if to fight back tears. Stung, Aryl touched her cousin's hand. *He doesn't know you as I do,* she *sent,* tight and private. And it was true. Power and Talent weren't the only strengths an Om'ray could possess.

I don't know how I know. Repeated mind-to-mind, the words

came laced with dread. *I feel—I feel them die, Aryl. I hear your voice and their screams at the same time. I—* Seru rubbed her arms vigorously. "I hurt with their pain."

Aryl's fingers left her cousin's hand, curled to meet her palm. The exotic Power of a Chooser, Seru's longing, her *need*. Easy to sense that, too. The disinterest of the only candidate for her Choice had to be a torment. The instinct consumed Seru from within, fought her valiant effort to restrain her Call and save her strength for the march.

For how long? A Chooser could wait, sometimes must wait, but there was always Choice. Wasn't there? She remembered a story, one of the glowlight scares for those too young to understand its true horror, about a Yena Chooser denied Choice. Her drive faded, then left. Her immature body remained as it was, infertile and barren, her mind partnerless and alone. One day she'd walked into a stitler's trap, and no one believed she'd been careless.

Not Seru, Aryl vowed to herself. She would have a future. Parth would have a future.

All of Yena's families would survive.

"I'll see what Weth found," she promised aloud, her voice steadier than she'd expected. She eyed her still-damp wraps with distaste and left them, grabbed her wet boots, and forced them on with a grimace. "Go tell Myris what you've told me." When there was no reply, she glanced up, not surprised to see her cousin's face had clouded. Aryl knew that stubborn look. "Please," she said softly, tying her laces.

"There's nothing wrong with me." Each word flat and hard.

"I didn't say there was. Myris isn't a Healer." But they both knew their aunt could ease the emotions of close kin. Worth a try, as far as Aryl was concerned. Maybe Myris could calm Seru, stop her dreams from affecting her while awake. At least keep her quiet. They had no Adepts of their own; no one who could repair a mind or protect the rest of them from its failure. "She's wise, that's all," Aryl said with care. "She might help you understand—"

"Understand what?" Seru scowled. "I'm not imagining this, Aryl. You think because my Power's less than yours, I don't know how to use it. I do. I have to. I've always had to. That's why I know this is real. Sona died." Her cousin stopped, her head rising to stare up the rise where Weth was now talking to Haxel. "Om'ray died. That's what you'll see."

Enris squatted at the near edge. Aryl noticed his hand hovered over the disturbed ground but didn't touch it. "Oud," he said at last, then turned his head to spit eloquently.

In disbelief, she stared at what should have been the road across the next valley floor. Should have been. From their feet—at the base of the hill Weth had climbed to meet them— to where it curved to disappear past the next abrupt rise of rock, the ground was no longer flat. Instead, its surface heaved and sank as if stone had momentarily become water, leaving ripples that grew in size toward the middle of the valley. The largest were, she estimated, more than two Om'ray high. Difficult obstacles, Yena or not. Worse, the footing between looked soft and treacherous. The disturbance stretched to either side, filling the valley.

They couldn't go this way.

"How?" Haxel asked, also staring ahead. "How did they do it?"

Enris rose to his feet. "Does it matter?" He brushed dust from his legs. "The reshaping was long ago. See the plants? The weathering on exposed rock? They're done. For now."

He spoke casually, but Aryl caught something restrained in his manner, a new tension. She was tempted to lower her shields and *reach* to him, but didn't. Even if manners seemed less important in this wild place, Haxel would likely notice.

"We can go around it," Weth offered. Leri's cousin, of the same height and slender frame but, unlike other Teeracs, her eyebrows and hair almost white against her tan skin. As with other Lookers Aryl knew, she was visibly restless, her eyes flicking from side to side as often as they fixed on someone else, her body tense, its weight shifting from one foot to the other. Possessed of an uncomfortable Talent, a Looker was alarmed by physical change in a remembered place. A band of tightly woven cloth hung from her neck, a blindfold Weth would use if confronted by too much change, too quickly. Her visual memory was so precise, she could close her eyes to retrace her own steps, and often did, as if memory was more trustworthy.

Aryl shaded her eyes with one hand, studying their options. Haxel, Syb, and Ael did the same. Enris didn't appear interested. He tossed a handful of dirt into the wind, then stared into the distance toward their goal, making a soft, irritating whistle between his teeth.

She ignored him. Weth was right. They could move along the slope of the ridge. Though wide, the disturbance created by the Oud didn't appear to extend all the way up the valley. Disturbing, to think the creatures might have focused their destruction on the road itself, as if to cut off movement in this direction. Why? Aryl couldn't forget Seru's feeling about this place. Had someone—or several someones—died when the Oud struck?

If so, how had her cousin known?

As for the other choice? This valley, like the others they'd passed, opened its mouth to the Lay Swamp. Cutting close to that dangerous shoreline would expose them to any Tikitik riding in the shallows. Worse, they'd have to be away from it before truenight, or face what might come out to hunt.

Aryl squinted up the valley again. Rock, rock, and more rock. Difficult and exhausting to climb. There was no way to know how much the detour would delay their crossing.

Or, she shuddered inwardly, if there were hunters hiding amid the rubble.

Ael spoke up. "Syb and I can take one route each. Report back—"

"We stay together," Aryl countered without thinking, then

gestured a hasty apology to Haxel. The First Scout led in this wilderness; she hadn't meant to usurp her authority.

She didn't want any.

Haxel merely raised an eyebrow, stretching her scar. "We've another problem, don't we, Tuana?"

The whistle ended. Enris tipped his head at the mountain ridge ahead of them, its top edge cloaked, as always, in heavy cloud. "Only if we're caught in the open."

"There's nothing but open," Haxel pointed out. "Such clouds on a changing wind mean an early winter storm," she clarified for the rest of them. "A hazard Grona's excuse for a First Scout did know. Enris is right. We'll need shelter before it hits. That's the priority."

"Winter? Will the water turn hard, like wood? The Grona said that's what happens." Syb was clearly entranced by the possibility. Aryl shivered. Water should behave like water, in her opinion.

"Not these streams." Enris sounded sure. "But there'll be a nasty bite to that wind soon. It's going to get cold."

Get cold? Aryl's legs were almost numb below the hem of her coat. "We could make a shelter," she suggested. "Pile rocks into walls, like the Grona do. Use blankets to fill any gaps, shield a fire—" If they could find anything to burn, she reminded herself. Everyone collected what dry vegetation they found as they walked. Twisted into compact knots, each day's gleaning barely let them heat water and light the way to their blankets. That trick . . . how to dig holes for their waste— there being no convenient swamp below . . . sharing their body warmth? All from Enris. She didn't doubt him. None of them did.

"Good idea—if we had bigger rocks or a cave." Haxel gazed up the valley for a long moment, her face expressionless, then looked over her shoulder at them. "That way."

"Up there? What we'll find are rocks to eat us in our sleep." Nothing could be trusted, Aryl thought. Not the ground. Not even the sky.

Haxel's scar twisted with her fierce grin. "One threat at a time. We'll go ahead. Find and prepare a shelter. You and Enris get them moving and follow as quickly as you can."

Decision made, the First Scout broke into an easy run, Weth, Syb, and Ael keeping pace. The wraps on their long legs flashed white as they ran parallel to the ridge, then, without slowing, up its slope to avoid the disturbed ground of the valley floor.

Aryl blew out a breath. "She didn't listen."

"She did," the Tuana said with a hint of his deep laugh. "Ravenous rocks or not, we don't have a choice." He put one big hand on her shoulder and turned her to face the ridge and its shroud of dirty white. "See what looks like mist dropping below the clouds? That's snow, Aryl."

Young Grona had excited Ziba beyond measure with their tales of playing in the fluffy stuff. "I've heard of it," said Aryl impatiently. "Frozen water. So what?" Hadn't she witnessed Enris' dismay at a little rain in the canopy? Om'ray like Tuana and Grona probably ducked inside their homes if the weather was anything but perfect. He'd learn. "We'll manage."

"Snow can be deadly." No laughter in his face now. "It can fill the air so we won't be able to see each other, let alone where we're going. Or," Enris hesitated, then went on, his voice grim, "it could be worse."

"Worse?"

"Winter storms from the mountains sometimes reach the edges of Tuana. What falls from them this early isn't snow. It's rain, a hard rain that coats whatever it touches in ice. Imagine being cold, blind, and unable to take a step without falling—"

"Yena," Aryl said stiffly, "don't fall."

"Yena haven't met winter." His grip became a push. "Let's get the others."

The click and rattle of disturbed pebbles. A deep breath of effort. The creak of a rope strap over a shoulder. Otherwise, the

exiles were silent as they made their way along the lower slope
of the ridge. Though Aryl kept close to her cousin when they'd
first come over the rise, Seru had said nothing more, her face
set and grim. Even Ziba remained hushed, making Aryl realize
how much cheer her lively babble had added to their journey.
She didn't blame the others, feeling the same. It was hard to
find words, faced with the evidence of a force that could stir
rock the way an Om'ray might a bowl of dresel.

The storm that so alarmed Enris and Haxel kept its distance.
Or, she thought anxiously, her gaze slipping up the mountain
to the torn edge of cloud, distance lied. The blue of the sky had
turned pale and the sun's power to warm was gone.

The exiles moved silently, but quickly. The more rugged terrain suited the Yena as the flat road hadn't. They leaped over
small gulleys and cracks instead of wading through the inevitable small stream, and ran up or down any vertical rise
worth the effort, rarely touching the gray-and-russet rock with
their hands.

Enris let them, choosing his path by flatlander criteria.
Though he made what speed he could, he soon fell behind.
He'd wave nonchalantly whenever she stopped to look back. At
times, he was out of sight.

Aryl didn't like it.

When she next looked for the Tuana, Cetto sud Teerac
paused with her on the ledge. "We should have split his load,"
the former Yena Councillor commented in his bone-deep
voice. "That pack would do three."

"It's not the weight." Aryl tapped her toe on the rock. "It's
the height. He doesn't like it."

"Ah." Cetto hopped down, nimble as Ziba despite being the
oldest of them. "Not much we can do about that, is there?"

She could wish Enris less stubborn, Aryl thought, but to herself.

Something cold touched her cheek. She brought up her
hand in surprise, bringing away a drop of water. A fleck of
white, like the fluff around some seeds, landed on her open

palm. It collapsed on itself, becoming another drop. When she looked out over the valley, she discovered that view now obscured by an oddly bright mist. Snow?

The others had come to a halt where they were, hands outstretched to intercept their own snowdrops. It wasn't easy. Wind followed the snow, tossing it up, spinning it around.

Much more, she realized, and Enris would be right. It was already confusing to look through the falling stuff over any distance. If it became thicker and continued to swirl in their faces, they'd be in trouble. At that worry, Aryl *sent* to the rest. *Stay close together,* she sent, pouring strength into the warning. *If it gets worse, move slowly and with care.*

Along with the sense of disquiet and firm agreement from all around, a wry amusement touched her mind. *Like me?*

Busy licking a snowdrop from her lips, Aryl didn't answer.

Slow and careful didn't send the exiles to Enris' flatter ground. Instead of moving independently, they tightened their group so that a couple chose the safest path for all, the Yena way when traversing a dangerous section of canopy. Parents kept their children close; foot- and handholds, however secure in appearance, tested before trusted. The damp left by melting snow might be no worse than during a light rain, but rock was still new to Yena.

New and cold. Aryl's fingers grew numb, less sensitive to texture. She could see her breath now if she puffed, a phenomenon they'd experienced thus far in the early morning, not midday. She guessed at the time; the sky was heavy with cloud as well as snow, imparting a gloom close to firstnight on the landscape.

Enris. She couldn't see him anymore.

Here. Strong and sure, as always. Few Yena could match his ability to *send* mind-to-mind over distance. Unless Chosen, most required touch to keep that sending private. *Watch your step.*

He was right. This wasn't a good place to be. She lowered her shields enough to *reach,* finding where the others were in

line. Gijs sud Vendan had taken the lead now, doubtless concerned for his pregnant Chosen, though Juo was the better
climber of the two. Gijs was paired with Veca Kessa'at, who was
their best.

Other than Aryl herself. She came last, ready to help anyone
ahead if they faltered. Or anyone behind. No doubting Enris'
strength and will, but he had no better view of his footing than
she did—and would have more trouble climbing out of a gully
should he fall.

This part of the ridge was gouged away, its surface scarred
by deep ravines, themselves cut by cracks. Loose material collected there, making them treacherous places to step. She noticed any snow that fell within these cavities or in deep shadow
didn't melt, accumulating in deceptively soft piles, cold and
dangerous.

To her inner sense, Haxel and her companions were *there*,
farther up the valley and lower down: four warm, distant
glows. Too distant. At least one would be coming back to meet
them if they'd found or made shelter by now. Aryl began looking for a cave or overhang, something to house them all. She
soon gave up.

There was no safety or protection here. They had to keep
going.

Suddenly, a scream rent the air, *felt* as much as heard. Aryl
recognized the source and threw herself forward.

"Seru!"

Chapter 2

"WE CAN'T GO THERE! WE can't! Don't—" the words dissolved into another scream.

The Om'ray clustered around the prone figure moved out of Aryl's way, letting her through. Seru lay on her back, hands pressed over her face, fingers tangled in strands of wet hair. She no longer screamed, but squirmed fitfully.

"Seru!" Aryl dropped to her knees. "Seru?" she repeated, gently. "Cousin." No response. She looked up at the others. "What happened?"

"We don't know." Taen held Ziba's shoulders, her face and voice grave. Murmurs of agreement from the other exiles, an ebb and flow of emotion that read to Aryl's inner sense as *concern* mixed with *pity*. "She was climbing with us, then she was down, screaming we had to stop. Why?"

"Seru's been talking to herself all day," the young Om'ray offered, eyes wide. "She wouldn't listen to me." This with profound distress.

"We're too exposed here." Rorn sud Vendan, Haxel's Chosen, traded looks with Cetto. "I can carry her," he offered. "She's little more than bone and clothing."

"Wait." Aryl pressed her hand lightly over Seru's, sending

her cousin's name through that contact. No shields barred her way. No consciousness responded. How was that possible? Her eyes widened in shock.

Seru was sound asleep.

An unnatural sleep. Aryl eased Seru's hands away from her face, then stroked strands of hair from her pale forehead and cheeks. Her cousin's lips quivered and tears leaked from the corners of her eyes, but she didn't stir.

Like last truenight.

Aryl laid her palms along her cousin's cold cheeks and summoned her strength. *Wake up,* she coaxed, as if it were a normal morning, as if this were a day when a pair of giggly young unChosen might sneak away from chores and spy on those who did work. *Sleepy Seru. We'll be late. C'mon. It's me. Aryl.*

A disgruntled huff of warm breath in her face.

Wake up. Lazy Seru. Wake up. She hid her own fear, did her utmost to project only *anticipation* and *pleasure*. Her awareness of the other Om'ray faded as they tightened their mental shields. It helped her focus; the reason for it didn't. She shared their instinct for self-preservation. If Seru's mind was damaged, contact risked them both.

Snow swirled and danced in silence; chill wind snuck between the legs of those waiting and found its way down the neck of Aryl's hood. She didn't move, didn't stop sending.

At last, Seru's eyelids fluttered open. She blinked away snowdrops. Her green eyes, their gaze vague, strayed until they caught Aryl's. "Why are you taking us to Sona?" Her voice, though hoarse with the aftermath of screams, was disturbingly calm and reasonable. A bead of blood marked a crack on her lower lip. "We can't go there. Everyone's dead. Can't you hear them warn us away?"

With a gasp, Taen drew Ziba back into the crowd. The rest exchanged troubled glances and Aryl didn't blame them. Her hands trembled as they left Seru's face. "Wake up!" she insisted, this time aloud.

Another blink, then Seru's eyes snapped into focus. "Aryl?"

Her brows knitted together as she noticed the others staring down at her. "What am I doing on the ground?" A look of dismay. She beckoned Aryl closer, then whispered urgently. "I didn't fall, did I?"

"Of course not." What could she tell her? Don't worry, Seru? You've been climbing in your sleep? You've had another bad dream? You said things none of us understand? It didn't make sense, Aryl fussed to herself. She did know none of this would reassure those hovering anxiously around them. "It's the cold," she improvised hastily. "You aren't used to it. You—fainted."

With perfect timing, snow swept between them, the wind tugging at their clothes. Seru's shiver reached her teeth and she sat with Aryl's help. "Sorry," she mumbled.

A touch on her shoulder that wasn't wind. *Aryl. We have to move.*

"Let's get you on your feet, Cousin." Aryl acknowledged Gijs' sending with a somber *I know.*

Husni, Cetto's Chosen, and Myris closed on Seru, chattering in anxious synchrony about the effects of such dreadful cold and how badly they felt, too. Seru, for her part, was unsettled by the attention of her elders; her cheeks flushed in spite of the cold.

How could she not remember shouting? How could she sleep while climbing in this difficult place—and not fall?

Only one thing was certain. It hadn't been the cold.

"Do you want me to stay—" Aryl began.

"We'll take care of her," promised Myris. Seru averted her eyes and started climbing with the others.

Lip between her teeth, Aryl watched her go. Their only Parth. Their only Chooser. Seru was young and strong. She shouldn't be the first to falter—shouldn't falter at all during what was—what had been—easy travel for a Yena.

She felt someone's attention and glanced up. Through the haze of falling snowdrops, Ziba regarded her solemnly from the top of the rise, her hand tight in her mother's. As the two turned to take their place in the line of exiles, the child twisted to look back. "What killed Sona, Aryl?" she called out, loud and frightened. "Is it going to kill us, too?"

Taen's head bent over her daughter's. Reassurance, Aryl supposed, wishing she had some. Whether inspired from dream or something more, Seru's shouts had shaken everyone's confidence in this path. But they had no other option.

Followed by Juo and the others, the two disappeared down the other side, leaving Aryl alone.

Not entirely. *Slowing down, Yena?*

Admiring the scenery. Aryl smiled. The snow made it impossible to see any distance. The ridge itself had vanished into bands of gray and white, along with the valley floor. Didn't matter. With a flash of her inner sense, she knew exactly where Enris was: farther down the slope, but closer than before. He'd made up time while they'd stopped with Seru; possibly found a superior route.

If the Tuana outpaced her on the flat, he'd be insufferable for days.

She wiped drops from her face and climbed hurriedly after the others.

The storm eased to sullen misery for the rest of the afternoon. The snow became little more than an unpredictable nuisance, drops to splatter into an open eye or mouth, mounds to fill nooks and crannies, so already numb fingers must push into the cold wet stuff to find a sure hold. The wind fretted at them, poked through ill-fitting clothing, unerringly found whatever was damp.

The Yena exiles maintained their pace. No one called for a rest; no place offered shelter if they had. Aryl followed the trail left by the others, the shape of a booted foot pressed into melting snow, the dark stain of soil where someone had yanked free yet another tuft of vegetation in hopes of a warm, evening fire.

These were the only traces held by rock and loose pebbles. She noted that, as she noted everything she could about this place. They had to learn to survive here.

They'd never last the journey to Rayna otherwise.

Gaining the high ground, Aryl paused to survey her surroundings before the plunge into the shadow of the next ravine. There were fewer such gashes in the mountain ridge this far up the valley; unfortunately, each was deeper and more treacherous to climb than the last. Aryl wasn't surprised to see those in the lead, already halfway up the other side, were angling downslope as well, to where the ravine walls weren't as rugged. At this rate, she thought ruefully, they might meet Enris after all.

The sun was a pale dot she could look at without pain, powerless against the cold that assailed her the instant she stopped moving. Her breath steamed from her mouth; the novelty had worn off. What interested Aryl lay ahead. She balanced the balls of her feet on the thin edge of rock and tried to make sense of the land before her.

Like the ravines cutting its sides, the valley itself narrowed and deepened as they moved toward its source, or rather the mountain ridge that was its far wall surged skyward here. Just as well they hadn't been forced along its jagged, shadowed face. No further sign of the disturbance caused by the Oud—a relief—but the valley's floor wasn't as smooth as where its mouth opened to the Lay Swamp. Traces of snow clung to the leesides of low, even hills, emphasizing the smallest wrinkle of ground.

No wonder Haxel had kept going. There was no shelter here.

Puzzled by a broad depression that wound its way up the middle of the valley, Aryl let her gaze follow its irregular edge. It looked like a giant version of the annoying small rivers they'd crossed, but held no gleam of water, only drifts of snow. Perhaps the Oud had made it. It curled out of sight behind the ridge.

At that curve, she spotted a cluster of straight and criss-crossed lines, stark against the muted brown-gray and whites of the landscape. Aryl's heart quickened. Only one thing she knew made that shape.

Nekis!

Too small to be the familiar giants that soared above all other growth in the groves. She refused to be disappointed. Possibly these were another kind of plant, or nekis stunted by the cold so high in the mountains. It didn't matter. Yena could work with wood of any kind.

Aryl shivered. Or burn it for heat.

Haxel would have found that grove, she told herself as she descended after the others, her steps eager and sure. Rather than retrace where the rest had climbed, she moved farther down the ravine to catch up, a more direct path. They'd be busy erecting a shelter for them . . . there was nothing Yena couldn't do with wood.

Distracted, Aryl almost stepped into a trap.

Almost. At the last instant, she glimpsed half-buried metal and flung herself away. She slid precipitously, grasping for handholds she'd marked as she jumped, missing the first . . . the second . . . There.

Hanging by one hand, Aryl froze in place, her feet suspended in midair. Pebbles continued to fall without her, pinging as they bounced off one another and the rock face. Before the last ping, she'd found a good hold for her other hand, a brace for one knee. A quick squirm and she was on her feet again.

She considered the piece of metal from a cautious distance, absently wiping blood and pebbles from her scraped palm on her coat. They needed to know the hazards here. Gingerly, ready to spring back, she crouched to brush snow, then dirt and small stones from around it, for the piece was set into a pile of such loose material. Some kind of snare, like those Yena hunters braided from wing threads. No. Something else.

Though the metal piece, a strap, did connect with others farther down, the whole was too fine and delicate to hold any prey worth catching.

Her fingers contacted something long and smooth to one side of the metal. She pulled it free, impatient for an answer.

Bone.

She laid it along her forearm, confirming her suspicion.

An Om'ray had died here.

"Some poor unChosen on Passage," she decided aloud, but didn't rise at once. The hem of her long coat collected snow as she reached for the piece of metal.

It resisted. Determined, she used the arm bone as a tool, first to loosen the dirt, then to pry at the metal. With a sudden pop and spray of stone, up it came, complete with skull.

Aryl rocked back on her heels. "Not unChosen," she whispered.

The skull was damaged, the jaw and back missing. The two deep cavities where eyes should be looked at her below a forehead-spanning strap of green metal. The ends of that met fine chain; more straps rose above it and fell behind, trailing down where a neck should be.

Only one type of Om'ray wore such an elaborate headdress. Only one type needed such restraint—designed to tame willful hair.

"You were Chosen."

Saying it made it no easier to comprehend. Mother, grandmother, aunt . . . a mature Chosen shouldn't be wandering alone, shouldn't be in this wasteland of rock. She'd heard flatlanders disposed of the empty husk by burial, but this lay on a path, as if it were where the Chosen had died.

What had happened here?

Aryl freed the headdress, leaving the bones where they were. She rubbed the front of the strap, feeling a texture suggestive of carving or inlay. It would have to be cleaned and polished, perhaps repaired. Remarkably light, for all its parts. Enris might know which Clan did such work.

Opening her coat, she carefully tucked the headdress inside her tunic. The cold metal stole heat from her skin.

Whatever Seru had experienced . . . was experiencing . . .

It wasn't anything so innocent as a dream.

Perversely, her cousin appeared anything but afflicted by dreams or visions of death when Aryl rejoined the exiles. They'd stopped where a hollow made a welcome windbreak, a few standing, most sitting on packs. Husni leaned against Cetto, only her bright pale eyes showing past the layers of coats and wraps she'd bundled around her body and head. A small waterfall trickled listlessly to one side. Seru was helping Ziba refill water sacs, the two giggling as if the same age.

Aryl watched them as she accepted what Grona's Om'ray called "travel bread" from her aunt. "How's she been?"

Hesitantly, Myris touched her tongue to her own piece of the hard, bitter stuff. She gave a resigned shudder instead of taking a bite. "Terrified. Angry. Confused." At Aryl's raised eyebrow, she colored. "I didn't pry, if that's what you think. Seru's emotions are—" a wince. "I'm not the only one avoiding her right now. No offense to the Parths, but I wish her shields were stronger."

"Then she'd be able to hide whatever's wrong." Aryl dutifully nibbled the bread, taking her own lack of appetite as a warning. "What if they aren't dreams, Myris? Some Om'ray can *taste* a coming change." She happened to be one of them, though it was a thoroughly untrustworthy Talent. The metal headdress pressed against her waist, its mystery prompting her to press on. "Have you heard of anyone who could *taste* what happened before?"

"Seru?" They both looked toward the owner of the name— presently juggling an armload of full sacs as Ziba laughingly piled on more—then back at each other. Though her shields were impeccable, Myris' hair squirmed in agitation within its net. "I've never heard of such a thing," she said after a moment. "I wouldn't believe it if I did. What's already been . . . surely it's done. Done and gone. What could be left to affect a living mind? Memories flying around?" She tipped her bread through the air like a flitter after a biter. "These fancies of Seru's will pass. It's difficult for everyone—worse for your cousin. She must restrain powerful needs and instincts—hard under the best of conditions. I cried for days." The bread wagged at Aryl. "One day, you'll know the stress of being a Chooser."

Impossible to argue with that, though Aryl resolved then and there she'd never cry when her time came. "Seru's lucky to have you."

"Maybe I can do more when we reach shelter," Myris offered bravely. Her Talent to affect the emotions of others might be restricted to very close kin; it still took its toll on her, regardless of outcome.

Aryl gestured gratitude. "What you should do is eat," she urged.

"I can't. Not without something to wash it down. Ziba! One of those sacs, please?" Myris left in pursuit of water, a little too obviously avoiding Seru.

Did the past leave its trace? Something to touch a mind in the present? If so, Aryl feared she knew where it would be. That *darkness* between minds, the whirling seductive abyss through which she'd sent Bern and traveled with Enris— whenever she'd allowed herself to enter it, she'd felt it wasn't empty. There was a sense of being observed, of some intangible presence.

Her mother, Taisal di Sarc, claimed the minds of the dead lingered there, able to lure the living from their bodies. She wasn't sure she believed Taisal, though it was true the *darkness* drew as much as terrified her. Just to think of it, standing here on this mountain in the middle of nowhere, brought it swelling into awareness, like the irresistible pressure of the M'hir Wind against her innermost self.

If she let herself go, it would carry her away.

Aryl worried her tongue at a stubborn crumb of bread lodged beside a tooth, studied the faces of those nearby, stamped her worn, damp boots against the ground until her feet were warm. She held to the *real,* to what was here and now. After a too-long struggle, the other place receded. All was improbably normal.

She shuddered. Dangerous. Deadly. That *darkness* was part of Taisal since the death of her Chosen, Mele, Aryl's father; it was part of those less fortunate Lost, whose minds no longer functioned.

And part, Aryl admitted, of her as well.

As for Seru? Was it the source of her dread?

Aryl knew better than to *reach* for her cousin. This was not the time or place for extra risk. She took another bite and frowned. As for her find? This wasn't the time or place to spread the news a Chosen had died here either.

She'd show Enris, but he was inconsiderately out of reach. Or . . . there was someone she could trust to keep this secret.

Aryl tucked away her bread and started to climb.

While the others rested, Veca Kessa'at had climbed to a vantage point to pick out their route. The tall, rangy Om'ray had been a promising young scout, until Joining Tilip Sarc. After Choice, like many, she turned to an occupation posing less risk to both their lives and became a woodworker like Tilip and her grandmother, Morla Kessa'at. Their quiet son, Fon, though younger than Aryl, showed the same interest. A valued, productive family.

Yena's Council had exiled him with his parents and great-grandmother—why, she couldn't imagine.

Veca's teeth bared in what wasn't a smile as Aryl joined her on the spit of rock. "Got any ideas?" she half shouted, gesturing over the edge.

"That bad?" Coat fluttering, Aryl braced herself and looked down, forewarned by a roar that wasn't wind.

The sheer drop at her feet wasn't the problem, though the scar in the rock was fresh and angry. They had sufficient ropes to get everyone down. Once at the bottom, though, they'd be trapped. Instead of the narrow ribbons of water they'd encountered thus far, barely worth a jump, here an angry torrent tore down the ravine. White fists slammed against huge boulders or bullied their way between in muscular currents. Directly below, Aryl watched the water plunge over a rock step. Clouds of spray, like snowdrops, obscured its fate.

And everywhere, the hard glitter of ice. It coated the boulders. It grew from the rocky banks like teeth.

"That bad," Aryl agreed. They couldn't cross this.

Veca squatted on her heels and rubbed one hand over her face. Weariness smudged the skin under her eyes; worry tightened the edges of her mouth. "Your friends' flying machine would be nice about now."

It was the first time any of the exiles had mentioned the strangers or their help. Aryl copied Veca's position, then gestured apology with sore, numb fingers. "Do you think I was wrong to tell them to stay away from us?"

Veca had deep-set blue eyes. Now they held a warning. "I'm no Councillor to say what others should do."

Implying she had? Aryl tucked her hands under her arms to warm them. "The strangers seek old things. They aren't interested in Om'ray." Or hadn't been, until they'd recognized some of their words, words she'd used in their first meeting.

Marcus Bowman, Human, Triad First, Analyst, Trade Pact: all those words named the stranger who'd brought his machine to save the exiles from certain death, carrying them through the air to refuge with Grona Clan. He and those with him were from other worlds, if she continued to believe what seemed incredible now, back among her kind. Om'ray in appearance, unreal to her other, deeper sense.

She'd saved his life. He'd saved theirs.

Friend?

Trouble, Aryl assured herself. Because of the strangers' curiosity, Yena's annual Harvest had resulted in the deaths of too many, including her brother Costa. Because of Marcus' interest in her words, one or more factions of Tikitik had turned on Yena itself. As a result, those deemed likely to cause even more change and disruption had been exiled.

"The strangers are no friends of mine," she declared finally. "Or of any Om'ray. We're better off without their machines or attention."

"Best we join your plodder on the flats, then." Veca's move to rise stopped, her eyes riveted on what Aryl held out for her inspection. She sank back on her heels, taking the metal headdress in both hands. "Where did you find this?"

"With the remains of its owner." Aryl gestured. "On our path, among the stones."

Veca spread the headdress across one broad, callused palm. Its simple counterpart wrapped her thick brown hair, braids of red thread connected by small wooden rings. Such a flimsy net could never control Taisal's opinionated hair, or Myris', Aryl thought, distracted. A Sarc trait. Kessa'ats were more restrained. "Did she die alone?" Veca asked, a wondering finger tracing the tarnished links.

Aryl shrugged. "I didn't see more bones, but I didn't stay to look. Have you seen—" she hesitated. What was she asking?

"All I've seen, young Aryl, is rock and snow. With more rock and snow. Despicable place. As for this?" The Chosen tipped her hand to pour the metal net into Aryl's. "A mystery too old to matter to us." She rose to her feet, Aryl doing the same. Standing, the older Om'ray easily looked over her head, and did so now. "Down it is," she mused. "That way." Louder, with a sidelong glance, "Did you show anyone else?"

"No."

"Don't." The word was said heavily. "Confidence is what stands between life and a fall. Might not be the Lay below us. Doesn't matter. These rocks will do the job just as quick. We can't afford doubt—not of the next handhold, not of where we're going. Not until we're safe for truenight." A tired smile. "Now, young one. Save my legs and call them for me, will you?"

How strange, to have others know and value her abilities like this, to use them at need. All her life, Taisal had taught her to keep her differences secret. The Adepts claimed new Talent, tested it, and locked it away in the Cloisters to maintain the Agreement. Her mother had wanted her to be an Adept. She'd chosen freedom.

Not that all secrets were out, she thought wryly, then concentrated. *Time to go,* she sent to the rest, adding with what confidence she could, *Veca's found an easier path.*

That worthy laughed. "Downhill, at any rate."

Aryl closed her fingers over the headdress. "What if Seru's not dreaming? What if we're going somewhere Om'ray have died?"

Another laugh, but this one bitter. "Haven't you noticed by now, Aryl? It's the living you have to watch out for. You needn't fear the dead."

Interlude

ENRIS MENDOLAR STEPPED OVER A tiny stream ribboned in ice and asked himself, again, what he was doing here.
He gauged the dark, roiling clouds with a wary eye. The snow
might be done; the storm wasn't. He refused to look up the horrible cliff. The Yena were beyond comprehension. There was nothing wrong with flat, normal ground. A few more steps, that's all.

More than a few, he admitted to himself. Keeping to the boundary between ridge and valley floor meant interminable detours
around barriers Enris glumly realized wouldn't bother the Yena at
all, from young Ziba to elderly Husni.

Fine for them. He took his extra steps, glad to confine his
climbing to walking over screes of shattered rock, his leaps to long
strides over the odd stream. When he had to wade, he did, his
good solid boots—the one item from home he'd managed to keep
intact—providing ample protection.

Home. Enris sighed, *reaching* involuntarily to find Tuana's place
in the world and his own. Against his will, he was farther from
home than ever in his life. Now he was moving away from the one
goal he'd set himself.

What was he doing here?

It wasn't the Yena Chooser. He felt nothing for Seru Parth, beyond sympathy for her situation. When she released it, her Call was faint, like the smell of yesterday's sweetpies. He barely heard it in his mind; he doubted it could summon any unChosen across this waste.

He stopped, his head turned toward Vyna. That's where he belonged. That's where he'd start finding answers. His fingers curled around the memory of a cylinder. An Oud had brought the strange device to his father's shop, demanded their help to discover its secrets. Enris was convinced the device was neither Oud nor Tikitik. It fit his Om'ray hand perfectly; it responded to his mental touch, revealing a store of voices and images.

He'd understood none of them. He had no idea how the device worked. All he knew? It was Om'ray, despite being a technology as far beyond those he knew as the workings of the strangers' flying machine.

The device was still in the shop, unless Jorg, his father, had returned it to the Oud. At the thought, Enris felt himself break into a sweat despite the coolness of the wind. The unrestrained power of the Oud was evident here as nowhere else he'd seen. They'd reshaped the road, or rather the tunnels beneath the road, as well as the lower half of this valley. If it hadn't been deliberate, then it was without heed to anything above. The result was the same. What had set them off, he didn't know or care.

He wanted Tuana safe. He had to believe it was. He couldn't breathe if he thought the device, what he'd done, might have aroused the Oud against his Clan.

What was he doing here?

Aryl Sarc.

Enris crouched to bring a palmful of icy mountain water to his lips, then another, savoring the taste. He shook the last drops from his hand as he straightened. Surrounded by rock, soil, and stray clumps of withered grass, where the only sound was the wind and his steps, he wasn't alone, not if he *reached* for her thoughts. He didn't have her Talent to identify an Om'ray at a distance, but he did have the strength to contact a known mind, especially a welcoming one.

Did she appreciate her own Power?

Did she think he was here because of it?

Was he?

"What I need," he said aloud, "is someone to talk to who isn't scampering over the mountainside like a—"

Crack!

Enris accepted Haxel's teasing about his feet—hadn't he teased his Yena friend Yuhas? But, though big, he wasn't clumsy by Tuana standards. He'd stepped on something that didn't belong.

A piece of broken wood protruded from the pebbles, worth more than the handfuls of grass he'd been dutifully collecting for tonight's camp. He bent to retrieve it, delighted when it took all his strength to wiggle it free. "Good size . . ." the words turned into a whistle of surprise.

Not a stick.

His hand fit perfectly around what had been a carved and finished staff, almost half his height. The wood was dark red and unfamiliar, its polish scratched and dulled by exposure and the rocks of its bed. Enris put it aside and dug for the rest of it.

Not a staff.

The remaining piece was a blade, long as his forearm and fitted to its bit of shaft so securely the wood had snapped under his foot, not that junction to metal. Enris grinned with triumph as he examined his treasure. "Aren't you the beauty?" The Oud's metal, right enough, but reworked by someone with skill and patience into a most unusual shape. The wide, thin blade, once razor sharp along both outer edges, ended in a forked tip. One portion of the tip was longer than its mate; not a break but made that way. Impractical for harvesting any crop he knew. Dangerous, that was certain.

Under the dirt, he discerned a line of ornamentation along the flat of the blade. A spit and hard rub revealed nothing so simple. A series of small, intricate symbols marched in a tidy row, some close together, some apart. Unique in design; not beautiful. He knew to a twinge in his shoulders the time and meticulous effort it took to inscribe metal. Why bother, if the result didn't enhance the finished work?

Pride, perhaps. Hadn't his father taught him to identify what he'd done? Not the everyday work, but those special pieces made after the routine blades and tools were finished, the adornments and art meant for Om'ray pleasure, not Oud—their creator should be known. Enris had chosen his favorite stars, hammering that tiny pattern discreetly into whatever was, to him, his best.

Nothing discreet about these symbols. He ran his thumb over them, achingly curious. Were they a metalworker's personal mark? He'd show Aryl. She'd seen the symbols the Tikitik used to represent words and those of the strangers. If they weren't the same . . . he felt a rush of hope. Could these represent words?

There were Om'ray who drew lists of names, crop yields, and such: Adepts, responsible for maintaining the Cloisters' records. The skill to write and read was provided only to those who accepted that role for life, to be used exclusively within the Cloisters, for the concerns of the Clan as a whole.

Ordinary Om'ray had no need. Surely a metalworker, even if an Adept, wouldn't abuse the knowledge simply to name his or her work.

More than pride. A message?

Enris shrugged off his pack and swung it to the ground. He went to one knee and untied his coat from the top. With a struggle—the pack already bulged in all directions—he managed to store the blade and its end of broken wood safely inside. The longer piece? He hefted it and grinned. No more wet boots.

As he reached for his coat, he spotted a pale speck among the disturbed pebbles by his foot. He brushed at it, hoping for more metal or wood, but it was only bone.

The bone itself didn't trouble him. Tuana carried their dead to the end of the world—namely as far from their village, and any other Clan, as was comfortable to go—across the wide nost fields to where the flat land of the Oud gave way to low, rolling hills. Though he'd heard some Clans practiced burial, Tuana's empty remains were sensibly left accessible to scavengers, present in abundance when the noisy clouds of *delits* returned to nest in their hillside burrows. Scattered Om'ray bones often greeted those bringing the latest to join them.

But no Om'ray would discard objects, or even wearable clothing, with their dead. This Om'ray must have died away from his Clan. There was only one kind who could. An unChosen on Passage.

A fellow fool.

A little digging unearthed more bones, most shattered or split. Enris was about to stop when he touched a softness among the fragments. It was a bag, its brittle material crumbling as he pulled it free.

Most of the contents fell apart as well, becoming flakes and fine powder, easily taken by the wind. He was left with two items. The first was a metal box the size of his smallest finger. He pressed its two longer sides together and a tiny, hot flame obediently bloomed from one end.

An ordinary firebox.

Enris pulled out his. The two were identical, save for the discoloration of age and dirt. Oud, as if he needed more proof the land between Grona and Rayna was theirs. He tucked both away.

The second item was as strange as the 'box was familiar: a featureless wafer that fit within the palm of his hand. It was thin but solid, with five unequal sides. Unlike metal, it didn't warm as he held it, instead stealing heat from his skin. The material was clear; it might have been cut from the window of a Cloisters, if that were possible. Unlike his other finds, the wafer glittered as if new. Baffled, he put it in the pouch with the fireboxes. It would be pretty, made into an ornament. When he had time to make things for their beauty again.

The grayed bones weren't fresh leavings. Enris frowned. The wood was still strong and whole. Despite its finish, it would have rotted quickly in hot, humid Yena; perhaps the coolness of the mountainside preserved it, the way it had the reshaped road and landscape. Though even in Tuana, such bared soil would be carpeted by tall, waving nost or other hardy plants within a harvest.

Despite the little mountain streams and dusting of snow, he guessed this was a dry place. No wonder it was barren.

Bones that weren't fresh. Intact wood. What else did he have? The Oud metal. Something he'd believed impervious; the darkened blade in his pack was proof it wasn't, though he'd never tried leaving the precious stuff outside on the ground.

Old. But how old?

Enris grinned. Other Om'ray wouldn't care. What was now, had always been. After all, the Agreement among Cersi's three races was built on things staying as they were. He wouldn't have cared before he met the strangers, with their preoccupation with the long-buried and longer past. But he'd seen with his own eyes the incredible structures from another time that they'd freed from a cliff face.

Things had been different once.

Faced now with his own puzzle, he began to see the fascination. Maybe he should keep digging. If this had been an Om'ray on Passage, there would be a metal token with the bones, twin to one Enris kept in a pocket. The tokens granted the bearer the freedom to trespass anywhere on Cersi.

He grimaced. Maybe not anywhere, after his experience with that crazed Oud in its tunnels. Instead of leaving him be, the creature had taken his original token from him. He owed the one he carried now to Yena's paranoid Council.

A token with the bones would make this a normal, if lonely, death—an expected hazard facing those who left their own Clan to seek a Chooser in another. If there was no token . . .

Enris gave himself a shake, then retied his coat to his pack with unnecessary force, almost snapping the tie. His imagination wasn't usually out of control. It was this place. What was he doing here? Of course there was a token. No need to waste precious time digging for what had to be there. He stood, settling the pack over his shoulders. A Clan couldn't abandon one of its own, any more than a member could stray too far. There would be family, a Chosen, who would feel and react to distress. Only those on Passage lost that protection.

"Bitter, are we?" He snorted and started walking.

It was the way things had always been. His family grieved him as dead, as was natural and proper. His friends might talk of him, tell stories. Hopefully, those fit to be heard. Naryn S'udlaat . . .

A mistake, to think of her when he was alone. Enris gritted his teeth and walked faster, driving the shaft of wood deep into the pebbles, his feet slipping with each careless stride.

Naryn . . .

She thought herself powerful. She'd make Adept; of that he had no doubt, if only so others could keep her in the Cloisters and under watch. She thought herself entitled to whatever and whomever she wanted; as a result, her failed attempt to force him into Choice had left him . . . damaged. Whatever she'd done, the Adepts warned he might never be able to Join.

He certainly didn't feel inclined to try.

No?

Enris blew out a harsh breath, unable to lie to himself. He was unChosen and eligible for Choice. Seru Parth might not interest him, but the mere thought of Naryn brought the heady remembered lure of her Call to speed his pulse, make his hands clammy despite the cool air. No matter how thoroughly she disgusted him, there was a part of him desperate to go back, to let her do whatever she wanted, turn him into whatever she wanted, if only he could touch her hand. . . .

The length of wood snapped, stinging his knee. One way to get his sanity back, he thought ruefully.

Enris picked up the broken pieces and put them in his pack. He walked at a more rational pace, finally paying attention to his surroundings. The freshening wind couldn't decide between a pleasant mildness—doubtless chill to the Yena—and a truly bitter cold.

He feared the storm played with them. Fine for those under a roof, with a warm fire, or for those used to such weather. On that thought, he *reached* to find the Yena. The glow of Haxel and her companions was still too far, farther up the valley. How long did it take to find some kind of shelter? The rest of the exiles were closer than he'd expected, and lower. Coming toward him. Maybe they'd finally grown sensible.

He lowered his shields and *reached* for one mind in particular. *Aryl.*

Here.

Strain. Worry. He could sense them despite her control, and couldn't help looking up the slope beside him. The mountain ridge was every bit as awful as he feared, an impassable conflict of vertical shapes and loose, snow-streaked rock, soaring into ugly cloud.

Distinct amusement. *That was the easy part.*

How had she *seen* what he saw? An image could be drawn from memory and sent mind-to-mind—this was something new. Enris surreptitiously checked his shields, though he should be used to surprises from Aryl Sarc by now. *Be careful,* he sent. *I don't trust this storm.*

Good advice. Here's mine. Walk faster, or we'll eat supper without you.

He laughed. *You forget who's carrying the pots.*

A whisper of contrition, quickly silenced. It left a warmth, like a smile. *We're coming down. Truenight's too close.*

Afraid of the dark? Enris shared his instant regret. The Yena had excellent reason to be. *Sorry.*

With the honesty he'd come to expect, *I'm afraid of everything until my people are safe. Move those big feet of yours, Tuana.*

His awareness of her faded and he didn't try to regain it. If this part of the ridge was "easy," he couldn't imagine what Yena might consider difficult.

Enris found himself walking faster, and smiling.

It wasn't only the reminder of supper, scant as that would be.

Chapter 3

THAT WAS . . . INTERESTING.

Aryl tiptoed along an edge to avoid a patch of loose stone. She came last, as usual, but now stayed with the rest of the exiles. If Enris needed help, she'd reach him faster going ahead, as they were. It shouldn't be long before they met again.

Very interesting.

He'd effortlessly shared what he saw—along with his aversion to it, which she chose to ignore. No denying his Power or skill. Few Yena could send with such ease in sight of one another, let alone at any distance. She'd learned to use the *other place* to reach her mother. Yet Enris took his ability to contact her at will for granted. Perhaps all Tuana were as gifted. Though this time she had the impression he hadn't realized what he was doing, that instinct, not concentration, had opened that path to his senses. Another new Talent?

At her turn, she jumped to the ledge below like the other exiles, arms out to balance her pack as she landed lightly. A few steps to the next. Another, longer drop. The eighteen moved almost as one, in a flow of confident quick steps.

Until they reached Rayna, there was no Council to dictate

what they were to do, she mused, and no Adepts to enforce those dictates. A freedom she didn't trust. Not that she . . .

Aryl focused on a tricky set of handholds as she climbed up, across a thrust of stone, then down.

. . . not that she agreed with Yena's refusal to permit new Talents and change. What could possibly be wrong in Enris letting her see through his eyes? If Haxel could do the same, they'd know where they were going.

They had to be careful. Without Adepts, they had no one skilled in the consequences of Power. A mistake out here could be fatal to both the user and those too close.

She refused to think about the consequences of upsetting the Agreement. One good thing about this land of cold and bleak, lifeless rock—it kept the neighbors away.

The scuff of boot on stone was the only sound. Whenever possible, fingertips brushed as holds were exchanged, exchanges of reassurance and encouragement. Ziba and Seru stayed together, the child unusually attentive. Juo lagged despite her best efforts. The previous Harvest, she'd been one of their group of unChosen, quick and surefooted, hard to beat at any game. Joined with Gijs, filled with child, she'd become more careful, not more patient. Aryl smiled to herself when Husni deliberately slowed to make the pregnant Chosen do the same. A slow pace for Yena was still a good one, especially on this stretch, where exposed ledges of some dark, harder rock formed natural steps.

Veca and Gijs had picked a route to bring the exiles to the floor of the ravine before it opened wide to meet the valley. Not far, but . . . Aryl frowned as she studied the descent left for the leaders. The final portion would be the most complex, choked with piles of fallen rock. The cracks between were full of snow. Couldn't be avoided without a long detour back the way they'd come; even then, there were few better choices.

Though the wind had died, at some point each of the Om'ray paused to stare at the wild shredded darkness looming above them. Something brewed in those clouds. She took

Enris' warning about the weather seriously; they all did. Whether more snow or rain, they'd best be off the rocky slope before it fell.

"Ow!" The loud cry came with a powerful flash of *pain,* quickly suppressed but enough to draw startled looks. Young Cader Sarc, climbing with his Kessa'at cousin. He gave a reassuring, if sheepish, wave, and she guessed he'd stubbed a toe. He was at that clumsy age.

"What?!" Another pained exclamation, this time from Morla's Chosen, Lendin sud Kessa'at.

As more of the exiles shouted and crouched, looking in all directions for their unseen attacker, something landed with a thud in front of Aryl.

She picked up a fist-sized lump of ice.

Before she could look for who might have thrown it, something slammed against her pack, knocking her off-balance. Another lump rolled between her feet.

They were falling from the clouds!

The path no longer mattered. Aryl and the exiles scrambled to find cover as lumps struck all around them, but there was none. Chosen shielded the children with their bodies. Some of the lumps smashed apart on rock, sharp pieces spraying outward. Most stayed intact and bounced, too hard to break. They struck flesh with the same force. Aryl's left arm was numbed by a glancing impact. She heard screams from others as they were hit. One, then another went down. She hurried toward the horribly limp forms, her feet sliding through loose stones and balls of ice, almost deafened by the clatter of ice against rock. She *reached* to know *who* . . .

Chaun sud Teerac was the one crumpled and motionless on a ledge. Myris—Aryl gasped with relief—her aunt was conscious and trying to sit up, though her face was dark with blood.

Weth!!! Fear drove the sending into her mind. Aryl staggered. Somehow she collected herself in time to catch Husni by the arms before she could rush past her. As gently as she could, she urged the older Chosen under the meager shelter of an overhanging ledge.

Stay. I'll look after Chaun.

Cetto . . . Husni's mindvoice wavered, but she didn't resist.

Stay.

Others were looking after Myris, drawing her to her feet. Aryl hurried to where Cetto protected Chaun's helpless body with his own, an act to save Weth, their granddaughter, as much as her Chosen. The loss of one would be the loss of both.

No one would die.

Aryl joined the elder Om'ray, laying herself over as much of Chaun as she could. He was so still. She *reached* through that contact and found . . .

PAIN! She winced, relieved by the strength of Chaun's inner self. Impossible to be heard over the crash and thud of the ice lumps. They were piling around them like the snow, chilling the air. She pushed her shoulder against Cetto's. *He's unconscious, but I don't think badly hurt.* For now, she despaired. How long could any of them endure this onslaught? Lumps continued to strike her. The long Grona coat and her pack took the brunt of it, but Aryl knew her head and neck were vulnerable. Cetto stoically endured blows she felt through their contact. Only bruises, she hoped.

The moment came when the thud and crash gave way to a high-pitched pinging, then a steady drone. Belatedly, Aryl realized lumps no longer fell. They were being hit by what felt like small hard seeds instead. She eased herself up, holding out her palm. Icedrops. Unlike lumps, they stung when they hit skin but didn't break it. Unlike the dancing snowdrops, they fell in sheets, a heavy white curtain that made it impossible to see any distance.

Cetto's relieved laugh was a deep rumble. "I see why Grona like their stone houses."

Shelter they'd left to follow her. Aryl added that to the tally she'd begun to keep, the one that measured the value of one stubborn, strange Om'ray against all the precious lives in her care.

She would get them to safety. Haxel would find shelter and be waiting. Nothing less was acceptable.

Aryl got to her feet, adjusting her hood to protect her face. "We have to go."

No one else moved from their crouch or hiding place. Were they afraid the lumps would start falling again? The icedrops bounced and pinged from the stone, collected in piles faster than the lumps. They'd make treacherous footing. She pushed aside her own anxiety, focused on confidence. *I thought we left biters behind,* she sent to everyone, making it a complaint.

A wave of startled amusement answered. *Time to get off this hill.* Agreement. Figures began to shift and straighten, icedrops slipping from the fabric of coats and packs.

Their strongest, Rorn and Gijs, would carry Chaun. As they prepared, Aryl checked on Myris, then made sure she touched every one of the exiles before they followed Veca, *reaching* through that touch as unobtrusively as she could to assess their state. All but the youngest bore bruises; all were shocked by the sudden violence of the storm. Morla's wrist was broken, a discovery they could do nothing about here. Lendin was at her side, a wicked gash on his temple, ready to help his diminutive Chosen.

Aryl quietly asked Tilip to stay close to the older pair.

They were descending again before she *reached* for Enris, only to find his thoughts were already close to hers, as if he'd been waiting for her attention. *Are you all right?*

I hid under the pots. What about you?

Icedrops bounced against her coat and hood, as noisy as the canopy after a rain. She rubbed her left arm, keeping the pain to herself. *At least it's over.*

No, it isn't, he corrected, letting her feel his dread. *Ice stones come* before *the storm, Aryl. Those were the biggest I've ever seen. Haxel better have found shelter. Forget walking. It's time to run.*

It was as well for their flight from the ridge that none of the Yena understood what lay in store. Aryl urged them to hurry, but didn't explain why. It wasn't as if she knew. But Enris had faced truenight and the swarm without the kind of fear she felt from him now.

They were steps from the ravine floor when the din of the icedrops abruptly ceased. Ears ringing in the silence, Aryl almost missed the start of the rain.

Rain they knew. Aryl felt the tension ease in those around her. Cold, sharp, and driving, hard enough to restrict visibility to those nearest, a vicious chatter against the rocks as they continued to climb down.

But just rain.

The dim light slowed them more. It wasn't firstnight yet, when the sun disappeared from sight behind Grona, but the dark heavy clouds made it seem more like truenight, when the only light came from stars and the Makers, Cersi's two moons. They had to go slower, touched one another as often as possible to share impressions of the next foot- or handhold. Ziba stayed close to her mother, Juo to Husni. Or the other way around. Aryl depended more and more on her inner sense to know where everyone was, *seeing* the slope, like the world, in terms of Om'ray life.

Until the first flash of lightning. Then she saw the rest.

Aghast, Aryl froze in place. *STOP!* she sent frantically.

The fierce white light had reflected from every surface. This wasn't rain. It was liquid ice. Like the boulders in the river they couldn't cross, the rocks all around them were already coated in a glistening layer. In the dark, in disbelief, she stretched out her hand to touch the slick chill of the nearest surface. Flakes of ice cracked from her sleeve to melt on her skin. Thunder shook the ground.

What kind of place was this?

Another flash. Another terrifying echo from the ice. The next roll of thunder seemed to never end.

She couldn't move a muscle. One slip. One. She'd fall.

Falling, she'd knock those below from their feet and they'd fall. All of Yena's exiled children, falling on the ice-crusted rock, cracking open like lumps themselves, fragments dying alone in the cold. . . .

Thought Yena could climb anything. Mockery, sharp and pitiless, lanced through her paralysis. *Thought Yena didn't fall.*

Stung, Aryl took one breath, then another. *Yena don't fall. And what's a flatlander know of climbing anyway?*

More than you know about ice. Oh, now he was smug. *Small steps, like a baby. I haven't all day to wait for you.*

Insufferable Tuana. She'd show him. *Don't get comfortable. We won't be long.*

Waiting for a pot of water to boil. The weary comfort before sleep claimed a tired body. The rest of their descent should have taken as little time; they were that close to the gorge bottom and safety. It should have been as easy, with only two wide ledges left.

But nothing was as it should be.

Anything flat and smooth was now an enemy, impossible to walk across. The exiles had to abandon the experience and training that worked in the canopy. The only way to move was to cling to one another, to form a living chain no safer than any one link. Without warning, feet would skid from underneath, taking the strength of all to hold and recover. It was terrifying.

Through it all, the unceasing rain. It built ice on their clothing and packs, adding weight. It melted and wicked through seams to add a chill misery to weary bodies.

Through it all, the blinding flashes. They alternated with a darkness akin to truenight in the canopy. Like the others, Aryl waited for each bolt of lightning, memorizing the few steps she dared take when the light was gone. Small steps, like a baby, as suggested by someone who did, after all, know something about ice. Tiring, painstaking movements.

How much worse for Gijs? They'd strapped Chaun's limp form to the younger Chosen's back. Rorn helped take some weight where he could, but most of the time Gijs had to manage alone. Aryl couldn't imagine that burden. Veca's wish for the stranger's aircar haunted her; her own untested ability was a constant frustration.

But how could she *push* Chaun to somewhere safe, if she didn't know where that could be?

All she could do was send *encouragement* to the rest.

Or was that all?

No, not all.

Her great-great-uncle, Yorl sud Sarc, had used her strength to heal himself. Stolen it. She'd been helpless for that draining, trapped until freed. A sensation she'd never forget.

Could she repeat it?

Aryl followed Gijs. She closed her hand on his arm and did her utmost to feel as she'd felt, to *give* strength to the weary, courageous Chosen. She thought she felt *something* drain from her, though he didn't react. As they waited in the dark, the exiles linked hand to hand to cross the ice, she tried a second time, tried to extend the sensation to include everyone.

When the next flash came, and they moved forward as a group, Aryl staggered and had to catch herself. Had she helped at all? She hoped her sudden clumsiness was a sign.

The drop from this ledge to the last was barely twice an adult's height, but jumping was impossible, too. One at a time, the Om'ray slipped over the edge and felt for holds that weren't covered in ice. Aryl came last, waiting to be sure all below had found safe footing before joining the chain again.

The final stage was a nightmarish tumble of ice-slicked boulders. The only grace was that a slip here, and there were many, couldn't send you farther than the next obstacle. No one would escape bruises, Aryl knew, feeling her own.

Easier ahead. An almost giddy relief spread with the message. Veca had reached the bank of the narrow mountain stream.

Soon, they were all free of the boulders. Level ground, but its scattered pebbles were still slippery as Aryl discovered, landing on her backside with her first incautious stride.

Small steps here, too, she thought ruefully.

Despite the need for care, those ahead of her moved more quickly, and Aryl agreed with their haste, just as eager to be free of the rock and ice. The storm, having failed to stop the Yena, admitted defeat, its thunder fading to a discontented mutter. The horizon grew brighter, then light began to stream through breaks in the clouds. The ice-rain glittered as it fell; the ice-encased stone glistened with deadly beauty, like some scaled predator basking in the sun.

Still day? The heavy cloud had fooled her. Aryl measured the sun's position against her sense of Grona's—it wouldn't be day for long.

Where was the sun through truenight? Before it woke the Pana and Amna Om'ray?

She shook her head, shaking ice and droplets from her hood. It didn't matter where it went—the Tikitik had toyed with her, mocked her understanding of the world and its light. What mattered, Aryl thought grimly, was reaching shelter before the sun abandoned them.

As for that shelter . . . she *reached* for Haxel and found her, confirming by that identification what her inner sense knew, that the others were now stationary. They'd found something—or been stopped by a barrier like that impossible river in the next gorge. She preferred the something, imagining a roof and snug walls while she was at it. And heat. Decent, comfortable heat. Glows would be nice.

She couldn't *send* to ask. It was beyond her range and theirs. Another reason to discover which of the exiles could be taught to access the *other place*. Distance didn't seem to affect it the same way—

Splash! Aryl looked down, surprised to find her foot in a shallow puddle. Was the ice-rain becoming something normal at last? She couldn't tell. Her fingers and toes were numb, as was the tip of her nose, but her body was damp with sweat as much as from seepage through her now-useless Grona coat.

What fell from the sky looked and sounded the same. It was the little river that had changed. The width of a stride a moment ago, it had swollen to three times that, in many places spilling over its rocky banks. Tendrils seeped along cracks and filled depressions.

Soon they were all splashing through puddles, a harmless nuisance to already wet feet, except when the puddle formed over ice. At least the ice was melting, adding its drips to the rain and rotting softly underfoot. Sheets of it slid from the rock walls in random smashes they quickly learned to ignore.

Harmless for how long? Aryl wondered, glancing back up the gorge. Its origin within the mountain ridge was masked by rain and mist. Fed by cloudbursts, the waters of the Lay Swamp could rise with terrible speed. And the Lay had all the groves to hold its flood, unlike this narrow, steep-walled gorge.

She wasn't the only one concerned. Veca had already set a quicker, more dangerous pace. Aryl moved even faster, making her way up the line heedless of risk. The older Om'ray gave her a harried look once they were side by side. "What is it?"

"Haxel and the others must be waiting for us to join them. What if they're on the other side of the river we couldn't cross?" Aryl gestured to the puddles spreading across the gorge floor. "What if it's flooding, too? We'll be cut off."

Veca shrugged. "There'll be a bridge."

Aryl raised her eyebrows. "A bridge?"

"Grona build them." As if this settled it.

"What makes you think this is part of Grona?"

Another shrug. "Could be Rayna, for all I know. Can you tell?"

Aryl paused while they used a pair of boulders to cross a more ambitious tendril of escaping river. She hadn't noticed any transition from Yena to Grona, not inwardly. She'd simply *known* they were in another Clan's domain. How?

Proximity to the village? It couldn't be that . . . not only that, she corrected herself. What defined a Clan's influence? The location of Om'ray minds, their glow—that was what she sensed. But with no Om'ray nearby but the exiles—and Enris—what made this bit of Cersi feel like Grona and not Yena?

Besides the fact that no Yena would want this lifeless heave of stone?

Though now that she considered the question—Aryl waited to let Veca consider the best route around a wider-than-most puddle—she realized this place didn't feel like Grona or Rayna or any other Clan. Not to her.

Were they nearing the edge of the world?

She felt no compulsion to stop, no dread of traveling too far from her kind despite being farther than she'd ever imagined. Yet from all accounts, the edge of the world revealed itself in that way—it was the limit of Om'ray existence, and Om'ray existence, after all, defined the world.

What of the world—the worlds—of the strangers? What of the world where Marcus Bowman had stood as a young Human, perhaps wondering such things, too?

Not, she reminded herself, that Humans were *real* in the way Om'ray were.

"We should wait for him."

Preoccupied, Aryl almost had to puzzle which "him" Veca meant. "Enris?" She *reached*. He wasn't far from them now. "He'll be glad. We took most of the food."

"He can help carry Chaun."

Her fellow exiles had a distressing tendency to value the Tuana's strength over any other of his virtues. Aryl hid a sympathetic wince.

The gorge opened without warning, its rocky walls plunged into the soil of the valley like longknives, its now-exuberant little river absorbed by a deeper, wider channel half choked with the stalks of some tall thin vegetation. Those stalks bent with the current, taming it, silencing it. On the shore, to either side, similar stalks lay broken and flattened to the ground by, Aryl assumed, falling lumps of ice. Why had she thought the valley would be spared?

The storm itself rumbled in the distance. Not done, but not immediate. The rocks and pebbles of the mountain ridge, like the river, disappeared beneath dirt, showing as scattered mounds in what was otherwise flat terrain. Flat terrain covered, away from the water, by a messy carpet of dead leaves and smaller stalks, none over knee height. The Grona spoke of winter as a time when their plants slept beneath the ground; spring as a time of regrowth.

She hoped they were right. It all looked dead to her.

Ziba left Seru to skip through the sodden leaves. The improvement in footing cheered them all. For once, Aryl admitted, she could appreciate what Enris saw in walking on flat, boring ground. Not that she'd tell him.

Thinking of the Tuana, she started to *reach* for his location, only to realize it was unnecessary. Instead, she let the others go ahead, to a slight rise Veca had indicated as a place to stop, and waited expectantly.

Enris appeared around the wall of the gorge a moment later, a distant figure her inner sense recognized. She thought he raised a hand in salute, as if he'd seen her, too.

We'll wait for you, she sent.

Don't. I'll catch up. Despite the heavy pack she knew he carried, Enris was indeed approaching at a steady, distance-eating lope. *We can't be caught in the open, not with injuries. Who was hurt? How badly?*

Aryl wondered how he'd known; she hadn't thought Chaun's flash of pain that strong. *Myris. Morla. Chaun's still unconscious.*

And you? You don't feel *right.*

Offended, she tightened her shields to be sure whatever the Tuana *felt* was what she intended to share and nothing more. *There's nothing wrong with me but having to walk on your dirt.*

Knew you'd see sense one day. Beneath the amusement, real concern. *Keep them moving, Aryl. The storm's not done.*

Thunder rolled down the valley, as if on cue.

No one argued, though the exiles delayed to let Veca and Rorn rig a sling for Chaun from ropes and a blanket. Gijs stretched out on his back while they worked, eyes closed. Like several of the others, Aryl forced herself to chew methodically on the Grona bread. Her aunt, who sat beside her, did not.

Aryl snapped off a piece, offering it to Myris. "Trust me. It tastes better now."

"I couldn't." Myris tried to smile. She fussed with her prized Grona scarf, its bright blue and yellow—dyes being one of that Clan's skills—now liberally stained with blood. The rain had washed most of it from her face, exposing a deep gash above her right brow. The eyelid below was horribly swollen and black. She was too pale, the darks of both eyes too large. Nothing they could help here, Aryl thought anxiously, refusing to believe it might be nothing they could help at all. "Stop worrying," her aunt ordered, nothing wrong with her perception. "You're as bad as Ael."

She considered her aunt, struck by an idea. "He's with Haxel. How much can you sense from him?"

Chosen were Joined. That permanent connection didn't make them more able to *send* words to one another across distance, since *sending* was related to individual Power. But Costa had assured her—many times—that the link gave each a special insight into the state of the other regardless of distance. Her brother had claimed to know when his beloved Leri was lonely or sad or happy. Aryl remembered being convinced this was only so Costa had a ready excuse to leave her for his Chosen.

Then she'd found her way into the *other place*, where connection mattered more than distance. She believed now, after

Costa was dead and Leri one of the mindless Lost. Aryl's fingers sketched apology in her lap.

"You know perfectly well I can't *hear* him," Myris protested. "I'm not like you or—or Taisal."

"Yes, but can you tell me how he feels—right now?" She felt the other's puzzlement.

Seru, sitting nearby, leaned closer to catch the answer. Aryl smiled a welcome. Her cousin's interest in anything about Choice and being a Chosen was reassuringly normal.

Myris didn't appear to notice. Her hands clenched on her scarf, then she spoke in a whisper Aryl had to strain to hear. "Afraid. So afraid. He can hardly breathe."

Seru scrambled back. "I told you we shouldn't go this way." Not quite a shout, but everyone looked their way. "I told you!" That was. She lurched to her feet and broke into a clumsy run, but didn't go far, perhaps daunted by the glowering cloud and dead landscape on all sides. There she stood, back to her kind, head high and free of its hood; the freshening wind whipped desperate locks of her hair from its net, as expressive as any Chosen's.

Though Aryl ached to go to her, she stayed with Myris. "We're all afraid," she told her aunt. "Do you feel anything more? Is he comfortable? Warm? Cold?" She had no idea what Chosen truly felt; she did know each Joining was unique. Myris might not have her sister's Power—but she had her own sensitivities. "Is he anxious to be with you, or for you to be with him?"

"What an odd—" Myris blinked. "With him," she stated, her eyes brightening. "Yes. Wherever Ael is, he wants me there. They've found a place for us, Aryl!"

Though Aryl smiled with relief, her gaze lingered on Seru.

What did she see, that no one else could?

Chapter 4

"NICE BRIDGE."

Aryl ignored the comment and the deep laugh that went with it, though Veca gave Enris a dour look. Which was hardly fair. He'd been as good as his word, rejoining them soon after they'd begun to march again. He'd willingly taken a share of Chaun's awkward weight, too. They'd made better speed with his help.

Just as well. The wind had a bite to it, and smelled of lightning. Sheets of rain obscured the ridge on the other side of the valley; it wouldn't be long before it reached this one and their coats were still damp. She hoped it wouldn't freeze on them. Firstnight was upon them, its shadows barely darker than those of the clouds, sure to steal what remained of the day's warmth.

As Veca blithely predicted, there was a bridge near the mouth of the next gorge, but it was broken. Luckily for the exiles, the riverbed it had been built to span was dry and empty.

Aryl wasn't sure which bothered her more: the twin arches that ended in midair above a tumble of smashed stone, or the missing river.

No, she was sure. "Where's the water?"

"Who cares?" Veca pointed to the other side. "Haxel and the others aren't far now. Let's go." She headed toward the river-bank; the others began to follow.

Aryl frowned. "Do rivers disappear in Tuana?"

Enris signaled Gijs he was ready to go, but words brushed Aryl's thoughts. *Show me.*

She retrieved her memory of the raging torrent she'd seen from atop the ravine wall. "Veca saw it, too. Impossible to cross. It should be here."

A flare of *curiosity*, as quickly damped. "A puzzle for another day," Enris decided. To Gijs. "I swear he's gained weight." He made a show of favoring his right shoulder as he slipped the sling's rope over what padding his coat and a folded scrap of blanket could provide, all the while careful not to jostle its pas-senger. "Sure he's not sneaking food on us?"

Gijs managed a weary smile at this. He'd refused to let any-one else take his share—he and Chaun were heart-kin.

Aryl tucked the unconscious Om'ray's hand inside his coat, pausing to *reach* and assess his condition as best she could. Chaun's pain had eased to a dull ache. She thought she might be able to rouse him, but didn't dare. Instead, she sent a little of her strength along that contact, more confident this time she was actually helping.

As she stood, she managed to touch Gijs and send him what she could. She thought he stood a bit straighter. Hoped, anyway.

Yawned.

She closed her mouth quickly, embarrassed. They were all bone-tired, but no one else moved like they felt their arms and legs were about to fall off, no one else yawned. She was young and stronger than most. They relied on her.

All of them.

Her fingers found Enris as he passed, but the instant she began to send him strength, his shields slammed in place, mak-ing him virtually invisible to her inner sense. Outwardly? He glared at her and jerked away from her touch. "What do you think you're doing?"

Furious. He was furious.

How? No one else had noticed. Why was he angry? Aryl took a step back, a stinging heat rushing to her cheeks. The step became a stagger, the ground unsteady beneath her feet. She swayed with it as she would with a branch in the M'hir.

What was happening?

Everything pulled away; voices muted, light dimmed, motions were slow and disconnected. She clung to what awareness she could, watching Enris shrug off the sling and come toward her. She put up her hands . . . he was angry . . . she'd done something wrong . . . why was she wrong . . . what was wrong . . .

As her eyes closed against her will, her shoulders were gripped with bruising force. Strength *flooded* her body until she gasped and jerked free, feeling her every muscle on fire. "What?!!" She stared at Enris, dumbfounded.

"We can't carry you both." Low and fierce. "Never give what you need. Use more sense!"

He turned and picked up the sling, moving, to Aryl's restored perception, with his usual vigor.

Impossible.

He had just done for her, much more effectively, what she'd tried to do for her people. Enris Mendolar, Tuana unChosen, metalworker, couldn't know more about Power and its use than anyone she'd ever met. Couldn't *be* more powerful than an Adept.

Could he?

Aryl let several more exiles step in between before she followed, paying little attention to the route Veca had picked to cross the empty river.

She caught herself smiling, and had no idea why.

Beyond the fractured bridge, the valley narrowed and bent sharply toward Grona, as if hiding a secret. Even here, it would take the better part of a day to cross. Anyone doing so would face a wall more cliff than slope, a steep barrier Aryl thought might be entertaining to climb in better weather. Not in this. She tucked her hands inside her sleeves, blinking away snow— that misery having returned with a vengeance—and wondered why any Om'ray would live where the worst of all seasons could pass in the same day.

They were close now. Everyone could sense the others, that one was coming to meet them. Only Aryl—and his Chosen— knew it was her uncle, Ael sud Sarc. She peered through the whirling snow, hoping for a glimpse of the grove of stunted nekis she was sure she'd spotted from the ridge. She'd told no one else, but it must be their destination.

A tug on her sleeve. She glanced down to find Ziba, her face contorted, tears streaming down her cheeks. The child was distraught to the point of invisible, her emotions swamped by the need to return to her mother. Aryl bent to comfort her, to learn why Taen sent her while so upset, but the child spun out of her grasp and ran back down the line of march.

Seru. It had to be.

Aryl *reached* for her cousin and found . . . nothing.

She followed Ziba, careful not to run and draw attention. With the promise of shelter, everyone was walking with cheerful faces and renewed energy, including old Husni and Juo, who'd stayed together. Morla smiled at her, her injured wrist cradled to her chest, her solicitous Chosen hovering at her side.

Those coming last weren't smiling. Taen, Ziba now clinging to one arm. Tilip and young Fon Kessa'at, both looking worried. Together, they surrounded Seru, walking with her, but at a distance. As Aryl neared, she could see why.

Her cousin's eyes were closed. It had happened again.

Taen nodded a greeting. "Thanks for coming. I didn't know what to do—"

Seru's GONE. With the desperate anguish of the very young.

Hush. The anguish vanished behind shields as Taen hugged

her daughter close. "One moment we were talking about Grona," she said quietly, "the next, Seru shuts her eyes and starts babbling nonsense. A stranger's name. Something about frost and harvest. How there's work to be done and we have to hurry. When I asked what she meant, she didn't say another word." A heavy sigh. "Better than screaming we're all going to die."

She wasn't so sure, Aryl thought as she studied her cousin. Seru walked in a straight line—in the direction they all moved—but she lifted her feet too high as if forcing her way through drifts of snow. Not slowly either. Wherever she was going—wherever she thought she was going—she intended to get there without delay. " 'Work to be done,' " Aryl repeated. "What 'work?' Why 'hurry?'" She wasn't going to try to guess what "harvest." Nothing could grow here worth eating.

"A dream," Taen dismissed with a shrug, one hand holding Ziba to her side as they kept up. "You woke her before," she prompted.

"I'm not sure she's asleep." Weth could walk blind like this. But even if Seru had that Talent, how could she remember a place she'd never been? Aryl frowned. Should she touch her? Wake her?

Could she?

A flash of *joy* sped mind-to-mind through the exiles. Voices rose in greeting and relief.

Ael must be in sight.

"Go," Taen said, smiling involuntarily. "We'll stay with her."

Ziba's eyes widened. "No," she protested. "You have to bring her back!"

Interesting choice of words, Aryl thought, giving the child a sharp look. "I'll do my best," she promised, unwilling to lie. "First, we have to keep her moving. Can you do that, Ziba?"

"But everyone's stopped." The child was right. Aryl cast an anxious look forward.

Taen laid her hand on her daughter's shoulder. Whatever passed between them settled the child. "We'll bring Seru. Go."

Their trust weighed on her heart; the blank *nothing* where Seru should be was worse.

It didn't take long to find the delay. A silent knot of Om'ray stood around Ael, watching patiently as he held his Chosen close. Her uncle seemed oblivious to everything and everyone else, including the need to show the exhausted exiles the way out of the snow.

The other Chosen were allowing this—this utter waste of time. Aryl sighed and wiped snowdrops from her lashes, pondering the best way to interrupt their bliss. Surely, somewhere in the happy cloud of hair that presently shrouded both heads was her more sensible aunt.

Myris! This with what force she dared. *We must go!*

A blast of *heat* and *longing* and *belonging* assailed her. Aryl clamped down her shields, annoyed enough to stamp her foot. Chosen had no sense of priorities.

"Ael came that way." Enris' lips twitched. They'd laid Chaun on the ground; Husni cradled his head in her lap. The Tuana pointed.

"That way" was somewhere ahead and to the left along this featureless plain, a destination obscured by swirling snow. Aryl *reached*. Haxel and the others were close. The mere thought of rest weakened her knees. The others could be in no better shape. Even Enris, despite his sturdy presence at her side, had to be wearing down. "We need to go," she said quietly. "If you and Gijs pick up Chaun again, maybe the rest will get the idea."

As quietly. "They'll follow you."

No, she wanted to say, but couldn't.

"Unfair," he agreed, as if she had. "Doesn't change the weather. They've come this far because of you, Aryl Sarc. You can't stop leading them now, just because you wasted your strength."

Lower lip secured between her teeth, where it couldn't tremble, Aryl glared at the Tuana. He gave her a wide, unrepentant grin.

She whirled and strode away, without waiting for anyone else.

Her feet crunched dead vegetation, the sound muted whenever she stepped in one of the growing piles of snow. Her breathing was too loud and too quick to her ears. Fine to believe they'd follow. What if no one noticed she'd left?

A tuft of taller vegetation ahead. Without slowing, she yanked it from the hard dirt, shook it clean, and tied it in a knot.

If Enris was wrong, she'd look a thorough fool.

If he was right . . . she stopped there.

Then, behind her, came the rustle and muted comments of people picking up their packs, sorting their marching order, starting to move. She blew a soundless whistle of relief.

A quicker set of limping steps as someone hurried to catch up. "Aryl—"

She glanced sideways. Ael's cheeks were flaming red. He began to gesture apology, and she touched his hand to stop it.

In the proper order of things, Myris wouldn't be walking in this nightmare of whirling snowdrops, shouldn't have been exposed to stupid lumps of ice, wouldn't have been hurt. More for her list. Aryl took back her hand, drawing her icy fingers within her sleeve. "Tell me you found a warm spot."

Ael's joyful laugh startled her. "Oh, it's warm," he promised. "Wait till you see. That way," he added, indicating a line of darkness that curved ahead, then bent to their right.

She squinted through the snow, making out a steep slope of dirt, weathered and loose. This had to be the near edge of the wide depression she'd seen from the ridge, the one that ran the length of the valley. "Another dry river," she guessed, astonished at its size.

"And frozen rain." Ael spread his arms to encompass the landscape around them—what they could see of it through the snowdrops. "Nothing here should surprise us, Aryl."

But something had. She *tasted* his excitement. Ael might be worried about Myris, but above all he anticipated the Om'rays' reaction when they saw . . . what?

"Warm," she repeated. She'd settle for that.

The wind faded to a whimper around their ears. The snow-drops, contrarily, worsened, becoming larger. They stuck together in the air, drifting down in soft clumps, deadening all sound. One landed on Aryl's forehead and melted to soak her eye and cheek, a drip tracing her jaw and sliding down her neck. She shivered. Truenight was almost upon them. They should be in sight of Haxel and the shelter by now, but the steady fall closed like woven panels around the exiles. She kept *reaching* for the others, reassuring herself they were together despite the poor visibility. She wanted to go deeper, to learn if Seru had regained her senses, if Gijs and Enris were tiring, if Myris and Morla were in pain—but refrained. She couldn't help, even if she knew.

Shadows appeared to either side, indistinct through the snow, irregular in height and shape. The grove she'd seen—this had to be its start. Aryl quickened her pace. Strange, that the ground was smoother and more level than before.

Strange, too, that what she'd assumed were tall nekis stalks leaned against one another. Aryl blinked away snowdrops, frustrated.

A flicker of light beckoned ahead. Warmth, comfort. She sensed *relief* as those following saw it, too. Ael's smile was in his voice. "There it is. Wait till you see—"

Do you see? The sending from Enris held none of the relief or joy of the rest.

A few more steps, another blink, and the indistinct shadows re-formed. Aryl slowed and stopped as she understood.

This wasn't a grove.

Others passed her, packs coated in white, eager for shelter. Aryl let them.

Thick drops of snow slipped and danced around her, playing hide/seek. She scuffed her toe through what lay on the ground to find a pavement of flat, well-fitted stone, then looked up again. What rose beside her weren't leaning stalks.

Though it was wood.

Huge splintered beams—some heaved upright and tangled, like sticks tossed by a child and let fall, others protruding from mounds—bordered this road. For road it was. Making this a place—a built place—before its destruction. Home to the forgotten Chosen whose headdress pressed against her skin.

Sona.

Only one word, but sent with a certainty she shared. Enris was right. This had been the home of a Clan. But what did it mean? What had happened? Were they safe or now in danger from more than the storm?

There, with the last group of exiles, came the only Om'ray who might have answers. How Seru Parth knew anything about this dead place, Aryl couldn't imagine, but she no longer doubted. She took a step to intercept her cousin, then hesitated.

Seru was chatting happily to Ziba, pointing ahead to the welcome light, laughing as if they'd been out for an afternoon's visit instead of a march across ice and rock.

As if she'd never left her body empty on the road.

"Come," Enris said softly. "Answers can wait for a roof."

Haxel had indeed found them a roof: the remains of a building with a few roof beams askew overhead. Stone and black wood rose as walls to shoulder height on three sides, barring the cold fingers of wind. The First Scout and the others had moved loose rubble to clear a flat, if not level, area within, in so doing discovering the remains of a stone hearth. It held a crackling fire for the first time in—none of them bothered to speculate how long this place had been a ruin. Om'ray lived in the known and the now; for the first time, Aryl understood the comfort that could give. A shame she couldn't bring herself to feel it.

Their carefully gathered twists of dry grass were put aside

for the future; there were abundant splinters of dark, wide-grained wood to burn. Splinters. As if the split and shattered remains of beams and floorboards were anything so harmless. Those still framing the door and inner walls were deeply inset with carvings, images of growing things twined around complex, unfamiliar symbols. They'd had meaning, once. The others ignored them, after commenting on the quality of work. Such always outlived its maker. They were comforted by that, too.

Aryl leaned in a shadow against the tallest portion of surviving wall and tried not to frown.

The rest of Yena's exiles sat shoulder to shoulder, chapped faces rosy in the light of the flames. Some opened their coats to coax what warmth the fire offered; others snuggled together under blankets. Close quarters for twenty-three, but no one complained. They were together.

Packs hung from the straightest beam to keep them out of the way. That, and because Husni fussed about crawlers spoiling what food remained. Despite seeing no other life for days, canopy habits persisted. Their assortment of mismatched pots, packed with snow, nestled near glowing coals. A trick from Grona. Before their arrival, Syb and Weth had made a soup from the bread they'd carried, letting it simmer and thicken while they'd waited for the rest of the Om'ray. The result had no taste but, Aryl decided, fishing the inevitable gritty bit from between her teeth, the hot moist stuff might have been fresh dresel by the speed with which the first offering disappeared. Their largest pot was stewing a second batch—Myris had volunteered her entire packet.

Their elders smiled wearily at one another. Ziba was snugged under Seru's arm, both with their eyes more closed than open.

She wouldn't disturb this hard-won peace, Aryl decided. Plenty of time to talk to her cousin in the morning.

At the thought of spending the night, she wrinkled her nose. The place reeked of wet boots and burning wood. The air glit-

tered, firelight caught by the fine, acrid dust they'd kicked up
on arriving, yet to settle. Shelter, indeed. How quickly she'd
grown used to sleeping outside. She resolved to be grateful—
and look for better tomorrow.

Enris propped himself against the wall beside her. He
shoved a lock of dusty black hair from his forehead, leaving a
streak. His eyes, bright and dark, surveyed the room. "Yena
don't build like this," he stated. "Not from what I saw in the
canopy."

So she wasn't the only one restless. "The Tikitik built our village," Aryl explained, pitching her voice to his ears. "Yena
Om'ray—" she paused to choose her words, "—made homes."

The Cloisters held records: names and Joinings, births and
deaths—collected and understood by Adepts. All ordinary
Yena knew of their past was the echo of those gone before held
in the beautiful cunning of their woodcraft: cupboards and
furnishings, forgotten hiding places, sturdy bridgework.
Homes where Om'ray feet polished floors to gleaming, themselves works of art. Homes entrusted to the First Chosen of
each generation, to be lovingly maintained for the next.

Homes. Ashes falling like black snowdrops into the Lay
Swamp, scorched remains abandoned in the canopy to be
overgrown by vines and thickles. To rot and be erased.

Stone was better. Aryl pressed her shoulder blades against
the wall for comfort. Stone, or beams like these, she thought,
following a dark line with her eye. They must have been made
from entire, full grown stalks, cut to lie flat atop one another
or fit end on end. Too heavy for a Yena home, carried high on
the living fronds of a rastis, but their thickness promised en-
durance and protection from the cold.

"You're right, though," she mused. "This doesn't look like
their work." The Tikitik coaxed living stalks to their bidding.
She'd seen it for herself. Yena homes owed their structure to as-
sembled pieces already in their final, useful shape, ready for
gauze-on-frame windows and dresel pod roofs. These beams?
Their initial shaping bore tool marks like those Yena wood-

workers left on the planks they trimmed to replace wear on bridges or ladders. "Do you see the carving? That's not Tikitik."

Enris made a pleased sound. "No? Then I've something else to show you—tomorrow, when we've decent light."

"Tomorrow," she agreed, trying not to yawn. She ran her hand along the stone. "Is this at all like Tuana? Oud work?"

"Oud dig holes," he snapped, as if insulted. "Tuana Om'ray build for ourselves. But not—" said more thoughtfully, "—not like this. We'd never waste wood on supports. It doesn't grow on the plains. All we have comes from the Oud—scraps from disused tunnels."

Aryl wrinkled her nose again. These dry lifeless mountains were bad enough. If there were no nekis or rastis, she didn't care for Tuana's plains either. Not that her preference mattered. "Where do the Oud get it?"

"No one knows." With a "who cares?" shrug.

So Tuana shared Yena's lack of curiosity about the not-*real* beings who lived on Cersi. She shouldn't be surprised; it was an Om'ray trait. One they couldn't afford, she fumed to herself. The exiles had to learn everything they could to survive.

"The Oud know," she challenged. "We should."

"I never wondered before," he admitted. "Maybe they trade with your Tikitik for pieces."

Tired as she was, Aryl straightened to stare up at Enris. "Oud and Tikitik?" He might have redrawn the world. "Together?"

That wide grin. "Hardly together. Trade's one thing. Getting along's another. From all I've heard, they like each other even less than they like us. Without the Agreement, who knows which of them we'd still have?"

"How do you know we'd still be here?"

Enris gave her a very strange look. "We are the world." As if she'd somehow forgotten who and what she was.

"Are we?" Aryl murmured. When he would have protested, she gestured apology, her hand heavy. "We're all tired," she said. "We've a place to sleep. Be glad of that."

"After going how far the wrong way?" A grumble like the storm outside. Fingers brushed the back of her hand. *Oud reshaped this place once.* Enris held back something more. She sensed its troubled edge.

Her people were safe and content, she fumed. Was it too much to ask to savor that victory? *Maybe Sona deserved it.* With a mental *snap* she instantly regretted.

Enris gave no sign she'd struck at him. *Did you?* he sent almost gently. *Do they?* This with an unnecessary nod at the Yena exiles sitting in front of them.

Though busy with pots and embers, Haxel looked up, the beginning of a question on her face. Aryl made herself smile back. "You're making people nervous," she said. Not quite a whisper.

"As they should be," he countered the same way. "Don't let them stay too long, Aryl. You can't trust the Oud."

"I'm not a fool." She might not have met one, but every Om'ray understood their world. Only Om'ray cared about Om'ray. "We can't leave until Chaun and Myris can travel. There are others hurt. Let alone Juo. We don't need her giving birth mid-journey. We'll use the time to find food . . . get some rest. All of which, I'm thankful to say, can wait for morning." With a yawn, Aryl leaned against the Tuana's comfortingly solid arm as she contemplated where to sleep. "Anyway," she continued idly, "what's this 'don't let *them* stay?' It's not as if you'd leave without us."

She'd meant to lighten the mood; instead, the words fell into silence, like a treasure let drop in the black waters of the Lay. Despite their physical contact, her inner sense gave her nothing beyond the *who* and *where* of him. She drew back and twisted to look at him. His face, smudged by exhaustion and dirt, was shadowed more than revealed by the flickers of firelight. Reflections like tiny flames danced deep in his dark eyes as he returned her gaze.

Then, predictably, the corner of his wide mouth crooked up, creasing a dimple. "I'm the one who's seen an ice storm before, remember?" he said lightly. "Delay too long and no one's going anywhere. Even Grona warned against travel late in the cold season. You've had a taste of it." Before she could respond, the Tuana pushed himself from the wall and her. "Speaking of taste—" a too-quick laugh, "—looks like there's more ready."

Aryl watched Enris squat beside Gijs, as if he had nothing on his mind but a still-empty stomach. The other Om'ray made room with a laugh and some comment she didn't catch.

She took her lower lip between her teeth, not hungry at all.

Enris hadn't said he'd leave them.

He hadn't said he'd stay either.

"Tomorrow," she said out loud. "Everything looks better in daylight."

"Which implies sleeping first." Haxel replaced Enris, her lean form taking much less space. Unlike the Tuana, her emotions—satisfaction, pride, determination—were easy to read. Deliberately so.

Aryl tightened her shields to keep in her own. The First Scout had a right to her pride: she'd found safety for true-night. No need to share her own foreboding—or Enris'. "I'll help keep watch outside."

"Leave it to those who've had some rest. You led well today, Aryl Sarc." A stronger flash of pride. "As I expected."

Before Aryl could utter a word, the other Om'ray was on the move through the firelight and shadow, touching shoulders, helping arrange blankets as more and more of the exiles stretched out near the fire. Haxel finally settled beside Weth, who'd managed to spoon some liquid between Chaun's slack lips before donning her blindfold. The conflict between her Chosen as she remembered him and his pale strange face must have become too much for her Talent to reconcile.

Led well?

If she'd hadn't led them at all, Aryl reminded herself bit-terly, Weth and Chaun would be sitting across a table, supping by the light of glows, not a fretful fire. He'd tell her one of his stories and she'd laugh—or they'd fall silent, as Chosen were prone to do, and gaze into one another's eyes, fingertips just touching, thoughts and selves mingled in a haven of their own.

Lie down before you fall down.

Her look of affront was wasted. Enris had his broad back to her, busy slurping his share of bread-broth with gusto. Aryl yawned involuntarily until her jaw ached and her eyes watered. Tempting to stay where she was. And prove what? Hardly a good example in someone who led. However unwillingly.

With a sigh, she went in search of room on the floor for her bed.

Before it left, the storm wandered the ruins. Snow curled around the base of stone, dusted askew beams to lines of white. Fingers of wind explored emptiness and rustled withered stems. A last chill breath guttered the fire that held back the dark, stirring the hair of those who slept like the dead.

On some level, Aryl heard the storm, shivered in the chill, but these were distant, unimportant things. The *other* pressed against her like a lover in the night, seeking entry, whispering seduction.

She resisted with all her strength, not knowing if she struggled to push the wild *darkness* away or to pull herself free of it, only that if she let it claim her, what she was would be lost.

As she fought, whispers became voices, clamoring to be heard. She refused to listen, heard herself moan and came half awake at the sound.

They—*something*—tried to speak to her through her mouth. She *pushed* harder and . . .

. . . was awake.

Aryl froze in place, her hand hard against her lips. When no further sound came out, she lowered her hand and eased herself up on an elbow.

The fire was banked; Enris had shown them how. The light

from its embers bathed the low rounds of shoulder and hip, the huddles of blanket and coat that marked where Om'ray lay asleep. She was the only one awake.

A dream. That was all.

She was the only one awake, she realized a moment later, but not the only one disturbed. Sobbing, so quiet Aryl almost missed it over the breathing of the rest. Seru. Did she dream, too?

Someone else squirmed and whimpered. Aryl *reached*, careful to lower her shields only enough to seek outward, not to send and disturb.

Ziba?

She shouldn't be surprised. What they'd faced today would give anyone bad dreams, even a youngling with the courage of any Chosen—

Yet another soft complaint. Aryl *reached* again.

Juo.

Even easier to explain, she decided. All the bedding they'd carried couldn't counteract the hard cold pavement beneath, cracked and heaved into sharp edges. Hardest on poor Juo, swollen with her unborn. Wise Husni had refused to lie on the stones, instead curling against her seated Chosen, who, to everyone's amusement, had began to snore at once. There they were on the other side of the fire, like a pair of ancient rastis whose fronds had intertwined until neither could fall alone.

There was light, similar to the radiance that found its way through curtains. A soft, comforting light.

Nothing was wrong. She'd dreamed.

That was all.

Aryl started to close her eyes, settling back down. She was so tired . . .

. . . light took a red tinge, like blood bathed the walls, then suddenly faded. *Darkness* assumed movement and form to tear at her consciousness, like a wind trying to tear her from a safe hold.

. . . Aryl thrust herself from the *other place,* her heart pounding, eyes wide. She sat up.

Impossible. It hadn't been real. Couldn't be real. Her mind couldn't slip into that *place* while she slept. She was safe.

She had to be.

They had to be—

She'd dreamed.

That was all.

Words formed, as if echoing her thoughts . . . *Bad dream?*

Bad rock, Aryl managed to reply, careful to add overtones of rueful amusement as she settled back down. She pretended to fidget and forced a smile in case Myris could see her face. *My bones need more padding.*

Her aunt couldn't afford to use her Talent until she healed, not that Aryl would have a choice if Myris detected turmoil. She had to trust her shields, being unable to move out of contact without disturbing Veca, close behind her.

A pillow would be nice. A flash of *pain,* quickly hidden. Ael groaned in Joined empathy but didn't wake.

Aryl cupped her hand against her aunt's soft cheek. Too warm. *Rest,* she sent, along with a careful sharing of her own strength, and felt more than heard Myris sigh in relief.

She waited until sure her aunt slept. Longer.

Then she lay back, eyes open, to wait for daylight.

When all darkness would be gone.

Despite breath-fogging cold at firstlight, no one lingered in their shelter. Their still-warm bedding went to the injured, while Ael and Weth rebuilt the fire. There was no question of leaving today. Myris was feverish and too quiet. Chaun had roused to open his eyes and smile, nothing more. Husni chided her daughter's Chosen for lying around while others worked, but when she turned away, her face showed every Harvest. They all shared the involuntary waves of *agony* when he moved; only Weth could persuade him to swallow. He was worse.

Sona was worse by the light of day, too. They used the name, though no one could give good reason beyond a wary look toward Seru Parth. In turn, she remained obstinately herself and refused to talk about what she called "yesterday's weather." That weather had blown itself over the mountain ridge and away, its clouds a tatter of wisps in the sky, its snow and rain little more than dark stains. In this valley, stone shed water or dirt sucked it down. As well, they'd collected what they could before truenight, Aryl thought, licking always-dry lips.

A long night indeed. She hadn't slept again for fear of dreams—in revenge, her mind might have been a wing on the M'hir for all the control she'd had over the direction of her thoughts. Seru. Ziba. The *darkness*. Bern and his Chosen. Myris. This place—its past. Her mother. Yena. The strangers. The headdress and bones. Tomorrow.

Enris.

No more of him, Aryl vowed, tightening her belt to silence her empty stomach. With daylight had come common sense, or its kin, pragmatism. The Tuana was a stranger, on Passage. Their paths had crossed, to the exiles' benefit. If he felt the need to continue his journey alone, it was his right and obligation. However long he remained, they'd take advantage of his strength and knowledge.

If she could avoid him this morning, all the better.

The exiles divided into groups to search for their most pressing need: food. Aryl had hoped to go with Seru, to talk to her cousin. Haxel and Cetto claimed her first.

"Reminds me of the nekis that fell one M'hir," Haxel said finally. "Took a good portion of Parth grove with it. Remember, Cetto?"

The former Yena Councillor stood with one hand shading his eyes, though the rising sun—and Amna—was behind them. "Wasn't this bad."

The three of them were atop the highest beam roofing last night's shelter, its wide surface secure, if tilted. It provided a useful viewpoint. Aryl found its height a comfort. She pursed her lips and surveyed their surroundings once more, this time looking for detail rather than absorbing the shock.

The valley narrowed here to perhaps an easy half-day's walk from one formidable cliff wall to the other. It drew tighter still not far ahead, where another twist hid what might be its beginning.

Two lines scored the valley floor. One, the dry riverbed, its pattern of tumbled stone hinting at the force which had once scoured its width; the other, matched to the river's course though set high above its bank, what had been a roadway of pale, cut stone, now fragmented and heaved. Aryl's gaze followed the ruined road and empty river to where they disappeared from sight around the valley's bend. Where did they go?

As for where they were . . . the road cut through what had clearly been a village, between this side of the river and the cliff, from its extent, more populous than Yena had ever been. The violence from beneath that furrowed and tossed the ground of the valley mouth hadn't so easily erased Sona itself. The buildings, though small, had been sturdy. From what she could see from this vantage point, most had been attached to one another by low stone walls and rooftop beams, providing extra strength.

Not unscathed, however. Most of those beams had come free of their supports, to lie like tossed sticks. Some of the stone walls had crumbled; others stood seemingly straight and untouched but spanned dark pits where the ground had been eaten away from below.

Homes, she guessed. Om'ray homes—another guess—of a style unknown to the exiles. Each opened to a narrow roadway off the main one; each shared walled open space with their neighbors, now choked with dead vegetation. Aryl watched Syb and Taen try to force their way through one such space.

They soon gave up and rejoined the rest, searching what homes remained accessible.

"Can we be sure this was once Om'ray?" Cetto rumbled. "There's no Cloisters."

"Here," Haxel pointed out.

She was right, Aryl agreed. Though Grona's Cloisters sat near their homes, Yena's was a good distance from their village—why, no one knew or wondered. "That could have been their meeting hall." The First Scout indicated a mound of shattered wood across the main road, half buried in soil and stone. A large building, set to overlook the river. If these had been Om'ray, it would have hosted every gathering of importance, as well as those for the joy of being together.

Aryl shuddered. Then her attention was caught by a gleam across the river. The rising sun had reached an area filled with white straight stalks—stalks with, she squinted to see, familiar branched tops. Many were toppled, most leaned in disarray, but she knew what she saw. "Nekis!" She hadn't been completely wrong.

"We looked." Haxel made a gesture of disgust. "Dead, like the rest of this place."

"How?" Aryl stared at the plants. She could understand those broken or buried failing to survive, but these were the canopy's most common growth. Nothing stopped young nekis surging from the ground, or regrowing in their multitudes from a fallen parent.

"In the groves, their feet are in the Lay Swamp," Cetto suggested, his low voice somber. "Perhaps when the river failed, these did, too."

Could strong, towering nekis—though none of these had been tall—be killed so easily? Aryl found the parched grove more a blow than the village. She'd thought of the groves and canopy as permanent fixtures of the world. Her home. At best, the swamp beneath them had been a nuisance, a threat to the careless. A new notion, that its black and dangerous water had been necessary to the growth above.

"Firewood." With that practical dismissal, Haxel directed their attention closer to hand. "There's something I don't understand. Those lines—they go under the buildings. See?"

Obviously something other than the crumbling walls or roadways. Puzzled, Aryl followed the scout's impatient finger as it indicated where they stood, the remains of the next building, then jabbed over to one closer to the other end of the village. At first, she saw nothing but the confusion of debris and time.

Then, she saw it. Haxel's "lines" weren't walls, but narrow depressions. They bounded the village, a course of small, similar stones. Once she recognized them, she saw they ran everywhere. If they'd been connected before the destruction, they would have formed an intricate network of shallow ditches. Some went beneath each home, reappearing on the other side.

Aryl's eyes flashed to the dry riverbed. She laughed, overjoyed by the simple elegance of it.

"I fail to see anything amusing about this place," Cetto grumbled.

She gestured apology. "It's only an idea . . ."

"What?" demanded the First Scout.

"When the river was full—" Aryl used her hands to mimic that flow, "—it would spill over at that point." She indicated where the boundary depression cut through the riverbank, what would have been upstream of the meeting hall and village. "Remember the ravine, after the ice rain? Water takes the low path. It would flow into all of these lines."

"Why?" Haxel asked. Both older Om'ray were frowning. "There are better ways to bring water to a home than this."

Aryl thought of her brother Costa, and the containers of growing things in his room. How they needed water brought to them to survive. "Not to the homes," she thought aloud. "To the spaces between them. This is a dry place—too dry for plants." The rightness of it made her heart pound. "Maybe these Om'ray grew their food like the Grona, but instead of fields and the chance of rain, they grew it here, between their homes, and took water from the river."

Haxel wasn't slow. "There are stone ditches like these through the nekis grove."

Om'ray who grew their own grove? Aryl's eyes widened. She couldn't imagine living like the Grona—or Enris' Tuana, for that matter. But this? "What if we could bring the water back?" she asked abruptly.

Cetto's deep astonished laugh lifted a few heads their way. "You never think small, Aryl Sarc."

Haxel didn't smile or say a word. But as they climbed down to rejoin the rest, Aryl noticed the scout lingered to look up the valley for a good long time, to where the outthrust of cliff hid the river's source.

Interlude

THEY WERE GOING TO STAY.

Enris stepped onto what had been a narrow, long porch and ducked to enter through what had never been a door.

They were going to make these ruins into homes and stay.

Carelessly he shouldered aside a half beam, dust and debris raining down on his head. His feet crunched something in the gloom.

There was nothing here, he fumed, nothing worth their lives or his to find. Nothing to sustain them, even if they'd be tolerated by the Oud. Broken pots, shattered sticks, anything and everything else rotted or carried away.

There was no future here. No answers.

"Any luck, Tuana?"

Enris bit back what he might have said. Gijs didn't deserve his frustration. "Not yet. You?"

The other Om'ray joined him, coughing despite the gauze they'd each wrapped over their mouths. Fine dust coated every surface; once disturbed, it hung in the air. "Nothing." Gijs began poking at a pile at the far end of the room. "Haxel claims we can boil our boots. Not ready for that meal, I tell you."

Enris' stomach chose that moment to growl and he was grateful the light was too dim inside to show his blush. "Baked glove for me."

Gijs laughed. "Don't worry. You've no bones showing, unChosen," as if this would be a comfort.

What it was? A reminder, Enris thought, of how tough and resilient Yena were. The longer he was with them, the better he understood how they'd survived life suspended in the canopy—and on rations scant for a child, let alone an active adult. But it was one thing to be a survivor and quite another to recognize your own folly. Coming here was bad enough.

Staying?

He had to talk to Aryl—they should be scouting the best way to Vyna together; instead, here he was, choking on dust.

Dust that turned darker as the light from the one window was abruptly blocked by a pair of white-clad legs. The legs were followed by a wriggling form in yellow who dropped to the floor with a cascade of pebbles—and more dust—to stand erect with a grin. "Did you find it yet?"

Trust the youngster to make a game of this grim search. Ziba Uruus was a match for his little brother, Worin, all right: a disarming mix of mischief and innocence. Enris grinned back, dust stinging his cracked lips. "Find what?"

"Breakfast!" With that, the tiny Om'ray marched confidently to a spot on the bare stone floor. She was still an instant, head cocked to the side like a curious loper, then began to move her hands in midair as if shaking something out and pressing the result flat on an invisible, waist-high surface.

Enris looked a question at Gijs. The other Om'ray shrugged and said gruffly, "This is no place to play, Ziba. Go outside. Find your mother."

"I am not playing," she retorted. "Everyone knows you have to squeeze the seeds out first."

Fascinated, Enris watched as her small hands mimed collecting something apparently sticky and then shaking it free over another invisible container. She wiped her fingers on her coat, leaving streaks of nothing but dust. "There." With relish. "The seeds are for planting," she explained, pointing to midair. "This is the good part." At "this" Ziba held up both hands, cupped as if supporting a round mass. "There's enough fresh *rokly* for you, too. I'll share."

Gijs appeared at a loss for words. Wait till Juo produced their firstborn, Enris thought with amusement. Well used to the antics of the young, he smiled and held out his hand. "Thank you. I'm hungry."

Instead of playing along, Ziba's smile faded and she took a quick step back. "You can't have any. You're not one of us."

"Ziba!" Gijs gestured apology at Enris. "She's repeating old lessons. Don't be offended. Ziba—" sternly, "—Enris Mendolar is no 'stranger.' "

A foot smaller than his palm stamped the ruined floor. "He is so!"

An unChosen arrived on Passage was by custom avoided by younger unChosen, watched by Adepts, assessed by all; he remained a stranger until the moment of Choice, when he would assume the name of his Chosen, Joining not only her life, but her family and Clan.

None of the exiles, not even Husni, that stickler for tradition, had made him feel like a stranger. The past fist of days? He'd forgotten his lack of official status. Someone hadn't, someone whose opinion mattered to Ziba. No need to ask who, he thought unhappily. Seru Parth. She had reason; nothing he could change.

The Tuana dropped to one knee, a move that brought his gaze level with Ziba's. Her eyes were huge and dark and challenging. "I'm not of Yena," he agreed. "But we aren't in Yena any—"

"This is Sona," she interrupted with scorn. "Everyone knows that."

Did they now? "What else does 'everyone' know, Ziba?"

"The Buas live here. They grow the best rokly of anyone." The words tumbled out, glib and confident, but Ziba stopped and looked startled, as if she hadn't expected to have an answer. "I want rokly for breakfast," she finished less certainly. "That's why I came through the window. But . . . there's no rokly here." With a glower, as if the empty room was his fault.

"Of course not, young fool," Gijs burst out. "There's no such thing. There's no family named Bua. Don't waste our time with your nonsense!"

Wait. Let me talk to her, Enris sent urgently, sure there was more going on. Too late. Ziba fled into the bright sunlight. The flash of *INDIGNATION* she left behind made both Om'ray wince.

"I'll make sure her parents hear about this."

"Someone should." And soon, the Tuana thought, staring out the doorway. This wasn't normal play. This was something else. "I'll—"

A pebble bounced along on the stone floor. Enris turned, half expecting to find Ziba back at the window, making faces. But it wasn't the child, he realized in horror as more pebbles and a choking dust began to rain down. It was the support beam he had so casually shifted from its ages-old rest earlier. A beam about to drop.

No time, no way to know how the beam would fall, or if the entire rotten structure might collapse with it. Grabbing Gijs, Enris flung the smaller Om'ray toward the opening. At the same time, he *pushed* at the wood and stone overhead with all his inner strength. Wanted it *away!*

As Gijs scrambled to his feet outside, Enris found himself bathed in sunlight.

There was no stone or wood overhead.

He grimaced. The pieces had to come down somewhere. Hopefully not on an Om'ray head. He *reached* anxiously.

No pain or alarm.

"Where did it go?" he wondered aloud.

"It's gone—the entire roof. Gone." Gijs stood in the doorway. His hand stroked one of its large stones, as if for reassurance. "You did that. I felt—I felt Power." He stepped back inside, staring at the sky before gazing in wonder at Enris. "What did you do, Tuana?"

Not quite what he'd intended? Enris shrugged. "I *pushed* it away from us." He stopped there.

Show me how. This with fierce determination. *TEACH ME!*

Stung and repulsed by the raw *need* of Gijs' sending, Enris slammed down his inner shields to keep the other out.

Was this how Aryl felt?

"Now's not the time," he said aloud. "Unless you want those boots for supper."

Gijs sketched a gracious apology through the air, but his blue eyes glittered like frost.

* ✳ *

"What's she done now?" Taen looked more harassed than worried. Dead leaves snarled her hairnet and one cheek was scratched.

Enris changed his mind. If Ziba wasn't with her mother, no point—as *his* mother would say—stirring that pot. Instead, he put on his widest smile. "Nothing at all. Do you need help?"

"Think you can get in there?"

"There" was one of the gaps between ruined buildings, on this side bounded by a waist-high stone wall. Beyond the stone was another wall, this of vegetation grown—and died—into a dense mass of vines.

With thorns.

"Why," Enris asked reasonably, "would I want to?"

"Aryl thinks these were fields, like the Grona's. If they were, maybe there's—" this with weary doubt, "—still something in the ground worth eating."

Fields? Enris studied the gap with this in mind. Had it once been filled with rows of crops instead of this wild tangle? A couple of narrow beams crisscrossed overhead, both wrapped in brown stems. He'd wondered about those. The wood was too thin and flimsy to take weight. Most had snapped and fallen long ago. But they could, he realized, have supported vines. He'd seen plants thrive in midair for himself in the canopy, strange as it seemed.

If there was anything left to harvest, though, it would be buried. Enris scuffed his toe against the hard packed dust and stone underfoot. The Grona had nice, sturdy digging blades. Al-

most as good as Tuana's. A shame neither he nor the exiles had
seen fit to bring one of those awkward-to-carry tools along. He
pulled his short knife from his belt and promised it a sharpening,
then eyed the thorns. "I'll give it a try. Where's Aryl, anyway?"

"She's gone looking for Seru. Our Chooser." Taen's delicate
stress of the last word sent Enris crashing forward, thorns or no
thorns.

He was more than aware the Yena Chosen waited for him to
pay court to their one and only.

They could keep waiting.

Forearms up so his coat sleeves protected his face, he drove his
legs into the mass, letting momentum gain territory. The thorns
snagged on the fabric and in his hair. Their source was brittle and
dry, stems that snapped as he pulled free. Four steps . . . another
two and a forward stumble . . . he was through the thickest part.
He stopped to look around, sneezing at the inevitable dust.

Fields, indeed. Away from the overgrown outer edge, order was
still discernible. Stalks with stubby tendrils at their top made one
line, clumps of leaves with wrinkled pods another, parallel to the
first. Dead vines hung in rows, too, a once-living curtain that might
have protected the plants beneath from the hot summer sun.

"We need Traud," Enris muttered to himself. Traud Licor and
his family tended Tuana's vast fields, and knew every kind of plant.

He'd just have to dig and . . .

Something wasn't right. Or too right.

The rows were straight. Straight and level. Ditches of small
stones ran between each, themselves straight, level, and undis-
turbed. The destruction that had heaved roadways and buildings
everywhere else had bypassed this place.

Not a good sign. Not good at all. A general reshaping was Oud
negligence, a threat to be ranked with flood or storm, impersonal
and relentless. But this? This could only happen if—Enris made
himself think it—if the Oud had attacked Sona's Om'ray.

The bones in the valley hadn't been those of a fellow un-
Chosen, leaving on Passage, but of someone desperately running
from death.

Long ago. Enris brushed thorns from his hair and made himself focus. Long ago. Sona had broken the Agreement, for what reason he couldn't imagine, and the Oud had reacted.

Those Om'ray were no longer *real*. What they'd done or not done no longer mattered. Only the living counted, and they were hungry.

Guessing that a plant with pods above ground wouldn't have a tuber, Enris went to his knees beside the tendrilled stalks and lifted his knife.

The Oud were below.

Sweat stood out on his brow. He couldn't bring the knife down.

Oud were below and all Om'ray stood on this shell of a world, pinned between sky and dirt, the only safety an Agreement older than them all, a promise not to change. But nothing stayed the same.

Which meant nothing was safe. Nothing.

Enris drove the knife into the hardened soil with all his might. It snapped below the handle.

A wave of concern. *What's wrong?*

Ignoring Aryl, he stabbed the broken blade into the ground, over and over again. With each stab, he made a vow.

He would find a better way. Stab!

He would find a Clan who didn't live in fear. Stab!

He would go to Vyna.

Chapter 5

"**W**HAT'S WRONG?"

Aryl ignored Juo's question. She wouldn't tell anyone else what Enris believed or what he'd decided. She wished she didn't know, but his mind had been appallingly open to hers at that moment. She could still taste dirt, thrown up by his furious, futile cuts at the ground, feel the prickle of thorns. She understood, as never before, why Tuana feared what lay beneath their feet as Yena feared what hunted the dark.

Oud had attacked Om'ray.

His reactions were hers, too. *Fear . . . disgust . . . rage . . .* finally, *resolve.* Too strong, too passionate, too destructive. She trembled and wished them gone, unfelt.

She didn't wish Enris gone.

But he wouldn't stay. She understood that, too. He believed they weren't safe, that no Om'ray was safe. He believed there was a Clan—somewhere—with technology of its own, free of the Agreement. That it was the key not to the future, but to their survival.

She wasn't sure he was wrong.

"Seru went this way," Juo said. "You coming?" She didn't

stop, though she kept to flatter ground. A concession to her changed balance.

Could the Oud hear their steps? Were they below, listening for trespassers? Aryl caught herself following in silence, as if stalking prey in the canopy, or avoiding becoming prey.

What difference would it make? Her next step was an angry thud that brought Juo's head around.

"You walk like the Tuana."

"Why would Seru come here?" Aryl countered, stepping over another dry ditch after Juo. By so doing, they left the village itself. Ahead was a series of dirt mounds, head-high, running parallel to the now-sheer cliff. Good thing they'd come down to the valley floor before this, she decided, looking up. The dark gray rock, shot through with specks of white, might have been polished to the smoothness of a fine table. They'd have needed more rope than all Yena possessed to descend here.

Juo's attention was for the mounds. "It's all here," the Chosen said, her voice strange. "Seru knows that."

When Juo had joined this hunt for her cousin, Aryl had been grateful for the company of a Chosen, even if a Harvest younger. She wasn't grateful now. Chosen shouldn't be risked. "What's 'all here,' Juo?" she asked cautiously.

"You know." Juo laughed. "Everyone does." Despite her swollen torso, the other moved quickly. Passing the first mound, she turned right and disappeared. "This way! She's already there."

Aryl felt a chill the warmth of the sun couldn't touch. They were alone here, the three of them. She dared lower her shields, slightly, and *reached* for Juo.

Nothing.

Like Seru. Not asleep. She could sense *where* and *who* they were, but their minds were untouchable, as if elsewhere.

What was happening?

Instead of following, Aryl scrambled up the mound. It wasn't an upheaval left by the Oud, but something more solid. Once on top, she crouched.

Not that Juo and Seru were looking her way. The two stood before another mound, their bodies rigid, their shadows merged along what Aryl now saw was more of the fitted paving stone the Sona used on their roadways, this stretch intact under its cover of windblown dirt.

What was this place? She dug her fingers into the mound by her feet. Wisps of vegetation parted; beneath were shallow roots, clinging tenaciously to hard lumps of dirt. Those came free, and Aryl touched stone.

A structure.

Enris! She made the sending tight and private. When he didn't respond, she added her *worry* and *fear*.

And . . . *curiosity*.

Here. His mindvoice was distant at first, then abruptly strong. *Where are you?*

Where she shouldn't be? Away from the rest in unfamiliar territory, with their only Chooser and a pregnant Chosen, neither of whom appeared sane? Aryl buried that twinge of guilt, sending an image of the mounds and valley wall. *Hurry. Something's wrong with Seru and Juo.*

Coming.

With the word, a warm rush of *reassurance*, as if somehow, he was already at her side.

She was going to miss that.

Someone else arrived first, someone small and fleet and the very last person Aryl wanted to see leave the safety of the village to run to this place. But she wasn't surprised. Ziba had been the other sleeper disturbed last truenight. It wasn't a coincidence.

What it was, she couldn't guess.

Ziba joined Seru and Juo. The trio stood before the mound without a word or look to one another. They might have been made of stone themselves. Not even the rapid drum of over-large boots disturbed them a few moments later, though it lifted her spirits.

When Enris reached the mound, she jumped lightly to the ground. "It's Seru and—"

Whatever else she'd planned to say stuck in her throat. He was so close she felt his deep steady breath on her face, could smell sweat mixed with dirt on his skin. He must have run all the way, doubtless alarming everyone he passed. They wouldn't be alone for long.

She gazed into his dark brown eyes, warm with concern, and suddenly knew—or had she always?—that no time with Enris Mendolar would be enough.

And hers was almost over.

"Vyna's not close," Aryl reminded him, proud of her even voice, her tight shields. "You should leave while the sun's out."

Enris' wide mouth turned down at the edges. "Aryl—" As if her name hurt to say. "I'm sorry."

She was no Chooser, to Call him to her side. She wouldn't if she could. He had a goal, a plan to benefit all Om'ray.

She was not so small as that.

Aryl lifted her chin. "I think Seru and the others have found something important—don't ask me how. It's this way."

He didn't say a word as he went with her around the mound, matching his stride to hers. Otherwise, they kept their distance.

The three Om'ray hadn't moved, as far as Aryl could tell, nor did they react as she and Enris approached. The freshening wind tossed Ziba's hair into her eyes. She didn't blink.

"What's the matter with them?" Enris sounded shaken.

She didn't blame him. "Don't try to *reach* them," she cautioned quickly. To her inner sense, the *darkness* was close, agitated, eager. Neither of them should risk it. "They had bad dreams last 'night. Seru's had them since we neared the valley. She and Juo seem—they seem to know things they couldn't."

"Ziba as well," he surprised her by saying. "Look. They're

staring at the same spot." He edged in front of the three, careful not to touch them, and brushed his fingertips over a place on the side of the mound no different from any other. "Ah."

" 'Ah?' " Aryl echoed.

Enris plucked the short knife from Juo's belt and used it to pry at the surface. Clumps of roots and dirt fell away. Casually, as he worked, "Did you dream, too?" When she didn't answer, he glanced over his shoulder at her, his expression unreadable. "Well?"

Aryl frowned. "Why ask me?"

"Because you're the only other one like them. Ugh." A satisfied grunt as a larger clod yielded to the knife. He began attacking higher up. "Ziba, Seru. Juo's unborn daughter." The shower of dirt became a tumble of larger pieces. "I thought so. A door," he announced, rapping his knuckles on what sounded like wood.

Aryl gaped at him, not the mound. "What do you mean, I'm like them? And how can you know what Juo carries?"

Enris grinned and sketched a bow. "One of the disadvantages to being eligible. My *sense* of Cersi has come to include an awareness of Choosers-to-Be nearby as well as Choosers themselves. Apparently," he added as he carefully replaced Juo's knife in her belt, near the restless bulge of her abdomen, "even those less able to speak for themselves." His grin disappeared as he looked at her. "There's something hungry about you all, something that reaches out. Maybe that's what finds these dreams. You did dream, didn't you? Tell me."

Aryl shuddered. "I don't know what it was," she admitted. "I felt—"

"Juo! Ziba!" Two, then four, then every Yena exile fit to walk appeared between the mounds, hurrying toward them.

Enris kept his eyes on her. "What did you feel?" Low and urgent.

She pressed her lips together and gestured a desperate apology. They had no more time for secrets.

No time left at all.

It seemed fitting that Seru Parth chose that moment to turn around and smile, as if to share a secret of her own.

"We could burn our way through."

"And lose what may be inside." Haxel turned to Enris. "Tell me again how you found this door."

Ziba pushed forward through the crowd of onlookers. "We found it!" she protested. "Seru and me! We knew it was there."

Seru flinched and clutched her coat tighter around herself. She'd stayed close to Aryl since waking from—whatever it had been. Her smile had vanished the instant she'd seen where she was, in the shadow of the strange mounds. It hadn't helped when the others arrived, full of curiosity and questions. Even now, her thoughts and emotions were chaotic, barely contained within her shields. Aryl felt a surge of protectiveness. Seru deserved none of this.

I'm here, she sent, stroking the back of her cousin's hand. *Don't worry. We'll find out what's happening. We'll stop it.*

Looking weary and equally confused, Juo leaned against Gijs who, for no reason Aryl could fathom, had his gaze locked on Enris.

Veca and Tilip, their woodworkers, stood in front of the mysterious wooden door, radiating frustration. Morla had pronounced it impossible. It wasn't their fault, Aryl thought. There was no locking mechanism, no rod on which to turn the door if unlocked. And they had only the knives in their belts.

"Have the Tuana open it."

Voices died away as Gijs left Juo to confront Enris. His face was pale and set. "Open it," he challenged.

Could he? Aryl wondered. He possessed the Talent to *push* objects through space. He'd used it to save her life. Haxel had been with them; there was no missing her attention to this exchange.

How did Gijs know?

Enris might have been carved in stone. Her *sense* of him faded as he tightened his shields beyond politeness.

"There's no need for the stranger's help," Tilip announced. He was a tall Om'ray, vine-thin before the days of scant rations—gaunt, now, with hollowed cheeks. In contrast, thick, fair hair curled at his neck and brow, tumbling into his pale blue eyes. His hands were long-fingered and skilled with any tool, but the Kessa'ats' tools had burned with their home, Aryl remembered sadly, in the fire she and Enris had set. "Fon can open it. Fon!"

Fon Kessa'at wormed his way through the silenced Om'ray, his head down. Their other unChosen, Cader Sarc and Ziba's brother Kayd, came with him. The three were always together now. Fon was four Harvests younger than Aryl; thin as his father but with his mother's coloring. Quiet and painfully shy. A poor climber.

Aryl was ashamed to admit that was all she knew of him.

Stepping past his friends, the young Om'ray peered through his hair at his father and mother.

Something passed among them. Veca's lips thinned and she shot a hard look at her Chosen before moving from the door. Fon took her place. He spread both hands—long-fingered, Aryl noticed—and pressed them on the door. Then . . .

POWER!

Someone cried out.

Messy, Aryl grimaced. Fon needed to learn some focus.

The result, however, was before them all—or rather, it wasn't. The door to the mound, however it had been secured, had disappeared. A puff of mist hung within the opening for an instant, then dissipated into the air.

Tilip ruffled his son's hair as he looked out at the rest of the exiles. There was pride in that look. Pride and defiance.

Aryl understood. They all did. The Kessa'ats hadn't been exiled by the Yena Council and Adepts because of Tilip or Veca. It hadn't been Morla and Lendin. They'd been exiled

because of their son. Here was the new Talent deemed too
dangerous for Yena. The change.

Curious. Had Fon sent the door somewhere else through
the *other,* or had he merely *pushed* it into that *darkness?* Was it
some other process altogether?

Haxel, practical as always, strode toward the opening as if
doors were supposed to get out of her way, collecting Enris and
Gijs with a gesture. The rest settled to wait, Cader and Kayd
rushing to Fon with congratulations that made the young
Om'ray blush.

Seru whirled and grabbed Aryl's hands. *I know what's inside! . . . How can I know? . . . What's happening to me?! FEAR!*

"Haxel, wait!" Aryl cried.

Haxel paused with a raised eyebrow and no patient feel to
her. "Why?"

Not a question she could answer. Not yet. She drew a breath
to try.

"Because we need light," Enris said, smooth and reasonable.
"We can carry fire. Lengths of wood—wrapped in cloth. Won't
take long to make."

His eyes met hers. *Go.*

Captivated by the Tuana's idea, no one appeared to notice
as Aryl pulled Seru away from the rest. Her cousin didn't resist.

Aryl didn't try to contact her mind. "What did you mean,
you know what's inside?"

Seru's eyes lifted. They were dark with shock. Her voice was
low and trembled. "Through the door are steps, like Grona's
meeting hall. Stone. Wide. But they go down, not up. Down,
down. Where they end is a flat space. On either side, an arch-
way of stone. The arch toward Amna leads to a long room. It's
full of things. Baskets. Gourds like the Tikitik bring. The
other—" she stopped, her hand over her mouth. *I don't want to
know this. I can't know this!* Frantic with fear.

Hush! But before she could comfort Seru, Aryl found words
spilling from her own lips. "The other leads to a second room,

as long as the first, with shelves." She could almost touch them, the image was so vivid in her mind. "On the shelves are bowls with lids, carved of wood. There are seeds inside, seeds for the next growing season." She knew their names. Knew which were husked in brown, which were shiny and black, which must be soaked for days or fail to sprout at all.

Seru gasped. "You see it, too! How?"

"I don't know." Aryl remembered the whispers in the *darkness*, her mouth trying to speak another's words—and fought back her own fear.

They stared at one another. Seru spoke first. "A storage place, like a Yena warehouse. Maybe," for the first time, her voice sounded hopeful, "there's food inside."

If any could last this long. "It's worth a look." Aryl wrapped her arms around her cousin and held her tight. *Whatever this is, Seru,* she sent, making sure the other felt her pride and love, *you may have saved us all.* When she stepped back, she added, "We'll go with Haxel—"

"No. I can't. What if what we—what we see—what if it isn't there?" Seru's eyes were bright with tears. "They already think something's wrong with me. Please, Aryl. Don't tell anyone that I—about this." *Promise!* The sending was as forceful as she could manage.

"I won't, unless I must." Aryl gestured apology. Lines of dark smoke rose, bending at the top of the mounds as the wind caught them. "They're ready. I'll go. Will you be all right?"

Will you?

She had no answer.

In that short time, Haxel had set everyone else in motion. The Kessa'ats and the Uruus, not coincidentally those with the youngest in their families, headed back to the village to improve the exiles' shelter before firstnight. The weather smiled on them now, but no one trusted the mountain sky. Weth and

Ael had already left, returning to their injured Chosen. Juo, who should have gone, refused. She sat with Husni, Cetto, and Lendin, their backs against the opposite mound. Morla paced, claiming her arm preferred it. Her tightly netted white hair caught the sun.

Rorn stood outside the opening, his longknife in hand. Guarding what, against whom, Aryl couldn't imagine, but Haxel took no chance she could avoid. Which left Enris and Gijs to enter with her, fire held high in their fists.

Motioning Seru to sit with Juo, Aryl followed hurriedly. She made it to the doorway before Haxel stopped to frown at her. "Wait here, Aryl. We don't know what's inside."

For some reason, Aryl glanced at Enris. Something in her face—for her shields were tight—made his eyes narrow in speculation.

"I do," she said, facing Haxel.

"You." The First Scout nodded toward Seru and Juo. "I thought they were the sleepwalkers."

Feeling her cheeks warm, Aryl stood her ground. "There are stone steps. Two storerooms. If we're lucky, they'll contain something still of use."

"Lead the way." Haxel sidestepped, motioning Aryl ahead.

With one stride, Enris was beside her. "Light," he explained, raising his burning stick. With a twist of his lips, *I hope you know what you're doing*.

She hoped so, too.

There were steps. To the unsuspecting, without light, the threat of a fall. With light, they were a broad roadway. Aryl took them without hesitation, hearing the others close behind. A bright circle bathed the stone before her feet; Enris' height gave that advantage here. Other circles bounced and over-lapped along walls she could touch, if she reached out with both hands.

"Cold," Gijs observed, a disembodied voice. The word echoed.

Silently, she counted steps. At twenty, she slowed. "We're al-most at the bottom."

"This shouldn't be here," protested Enris. "Om'ray don't trespass underground. The Oud forbid it."

"They didn't destroy it," Haxel countered.

"They'd killed everyone. Why bother?"

She laughed. "Comforting, aren't you, Tuana?"

"Here we are," Aryl interrupted. The mound's heart was as her mind expected. The firelight pushed back the dark on either side, through wide archways easily two Om'ray high. Colder here, much colder. She could see her breath; her warm Grona coats did nothing to stop her shivers. Or was it fear? She made a choice. "This way."

"Wait." There was a sound of metal sliding, a faint *whomp*, then the steps were illuminated in warm, yellow light. "Good. Still oil," Enris commented, using his stick to ignite another of the round fixtures. There were a pair on each arch. "Glows don't last long in the cold," he said self-consciously as he noticed the others, including Aryl, gazing at him in wonder. "We make something similar. Good for working outside in winter."

Gijs snorted. "You go out in truenight."

"I do many things you don't, Yena."

Tension. Aryl hesitated, looking from one to the other. Something was wrong between them. What?

"Let's go," Haxel ordered.

The first room wasn't, as Seru had feared, empty. As Enris hunted more of his oil lights to ignite, Haxel and Gijs walked a wide aisle between tall baskets and gourds, opening lids, exclaiming at what they found inside.

Not empty—but not the same. Aryl clung to the arch, feeling empathy for Weth, their Looker. Her mind demanded to see what it "remembered," arguing against the reality before her eyes until her stomach threatened to lose the nothing it contained. The baskets should be shorter, wider. The gourds should be in clusters nearer that side, and why were they colored in elaborate symbols instead of plain?

Whatever was in her head, it wasn't this moment, or even a moment close to it.

"Seru's dream or yours?"

Aryl focused with relief on Enris, who was as he should be, though with a thunderous scowl she ignored. He was leaving; let him worry about Vyna, not her.

"Mine," she told him. It wasn't a lie. "But not like a dream. I know things about this place—I can't explain how. The other storeroom—somehow I'm sure it was used for seeds and tools. I can tell you names, words for things I never learned. This room was for food and—" as Gijs pulled out a length of fabric, "—other supplies. But it's not the same. It's changed . . .

" . . . I think," she warned hastily, feeling an abrupt lurch inside, "I'm going to be sick."

She shut her eyes, numb with more than the cold, and fought her unhappy stomach.

Aryl . . . Fingertips brushed her cheek. *Power* followed, a shock like icy rain down her back. She opened her eyes and glared. "Why did you do that?"

"You don't feel sick now, do you?" Enris smiled at whatever showed on her face. "I'm hungry. As the one who 'knows things,' how about finding food?"

About to deny any such ability, Aryl found herself walking forward. The Tuana was right. The room grew longer as Gijs and Haxel continued to find more lights on its walls. There had to be dozens of baskets, some shoulder-high. Even more gourds. Whatever else Sona had been, they'd been rich beyond any Clan she knew. "Why so much?" she mused, fingers leaving trails on a dust-covered lid.

"This?" Another laugh. "You should see what my Clan stores for the winter—and we barely have the cold. Grona spends most of the warm weather putting away supplies and still has lean times. You Yena are spoiled. Food grows for you all the time."

"Dresel can only be harvested once a year," she reminded him. Om'ray couldn't live without it, not in the canopy. Once a year, the M'hir Wind would blow over the mountains. The

Watchers would sound their alert and Yena would climb. They'd risk their lives to snatch pods from the air. Once, she'd never imagined or wanted another life.

Would any Yena climb a rastis in the coming M'hir? Would any hooks flash, stealing treasure from the snatch of a wastryl?

Would she even know?

"Starving," Enris prodded. "Skin and bones."

Aryl flushed and lifted a lid at random. "Here."

He peered inside. "You're not serious."

She looked, too. The basket was filled to its brim with wizened red lumps the size of her smallest finger, utterly unappealing.

Aryl popped one into her mouth before she realized what her hand was doing. About to spit it out, she stopped, entranced by a sweet, rich flavor. A tentative chew released more.

Seeing this, Enris put two in his mouth, his face taking on a comic look of rapture.

Aryl swallowed and smiled. "They called it rokly. It grows on a vine, like sweetberries."

"So it wasn't a game." He wiped his lips with the back of his hand. "I was afraid of that."

"What do you mean?"

"Ziba." Enris sighed heavily. "She's too young to sort dreams from real memory. Taen and Syb should be told. Maybe they can shield her." He glanced to where Haxel and Gijs were moving a gourd into an open space, both of them needed to tip and turn it on its base. "You should all be careful," he urged quietly. "Something's put this knowledge in your heads, Aryl, or put it where your mind can find it. We don't know how—or why."

She brought her lower lip between her teeth.

He gave her a quizzical look. "You do agree, don't you?"

"About Ziba? Of course. And Juo's unborn. We should protect them. But I don't see the harm, Enris. Look at all this," she gestured at the room. "We'd never have found it on our own."

She felt a jolt of *dread* before he buried it behind shields.

"Tell me you aren't planning to stay here," Enris demanded, leaning forward. A lock of black hair fell over one eye, and he shoved it back impatiently. "Tell me you're going to pack all you can and leave for Rayna as soon as Chaun can walk. Aryl, please."

Her heart raced. "Om'ray lived here once—"

"And the Oud ended them!"

"Tell me Rayna will take us," she retorted fiercely. "Tell me they won't be sorry if they do."

She hadn't meant to say it. She hadn't, Aryl thought with a pang of guilt, known she would.

Enris drew back, his eyes bleak. "Is that what you believe? That Yena's Council was right after all? That your people deserve to be thrown out on their own?"

Insufferable Tuana. "Think what you like. You're leaving." She started to turn away. His big hand trapped her arm. "Let go of me." It was like trying to shake off a mountain. Haxel and Gijs were ignoring them—too obviously. Aryl felt her face grow hot. "Let. Go."

His fingers opened, but stayed on her arm. "I'd like to think you'll be safe. All of you." His voice deepened to a distressed rumble. "Staying here isn't the answer, Aryl. Listen to reason. You're too few. You need other Om'ray, a Clan. Your people will go wherever you lead—"

Let GO! Her sending hurt him; his hand dropped to his side and he gave her a stricken look.

She didn't care. "We're no longer your concern, unChosen. Take your Passage. Find joy." If the traditional farewell came out as a snarl, the Tuana deserved it.

Maybe he'd leave now. Aryl half ran past Haxel and Gijs, both of whom exchanged looks but didn't say a word. She stopped at a group of baskets and began tossing lids aside without seeing what was in them.

He didn't understand. It wasn't about fault or guilt. It was about what they were. The exiles would change whatever Clan they tried to join. They'd bring Yena names. They'd bring new

Forbidden Talents: hers, Fon Kessa'at's, others' yet to be revealed. By existing, they'd upset the Agreement.

Sona offered what she'd never imagined—the possibility of living apart from other Clans, to be themselves, to risk only themselves.

To become something new.

Chapter 6

IT WAS CLOSE TO FIRSTNIGHT before they finished exploring the mound and returned to the village. Ziba pounced on the rokly, but made faces at a stone jar of a spicy paste she personally detested but others could eat if they wanted. Her parents had been appalled, Haxel amused. With Aryl's help—as best she could offer—they'd sorted the bulk of their trove into what could be carried back to the village and used immediately, and what should be left. Stones were used to seal the opening. Ideally, they'd enter the next mound through its door.

For there was no mistaking the value in what they'd found, or where. Whether by some unknown technology within the mound itself or a combination of excellent packing and the cool mountain air outside, the stored goods were remarkably intact. Along with still-edible, if unfamiliar, preserved food—most from plant sources, though there were hard purple twists Aryl "remembered" as flesh from a kind of swimmer—there were thick woven blankets, tools, clothing in various sizes. The big sealed gourds were found to contain a fine oil. There were devices to use it for cooking as well as light.

Everyone who could helped bring baskets and gourds to the

village. Enris carried more than his share, conversed easily with others, laughed his big laugh.

Kept his distance.

Those who'd gone back to improve their shelter and care for the injured found themselves with supplies better than anything they could have brought from Grona.

By truenight?

It wasn't the same place, Aryl thought, leaning exactly where she had the 'night before.

Blankets of yellow and green and red lined the floor and hung from the walls to keep out drafts. On advice from Enris, the roof was left open above the fire, but elsewhere?

Let it storm. The Om'ray would stay snug and dry beneath Sona winter coats, woven and warm.

There was ample space to move as well. A neighboring building had been cleared of rubble and made habitable. Their packs were there, as well as their wounded and youngest, resting comfortably on extravagant layers of blankets. By the cheery oil light—as good as glows, Husni proclaimed the new devices—there was animated talk of two more homes in need of nothing more than roofs and doors, simple to accomplish with tools now at hand. The search for a water supply would begin at dawn, but no one seemed to doubt Sona would provide that, too.

As for food? Aryl wrinkled her nose. Only the dried fruit and swimmer twists were ready to eat. Everything else needed to be soaked or combined or cooked. Inconveniently, nothing had come to her or Seru on how to prepare what they'd found while Ziba's explanations centered on rokly and sweets they hadn't. Juo had only the faintest sense of likes and dislikes.

Leaving Haxel and Ael to experiment.

From the smell of the current concoction, something they were cooking was either in the wrong combination, or intended to wash cloth.

Seru slept now, in their other shelter, a true, deep sleep. She was happier, Aryl thought, to see something good come from something so frightening. They were no closer to understanding what had happened here, but most agreed Seru's first dreams must have been a warning, generations too late. The latest, though, seemed intended to help Om'ray survive here.

For her part, she hoped for more—so long as they didn't involve the *darkness*. One to tell her where to find water. One to tell her what to expect from the weather. One to explain how to avoid angering the Oud. She had a growing list.

Aryl relaxed and watched the others. She watched Enris, too, when she thought he wouldn't notice. His pack wasn't with the rest; it leaned casually near the door. She was the only one to know why.

While he'd been busy helping move Chaun and the others, when no one was watching her, she'd added a few things. No sense having him stint himself on food, when they suddenly had so much. No harm giving him the Grona bread, some of the dried twists of swimmer, a bag of sweet rokly.

Her longknife.

A new blanket, tightly rolled and tied. A coil of rope. He might not climb willingly, but sometimes it was necessary.

A lock of her hair, tied into a Highknot. Every Yena child made one to leave at the top of that first true climb away from their mother. It was a matter of pride to go as high as you possibly could before the longing drew you back.

It didn't matter that Enris wouldn't know its purpose. She did.

Enris himself was presently Haxel's most willing taster. While he waited for his next spoonful—the Tuana had the constitution of a rock—he filled another kind of light. It had the ropelike wick of the wall lights and a reservoir for oil, but within a small, sturdy metal frame with a handle. His head lifted and she looked away, sure now.

Such a light was meant to be carried.

He wasn't going to wait for dawn. Enris would leave when no Yena would dare, in the middle of truenight.

Aryl settled herself against the blanket-shrouded stone.

The wonder was that the big Tuana didn't wake everyone else. Aryl listened to Enris' attempt at stealth, grinning as he put a foot squarely on a scrap of wood, then set a row of hanging tools in motion with his shoulder. When he picked up his pack and boots, half the Om'ray in the room grunted or turned over. Passing through the doorway would have been silent, except that its blanket curtain caught on his head and he muttered something desperate under his breath as he struggled free.

That made her stifle a giggle with her hand.

She gave him time to put on his boots, coat, and pack. Another few moments for his light and orientation—and to negotiate his way past Syb, on watch outside. One more for her own courage. Then she slid from under her blanket, fully dressed and booted, and moved to the door without a whisper of sound.

Even so, a hand found her ankle. *He'll be back.*

Haxel's mindvoice. Did the First Scout ever sleep? Aryl looked down to meet the gleam of very alert eyes. *There are things I need to say.*

It's truenight. Curiosity.

I've been out in it before.

True. Amusement. *Tell the flatlander his walk's improved. Slightly.*

Before opening the curtain, Aryl *reached* with care. As she'd expected, Enris and Syb were standing together, away from the door. She slipped through, careful to avoid the twinned circles of light from Syb's small fire and Enris' device. The older Om'ray had his hand on Enris' broad shoulder. While they conversed, she moved around the corner of the ruin, close to the wall, placing weight on each foot only when sure she was on solid stone.

It wasn't shadow here, it was truenight. Darkness pressed against her open eyes, real and tangible. Her nerves sang desperate alarms along her skin. Despite the heavy Grona coat, she could feel the hairs rise on her arms and neck. It was bitterly cold. She'd see her breath, if there was any light. But there was no light. No Om'ray should be outside in this . . .

Listen, she scolded herself. No screams. No screams meant no swarm. There was nothing here that hunted in the dark. Nothing. Her worst enemy was unfamiliar ground, where a false step could land her in one of the Sona ditches, or worse, one of the deeper pits left by the Oud.

Her heart slowed its hammering. Slightly.

She *reached* again. Enris was on the move; Syb by his fire.

Time to go.

Om'ray defined their place and world by each other. It was simple to follow Enris—the effort came in moving away from the comforting *sense* of so many more of their kind behind. As for avoiding Syb's well-intentioned interference?

Climb and seek, Aryl smiled to herself. Few could discern one Om'ray from two or three—she was the only Yena who could discern who. She ran on her toes to the second shelter, guided by a hand on the wall between them. Those asleep inside would hide her glow from Syb. Once past that?

Aryl felt the door curtain, then the rest of the wall. There should be a beam leaning here; Tilip planned to use it tomorrow. She crouched to pass underneath, growing more confident in her memory as a guide. Three more steps should . . . her outstretched hand found stone and she turned to face the road.

Her breaths were drowned out by solid footsteps, though to be fair to the Tuana, sound was exaggerated in the still air. The tiny light from his hand danced over the paving stones and his boots, as strong a beacon as the lives behind her.

Enris slowed and lifted the light, sending brightness skittering over the ruins. Aryl backed out of its reach, making her inner self as invisible as she could. She saw his face, how his eyes searched the shadows for a moment. He lowered his hand and continued walking, footsteps echoing.

The brief illumination had reflected from the metal disk Enris now wore on his coat. A token.

Aryl sank down and hugged her knees to her chest.

She should go back.

Tokens were for those on Passage. Those who were as dead to the ones left behind, on their way to a new Clan, a new name, a new life. It was Forbidden to say more than farewell to those departing, Forbidden to interfere in any way. She'd watched Bern leave her and obeyed.

Who did she have to obey now? Aryl rose to her feet. This was Sona.

She gazed down the road. A light bobbed in the distance, moving farther and farther away.

There was no Council here.

She started walking slowly, then broke into a run.

Nothing was Forbidden.

His long legs and light gave the Tuana the advantage. Aryl wasn't able to catch up before the point where paving stones split around a heave of rock and dirt, forcing her to a cautious walk. She knew where she was. The heave marked where the roadway bent to follow the empty river, and where what had been homes were now piles of rubble and sticks. It made no sense for the Oud to strike harder at the edge of Sona than its core, unless their intention had been to prevent escape.

Not a happy thought.

Nor was how Enris kept on going, farther and farther. She'd been confident he'd stop for truenight once a few steps away from the exiles, take shelter in the ruins, make a bright, warm fire she could enjoy while they talked. He should be exhausted, having carried more per load than anyone else.

Hadn't he managed to slip out with—so he thought—only Syb aware so far?

The Tuana had his own ideas. Aryl was forced to follow, sure of her direction, if less so of her footing. At least it wasn't the truenight of the canopy, with its utter dark. There were bright holes in the sky above—stars—the effect like the open weave of a black curtain. Not enough to show details on the ground, though she could see the tall, jagged silhouettes of the mountain ridges that walled the valley. She didn't know why the Makers failed to rise—they would have bathed the land in light.

The only grace was the terrain between Sona and the first dried riverbed, with its tumbled bridge. She never thought she'd be glad of flat.

Flat . . . almost. Aryl's step went deeper than she'd expected, turning her next into a lurch to recover her balance. Pebbles skittered and she froze in place.

The solid *crunchcrunchcrunch* of Enris' boots stopped.

Aryl crouched and held her breath.

She really should call out. Was it fair to make him wonder who was here?

She grinned.

Then again, she always won climb and seek.

Crunchcrunch She began to follow again, at a comfortable distance.

Suddenly, his footsteps came faster and faster. He'd broken into that ground-eating lope of his. Aryl hurried as much as she dared, but his light slipped away.

Did he want to leave her behind? Truenight pressed at her from all sides. Leave her in the dark?

She was about to give up the chase and shout when he halted, his light held chest-high.

At last! Aryl rushed into the welcoming glow. There was the light, on a rock. The tiny flame fluttered within its metal case so the shadows around it came alive. "Enris?" She looked around wildly—*reached*.

There.

The Tuana stood beyond the ring of light, impossible to see. His shields were enough to almost—not quite—make him impossible to sense as well. "Aryl?" He sounded startled.

Who else? she wondered, then pushed the thought aside. Now that she'd caught up with him, she found herself fumbling. "I—we've—I—Come where I can see you."

He loomed from the shadows, gave her a cryptic look, then stalked to his light. Picking it up, he held it out. "Here."

Aryl took it.

"Now go back."

"Wait—"

Enris pointed up. "I've been out in truenight by nothing more, Aryl Sarc. Many times. You need the light—take it and go. I've made my decision."

By "nothing more" she guessed he meant the stars, the little bright holes in the sky. As for his implication? She replaced the light on its rock. "I know you're on Passage," Aryl told him stiffly. "It's Forbidden to interfere."

"It's Forbidden to follow me," with a hint of his laugh. "So why did you?"

Why had she? Aryl watched the flame, struggling to find words for what had been clear and imperative before. "Because you were wrong about me," she said finally. "I want more for my people. For all Om'ray. Like you, I seek a new future."

"Here. In Sona."

"Here," she insisted. "Where we can be what we are without fear of harming anyone or upsetting the Agreement. Use whatever Talents we possess or learn for our own good. Think about it, Enris."

"Put aside the fact that you're being influenced by dreams you can't explain," no laughter in his voice now. "Or that you don't know what the Oud will do. You can't start a Clan with twenty-two Om'ray. Be reasonable."

"We're already a Clan," she replied. "By the next M'hir,

we're either all that remains of Yena—or something new. The name doesn't matter. Don't you understand? The others didn't leave Grona to follow me. They left because deep inside we know we belong together. Now—" she took a deep breath, "—we have a place of our own."

"This Oud-reshaped pile of broken wood and stone? It's not possible. You can't stay here—"

"It's not possible Om'ray have technology like the Oud or Tikitik," she snapped back. "It's not possible Vyna is the only Clan who still has it. It's not possible, Enris Mendolar, that they'll accept you on Passage as their own, then give their wisdom to you to share with the rest of us. Is it?"

Enris burst out laughing, deep and loud enough to echo in the distance. Despite herself, Aryl's mouth twitched up at the corners. "We're a great pair," he chuckled. "Come with me, Aryl. Vyna won't stand a chance."

He didn't mean it.

Knowing that, Aryl had no problem finding a smile. "Make a proper fire, Tuana," she told him, "and I'll do better than that."

She had a promise to keep.

They made camp where an upthrust of paving stone reflected the warmth of their small fire and protected it from the wind. Easy to scavenge dry splinters of wood here; not so once Enris left Sona. As well, Aryl decided, he'd agreed to linger here until dawn. When the Tuana, apparently always hungry, went to dig in his pack for food, she offered the rokly she'd tucked into a pocket, along with her last chunk of Grona bread. The way he ate, he'd need all his supplies and more.

Yawning, Enris stretched his legs and arms, then shifted with a grunt to retrieve a sharp rock from where he sat. He tossed it into the darkness that walled their bit of light. "You sure you want to sleep out here?"

"We're not going to sleep," Aryl warned him, then temporized, "not until you've learned what I can teach you. If I can teach you."

He shoved back his hood, as if too warm. Aryl sat as close as she could to the flames and left her head well wrapped. "I'll have you know my father considers me a quick study."

Her father had died when she was young. Her mother had somehow recovered and grown strong . . . Aryl pushed away thoughts of Taisal di Sarc. Her mother could touch the *other*. Not attention she wanted to court.

"Think about when I moved us from the strangers' camp on the mountain to Yena. Did you sense the *other*?"

" '*Other?*' Someone else? No."

"A place. A moving *darkness*." That wasn't the word she wanted. Taisal called it the Dark, but it wasn't. Aryl raised her eyes from the fire and stared into the real thing: nothing, black, an absence of light. Even peaceful, without hunters. The *other place* wasn't like that. Its *darkness* was ablaze with sensation, churning with powerful, chaotic movement that affected everything in its path. Like the M'hir Wind when it struck the canopy—a force to be understood and resisted, or it would destroy.

"Call it the M'hir," she decided. The naming gave her comfort, as if it brought the inner *darkness* into the light of day, harnessed it for her people's good. Her fiches were designed to ride one wind—maybe Om'ray were, too.

"The M'hir, is it?" Then he startled her by adding matter-of-factly, "Guess that's where I *pushed* the roof this morning. I was afraid it would land on someone outside. Good to know it's really gone. It is really gone, isn't it?"

Aryl blinked. "Roof?"

"What was left of the supports. About to collapse on us." Enris paused and his voice took on an edge. "Impressed Gijs." He'd relaxed his shields. Now she felt *anger* and a curious *shame*. "Too much."

That reaction, she understood. And something else. "You thought I was Gijs, didn't you? That he'd followed you to demand you teach him."

His lips quirked as he gestured apology. "Don't ask me why. Gijs has young Fon now. I wonder who'll be the next surprise? Oh, yes. You." This with a sly glance. "Wish I could be here to see their faces. Haxel's in particular."

Insufferable Tuana. Aryl refused to react. She'd tell the others about the M'hir when she chose and not a moment sooner. "Are you ready to learn this or not?"

"If you won't let me sleep—" a dramatic sigh, "—I'm ready. Do your worst, Aryl Sarc."

If he could use the *darkness*—the M'hir, she reminded herself—this might be easy.

Or not.

She'd promised to try. "There's more you should know about the M'hir before you touch it. It—it hungers. It will take you into itself, make you forget who you are. The Lost. Somehow they are part of it, or it's part of them. I felt it."

"Dangerous. What else?"

"This is no joke, Enris!" Aryl felt her cheeks warm. "The longer you touch it—the closer you let it come to who you are—the easier it is to let go. It came in my sleep last night, and I—" She stopped there. "It's more than dangerous."

Instant *concern*, deep and real, proved he wasn't taking this as lightly as she'd feared. "Aryl, you don't have to do this."

"Yes, I do." Aryl laid another splinter on the fire, just so. "Don't be careless. That's all. Don't look at the scenery. Treat the M'hir like fire. A tool that can burn you."

"So how does this tool work?" Enris picked up a pebble, shot through with sparkles. "How do I move this from here," on the flat of his right hand, "to here?" a quick toss to his left. "You need me for that?"

Enris grinned. The pebble lifted from his palm, moved through the air between them, and landed with a quiet *click* among the others in front of her boot. Aryl barely sensed the Power he expended. "But that's not what you do," he pointed out. "Not how you brought us faster than a heartbeat to Yena."

"No." Nor was what he did something she could do, Aryl

thought wistfully. Her mother could *push* with her mind, like Enris. So far, she hadn't found that useful Talent in herself. "To move us—" or to move Bern Teerac, that fateful Harvest, "—was what I wanted most at that moment. I wanted us in my home, helping my Clan. I pictured us already there, until that image was more real to me than being on the cliff with the Humans. And there we were."

She'd wanted Bern safe on the bridge, not falling to his death, wanted that to be real more than anything in her life. Bern, but she hadn't thought of Costa, or the others who'd fallen . . . screaming . . .

Aryl forced the memory away. "Somehow," she explained as best she could, "it means going into the M'hir, then out of it almost at once. It's as if the M'hir is a place, but one where distance doesn't matter, only will, so it lets a traveler ignore distance, too." She threw up her hands. "Which probably makes as much sense to you as it does to me."

Enris' eyes almost glowed. "An image of your destination. Perhaps it's necessary to have been there in person. To know the place well."

"Why do you say that?"

"You said it: first, you envisioned a place you wanted to be. Then, you used your strength of will—which I'm guessing means your considerable Power—to *move* there through the M'hir. If you didn't have a strong, clear location in mind, a target for your will, maybe you wouldn't go anywhere." He chuckled. "Or maybe you'd vanish like my roof. Go in, but not come out. Wonder what that's like."

She glowered at him. "Not funny, Tuana."

No smile now. "I think it's important to consider what could go wrong."

Maddening unChosen. Bad as her brother for being ridiculous one moment, serious the next, without bothering to let her know which to expect. Enris returned her look with one of complete innocence.

Aryl pressed her lips together. He was right. She knew almost nothing about traveling through the M'hir, nothing of the risks. How could she teach anyone else until she'd learned herself?

"We'll start with sending." Before he could object, she went on quickly: "Yes, you can *send* mind-to-mind an impressive distance. But even you have limits." Her glare defied him to argue. Enris merely smiled. "The M'hir can carry your thoughts like the wind, to anyone else able to touch it. I've found no limit, no effort except to keep from being swept away. Interested?"

"Very." He held out his right hand, palm up, the gesture natural, as between trusted friends. Offering touch.

He meant nothing more by it. After all, who better than an eligible unChosen to know she wasn't a Chooser?

Yet.

If not now, it didn't matter when. It would be too late. Enris would be gone.

Within a fold of her long coat, Aryl's right hand curled into a fist, nails digging into her skin.

"Close your eyes," she ordered, proud the words sounded normal. She laid her left hand on his. Different calluses marked his palm; his hand was wider and longer than hers. Warmer. The irony that someone so physically strong should possess the Talent to *move* what he wanted by Power didn't escape her.

But not everything required force.

Wait for me, she sent.

She'd spent the day avoiding the *darkness,* but it was always there if she dared look for it. The M'hir. The instant Aryl turned her perception inward, she found herself fighting to keep her place within its now-familiar confusion. She concentrated, then *reached.*

Enris.

Here. Unmistakably his inner voice. The link formed between them as effortlessly as a smile. She *saw* his presence, a bright, distinct whirlwind in the *darkness.* It suddenly rushed toward her; she instinctively kept her distance, though there was no true movement here. Only the surge and conflict of the M'hir itself.

Listen to me, she sent, feeling the exchange forge tighter the connection between minds, perversely calming the M'hir. *There. Good. Very good.* Enris was as able here as anywhere. Somehow, Aryl wasn't surprised. *Welcome to the M'hir.*

You look like the inside of our vat. With the unflattering description came an image of metal melting into glittering pools.

Could be worse. *Pay attention,* she warned. *See what's here, but stay with me.*

She felt the shift in his attention by the attenuation of their link. She poured more of her own strength into it, letting him be. He was confident, curious . . .

Horrified.

I know this!!!

On that recognition, the M'hir became a storm, lashing out. Aryl fought to hold Enris, but he was being ripped away . . . she *felt* him scream . . . or was she an echo . . .

PAINPAINPAIN . . .

. . . hidehidehide . . .

He was coming apart . . . dissolving into the M'hir . . . pieces of Enris began to scatter . . . she fought to hold them . . .

. . . can't let her . . . don't let her . . . hidehidehide . . . DIE FIRST! PAINPAINPAIN!!!

Somehow, Aryl struggled free of his agony. She concentrated. She had to hold what she sensed was Enris. He was like a wing fraying at the edges, threads come loose in the wind. The touch of him *burned,* but she wouldn't let go, couldn't let go.

The M'hir itself *stirred.* She felt *others* . . . Felt . . . *interest* . . .

They had to pull free of the M'hir. Now. They had to . . .

They did.

The fire snapped and crackled cheerily; the dark of truenight outside its circle was silent, almost soothing. Stars winked above. The wind caught a spark and swirled it out of sight.

Aryl savored the smoke-scented air, relished the chill of tears on her cheeks. Her hands ached. They were tightly clenched—on what? After an odd delay, she realized she was lying on top of Enris, as if she'd flung herself over his prone form. Her hands still gripped both of his with all her strength.

She let go, gently, and eased to sit beside him. The rise and fall of his chest matched his ragged breaths, as if he dreamed he ran. From what?

Her first experience in the M'hir had been filled with the screams of the dying.

What had happened to Enris there?

And who was "her?"

Enris went from unconscious to his feet. Aryl hurried to save the blanket she'd placed over him from the fire. "What happened?" he shouted wildly, staring at her. "Where are we?"

"Not that far from Sona. Hush." She patted the solid ground. "Sit."

He sank down, crossing his long legs. "Aryl." Distantly, as if he had trouble remembering her name. Then in a more normal voice: "Are you all right?"

"I'm not the one who—" Aryl decided "fell to pieces" wasn't tactful, "—who slipped. How do you feel?"

"Hungry." With a rueful smile. "Foolish." He ran his hand through his hair and shook his head. "Guess I panicked. Lost control . . . was careless. Don't worry. Next time, I'll—"

"There's no 'next time'!" He couldn't be serious. "Don't you remember? You were almost Lost, Enris Mendolar. Lost! I had to pull you back together. I barely managed to free us both. I—" she struggled for calm, to be convincing. He had to listen, had to believe her. "Enris, you've been in the M'hir before."

"Of course I have." He looked more puzzled than concerned. "When you moved us through it, to Yena. But I didn't see anything like—" He stopped abruptly. His shields tightened until he faded from her inner sense; all expression left his face. When he spoke again, his voice was flat and deliberate. "I didn't see what I saw tonight. Why?"

"You weren't aware of it then," Aryl guessed. Her fingers sketched an apology against her coat. He had to understand. "This time you were. When you stop and notice the M'hir, it—it notices you. Things become . . . complicated. It's easy to be distracted, confused, to forget who you are. I know. Strong emotion—" She had to explain, to warn him. "Strong emotion makes it much worse. Enris, you were safe until you recognized the M'hir. Until you remembered what happened to you there, and why, and mixed before with now. You felt . . . what you felt then." She shivered, having shared that terrible *pain* and *dread*. "That's how the M'hir almost took you."

"I know." His big hands shook as he stretched them to the fire's warmth. He stared at them as if surprised, then drew them inside his coat.

Enris had met the strangers, flown in their aircar, traveled the M'hir with her. He'd fought the swarm and climbed—however badly—high in the canopy. What could disturb him like this was beyond her imagining.

Aryl sat perfectly still, eyes locked on the fire, and waited. The silence between them grew desperate.

Finally, she pulled the metal headdress from her pocket and ran it through her fingers. Though dull, its links and straps glinted rich green in the firelight. It must have been beautiful once. "I found this high on a ridge." Easy, quiet, not looking at him. "With a Chosen's bones. I suppose she thought she could escape that way." A dangerous climb, for someone used to flat ground. Or maybe the daring Om'ray had made it that far, Aryl thought with a rush of sadness, only to be doomed by the loss of her Chosen in Sona. She laid it flat on her hand, rubbing her thumb over the forehead band. "There are marks in the metal."

Enris rose to his feet, but not to leave her. He went to his pack and brought something from it to the fireside. "I found bones, too. And this."

"This" was a strangely deformed blade, point divided into two, one tip longer than the other. It was attached to a broken wooden shaft. Enris had also brought the two sticks he carried tied to his pack, the ones he'd refused to donate to the fire. He fitted the three together and demonstrated the original length against himself. The tips reared over his head.

Awkward to carry. "What was it for?"

"I've no idea," he said, sounding remarkably pleased. He tossed the sticks at his pack, then squatted beside her and held out the blade. "There are markings." He wet his finger and ran it over the metal. "Like the ones carved into the Sona wood."

At least he was talking again. Aryl dutifully glanced at the thing, then took a second look that developed into a stare. She didn't realize she'd reached for it until she felt its weight in her hands.

"These are words."

"I knew it!" A definite resurgence of the Enris she knew. "Can you read what they say?"

She sent him an annoyed look from the shadow of her hood. "Of course not. I'm no Adept."

"But you've seen writing."

True. She'd seen the plates used in the Cloisters, glimpsed from a distance the lines and circles that made sense, somehow, to those with that skill. She'd seen the writing used by the strangers—sharper lines and angles—and thought she might be able to reproduce a word or two. The Tikitik used all manner of wild swirls and lines, some to decorate—or label—the door panels they made for Yena homes, and wore their names on wristbands of cloth. From Thought Traveler, she'd learned there was no Talent needed to read, only a knowledge of what each symbol represented. He'd shown her his name, then what he took to be hers from the little drawing she'd used for herself. A bowl containing a small dot, neither touching.

Apart-from-All.

Enris, perhaps impatient, tapped the blade. "Does it look familiar?"

Pushing back her hood, Aryl tilted the blade to the firelight to study each intricate line. "I can't tell," she admitted. "What I've seen before wasn't cut into metal. If it's from Sona, it could be Om'ray. But why would an Om'ray do this?"

An image formed in her mind: a memory offered. Aryl saw a pale green ring, large enough for a wrist, polished to a rich gleam. Its surface rippled in a never-repeated pattern. It was as if the metal was water, curling around small round rocks. A mountain stream. She felt Enris' *satisfaction* and *pride,* watched his hands painstakingly hammer a design into the inner surface of the ring. Three tiny dots in a row; two others, above; one below.

"You made it." She'd never imagined such an ornament, for it was clearly of no other use. "Tuana trade for such things?"

"All the time."

She'd sneered when he'd described his Clan's wealth, how farming gave them leisure to create and specialize, how one Om'ray could trade the makings of her hands for the work of another's. She'd thought Yena, who shared everything—including hunger—superior.

While not ready to declare Yena any less, Aryl knew she'd gladly have "traded" anything from the Sarc storage slings and cupboards for what Enris had made. "What does the pattern mean?" she asked. "Is it your name?"

"No. They're my stars. Would you like to see them?"

"See them," she repeated doubtfully.

Trust me.

Aryl let Enris take her hand and pull her to her feet. She was less sure when he turned her from the comforting brilliance of the fire to face the dark, but there was no arguing with his firm grip on her shoulders.

The fire crackled; she could hear her heartbeat. The silence was suffocating.

Patience.

Her hand found the hilt of the short knife protruding from her belt, every instinct warning her of danger. His breath tickled the top of her head. The Tuana's size would be a comfort, she grumbled to herself, if he showed the slightest comprehension of the risks outside his village, especially during truenight. How had he stayed alive?

Maybe anything hunting him suspected such too-easy prey had to be a trap.

She'd lived her life among hunters. Truenight should be a cacophony of song and screams, sounds she'd learned to ignore as normal, protected by the glows of Yena, safe within the inner glow of her Clan. Everyone should be together.

Aryl let her inner sense *reach* for that reassurance. Close, but not close enough, those asleep in Sona. Close, but not close enough, Grona and Rayna. They faced distant Pana and Amna, Tuana to one hand. Vyna faint but there, to the other.

Yena—Aryl found the glow that sang *home* to her innermost self and retreated. Those left lived within the Cloisters now, the safest place in the world. They no longer needed her.

Even if she needed them.

Where did unChosen find the courage to walk away from their Clan? Did the drive to find a Chooser really overwhelm fear? There was so much to fear—

She hoped that was the truth. Passage was fraught with enough peril; she couldn't bear to think all the young Om'ray who'd walked away from their homes had felt like this, had stared as she stared now into unknowable darkness, had ached for those left behind as she ached.

Because if they had, Aryl decided with abrupt fury, Agreement or no Agreement, she'd never let Kayd, Cader, or Fon take Passage. Not like this.

Not alone.

I'm never alone when I can see my stars.

Shame flooded her; she hadn't meant Enris to *hear* her thoughts. Too tired. Careless. But his sending was calm, if nonsense. He understood her. She'd miss that most of all.

I don't see any stars.

You will. Patience.

An urging for now, or the future? Aryl smiled.

Gradually her eyes grew accustomed to the lack of light, and stars made their chill appearance overhead. More and more of them, until they might have been the flower dust that coated Yena's bridges and rooftops in early summer. Once, she'd believed the specks were all of a piece: the sun's light leaking through the gauze of the sky. Thought Traveler had mocked her—any Om'ray's—understanding of the sky and this world. The strangers claimed there were more worlds than Cersi.

Aryl frowned. Stars complicated her life.

There. Enris dug his big chin into the collar of her coat and pressed his ear against hers. *Little more that way.* He tilted her head with his, sending the image of his pattern. *See them now?*

Typical Tuana. Aryl didn't bother being offended by his un-Yena-like familiarity; he'd only laugh. Besides, her back had been cold. As for his stars . . . "How can you expect me to find six? Look at all . . ." Her complaint faded away.

There they were. Among all the rest, she could see them. Five were bright: two above, three in a row below. Two Om'ray, she imagined, standing on a straight branch, Fainter, but still distinct, a blue dot beneath the rest and to one side. That was harder. "A fich!" she exclaimed and laughed.

"A what?"

Aryl shared her memory of being on a branch, high in a nekis, tossing her creation of wing and thread into the air above the Sarc grove, watching it sail into the distance, free as any flitter. She remembered the child with her, Joyn Uruus, full of enthusiasm and joy, both LOUD. She remembered the arrival of the aircar and . . .

Shields tight, Aryl lurched away. She went to sit before the fire, her eyes partly closed against what now was too bright, her back again cold. "A foolish notion." Bitterness rose in her throat. "Others rule the sky. There's no room for Om'ray in it. Only stars."

"Aryl . . ."

"The fire's hungry."

Enris was silent a moment. Then, "I'll look after it." A home lay shattered steps from the roadway. She listened to him move, heavy-footed in the loose stone, and refused to yawn. Dawn would be too soon.

He returned to drop an armload with a triumphant *clatter,* then went for more. On his third trip, he tossed the splinters directly on the fire, the flames licking the lengths of jagged black wood as if famished. Light spilled over the road. Not done, he added more wood until Aryl had to move or risk her boots. Soon flames shot above the Tuana's head. Sparks popped and snapped, landing in every direction. Against the stone they looked like eyes caught by a glow.

Aryl brushed one from her coat. "Syb'll see this," she disapproved. "You'll give him ideas." The exiles absorbed every word and action the Tuana provided about the care and maintenance of fire, their newest, most vital skill. Those instructions hadn't promoted waste, till now.

Enris laughed for the first time since entering the M'hir. "I only follow your example."

He was on the far side of the flames; if she couldn't see his face, he couldn't see hers, hot from more than the Tuana's immense fire. Was he right? Was she daring too much, too soon? Was the freedom of Sona nothing more than the trap her mother and Yena's Adepts had feared all along: the release of Talents and ideas too dangerous for Om'ray to survive?

"I intend no harm," she said finally, cold inside. "I want the best for my people. For all Om'ray. To stop us dying needlessly."

Enris came and sat beside her, making a show of looking for rocks first. He tossed a few aside. Once settled, he nudged her with his wide shoulder. "You want us to fly, Aryl Sarc. The only harm I see is if we fall."

A Yena caution. To check a handhold before trusting your weight to it was the first, vital training. She'd nearly cost Enris his life, drawing him into the M'hir when she hadn't checked it was safe, and he knew it.

Aryl raised her hands to gesture a profound apology. Enris trapped them in one of his. "Don't. What happened to me wasn't your fault. You saved my life."

She tugged free. "After almost losing it!"

"What matters to me is the M'hir. How you move through it. Whether I ever can." Enris used a giant from his pile of splinters to prod others deeper into the fire. "The truth, Aryl?" with a wary glance her way and a sense of *determination*. "You were right. Back in Tuana, something did happen to me. I was . . . there was a Chooser. Powerful. Beautiful." His voice became a low rumble. "I wasn't ready. She was. I didn't want her." This with a twist to his lips as if at a foul taste. "She wanted me. Maybe she couldn't stop herself. Maybe she didn't care." When he paused, Aryl held her breath. "She tried to force me to answer her Call. I refused." He shoved the heavy length of wood violently into the rest, showering sparks into the air. "That's when my mind fled into the M'hir."

Aryl struggled to grasp what he was telling her. She'd never heard such a thing. How could an unChosen refuse Choice? Why would he? Wasn't it the most wonderful moment of an Om'ray's life? Whatever you'd felt about each other before, heart-kin or stranger, Joining made you one for the rest of your lives and ridiculously happy to be so.

Didn't it?

"Afterward," Enris continued, his voice flat, "the Adepts told me I was damaged. They couldn't promise I'd ever be able to complete Choice—that it would be better for Tuana if I sought a future elsewhere." He shrugged. "So I did."

"There's nothing wrong with you," she said without thinking.

His laugh was bitter. "While I appreciate your high regard, Aryl Sarc, you're hardly—"

"I know. I *saw* you. In the M'hir." She'd held the fragments of his mind together, *felt* them. There'd been no flaw, no injury. Whole again, Enris had been solid Power, a boulder the dark currents could only fling themselves against or pass around, not force out of place.

Hurt and terrified—she'd *seen* that, too. All of which explained why he took Passage to solve a mystery, not to seek Choice.

It didn't explain why he'd been sent on Passage in the first place. Her heart thudded heavily. Could she? "Do Tuana un-Chosen often refuse a Chooser?" Aryl asked carefully.

She'd startled him. "What?" A hint of *embarrassment*. "How should I know? I don't talk about such things."

Making Enris different from other unChosen of her experience—not that Aryl was surprised. "I'd think a—" she hunted a word that wouldn't offend him, "—an ability like that would be noticed." Without delight by Choosers, she was quite sure.

" 'Ability?' " If she'd startled him before, he was appalled now. "I've seen my cousins lose all sense about each other, but that's their decision, not mine."

"Didn't your parents teach you anything about Choice?"

Enris managed to grow larger, though he hadn't moved. Like a brofer puffing itself up in self-defense. "I had," he said stiffly, "more important things to learn."

"Apparently not."

"And I suppose you're going to teach me?"

No. Not. Never. Aryl didn't bother to say any of that aloud. Instead, she circled back to where they started. "You weren't damaged."

Enris flicked an escaping ember back to the fire. "The Adepts—"

"Lied."

"Not every Adept is like your mother!" He gestured a quick apology. "Aryl, I—"

"You're a fool," she retorted. "Like I was. Adepts protect the Agreement by preventing change. Change like me—and like you, Enris Mendolar. I've never heard of an unChosen able to refuse a Chooser's Call. I can't imagine it. But you did it. You still do. You ignored Seru. You dismissed Grona's Choosers. Let alone how you entered the M'hir." He took a sharp breath as if to argue. She didn't let him. "Don't you see? You proved yourself a threat to be removed for the good of your Clan.

"You're right, Enris," she finished. "Not every Adept is like my mother. Tuana's gave you a chance to live."

He jumped up and strode away without a word, the crunch of his boots ending a few steps into the dark. She let him be and watched the flames, careful to keep her thoughts to herself. Not easy, remembering the moment she and the others had been exiled. None had believed they'd survive the first truenight; without the Human's help, none would have. Yet was it Taisal's fault that Yena had had no supplies to share, no safe road of dirt and stone for their feet?

She couldn't forgive the decision, but suddenly she wondered. Was it one only a Yena could have made? Despite its beauty and lush life, the canopy was a harsh existence. She doubted other Om'ray faced death every day or fell asleep to screams. It made Yena strong. Had it made them ruthless, too?

If she believed it necessary for the good of her people, would she do what her mother—what Yena's Adepts—had done?

No, Aryl assured herself. In Sona, they would find another way. She would protect her kind, never waste their lives.

The fire snapped and crackled to itself. Then, from the dark, a contented "Hmm," as if Enris had discovered a forgotten sweet in his pocket.

Crunchcrunchcrunch. When the firelight caught his face as he sat, he looked younger. His face might have shed lines of grief or anger or both. Noticing her attention, the Tuana flashed his grin. "So you're saying I'm special."

Her lips quirked. "What you are is annoying."

"More than special." The grin widened. "Unique. Perfect!"

"Insufferable," Aryl countered.

"With, according to you, my wise little Yena, my pick of Cersi's Choosers!"

"How could any be worthy?" That made him laugh. Her chuckle died in her throat.

What would it be like, to offer her hand and have an unChosen refuse it? She felt a rush of sympathy for Seru—and for the unknown Tuana who'd wanted Enris so desperately.

What would it be like to have an unChosen—no, not any unChosen, but Enris Mendolar—have him take her hand, knowing it meant he wanted her more than any other?

Suddenly too warm, Aryl coughed and sputtered in an anguish of embarrassment. "S–smoke," she managed in answer to his quizzical look, glad her shields must have kept the wildly errant thought private.

Enris laughed, then bumped her shoulder companionably once more. "Choosers will have to wait. I'm in no hurry to complicate my life. What matters is the M'hir. You're the Adept there. Do you believe I can ever use it?" Lightly, as if all he asked was for another rokly stick.

"It's not safe," she evaded hoarsely.

"What is?" A pause. "Your turn. The truth, Aryl Sarc. Can I try the M'hir again? When I'm ready," he said in hasty addition. "My head still spins."

She could say no. Should say it. Protect him from himself.

Her teeth caught her lower lip. For how long? Until curiosity overwhelmed caution? Oh, that would be the first moment the Tuana was bored. Until he was truly desperate, with no other choice but to try again? Courage, Enris had in abundance.

Doubt made any handhold fail.

Aryl bumped her shoulder into his. "You've *touched* the M'hir. Sent a roof into it," she reminded him. "You're as much an Adept there as I am. Learn from what went wrong, like anything else. Be careful."

As she would be.

The giant fire was a heap of pale, ember-studded ash, firstlight little more than a promise toward Amna, when Aryl gathered her feet under her body and rose without a sound. Enris half lay against his pack. His head was bent at a painful-seeming angle, his mouth open, his arms spread wide. She had to step over his long legs to get by. The Tuana consumed the space of two normal Om'ray, even asleep.

They'd spent the rest of truenight talking about silly things, laughing at each other's stories. Climb and seek in the light-kissed canopy. Pushing a cartful of giggling cousins in a race. Sweetpies and dresel cake.

Brothers lost.

Homes left.

Why not to polish your father's hammer. Where not to store a fresh, wet hide.

Rain that filled the world. Dust that did the same.

Somewhere during a lengthy discussion of Tuana boots—more precisely the clear superiority of Yena footwear—Aryl had received a snore instead of answer.

She'd stayed awake, to watch over him as long as she could bear.

To watch him wake up, see him realize he had to go, try to say good-bye?

She'd keep her memory of this truenight instead.

"Find joy, Enris Mendolar," Aryl whispered, this time meaning it, and walked away.

She didn't look back.

Interlude

"FIND JOY, ENRIS MENDOLAR."

Enris kept his eyes closed. If Aryl wanted to leave like this, he'd make it easier for her.

Easier for whom?

He couldn't hear footsteps. No surprise; she walked like air.

Was she gone?

His head rolled to face the glow of Sona's Om'ray. Her inner warmth would be part of it, indistinguishable unless he *reached* to find her. If he did, if he touched her thoughts once more, if he felt her brilliance, her passion and strength again . . . he'd stay.

"Find joy, Enris Mendolar." Had it been her voice or a sigh of wind across the barren stone?

He should stay. Vyna and the Om'ray artifact were impossible hopes, even if Aryl believed. Sona needed him; he needed them. No Om'ray should live alone.

Aryl Sarc's time of Choice would come.

He could stay. Be there when she was ready. She believed him whole, even if he had doubts. To Join with her?

His breath caught.

No Om'ray could live alone.

He closed the fingers of his right hand around sharp, frozen stones. That was the reality. A future with no Sona. No Aryl. No Om'ray at all. Unless impossible hopes could be true.

And he could find them.

* ✳ *

Pushing a loaded cart up the ramp, walking away from home, leaving Sona. One step at a time. If Enris made them long steps—careless, driven, hurried steps that splashed through rivulets and skidded over stone—there was no one to comment on his flatlander clumsiness.

When he fell, only his gloves saving the skin of his hands, only his outthrust hands saving his nose, he broke out in helpless, bitter laughter.

"Fool," he gasped, climbing to his feet. "Break a leg here and you'll be supper."

Though there didn't seem to be anything interested. Or anything alive at all. His shadow, the only thing taller than a boot, stretched over a numbing sameness of gray pebbles, drifted dirt, and isolated tufts of dead vegetation. The wind, a constant now, tugged at his hair and lifted the ends of his coat. The sun hung in a faded arch of sky, flattening the distance from one side of the valley to the other. He thought he should be halfway by now, but the far wall seemed no closer.

Maybe he'd wind up as a mystery among the pebbles. Tatters of cloth, a pack, a few longer-than-most bones. A token that lied.

"I should keep walking," he told himself, not yet ready to be bones.

Enris had no particular reason for striking out across the valley, other than it was the most direct route to Vyna. And flat. He was fond of flat, and this place rivaled the plains of the Oud for level terrain. The Oud. They hadn't reshaped here. Why?

"Oof." He stumbled and caught himself. Flat except for the little ditches. They were everywhere. Traps, more like it. Being filled with smaller pebbles, they blended with the ground and were just deep enough to catch his foot every single time.

Another of Aryl Sarc's ideas: that the Sona Om'ray had used

the ditches to spread the water of the river to where they wanted it.

He'd walked through it: a river remembered in sand and rock. Where the tiny mountain streams trickled down its crumbling banks, their flow ended in mats of bent reeds, dead and brown now, but perhaps they would grow again in warm weather. Unless the warmer weather dried the mountain streams. Tough place to be a plant.

Tougher place to be an Om'ray, let alone be Yena, used to such frantic abundance of growing things.

The problem with Aryl was that an idea wasn't enough. She saw a sky and wanted wings. She saw an empty river and parched land, and wanted water and growth. She saw a homeless group of exiles, most too old or too young, and wanted a Clan.

Given any chance at all, she'd do it, too.

Enris tugged his water sac from its loop—an idea of his own. If she could do the impossible, he could. No slip of a Yena was going to best a Tuana!

For no particular reason, he found himself humming through his teeth as he walked.

* ✳ *

The mountain loomed taller but no closer by late afternoon, as if it toyed with him. Enris had expected to reach its feet by first-night, to drink fresh cold water from one of its streams and camp where outcroppings of rock would shelter a fire. At this rate, he'd be lucky to reach it by tomorrow's sunset.

Sona had faded with every step. Rayna's glow was now the brightest and warmest. He ignored the urgent pull of both as best he could. Vyna lay ahead. On the other side of the mountain.

The mountain that wasn't getting any closer.

"Patience," he told himself.

Expectation meant nothing. Perseverance was what mattered. Pay attention to the details. Do your best at each moment. Nothing worth the making could be rushed.

His father, Jorg, was fond of such sayings. He'd look up from his

bench when Enris muttered with frustration—a frequent occur-
rence during the year when rapid growth undid all he'd learned
and made him doubt his awkward fingers would ever do what he
wanted again—and send *calm encouragement* with the words. A
young, proud Enris had been less than grateful. He blushed to remember how quickly he'd slam tight his shields and stomp from
the shop, how he'd roam the fields like a storm cloud until an
empty stomach brought him home. Ridersel would feed him. Jorg
would pretend not to notice he'd ever been gone. Kiric, his older
brother, would laugh and ruffle his hair, a loud, warm laugh that
somehow took away the day's sting.

From what Aryl had told him of her brother, Costa, maybe the
two had been friends for the time Kiric lived with Yena. The peace
of that thought startled him. His brother's loss had been an open
wound for three Harvests; he'd shared Kiric's despair as well as his
death agony.

What had changed? He'd seen Yena for himself. He'd felt a
Chooser's Call. Perhaps, Enris thought with a wry twist of his
mouth, he'd needed to grow up himself to forgive Kiric's leaving
him.

Those on Passage had their reasons. His happened to be a little
different. He snugged up his Grona scarf. He'd be happy to find
shelter from the wind tonight. Even happier to find a way around
the appalling mountain that wouldn't mean forcing his way
through the landscape torn by the Oud. After that?

One detail at a time, he told himself.

At last the footing improved. Fewer ditches. In fact, now that
he noticed, there were no lines of pale pebbles ahead. The ground
beneath his boots was still stony, but these were larger, flat
stones, embedded in hard, cracked soil. As good as a road. Enris
shrugged his pack from one shoulder and pulled out the blade he'd
found. Time for a good look by daylight, now that his feet could
look after themselves.

Aryl agreed the symbols were words. Not a name—or not just
a name. Enris puzzled at it as he walked. A list, like Tuana's
Speaker prepared for the Oud's Visitations? He couldn't imagine

one kept on a tool. Something important to be remembered? That didn't make sense either. What Om'ray needed to know was shared mind-to-mind: parent to child, between Chosen, to some extent among those doing the same work. No one Om'ray could know everything. He didn't know how to operate an Oud harvester in a field; Traud didn't know how to pour metal into a mold, let alone properly sharpen the machine's blades.

Everyone knew what was dangerous, and who belonged.

Daily happenings and advice were part of ordinary conversation. Strangers newly Chosen might share recent events from their Clan, if approved by the Adepts, and Council made announcements of import in front of all.

Or so he'd believed. What did his Clan know of his Passage? He'd entered the Cloisters unconscious; once recovered, he'd been told to leave in the dark, alone. Mauro Lorimar and his followers had known enough to lay ambush, to send him on his way bloody. How? Yuhas sud S'udlaat, once Parth and Yena, had been the only well-wisher, saving him from a worse beating. Had Yuhas told his family the decision of Council?

Had his grandmother, Councillor Dama Mendolar, known the truth about the Adepts' reasons, as Aryl claimed?

Ridersel's relationship with her mother was strained at best. That would end it.

The past . . . Enris rubbed the dull edge thoughtfully. The Eldest told their stories—most, including his grandmother's, laced with warnings about proper behavior for unChosen—about Om'ray they had known. To hear them was to believe nothing ever changed, including the foolish risk-taking of young Om'ray. Only Adepts collected everything there was to know, to be recorded so only they could read it.

Why?

A new question. A radical one. The sort Aryl would ask.

Enris pondered it as he tucked the blade inside his coat and took a carefully small sip from the sac, leaving the water in his mouth as long as possible. Adepts were the gifted, most powerful Om'ray. They received training to enhance their inner abilities,

abilities to be used for the benefit of their Clan. He could have joined their ranks, had he not preferred the work of his hands over his mind. And preferred being able to wander the fields instead of work at all, should the mood strike him.

If he'd become an Adept, would they have let him stay?

Enris shrugged. More to the point, as an Adept, would he have known about Sona? The death of an entire Clan should have been felt by all Om'ray alive at that time. Wouldn't such an event be recorded?

Unless each new generation of Adepts merely recorded their own time, without reading what had passed before.

He would, if he had the chance. Enris added reading to his own list, the one of questions he hoped Vyna would answer, and problems they would solve.

Once he got there.

* ✳ *

Enris didn't begrudge the lack of sleep last truenight. He'd never forget a moment: how firelight burnished Aryl's hair, the quickness of her thoughts, her warm slow smiles. He might not want to remember the trauma of his encounter within the M'hir, but that memory was also of her courage and Power. Her insights. It was the leave-taking he would have wanted from his family.

But—a yawn cracked his jaw—he was paying for it.

The sun had melted into its mold beyond Grona, to cool overnight so it would be ready to rise over Pana tomorrow. Worin had earnestly presented this explanation at the supper table, after his first time operating the vat controls. Enris grinned, wincing as his chapped lower lip split again.

All he could see was the dirt within the splash of brightness ahead of his boot. And his boot. And sometimes the cold puffs of his breath. He'd shortened the twist of rope inside the Sona light, hoping to conserve its oil. Walking—if the ground was cooperatively flat—was one thing he could do half asleep. If he was half awake and not dreaming he was walking while really he was asleep . . .

" 'Nuff of that," the Tuana said aloud, raising the light. He'd tried securing it to his belt, but if tipped to one side, it went out. Running low on oil, he suspected.

Something caught his eye. He took an eager step forward, swinging the light from side to side trying to find it again.

There, right in front. He would have walked into it in another step or two. "Finally!"

Not much as rocks went: roundish, gray, and plain. Barely up to his waist, with a flat top. But it was the first object larger than his fist he'd seen since leaving Sona and the first hint he was close to the other side of the valley. Enris dropped his pack on the rock with a relieved groan.

There would be more nearby, big and small ones, with streams trickling between them. Lovely wet streams.

Light in hand, he walked outward in a series of arcs, glancing back every few steps to be sure he stayed in sight of his rock. Nothing but flat dirt. He widened his search in disbelief. Nothing.

Surr-PLUNK! Clatterclatter.

Enris halted. When there was no other sound, he turned, slowly, and brought his light high over his head.

His pack was lying on the ground. The *clatter* had been his sticks.

Odd.

He might be bone-tired, but he knew he'd put the pack securely on the rock's flat top. Grumbling, he walked over to his pack and picked up the sticks. He put his light on the rock.

Where it tilted and guttered.

And went out.

Because the rock was no longer flat.

Abandoning the light and sticks, Enris scooped up his pack and broke into a run, trusting his memory of the ground he'd walked, using his *sense* of place to guide him in the pitch-darkness.

After a few hasty strides, he slowed, then stopped. What was he doing? So his pack slid off a rock. So he'd put his light down on some unseen bump. It was a rock, not a table. Not a hunter. He wasn't a frantic Yena. Truenight was safe.

Still.

Holding his breath, feeling the fool, Enris listened for anything louder than the pulse of blood in his ears.

Surrrrr-tinkle CRUNCH!

Like that: the sound of the small metal light being crushed by something heavy. Something alive.

This time, when he started running, Enris didn't plan to stop any time soon.

A shame there was a ditch directly ahead.

His foot caught and he flew forward with the momentum of his last stride, unable to drop the pack fast enough to bring his hands up to break the fall.

He'd never live this down, Enris thought with remarkable calm before the ground and truenight claimed him.

Chapter 7

A RYL YAWNED. CATCHING HER aunt's frown, she said
as contritely as possible, given she hadn't been paying the
slightest attention, "I'm listening."

"Then what did I say?" Before Aryl could reply to that,
Myris went on, *exasperation* beneath every word. "I said Enris
shouldn't have left us. I don't care whose Call he heard. And
you shouldn't have followed him, Aryl. Outside in truenight?"
A shudder. "You could have been eaten!"

"By what?" Aryl asked innocently.

Myris hesitated. She remained pale, the gash above her eye
angry and swollen, and her hands trembled. That hadn't
stopped her from intercepting Aryl on the road to Sona and
escorting her back—as she put it—to safety. She drew a quick
breath before resuming her argument. "The point is that you
used poor judgment. As First Chosen, I'm responsible—"

" 'First Chosen?' " Aryl stopped in her tracks. Those exiles
near enough to overhear made a show of being very busy at
their tasks. Her mother, Taisal, was the First Chosen of the
House of Sarc. Myris had left the Sarc home to seek her own
place, as was proper.

Reality, Aryl realized, had changed. The Sarc home no

longer existed. Myris was the only Sarc Chosen among the exiles. The title was hers by every right, even if it had no real meaning.

The duty to her younger kin was hers as well. Aryl gestured a gracious apology. *I'm sorry to have upset you,* she sent. *I couldn't let Enris leave without wishing him joy. He is . . . he was my friend.*

Her aunt's eyes glistened. *I wish he'd come back with you, Aryl. I wish he could have waited.*

If wishes were dresel . . . even now, she knew *where* Enris was. The *how* he was remained locked behind his shields. She doubted he'd ever *reach* for her mind again—certainly not through the M'hir. She would not *reach* for him. Those on Passage had to focus on their own future, not those left behind.

Left behind, in a world gone quiet and cold.

Annoying Tuana.

Aryl felt her pain fade and resisted, clutching her grief. "Please don't," she asked gently. "Let's get you back to bed before Ael scolds me."

As always, the mention of her Chosen brightened her aunt's face. Aryl buried the twinge of envy she couldn't help.

She had work to do.

Dry leaves muttered to themselves. Dead stems clattered against one another, frozen and hollow. The plants offered more questions than answers, Aryl decided, squatting on her heels to drop below the wind. She'd hoped the small field would give her another vision of the past, something to tell her where Sona's Om'ray had found water, something to prove this place could become green again. She trailed her fingertips along fresh scars in the dirt. Enris didn't believe in Sona's future. Here, then, alone, he'd made his decision to seek another path. Not one they could follow, even if they would. Myris was unfit to travel; Chaun . . . wasted away. Weth didn't leave him.

"There you are!" Seru wriggled through the gap the Tuana

had forced between the thorns, an effort hindered by her too-long Sona coat. "Myris said you were upset." Tugging her bright scarf free of an avaricious twig, she plopped herself on the ground beside Aryl. "Are you?"

"I haven't found water, if that's what you mean."

Her cousin's eyes sparkled within their nest of scarf, hood, and hairnet. "Of course not." She pushed her right sleeve up to expose her hand, wiggling her fingers suggestively. "Tell me you at least tried."

"Seru, you know I'm no—" Aryl caught *despair* and stopped. In another life, they'd tuck themselves into bed and talk until firstlight. Brainless flitters, Costa had called them, not appreciating the importance of such conversations. How to glance just so at handsome unChosen. How to tip a wrist in a manner subtle yet alluring. How not to be caught doing either.

She made herself comfortable on the dirt, cross-legged, hands flat on her knees. "I would have tried, if I could," Aryl admitted. Her own hood was down. She was, she realized with a vague surprise, no longer as troubled by the cold. "But Enris isn't ready for Choice." True, in a sense.

"He's on Passage." As if Aryl had missed some vital lesson. "How could he not be ready? That's why unChosen go."

Easy to sigh. "He told me about his family. How Mendolars can seem eligible to others before they really are." Glib and almost true. Aryl tucked away her guilt. There was no harm in shaping words to undo pain.

"I've never heard anything like that."

"His brother?" She waited. Seru had loved every version of his story.

"Kiric?" Her cousin sighed, too. "I'll never forget him. Such a waste. He arrived too late, you know." As if Aryl, equally fascinated by the sad-eyed stranger and far more willingly inventive, hadn't been the source of most rumors. "There were no Yena Choosers left for him. He died of loneliness. I can understand that . . ."

"What if that wasn't true?" Though they were alone in the

field between buildings, she leaned closer. Seru did the same until their noses almost touched, her green eyes wide. "What if Kiric was like Enris," Aryl whispered, "and couldn't."

Her cousin drew back with a gasp. "Aryl! What a dreadful—" another, calmer breath "You mean . . . But if that's true . . . ? Oh." She sniffled. "Poor Enris. He must have been so unhappy to be near me, to want me yet be unable . . ." Another, wetter sniff. "No wonder he had to leave. I mustn't Call again, not until he's very far away."

Seru Parth might not have the Power of others, but she had kindness enough for a Clan. Aryl managed not to smile. "I didn't let him go without saying good-bye." She let a tiny portion of *loss* leak through her shields. "Enris was a good friend to all of us. I told him so. I think he feels better about himself now." She hoped. The biting anger she felt at his Clan's betrayal was something she kept very much to herself.

"May he find joy." Seru laid her hand over Aryl's. "And may we find it, too, Cousin." A breathless laugh. "Though it might have trouble finding us here."

Aryl turned her hand and gripped Seru's, hard. "I promise, Cousin. You'll have Choice." Even if she had to travel to another Clan and drag an unChosen back through the M'hir by his hair. "I promise."

"No." Seru drew herself up straight. "You can't. You'll be a Chooser soon and then you'll understand. It's up to me to Call. It's up to him to hear me and come. However long it takes." She pulled something from under her coat and smiled shyly. "I'm going to show him. How long I waited. See?"

It was a loop of braided yellow thread, hung around her neck. The braid was dotted with fine black knots. Seru's hair. Between the knots were tufts of frayed red thread. "It's pretty," Aryl ventured. The frayed thread—likely from an undershirt—looked like small bursts of flame.

"It's more than that." Her cousin touched a knot. "I tie one each truenight, before I sleep. With a wish." Her cheeks went pink. "I'd like someone . . . you know what I mean."

Aryl fervently hoped not to, for some time yet. Bemused, she touched one of the tufts. "What are these, then?"

"A fist." Seru ran her fingers along the loop, her lips moving soundlessly. "Eight fists and a day since I became a Chooser." Her smile faded. "A fist and two days since we left Yena."

Seven days. Was that all? It might have been another life, lived by another Aryl, another Seru. Three days at Grona. Three on the road. Their first day at Sona.

Yena had no need to mark days. The only change in their lives came with the annual M'hir, which the Watchers announced. The steady growth of rastis and vine mattered more, the constant decay of bridge or roof, the cycle of biters. But now—in this exposed place, where storms swept away the sun at whim, where nothing grew in winter? They had to hold every day, Aryl realized, or lose track. They had to learn to remember, to warn themselves of the season's change, to prepare. Her mind felt swollen by the possibilities. "Clever, Seru," she praised, adding *warmth*.

"I didn't think of it," the other admitted. "Mother . . . she taught me. It makes it easier to wait. Parth Choosers must be patient, especially if there's—you and I—we were always together, Aryl. Mother knew I couldn't avoid you." *Grief* beneath the confusing rush of words.

Ferna Parth lived—her body lived. That was all. The rest of what she'd been had been Lost with her Chosen, Till sud Parth, killed by the swarm during the Tikitik assault on Yena. Aryl shielded her own emotion and tried to understand. She'd never doubted her welcome at the Parth home. Ferna and Till treated her like a second daughter. Had. She and Seru weren't heart-kin; they were dear friends nonetheless. "Why would she want you to do that?"

"You're Sarc." As if that made everything clear. Something in Aryl's expression must have told Seru it didn't. "I'm not saying you ever push yourself up the ladder, Aryl." Another rush of words. "You aren't like that. But everyone knows. It's about Power. Always is. To be a Parth, near a Sarc Chooser?" Seru tucked away her loop of hair knots and thread. "UnChosen have to answer your Call first. They can't help it."

Fighting back a strange, fierce *joy*—where had *that* come from?—Aryl placed her fingers on Seru's. *Not a Chooser yet.* With careful *reassurance*. "Now let's go find Haxel. I've a feeling she'll be interested in this clever idea of the Parths."

The First Scout? Interested? Seru pretended to shiver. *Oh, no. You show her.*

Coward.

Smart. And fast. With that pronouncement, Seru leaped to her feet, scattering dead leaves. "Race you!" A jump, grab, and twist put her on top of the nearest beam.

Aryl laughed and gave chase. The beam, used to vines, not playful Om'ray, creaked and cracked in protest underfoot. A hop took them both to the shelter's makeshift roof. Which shook and shuddered.

Someone inside shouted a protest.

Seru glanced back, hood down and black hair flying wild, balanced on one foot. Her teeth gleamed in a wicked grin, then she dropped lightly to the porch. Aryl tried to hurry. Too late. Looking oh-so-innocent, her cousin helpfully pointed up as the blanket door opened and a dust-covered head peered out.

Not dignified to leap on her so-helpful-cousin and roll her in the dirt.

But, Aryl decided, hands full of squirming Seru, it was worth it.

"Water's the problem."

Aryl nodded. Freed from the threat of starvation for the first time since last Harvest, sheltered and safe, they had yet to find that final necessity. "We could move down the valley," she suggested with reluctance. The nearest of the mountain streams was a half day away. The three unChosen—Fon, Kayd, and

Cader—were there now, refilling every portable container they could carry. The next group—Rorn, Syb, and Veca—would leave soon, to return by firstnight. If the clouds building over the mountains meant another storm, best only their toughest, most experienced Chosen were out in it.

Haxel's scar whitened with her grimace. By tradition and inclination, she'd be with those after water, but they needed her here. "If we did, we'd have to come back here for supplies and oil. Let's hope for better. Are you ready to go?"

"Yes." Aryl hadn't slept, but otherwise judged herself well rested. She checked the ties on her small pack. There'd been no need to discuss who should explore the head of the valley. No one else with any scouting skill could be spared from carrying water or improving their shelter. Also unsaid . . . no one else had her range to *send* for help if need be. Haxel held out a pair of ropes and she slipped one coil over her shoulder, securing it with her belt. She declined the second, wishing she could leave the pack, too, but she wasn't a fool. If necessary, she'd spend her second truenight away from the rest. And there was that brooding sky.

"It may end in a cliff around the corner," the First Scout warned. "Nothing more."

Aryl shrugged. "I'll be back for supper, then. If they've finished complaining about Enris." She'd thought Grona's infatuated Choosers a nuisance, the way they'd cornered her for any detail about him, but the exiles were worse. Or made her feel worse. Even Husni wasn't beyond a sly comment on how in her day a sensible Chooser-to-Be would have found a way to keep such a fine catch happily waiting. Had anyone but Seru and Gijs missed telling her, at length, the wonderful qualities of the Tuana and how tragic it was he'd had to leave them to seek Choice?

As if she didn't know.

"You'd think they'd wish him joy and be done with it."

A grunt. "They wished he'd found it here. Do you blame them?"

Aryl looked back at Sona. Ax strokes and cheerful shouts gave new life to the ruin; a line of billowing blankets, new movement. The same wind—always a wind here—blew an errant strand of hair into her eyes. She tucked it away, wishing the Sona supplies had included a decent net. "I suppose not. But Enris believes the future—our future—is elsewhere. What he seeks may help all Om'ray."

"A Clan with its own technology." She'd told the First Scout that much. Whatever her opinion of his feet, Haxel had been pleased Enris hadn't abandoned them for, as she'd put it, some useless Chooser on the wind. "He has courage," the older Om'ray conceded. "Myself, I'd test that limb before I put weight on it."

"Vyna exists. He'll find out the rest for himself." Aryl stirred. "I'd better go, too." She hefted the thin strand of rope she'd attached to her belt. Seven knots at the top; room for more below. Haxel, who'd instantly grasped the value of such counting, wore its twin. "Two days, then I'll turn around."

Fingers brushed her hand. *Make sure you do, Aryl Sarc.* Concern in the First Scout's pale, crease-edged eyes, or sudden doubt?

My future is with my people, Aryl promised. *It always will be.*

Despite the wind and cloud-ridden ridge, the day was bright and warm, for the mountains. As Aryl strode away from Haxel, she left her Grona coat open, its hood thrown back. She followed the road; it followed the dry riverbed. Both bent around an outthrust of unclimbable rock. Despite Haxel's warning about a dead end, it was unlikely. She found herself taking longer steps and deliberately slowed her pace.

Aryl passed the heap of rubble Cetto thought had been the Sona Meeting Hall. Nothing worth salvaging here, beyond slivers of wood to burn. They'd have to build their own.

If they stayed.

The road crossed the river before heading into the grove of dead nekis. If there'd been a bridge spanning the riverbed, it was gone now. Aryl jumped lightly from the last paving stone that jutted out, landing on fine gravel and dirt. No bent reeds. She gauged its depth by her jump. Two Om'ray here, perhaps two more in the center of the course.

The footing took concentration, if not effort. Larger boulders lay scattered among the rest, along with broken spars of wood. If such were the remains of a bridge, it had been thoroughly destroyed by the Oud. Preventing what?

Aryl kept her distance from any stone of size. They hadn't seen a rock hunter. Didn't make the memory any less fresh or her careless.

She tried to imagine the river full of water. Would it be clear, like the Lake of Fire, or impenetrably black, like the Lay Swamp? Would it tumble and roar like the torrent they'd seen up on the ridge? Or be smooth and slow, only dimples in its surface revealing any movement at all?

Aryl picked up a pebble and sent it flying ahead. It didn't reach the other side. She should, she decided, be glad the river was empty at the moment.

The other bank was an easy scramble to the top. Once there, she found the paving stones flat and in place, spared by the Oud. Dead nekis stalks tilted and towered on one side of the road, separated by more ditches. The grove-that-had-been stretched across the valley, row upon row of old bones.

After that one look, Aryl kept her eyes on the paving stones. The wind whistled through the stalks, unsoftened by leaf or flower. The sun beat down, its light unfiltered by green or brown.

The road turned sharply, angled toward the river until she walked almost on its bank. She didn't look back, although she *sensed* those behind her. There were, she realized abruptly, no Om'ray ahead of her at all.

The world's end.

"We'll see," Aryl whispered to herself, and lengthened her stride once more.

Although the road climbed, the rock outcrop that hid the valley's upper reach rose faster. Very soon, it blocked most of the sky and Aryl had to tip her head to see its top. To the side, the valley's other wall closed in until only the river—narrower and deeper here—the road, and an edge of fallen stone could fit between.

The shadows were deep and permanent here, brightened only by drifts of unmelted snow. Aryl, coat now fastened and hood up, used mouthfuls of the stuff to assuage her thirst, saving the water she carried. She tried not to do it often. Walking didn't warm her, and she was afraid the snow would chill her body even faster.

Difficult to keep her mind from wandering; harder still to keep it from where she didn't want it to go. Lack of sleep. Lack of challenge. Climbing would be better. She almost—almost— wanted some of the rocks she passed to move, simply to help her focus. Though every step took her farther from the comfort of her kind than she'd ever been, so far she felt no dread, no overwhelming impulse to return to their glow.

"Day's young," she reminded herself.

Difficult to keep track of time, wedged in this deep cleft between ridges. In the wider valley, she could have used the steady climb of shadow up a rock face, but here those walls overhung and shaded one another. Likely less than a tenth since she left Sona. Her stomach hadn't complained; not that Aryl planned to eat before truenight if it did. Haxel had given her one of the Grona fire starters, and wood filled most of her pack. Good thing. There hadn't been more since the nekis grove; the pieces she could see down in the riverbed were too massive to move or set on fire.

The chill shadows, the soaring rock walls ahead and alongside her, the complete silence other than her soft footsteps on the smooth stone of the road . . . this was nowhere she'd been or imagined. Yet Aryl found herself more and more at ease, as if this place somehow held a welcome.

Or she remembered one . . .

She stopped, waiting for the echoes of her footsteps to stop as well. Was she dreaming this, the way Seru had walked and dreamed?

"I am awake!" The reverberation of that defiant shout bounced and blurred; definitely not something she'd dream.

Aryl blushed and started walking again. Regardless of how she felt, the road was reassurance. If the Sona had built it, they'd had a reason. An Om'ray reason. Something she'd find and understand.

"With water," she promised herself, around another icy mouthful of snow. It wasn't an idle hope. The uncrossable torrent in the ridge gully they couldn't cross had been flowing toward the valley. It didn't reach it—she didn't know why—but she'd seen its water. If there was a similar source for Sona's river, it might be closer. The road was an easier path than the ridges for those carrying water.

Even better, maybe they could fix whatever stopped the river and make it flow into Sona again.

She could hear Enris now. He'd laugh his deep laugh—not to mock her but because she'd surprised him with another of her "ideas." Then he'd have questions—not to discourage her but to explore possibilities.

They moved apart with every step—she could *feel* the distance between them stretch. He was heading straight for Vyna. He couldn't plan to climb the mountain that lay between. The powerful Tuana's climbing skill, as Haxel would say, made his walking look good. No, surely she'd *feel* him turn toward Rayna, go in that direction for a day or more, stay to flat ground.

Difficult, moving through the destruction left by the Oud. Dangerous, passing close to the Lake of Fire and the Tikitik. She couldn't help him. Could she?

No.

Aryl's hands became fists.

She wasn't doing this again.

She'd ached for Bern when he'd left Yena on his Passage—

had almost followed him. What had that longing gained her besides pain? Hadn't he Chosen Oran di Caraat of Grona? Hadn't he abused their link as heart-kin and tried to force her to share her Talent?

What she felt for Enris Mendolar promised a greater agony, unless she let him go.

"Those on Passage are dead to those they leave," she whispered.

Fighting back tears, Aryl withdrew her inner sense until all she felt were those behind in Sona.

The riverbed didn't go tamely around the outcrop. Where the cliff's curve thrust into the valley, the river had gone through it. Gray rock hung above the river's deep and jagged course, the entire height of a mountain suspended in midair.

Aryl pushed back her hood to better stare at the mass of rock overhead. Water had power. No one climbed during the heavy rains: the force could knock an adult Om'ray off a branch or wash anything unsecured from a platform. Missing roof pods had to be replaced or the resulting flood could destroy a home's contents.

Could water wash away stone? She shook her head. Another of her "ideas;" a more foolish one than most.

She wasn't surprised when she came around the outcrop only to face another, this thrust from the opposite wall of the valley. Over the past days she'd seen for herself how repetitive this mountain landscape was: hollow and peak, valley and ridge, without an end in sight.

The road became steeper, though still even and paved in those matched flat stones. The riverbed writhed to the opposite side as if it fought the constraint of the mountains. The road rose over it, carried on an arch of perfectly fitted stone.

The how of it baffled her. Perhaps Sona's Om'ray had been like Enris and Fon, able to *push* heavy objects with Power.

Better that, she thought grimly, than imagining Sona had trusted the Oud, had worked with them to create something this impressive, only to be betrayed.

The answer might lie ahead.

More twists, more arches. The shadows grew longer or the mountain to either side taller—Aryl couldn't tell which. The result was the same. The rare glimpses of sky only proved it wasn't firstnight. She might have walked three tenths or five.

While she had light to travel, she would. She felt no fear or exhaustion during this easy walk, only anticipation. Careful of her body, she'd chewed one of Haxel's swimmer twists and drank at intervals, but stopping to rest was out of the question.

Why build this road?

Homes, places to grow plants, a meeting hall, storerooms sunk into the ground: these made sense. A road for Passage to another Clan made sense.

There was none of that here, just the road and the river, the glow of her kind receding with each step. As she walked, Aryl studied the walls to either side, searching for doorways at ground level or caves higher up, like Yena's Watchers. These walls were sheer or jagged; she found no sign they'd ever been touched. The "before-now" structures Marcus and his Triad had freed from the cliffs beyond Grona—another how she couldn't imagine—had been embedded in rock that crumbled rather than split along clean lines. If any such buildings were buried here, they were staying buried.

She tightened the scarf around her neck against the wind whistling down the valley. It grew stronger as the walls narrowed. Louder. The M'hir Wind must roar through here—not a place to be at summer's end. Didn't the Sona have Watchers to warn them?

The Tuana had drums, Enris said. Those didn't sound a warning of the M'hir. They announced the Oud.

Useful, that. Aryl scuffed her toe pensively. There might be Oud beneath her right now and she'd never know. "No Tiki-tik," she assured herself. They stayed in the groves, or on the borders of the Lay Swamp, where they could tend their growths and beasts.

Didn't they?

She'd hear any pursuit.

Or would she? The wind made odd noises where it slipped along the river's deep empty channel or under rock overhangs. Her footsteps and breathing, however quiet, were caught by the stone and reflected back at unexpected moments.

Aryl shook her head. She was alone, more alone than she'd ever been in her life. Those on Passage sought a living goal; she followed a road made by the long-dead and forgotten. Their purpose, however, was the same: to find a future, no matter what stood between.

She swung her pack around to retrieve a piece of rokly, food left by those who'd last walked as she did. Dresel was what her mouth wanted—fresh, moist, and sweet—but the wizened fruit answered the same craving.

They'd taste fresh rokly, she thought as she chewed, if they could get it to grow again. Ziba "remembered" it fondly. She didn't.

Aryl's mind skittered from fruit to Choosers and those to be-come Choosers. No one else had dreamed or had visions of Sona's past. If something about their minds made them more susceptible or reached out, it didn't explain to what.

Or why the M'hir had come perilously close in her sleep.

She stopped on the next arched bridge, toes over the edge, and gazed down into what was now a black abyss. Life should be lived high above the ground, she thought wistfully. There should be a reason to step with care; balance and strength and skill should matter.

If she found water, if Sona could become green again, would Ziba still run the rooftops? Or would the Yena lose that part of themselves?

"Survive first," Aryl reminded herself.

About to move, she paused, suddenly aware of a vibration beneath her feet. She crouched to flatten her hand on the stone.

Faint. Steady. Like rain on a roof.

She looked to where the valley twisted around yet another slab of mountain. Was there sound as well? Aryl held her breath and strained to hear.

Still faint—more imagined than heard—but there, she was sure. A low, heavy thrum.

Aryl rose to her feet and eagerly took to the road again. She had to force herself to keep to a walk, prepare herself for disappointment. Nothing promised the next turn would be the last.

But it was. Aryl knew it by the time the road and river turned around rock. The vibration here came up through her feet, matched to a growing rumble.

The air took on a scent. Heady, rich, moist.

Alive.

About to run forward, Aryl hesitated, then left the road for a shadow darker than most. Shedding her pack and rope, she tucked them against the rock wall. She pushed back her hood and drew the short knife from her belt, then relaxed. From this vantage, it was easy to watch the road she'd just walked.

Shadows moved and lengthened. The wind tugged at her hair. She felt disoriented, without Om'ray in every direction, but it wasn't as if she could be lost here, where there was only one path.

No pursuit. Satisfied, Aryl continued on. Keeping to shadows, now avoiding the road, she moved with every bit of stealth she possessed.

With each step, the vibration grew stronger, the rumble louder, the scent of the air more intense.

Nothing prepared her for what waited around the turn.

The valley walls faded back, embracing a vast open space. Their towering reaches were hidden in mist and cloud. The mist came from the source of the vibration and roar: a river that fell from the sky.

Not the sky, Aryl realized as she walked forward, the hand with the knife limp at her side. She faced a cliff whose upper height she couldn't see. Its sheer face streamed with lines of writhing white and black that glistened and sang with unimaginable force. The amount of water pouring straight down in front of her mocked any understanding she had of her world. This was the Lay Swamp and the Lake of Fire . . . this was every flood and raindrop . . . every melting snowdrop . . . and it went—

Nowhere. The water fell. And vanished.

It couldn't. That much water had to go somewhere. It should be filling the empty river, racing down the valley to Sona and beyond.

The road, and empty river, ended at a hill of loose rubble and dirt taller than three Om'ray. Aryl ran to it, then up it, her boots digging in with every stride. The roar of the waterfall grew deafening. She met mist, chill and clinging, that turned the footing slick and treacherous. The slope steepened and she grabbed for handholds. Only after the second reach did she recognize what she grabbed.

Aryl froze, one hand on a piece of dark wood, identical to the splinters from the beams of Sona, the other on a skull.

This wasn't a hill. It was another ruin.

The Oud had struck here, too.

Suddenly the urge to turn back, the pull of living Om'ray overwhelmed her. Aryl blinked tears from her eyes and leaned her forehead against the hand on the skull. "Soon," she promised herself. "But not yet."

She climbed the rest of the hill with a heavy heart, making no effort to avoid the gray skulls and bones that dotted its surface, though they cracked underfoot. Their appalling number answered one question: why they'd found none in the homes. The exiles had assumed all of the Sona Om'ray had fled into the mountains and died there. After all, that would be the Yena preference, the safety of height. But Sona had come here, in a final, desperate flight along their road.

Why?

What refuge could protect them from a terror underground? Where would Om'ray run?

The Sona Cloisters. There was no other choice.

Sure now of what she'd find, Aryl came to the top and stood, staring through layers and swirls of mist. Her hand rose to her mouth.

She hadn't imagined this.

Water dominated everything. It dropped from the sky, barely touching the immense cliff, its spray like plumes of smoke. Where those plumes touched rock, there was life. Gnarled stalks and sprigs of still-green leaves burst from cracks. Vines thicker than her body somehow found hold on the stone itself. Their tendrils, heavy with clusters of wizened brown fruit, hung out in the spray as if to catch it. The air itself was like a drink.

A drink that vanished. The water plunged into a great black hole, choked with spray and rimmed by more ruins. Nekis sprouted in thick groves along that crumbling edge, their stalks short and twisted, leafless in this cold season but alive. Several were about to fall, their roots washed bare.

Aryl worked her way down, wary of the footing. When she came to the first of the groves, nekis barely over her head, she ran her fingers greedily over the tight buds that tipped every branch. This was what water could do. Bring life even here.

As to the hole? Knife in her belt, her woven coat collecting droplets from the plants, Aryl pushed her way to its edge, forcing a path through the stalks. Without conscious thought, she slipped into old habits, checking as she moved for what might fancy a taste of Yena or merely have thorns. The stunted grove seemed barren of dangerous life; "seemed" couldn't be trusted.

Once at the edge, she found a sturdy, if doomed, stalk leaning over the chasm and walked out along it as far as she could before peering down.

It was like being in a storm where the rain came up as much as fell properly from above. She had to gasp for breath and wipe her face constantly, her bones vibrating with the roar and crash of so much water going . . . where?

For all she could see, it went through the world to nowhere. There was no flash of white, as if the water struck bottom and boiled. The torrent simply fell into the dark.

Thoughtfully, Aryl walked back up the stalk, leaning with its tilt.

Now she knew where the water from the river had gone—if not why or how.

Returning it to the river was going to be a problem . . .

Snap!Pop! The stalk's roots began to give way, and Aryl absently jumped to its neighbor. Maybe there'd be something about moving rivers in a dream, she told herself.

Once more above the grove, she moved along the hill itself, hunting what had to be here. Every living Clan had a Cloisters. Finding Sona's would be irrefutable proof there had been Om'ray here once.

And could be again.

Rock, shards of wood and bone. The destruction here had been horrifyingly complete. But a Cloisters wasn't made of rock or wood; didn't suffer weathering or damage. She'd find it.

Every so often, Aryl checked the sky. There wasn't much to see other than mist and hanging cloud; it was still daylight. For how long? She should retrieve her pack and make a camp. Wood wouldn't be a problem. That would be the prudent, sensible plan.

Something in her couldn't stop. Not yet.

The hill didn't ring the entire hole. It rose highest over the road and the old river, then flattened as it approached the cliff and waterfall on either side. There, the nekis and other, unfamiliar growths took over, cloaking the ruin. To continue, Aryl found herself once more forcing her way through spray-drenched vegetation.

She couldn't stop.

Her coat caught and held on a leafless branch. Impatiently, she tore off the sodden garment, leaving it to hang. It had started to smell anyway. She kept her belt, using it to hold her knife, and shivered as she pressed forward.

"Not yet," Aryl muttered. She protected her face with her forearms as she pushed through a particularly thick stand of young nekis. A twig snapped against her ear.

She stumbled into the open, at once sinking knee-deep in freshly loose soil and pebbles. Trapped! Her hand flashed to the hilt of her knife. It stayed there.

The Oud reared, black limbs flailing, dust and dirt pouring from the dome and fabric of its covering. "Who are!? Who are!!?"

Aryl coughed and spat dirt from her mouth. The creature rose so high she thought it would topple over backward. "What do!!? What do!?"

The voice came from its . . . did she call them arms or legs?

"Me? What are you doing?" she demanded, trying her best to portray dignified offense, which wasn't easy, half buried and terrified. Though she could see for herself.

Sona's Cloisters stood beyond the Oud. Not lifted on a stalk like Yena's, but set on the ground, like Grona's or Tuana's. What she could see of it was achingly intact, both levels within their encircling platforms, their petal walls broken by a series of tall wide arches; each of those a triplet of smaller arches: two of a clear window taller than three Om'ray, the centermost a door of metal; the whole roofed by a series of overlapped white rings.

Beautiful.

Once. Now it was, like her, half buried in newly turned dirt. The lights within shone, but to her inner sense it was empty, either abandoned or full of the dead.

There were abundant signs of a prolonged and vigorous attempt to find a way inside. Unsuccessful, since what showed of the Cloisters looked unmarked, though its walls and windows were filthy, muddied with strange tracks. The creature must have been digging for days to move so much rock and dirt. The lowermost platform was filled. She couldn't tell where its paired main doors would be.

It would take Om'ray days to dig it back out again.

The Oud had turned still as stone, though still upright. Then, "Way in? Yesyesyesyes?"

Even if she knew, she'd die first. Aryl thrust out her arm and pointed, her hand shaking with fury. "That belongs to us, not you!"

"Us?" The Oud dropped with a thud, then raced back and forth in front of her, every limb a blur of motion and flailing dirt. It didn't turn around, merely changed direction, as if it didn't matter which end went first. The loose ground didn't slow it at all.

She had no idea what the creature was doing, but while it was doing it, she wormed her legs free.

The Oud plowed to a stop in front of her and reared. "No us!" it declared. "You. Only."

A threat? Was it telling her she was alone and defenseless?

Or confusion, that until it "looked"—however it managed without eyes—it hadn't been sure how many Om'ray had surprised it?

She needed Enris. Or her mother. Someone who could talk to something not-*real*.

As she'd talked to the strangers.

Remembering that, Aryl stood a bit straighter. The Oud was of Cersi. A neighbor. If they still lived beneath Sona, the last thing she should do was antagonize the first one she met. Say something, she told herself. Anything. "My name is Aryl Sarc." Her voice sounded weak. She firmed it. "I came to find water for my Clan."

"Water too much." It sounded annoyed.

Maybe it was. Drops of spray smeared the dusty dome covering its "head" and were rapidly turning the loose dirt around them both into mud. Aryl's lips twitched. Her own face was clammy with it. She must look like a lump of mud herself. "There is water here," she clarified, "but the valley is dry."

"Yesyesyesyes. Way in?"

Stubborn. Determined. Did this Oud know what had happened so long ago? Did it care? Or were they like Om'ray, interested only in what was happening now, to those alive? Vital questions. A shame she didn't dare ask them.

"Why do you want to go in the Cloisters? Not," she added quickly, "that I'm offering to let you in."

"Curious."

One word. A good word. Possibly the only one she would have understood from it.

Aryl tugged her boot free of the dirt and took a cautious step toward the Oud. It lowered its "head," lifted its midsection, and humped itself rapidly away, stopping a body's length from her. Afraid of her or loath to have an Om'ray so close? She stopped and regarded it for a moment, at a loss.

Finally, desperate. "Do you want us to leave?"

Rearing, the Oud fastened on one word in return. "Us?"

This wasn't going well.

Maybe she should try something else. "Are we safe?"

Its limbs moved rapidly, the lowermost churning through the dirt with such force she had to step back to avoid being showered in it. It sank backward—if that was backward for an Oud—into the ground.

"Wait!" she cried out. "You didn't answer me!"

It paused, its "speaking limbs" barely free to move. "Goodgoodgoodgood. Wait."

Then, in a final flurry that made her duck to protect her eyes, it was gone.

" 'Wait,' " she echoed.

The creature was ridiculous. Insane. She should ignore it.

What if it had left to confer with others of its kind? What if they discussed the upstart Om'ray who dared reinhabit Sona? What if it returned with some ultimatum that she must be here to answer or her people would suffer?

What if it forgot she was here and went to dig another stupid hole?

"This—" Aryl kicked dirt into the oval depression left by the Oud, "—is why—" another kick, "—I hate—" kick, "—talking to—" kick, "—not-*real*, not-Om'ray, not—" She stopped.

What was that?

Careful to move only her eyes, she sought what had caught her attention. It couldn't have been a sound. The rumble and drone of the falling water masked all but a shout at any distance.

Had she *sensed* something?

Enris warned her not to use Power near Oud. He hadn't been clear if that meant near any Oud or only certain Oud, not to mention reared-and-talking-to-your-face Oud as opposed to might-be-in-the-general-vicinity-don't-care Oud.

A giggle worked its way up her throat, and Aryl pressed her lips together.

Avoiding the worst of the Oud's work to keep her feet from sinking again, she walked as naturally as possible toward the Cloisters. A reasonable goal, being the only shelter outside of the shadowed grove. Mist hung over its round roof, distorting the shape, but the ground grew drier as she approached— farther from the waterfall and spray, though closer to the gigantic wall of rock that ended the valley. The Cloisters had stood before that rock, gleaming and full of life. Sona's Adepts. Its age-weary Chosen, seeking peace. Newborns, to take their names and be recorded. The newly Joined, to give theirs.

There. To the side where the grove bordered the open space.

Aryl did her utmost not to react, but she was certain. Something, or someone, watched. She didn't know how she knew— it wasn't quite a *taste*. The sensation followed her, as if her watcher mirrored her steps.

The ground became more pebble than dirt, those pebbles familiar despite the best efforts of the Oud to overturn them all. Belatedly, she realized she was walking across another of the ditches, but this was much wider and curved. Shallow, she thought, though that was difficult to gauge after the creature had plowed its way back and forth and, from the disturbance, in circles.

If she imagined the space full of water . . . for an instant, Aryl could *see* what had been here before . . .

The Cloisters rose like a blossom before a still pool, its lights reflected on itself so that it glistened in welcoming splendor against the dark stone of the cliff. Sweeping groves of nekis and other plants, fragrant and full, rose behind and to the side. Paired paths of stone, white and clean, curled around the water and soared over arched bridges to link the building to the road from Sona. The road was filled with laughing figures, some carrying baskets, others bearing oillights high on poles. More Om'ray than Tuana or even Amna could claim. So many, there was a second settlement behind her, across this made-lake, where the elderly could take their ease close to care, and those waiting to give birth could be watched.

The waterfall had its own lake, wide and churned to perilous froth, spilling and tumbling and babbling where it overflowed down the valley, contained by the river channel, celebrated by Sona. There should be a festival to mark the end of ice and cold, that day when fields and gardens received their first gift of flood and seeds began to grow . . .

Aryl came back to herself with a jerk of dismay. She'd moved forward; she didn't remember the steps. The M'hir! It was smotheringly close, pulling at her, *demanding* her attention. She refused and shoved it aside, an easier effort this time.

Her slip into it had been easier, too. Was her skill growing, or was it consuming her?

What mattered was here and now, she scolded herself. First-night was coming. Water and wood weren't problems, but she'd left her supplies—oh, so cleverly—on the other side of the last outcrop and her coat somewhere in the grove, for what good its soaked mass would be. The Oud had said, "Wait." She had to believe it had meant to stay here as long as she could.

And she was being watched.

Ambush hunters were common in the canopy. As Aryl continued toward the Cloisters, she kept her distance from likely cover, watched for any trace. The flutter of web or hair on a branch. The remnants of digested bone or skin.

Nothing.

The hairs on her neck rose as she walked over the buried lower rail and platform of the Cloisters. The digging of the Oud had left a wide ramp of dirt and stone over the upper rail on this side. Elsewhere, that rail curved upward, too smooth to climb. Aryl took the ramp and found more dirt and stone. The Oud had filled in the upper platform as well, for what reason she couldn't guess.

The windows arched ahead of her were too dust-smeared to offer a reflection. Wrong, wrong, wrong. They should be clean. There should be life.

Despite her dread, Aryl lifted her hand eagerly as she approached and laid it on the window, expecting . . . what? Cool, hard, solid. Nothing more. She tried rubbing dirt away with her palm. There was light within, too faint to reveal more than hints of a wall and floor inside.

She went to the door next to the window. Familiar—the same multicolored metal, same shape. It would turn, thus. This could be Yena, if she weren't standing on Oud leavings. She knocked on the door, hearing only the dull thud of her fist. How did it open? Adepts had the secret. It was something an Om'ray could do. Frustrated, Aryl studied the door and its frame, looking for any clues.

What she found were scuffs in the newly disturbed ground at its base.

Leading away.

She followed, pretending to examine each window arch and doorway. The ground—the Oud's pile—descended until her feet touched the metal floor of the upper platform.

Darker here. The platform rail normally admitted light, but the Oud had thrown dirt against its outer surface. Stupid creature. The dimness made it possible to see more through the windows. She gazed with longing at pale walls and floors, the unique lighting that ran at the junction of wall and ceiling. There were no furnishings, no objects in sight. An unreachable, vacant perfection.

She would open its doors, Aryl vowed to herself. It wasn't merely a symbol of a Clan's existence—the Cloisters promised shelter and safety for her people even from the Oud.

After she learned who or what was trying to get there first.

The platform was coated in fine dust, another result of the Oud's diligence; the waterfall's spray didn't reach this far to mottle it. Lines of paired steps made a beaten path. Aryl grinned without humor. She didn't need Haxel's training to read these tracks. Multiple trips, the most recent crossing the rest.

Aryl bent to take a closer look. No beast or Oud. She'd seen a Tikitik's long-toed foot. These tracks had been made by a boot—an Om'ray boot.

She lowered her shields and *reached* at once, finding the exiles and the distant solitary glow that was Enris, no Om'ray closer.

These were fresh tracks.

Aryl frowned. Only one kind of being on Cersi had a foot like an Om'ray, while being as not-*real* and invisible to her inner sense as an Oud or Tikitik.

He wouldn't, she told herself, shaken. Marcus Bowman had promised to stay away—to keep his people away. Besides, with the stranger-technology at his disposal—aircars, flying eyes, distance viewers, who could guess what else?—why wander around in Om'ray boots?

Alone, too. Each pair of tracks was identical.

The most recent led to an arrangement of wood pieces, arranged as a stair against the rail. Since the rail was only waist-high, Aryl didn't see the point. She jumped lightly to the rail top, crouching as she landed to present a smaller target. Beyond was the start of the nekis grove.

Through which had been cut a nice, neat path, straight as a beam.

She almost laughed. Had the wanderer wanted to be conspicuous?

No taking that path. Not because it was a blatantly obvious site for a trap—she trusted her own ability—but the Oud hadn't returned. Might never, she realized, but she couldn't go out of sight of this open area until sure.

There was, however, another kind of ambush. Aryl stood on the rail, making a show of fighting for her balance. She took one step along it, then missed the next and fell through the air.

"Ooof!" she let out as she landed on her back, body twisted in a position she hoped looked painful, though it wasn't.

Her eyes had to be closed for this to work. Easy enough. She'd picked a spot free of sharp pebbles. Remarkably comfortable. Not that she planned to sleep, but it had been a long day. And truenight. And day before that.

She chewed her tongue for distraction.

The waterfall's deep vibration traveled through her bones. Its damp breeze stole warmth from her coatless body and left an acrid taste on her tongue and lips. Aryl didn't move, barely breathed. She'd always won Fall/Dead. Her playmates would leave in search of dresel cakes long before she tired of the game.

The sensation of being watched never left her. She sought to grasp how or what she felt.

Elusive. A *scent* more than a *taste*. Her inner sense responded, but it was like trying to catch a flitter with a dresel hook. The effort was too quick, too slow . . . or was it too violent? That was it. Whatever she *touched* disappeared if she *reached* for it. If she let her inner self still, be less attentive, the sensation returned.

Snap! A branch. *Crunchcrunch.* Boots on pebbles. Bad as the Tuana. The footsteps grew hesitant. She didn't move.

They stopped short.

Patience, she told herself. Her hand was on her knife hilt.

Now she tightened her grip, tensed every muscle. Her position was part of the ruse: far from being helplessly on her back, one lithe twist and she'd be on her feet, knife out, ready to strike or run.

The footsteps started again, moving away with clumsy haste. Aryl snapped to her feet, hitting a run by her second stride in pursuit.

A figure—Om'ray shape and size, Grona clothing—struggled to keep ahead of her. He—she guessed that much from his movement—made it no farther than the start of his path before she launched herself.

They fell together into the shadows. Aryl dug a knee into his spine and pulled his head back with an arm around his forehead. Her knife edge found his throat. "Who are you?" she asked politely.

His hand clawed for something on the ground and she pressed the knife in warning, waiting for him to subside before she looked to see what it was.

Not a weapon. A hand-sized box, aglow with tiny lights. A familiar box.

Aryl jumped up, giving his backside a hard shove with her foot. "You promised to stay away, Human!"

Marcus Bowman grabbed the bioscanner and rose to his feet, his so-Om'ray face a mix of chagrin and offense. "Aryl not hurt!" he proclaimed fiercely, brandishing the device. "Trick!"

"Spy!" she shouted back.

"Not spy! I promised. Not interfere. Not visible. No Om'ray here." He gestured at his clothing. "Disguise, me."

Her lips quirked. "How could wearing our clothes—" a closer look, "—clothes like ours—hide you from us?" Silly Human. "You know we can sense one another." Though he had, she admitted, gone to considerable effort to fabricate a Grona coat and Yena leg wraps. And boots. Too new, with stranger fasteners and fabric, but at a distance they might pass. She sniffed. As for smelling like bruised flowers?

"I remember," Marcus said with dignity. "Not my idea. *New*

policy. Hide being stranger. *Discretion.* Stop problems. Only Human allowed *inthefield.* Look like Om'ray." He tucked the bioscanner into his belt, a wide un-Om'ray-like affair of loops and hooks, most filled with more devices. "Maybe work for not-Om'ray."

If he dressed like an Om'ray to hide his Human identity from the Oud, what had the Oud thought? Aryl didn't want to imagine. "Better stay out of sight," she suggested.

He rubbed his throat. "I was. Then you fell. I worried—" this with a grim look, "—you hurt."

"Yena don't fall," Aryl reminded him. "You should have remembered that, too."

For some reason, this produced a smile. He had a nice smile, for something not-quite-*real*. It crinkled the skin beside his brown eyes, and produced a dimple in one cheek. "So what do?"

A general question, about why she was here? Or a more specific one, about her immediate intentions?

Embarrassed, Aryl put away her knife. "I'm waiting for the Oud to come back."

An anxious glance around. "Night soon." He paused and said carefully, "Truenight is soon. Dangerous for all."

The Human had been practicing proper speech, a distinct improvement over the Oud babble the strangers had learned first. They had their own words, bizarre but fluid-sounding. They knew others. Before meeting Marcus Bowman, she'd believed there was only one language, one time. Aryl felt a chill that had nothing to do with the cold air and her lack of coat. "Do you know where you are?"

She'd seen that wary look in his eyes before. "Mountains. No Om'ray," with emphasis, to prove he'd followed her rules. "Old place." A casual shrug. They had that gesture in common.

Aryl didn't believe words or gesture. "Where are the others?" Marcus had lost the two colleagues of his Triad, killed when their aircar crashed near the Yena Watchers after a disastrous encounter with the Tikitik, but he was by no means on his own. While with Enris, Aryl had seen several, Human and not, and buildings to house more.

"No others. Aryl, it will dark be soon."

"It will be dark soon," she corrected, then frowned at him. "You're alone? Why?"

The tracks by the door.

Aryl stepped up to the Human, put both hands on his chest, and pushed with all her strength. "You're as bad as the Oud!" she accused as he staggered to stay on his feet. "You want into the Cloisters. You can't. It's Om'ray. Ours!" She began walking backward. "Go home. Go back to your Hoveny and leave Sona alone."

Marcus froze, whatever protest at her behavior he might have made dying on his lips, his eyes fierce and bright. "So-na." Breathless. "This? So-na?"

"Sona," Aryl corrected, then was furious at herself. She couldn't take the name back. He was too intelligent for that.

"Vy, Ray, *So*, Gro, Ne, Tua, Ye, Pa, Am." With each syllable, his excitement grew, as it had the first time she'd told him the names of the Om'ray Clans. "So-NA! This wonderful, Aryl. Wonderful! Word we seek. Word I seek long long long time. Thank you!"

Wonderful wasn't how she felt. "I don't care about your words. I care about my people." Suspicious, she looked all around, then upward. "Where are yours?"

"No people. I am alone." As if realizing it wasn't enough, Marcus licked his lips, then went on, "Need new Triad. Recorder. Finder. Coming soon. I wait, can't work. I—" he put a hand on his chest, "—not good, Aryl. Sad. Came here to be alone a time. To explore. Surprise to find Aryl. Sorry."

From no information to a flood. Aryl blinked at him. Replacements were coming—from where? She didn't want to know. He was still recovering from the loss of his friends? No offense, but she'd lost more. This was his chosen spot to explore, of all Cersi? She fastened on that. "Here. Where the only ruins are Om'ray. You told me you were looking for these Hoveny."

That shift in his eyes. She'd learned it meant evasion. But he answered readily. "True. Om'ray, Oud, Tikitik. Not matter to First Triads. Not matter to Trade Pact. *Vestigial populations.* No connected history. Chance. Remains. Left behinds. Understand?"

She glowered and didn't answer. The Human's notions of past and time had nothing to do with reality. That he'd insulted her kind? He probably didn't notice.

"But I—" that hand to his chest again, "—am curious."

The Oud's word.

Aryl wanted to strangle them both. "About the Cloisters. Because you don't believe the 'remains' of Om'ray could have built them."

He dared smile. "Curious."

Tired, unsettled, and quite sure she shouldn't be having this conversation, Aryl nonetheless felt the stir of her own question. "The Cloisters have always been," she said roughly, denying it. "As Om'ray have always been. As Cersi has always been. Only you are new and different and dangerous. Go home!"

"In truenight?" The Human could be charming. He gave a slight bow and swept his arm in invitation toward the cut path. "Safe there," he assured her. "Stay."

His camp—if he meant that and not one of their flying machines—would be a wonder of stranger technology. Enris would love it. Aryl was . . . curious. That dangerous word again. She took another step back. "I'm waiting for the Oud. I've supplies over there." She indicated the hill.

Marcus shook his head, the Human "no." "Not safe."

Aryl laughed. What did this Human in his pretend-Om'ray clothes know of safety?

Another head shake, as if he read thoughts like an Om'ray. "Show Aryl." Marcus removed two objects from their belt loops. One, a small featureless disk, he flung into the air. It continued rising, then hovered in midair a considerable height above them.

He glanced down at the second device and swallowed. "Look, Aryl," earnestly. "Please."

With reluctance, she took the thing in her hands. Its surface held an image. She'd seen such before: a viewer, tied to the "eyes" overhead. The image showed the other side of the hill. Bones, wood, dirt, stone. The beginnings of the road and river . . . About to hand it back, she noticed something else.

The road was littered with rocks. Small ones. Big ones. Piles of rocks of every size. Rocks she'd passed lying at the base of the valley walls.

She'd been right to fear an ambush—just wrong about where.

Her pack was likely crushed beneath another pile. "So much," Aryl said wryly as she returned the viewer, "for my supplies."

"Alive-rocks stay that side," Marcus assured her. At her skeptical look, "Promise. Maybe they not like Oud."

If the Human attempted humor, Aryl was in no mood for it. "You'd better be right. I have to stay here." She stamped the ground with one foot.

He gazed wistfully at his path through the grove, then back to her. "Aryl sure?"

"Yes."

Definitely unhappy. "I bring my things."

Chapter 8

ARYL MADE A FACE. "I don't know how you can eat that." With a chuckle, Marcus took back the stick of what he called *e-rations* and offered her a shiny box. "Try this. It safe for your *metabolism*."

" 'Metabolism,' " she repeated dubiously.

"Means Om'ray body. This good."

Good, Aryl had to admit, described most of what Marcus had laboriously carried down his path to where she waited. They sat beneath a bright yellow fabric roof, protected on three sides by walls of a similar material. It had been limp cloth until the Human had attached one of his devices to it, then became rigid and strong enough to block the chill wind.

Her feet rested near another marvel. Not fire, but a heatbox unlike any Aryl had seen. Heat radiated from whatever side Marcus chose, to the degree he selected. Better still, the fabric *tent* reflected the heat around their bodies until Aryl was warm to her core for the first time since leaving the canopy. The Human shed his coat and wiped sweat from his forehead, but didn't complain.

There was water, cups whose interiors heated it—without warming the outside—for the dark and fragrant stranger-

beverage called sombay, and sitting pads of decadent softness set by buttons. An *accommodation,* as Marcus called it, sat discreetly behind the tent—a marvel of compact tidiness.

And protection. Three small metal rods pushed into the dirt formed a triangle around them. Marcus had fussed over their placement, trying several spots before being satisfied. He'd declared the flimsy things would keep away any threat.

While intrigued by this claim, Aryl kept her knife at hand and hoped for no threat at all.

They'd established their tiny camp in front of the Cloisters, facing the depression into which the Oud had disappeared. Since truenight, two of the stranger-glows hovered in the air to illuminate the disturbed ground. Aryl had argued against them, worried the Oud would refuse to return. Marcus worried more about being surprised and insisted.

Aryl took the shiny box and opened the lid. It was half full of hard green balls, the size of the tip of her littlest finger; they rolled noisily when she tipped it from side to side. "This is food?"

"Full *supplement,*" the Human assured her. "Food, yes. Do this." He dropped one into his steaming cup, waited a moment, then drank. "Aaahhhhh. Try! All need."

She sighed. "Don't you ever cook?"

Marcus laughed. "Waste time. Risk local *contamination.* Better this."

More of his words. More of his ideas. Thoughtfully, Aryl put one of the balls into her cup of sombay, watching as it fizzed then dissolved. She took a small sip. No perceptible change in flavor, but the liquid had thickened to the consistency of soup. The strangers' technology pervaded everything they did; there was no telling what they were capable of, no way to hold them to their word.

"Aryl should not worry. Safe are."

Marcus had read something from her posture or expression. She studied his face, wishing in vain it wasn't normal and proper and thoroughly Om'ray. The Human was not-*real* to her inner sense, disconnected from her reality of place or self.

But if she touched his skin, she could touch his thoughts. She could read his emotions. She'd done both, once before. Which made Marcus *real*, didn't it? Real and vulnerable in the most devastating way possible to any Om'ray, despite his devices.

"Safe are," Marcus insisted, blind to the closest threat of all.

Not that she'd ever—she'd never let anyone—

Aryl stopped there, thoroughly disturbed. "I appreciate the shelter, the food," she said, gesturing with her cup. "But I don't understand why you're helping me."

He ducked his head then looked up at her with a small smile. "Om'ray need reason to help?"

"No, of course not." She hesitated. "Not to help other Om'ray. The Oud and Tikitik—they don't ask or need our help."

"You helped me."

Aryl squirmed inwardly. "You wouldn't have survived."

"Ah." The smile widened. "Good reason."

"I don't need your things," she asserted, unsure why she felt off-balance. "I'd be fine without them."

Marcus nodded his head again. "Know this. Yena don't fall. I remember now."

Was he making fun of her? Aryl stiffened. "This is my world, not yours."

The Human moved his hands in a fair approximation of an Om'ray apology. Observant, or a ready mimic? Both, she thought. "Like help, yes." Marcus turned his face to look sideways at her, his expression grown earnest. "Like you, Aryl Sarc, Yena, Om'ray. Yes yes yes. Like you. Understand?"

She hoped not, suddenly aware of him in a way she hadn't expected. His familiar face and form were too close. His green-brown eyes, too intent. The slow gentle smile as he waited for her to reply? What did that mean?

She could touch him and find out.

Instead, she eased farther away. "A friend," she suggested. "Like Janex."

The reminder—or her avoidance—wiped away the smile. Marcus gave an exasperated sigh. "Janex friend. Good friend. Janex never need help, mine." During this confusing sequence, the Human palmed a small disk. He held it out and a group of figures appeared on the other side of the heat box, standing slightly above the ground. Images, she realized immediately. Humans, by their stranger-clothing.

Marcus stood and went into their midst, his hand passing through each face as he provided a name, as if he longed to touch them. "These need me. Understand? This Cindy." A female with a wide smile and cheerful, round face. His voice grew tender. "Howard." A lanky, intense child, with Marcus' eyes. "Karina." A younger child, curled in another's arms. "Kelly," he named her, his hand lingering within the image of a tall elegant female, with flowing red hair.

"You're Chosen?" Aryl blurted. Not only Chosen, but a parent twice over? Maybe he'd attribute her flaming cheeks to the heat. An unChosen couldn't be attracted . . . like that . . . to a Chosen. Or a Chosen to anyone but his or her mate. It was the nature of being Joined; no other pairing was possible. She reassured herself. He was not-Om'ray. How was she to know his state?

She should have. He was in charge of others and their machines. He had expertise and training. Marcus Bowman was no unChosen like her, bumbling through lessons and life. He was adult, respected, accomplished.

Claimed.

Then why did she feel . . . vulnerable?

The Human couldn't read her thoughts. That mercy at least. Although he could be uncannily perceptive for a not-*real* stranger.

"Not understand 'Chosen.' Oud not have right words. Kelly is me. My heart. *Lifepartner.*" Tucking away the disk, Marcus returned to Aryl. The images took a moment to fade and disappear, leaving rubble and truenight behind. "Far far away," he said in a faint voice, reaching for his cup. "All."

How could a family be so shattered? Her father had died, otherwise he could never have left them. It distressed Chosen to be distant. Ael and Myris had been apart for half a day and suffered. Marcus must be in agony. "What happened?" she asked gently.

"Work." This with a casual shrug. "Send *vids* between. Message on special times."

She was appalled. No Om'ray would leave his family except to seek Passage. No Om'ray would voluntarily leave their Clan. Even in exile, the Yena families stayed together. Being this far from hers was an ache inside. "How could you leave them?"

His cheeks colored. "Human way," he said brusquely, as if stung by her disapproval. "Analyst. Triad First. Long time to be this. Opportunity here of my life. Family happy for me. Proud."

"But to leave them—" Aryl shuddered. She had no idea how far away Marcus Bowman's family was, but she feared it was a distance beyond her comprehension. "Om'ray would not," vehemently, "could not. It would be impossible."

A sharp look. "Explain."

"Explain what?"

"Om'ray family. Help me. Need proper words." A wry smile. "Curious."

"I've noticed." Aryl settled herself in the warmth and considered "words." "I am unChosen," she began, putting a hand on her chest. "Not yet a Chooser. Your Kelly-*lifepartner*—she Chose you. You are her Chosen. She is yours."

"UnChosen mean—" he pantomimed someone very small, then pretended to rock his folded arms as if holding a baby.

"No," she frowned. "UnChosen means unChosen. That's a child. Your Karina is a child. Howard—" the image wasn't much to go on. For all she knew, Humans and Om'ray grew at different rates, like rastis and nekis. "If he can leave his mother, Om'ray would call him UnChosen, not child. Do you understand?"

"What 'mother'?"

"I thought you had words from the Oud."

"Life words no. Rude to ask." Not rude to ask her, apparently. "What is 'mother'?"

Aryl copied his holding-a-baby motion, then put a hand to herself. "Mother. Kelly?" An assumption.

"Yes yes. Wonderful words, Aryl." Marcus beamed. "Child. Mother. UnChosen. My childs. What me?"

"Your children. You're their father."

"I, Father. Aryl, unChosen not child. She can leave her mother. Aryl not can before. Why?"

"Why" was becoming his new favorite question. "Why couldn't I leave her when I was a child?" she corrected, buying time. Some things everyone knew. Didn't they? "That's what a child is—someone who can't leave her mother. It's impossible. There is a bond—" she wrapped her arms tightly around herself, "—that pulls them together, always. Only with age does the bond weaken enough for the child to become unChosen, and go anywhere. Is it not the same for Humans?"

"Same. We not call it bond. What word for more than like? For like most of all?" His eyes glistened. "More than any."

She sat in a stranger-tent, waiting for a crazed Oud, outside in truenight for the second time in a row, discussing word choices for affection with a not-Om'ray. Aryl chuckled. "Love. The word is love."

"Good word. I love Cindy—same mother, me. I love my children. Kelly love children. I love Kelly. Kelly love me. Family hold together with love. Human. Om'ray. Same."

Love was only a feeling, an emotion that could be kept behind shields or shared at will. What did he mean? Curious herself, now, Aryl elaborated, wondering what he'd say. "Love isn't the bond between children and their mother. Or between—" her cheeks warmed, "—Chosen. Love—" led where she couldn't follow. She coughed and continued. "Om'ray feel love," she told the Human. "The bond is Om'ray." She stressed the "is."

To her surprise, he nodded his head. "Is part of how you know where others are. Sense. I remember. Right?"

Clever Human. "Yes. The bond between Om'ray is strongest between mother and child—between Chosen pairs. Less for all others, but there. You don't have this, do you?" However incredible, she'd seen for herself that Marcus couldn't find those of his own kind. To exist in complete isolation . . . Aryl shivered. "I can't imagine what it would be like—to be so alone."

"I can't imagine what like for you." Wistful. "How not-love bond feel."

He hadn't asked, but Aryl found herself hunting a way. "The heatbox," she said triumphantly.

"I don't—"

"Close your eyes." Once he did, she took his hand, careful to stay behind her own shields and away from his thoughts, and positioned it so his palm faced away from the heat. "Where is the heatbox?"

His hand turned in hers to point. "There." Marcus opened his eyes and looked at her.

Aryl held up her hand and pointed toward the exiles—hopefully safe and within the shelters by now. "There. My people. Every Om'ray has a warmth, a glow, we feel deep inside."

"Location. Not *telepathy*." He sounded disappointed.

Another of his words. "What's 'telepathy?' "

"Talk without words. Mindvoice." The Human tapped his forehead, then jabbed his finger at her. "Trade Pact has *telepathic races*. Only few. Special."

Making Om'ray "special." Making Om'ray potentially interesting to this Trade Pact. Not an interest she deemed prudent in any way. "Strange," Aryl commented. "Are Humans—are you—telepathic?"

A shadow seemed to cross his face. "No." Marcus rose and picked up his sitting pad. "Sleep. We talk, morning." A sharp shake and the pad elongated to a length longer than he was tall. "Aryl need so much heat?" This with a plaintive look at the glowing heatbox.

Aryl copied his negative gesture, turning her head from side to side. "Not if you lend me your coat," she suggested. As for sleep? She could miss another truenight without harm. This was no place or time to close her eyes. Or company. The Human slept like the dead; he'd be useless. "I'll keep watch." And wait for the Oud.

"No need. *Perimeterfield.*"

The three sticks? "I'll keep watch," she repeated. "Your coat?"

Instead of handing it to her, Marcus laid the garment across her back, tucking it against her neck. She felt the pressure of his hand briefly on her shoulder before he went to adjust the heatbox. "Keep warm, Aryl. Need more again, do this." He showed her the control.

Like a father, she thought abruptly. Was that why the Human offered his help? Not for what he could gain from her—not entirely—but because he missed his own children?

Aryl slipped her arms into the sleeves. The stranger-version of a Grona coat was warmer and lighter than the real thing. Was it wrong to accept his gifts, to enjoy being cared for instead of needed?

"What about you?" she asked.

Marcus smiled. "Watch." He ran a finger down the side of the pad and it split open. "*Thermobed.*" He took off his boots and slipped into the pad, giving a blissful groan as he stretched out. "Nice. You try?"

"Maybe later."

Without their voices, truenight filled with the powerful rumble of falling water. Not unfamiliar. During the rains, water hammered roof tiles and bridges, and poured in aerial rivers along fronds and branches. This was deeper, no louder. She'd hear screams over it. Their camp was lit by glows, again normal, and she was warm. The only sensation out of place?

The ground. Other than the faintest, constant vibration, it was immobile and hard. Wrong. It should sway, like breathing. There should be life all around her, especially beneath her. A Yena belonged high in the canopy. She missed its life. Missed color and movement. Vines and fronds and clusters of flowers. She even missed biters.

Maybe not biters.

But she did miss flitters. And wysps.

Her family.

Without conscious decision, Aryl lowered her shields, relaxing her *inner* guard the smallest possible amount, and *reached* farther than before. Not to contact her mother, she thought, only to find her, be sure she was safe.

That she lived.

Her unexpected awareness of the Human, though dim and vague, had come when she hadn't used strength to find it. Now, Aryl did the same. Relax rather than concentrate. Better to be attracted to the glow of Om'ray than seek it. To let the *here-I-am* become the *who-I-am* . . .

To this Talent, those were the same, she realized abruptly. Had it been a habit, all her life, to ignore that extra information, the way she'd ignore the drone of biters or drum of rain? There'd been no need to consciously *know* everyone nearby—unless, of course, she wanted to win at seek. There'd been every reason to hide that ability, according to Taisal. What was new, was likely Forbidden.

Not here. Not anymore.

Aryl *reached* for Yena's Om'ray, ignoring every other glow, paid attention. Names filled her mind . . . no, not names. Identities, resonating one to another. No Om'ray existed in isolation, not even the Lost. Each came with bonds. Chosen to Chosen. Mother to child. Families. Heart-kin. Their connections crossed and blended, like a net woven in light.

Within it, she might have been home again, surrounded by those who belonged together. Rimis Uruus. Her Chosen Troa. Their son Joyn. Tikva, their grandmother. Alejo Parth, Seru's tiny brother. More. Aryl *reached*. Vendans. Kessa'ats. Teeracs.

Sarcs.

Among them. There. Her mother.

Alive.

But it wasn't like home. The more Yena Aryl found, the

more wrong they felt. Bonds were strained or too thin. Connections were missing.

The exiles. Too many had been torn from the fabric of Yena itself for it to stay whole. Whole as it had been, for as she recognized the tear, she could *feel* its shape changing. Bonds thinned beyond comfort were being turned toward others. Connections lost were being replaced with new ones. Yena mended itself without regard to those now outside its reach.

Excluding them. Excluding her.

There could be no going back.

Aryl *pulled* away.

As she did, her *awareness* stumbled into another cluster of identities. Six Om'ray, closer to Sona than anywhere else.

Strands of interconnection . . . *Chosen* . . . *mother/child* . . . *brother/sister* . . . *cousin* . . . *aunt/uncle/niece/nephew* . . . *heart-kin* . . .

Bern.

Shields tight, Aryl rose slowly to her feet, facing the dark toward Grona. Did he look this way, she wondered? Had he *seen* her, too?

"Trouble?" Marcus wriggled free of his thermobed in a noisy, time-consuming effort that convinced her never to sleep in one.

"Someone's coming," she said before she thought.

"Oud?" He stared at the well-lit depression.

"Grona Om'ray. They won't arrive until late tomorrow 'night—or the day after," she corrected, guessing they'd camp another truenight.

She'd worry about them then. Him, then.

"Trouble?" Marcus asked again, his eyes wide.

Her quick denial died on her lips. "Change," she offered, the truth, if hardly reassuring. The time she'd believed Om'ray incapable of harm to one another was long gone. Like the Sona.

The Human plopped down at the end of his thermobed and pulled the remainder of its soft mass awkwardly over his shoulders. "Not sleep." A declaration of intent.

"As you wish." She'd be glad of the company, Aryl admitted

to herself, sitting again. After *reaching* Yena, the dark beyond the lights pressed too close, even if all it hid were the scars of Sona's violent passing. She regarded the nervous Human thoughtfully. He studied what was long gone, a concept she was still fighting to believe.

He returned her gaze for a moment, then said quietly, "Ask."

Perceptive, indeed. She half smiled. "I have a question about this place. About Sona."

"To know what happened here?"

"The Oud happened." As she'd mention a storm. The Human gave the nearby depression a worried look. "The Sona Om'ray disturbed the Agreement. Upset the peace," she added, when he turned the worried look on her. "We're safe." Not that she was sure, but it was better than having Marcus run for higher ground. "How long ago? Can you tell?" He'd tossed his belt of devices into a corner of the tent—a revealing lack of respect for such technology. Ordinary to him, however extraordinary to her.

"Om'ray not know?"

Question for question, was it? Aryl made herself comfortable, willing to play for now. "None of us knew Sona existed before coming here."

"You know name. How?"

One she didn't want to answer. "When?" she countered.

Marcus took a handful of dirt and let it fall. Dust rose like smoke in the lights. "Recent. This *century*." At her frown, "Wrong word for Om'ray time? How you count how old?"

A knot for a day. Age? "Yena count the M'hir Wind and the Harvest," she offered dubiously. "There's only one a year."

He smiled. "Ah. Good. Same thing. All seasons pass one time, count one year. Same all your world."

On her world. Implying other worlds. As if the "past" wasn't enough to make her head feel swollen inside. But she had to ask. "A year isn't the same on yours?"

"My world closer to its sun, shorter *orbit*. Makes my year

faster. Trade Pact use *standard* year so all worlds have common *reference*. Otherwise, every time be different. Everyone be too early, too late!" Marcus paused his enthused babble. "Aryl not happy?"

Aryl was decidedly not, the "sun" and its behavior being a particular sore point and everything else he said making matters worse. "Om'ray are the world," she informed him testily. "Nothing else is real!"

Foolish Human.

Who pursed his lips and appeared fascinated by the heatbox. "Is this Aryl truth—your truth?"

If there'd been condescension in his tone or manner, any hint of amusement at the "ignorant Om'ray," she would have insisted what the Adepts taught was exactly that: her truth, too.

But there wasn't. Marcus Bowman, Analyst and Triad First, seeker after the unimaginably old from another world, Chosen and father in his Human fashion, passed no judgment.

Forcing her to do it instead.

Aryl chose words with great care, more afraid of her own daring than of being misunderstood. "The truth is that Om'ray are always aware of each other. Part of each other. We must be."

"Must be?"

"I'm uncomfortable," she admitted with a pained expression she hoped he could read, "to be this far from my people. The only ones who willingly leave their Clan—" except Yena's exiles, "—are unChosen. And they only travel to find another Clan." Except Enris. "I think—maybe we speak of ourselves as the world because we can be no other place. Do you understand, Marcus? But I—" She broke into a sweat beneath the Human's coat. "—I don't think the world ends beyond us. Not anymore. There must be another side to this mountain. The waterfall must come from somewhere. You do."

"I do." Marcus leaned his chin in his hand, his elbow on one bent knee. A thoughtful pose. "Other side of this mountain are more. Many more. Mountain *range*. This waterfall come from river that cuts through *range*. I have seen. Aryl right. World bigger."

She felt giddy, a reaction probably due more to terrified exhaustion than the thrill of discovery. No, she admitted, the thrill was there, like leaping for a chancy hold. "If," she dared, "Om'ray have believed Cersi—the world—is only where we can sense one another, maybe that is why Om'ray history is only about those who are *real*—who we can sense."

"What do you mean?" he echoed, eyes shadowed and intent. "What is Om'ray history?"

"Stories. We tell each other what's happened to us. UnChosen on Passage take their Clan's stories to their new one." She felt foolish and hesitated.

"Same for us," Marcus offered immediately. "Stories important. How else know long ago time? Stories live after we dust." He lifted and released another handful of dirt, then held out his tight fist. "Stories live forever."

"Of course not. Not ours," Aryl corrected hastily, seeing the difference. The air around them seemed to listen. She shuddered but continued. "Ours stop."

With a puzzled frown, the Human lowered his fist. "Why? Not understand."

How to explain what she barely grasped herself? "Costa. The others. The ones who died during the Harvest. You remember them?"

This softened his eyes. "Sorry, Aryl. Will always remember."

"Always?" Her envy at that easy promise thickened her voice. "Om'ray will not. Cannot. Once everyone who ever sensed them as *real* has also died, they will no longer exist to other Om'ray. Their story will be tossed aside and forgotten, like the empty husk of a body. For us, history is bound to the living, Marcus. That's why the Eldest of each family is on Council. They connect us to all there is of our past."

She'd upset him somehow. "History is more," Marcus protested. "History is all who lived, ever. All they did, ever. Our work here—we make *vidrecordings* so others will know. Vital. Important! Can't forget!"

"Why?"

From his stricken expression, she might have asked him why he kept breathing.

"If we don't live in a place, why should we care if it exists?" she went on, perversely enjoying playing the Adept. "If we can't sense for ourselves someone is *real,* why should we care if that person ever existed?"

"Aryl not believe this. Not!" He bounced up and down on the thermobed.

Aryl almost smiled. "When I'm with you, Marcus," she brushed her fingers along his sleeve, "I don't. But my people do. They always have."

Though mollified, he wagged his finger in her face. "Ah, but you not know that. If no Om'ray history before elder's experience, how can know that?" Definitely smug.

"Our Adepts teach us that nothing has changed." She didn't add that the Agreement between Om'ray, Oud, and Tikitik held that nothing should. A new problem: what to tell someone who would remember always.

An eyebrow lifted. "Truth or what they decide is truth?"

Ideas were dangerous. This one, Aryl was quite sure, would be Forbidden. "The Adepts are trusted," she assured him, despite the sour taste the words left in her mouth. "They keep a Clan's Record. Who was born, who was their Choice, their children." Who caused trouble . . . who did the Forbidden . . . who was exiled to die . . . did Yena's Adepts write those words, too? "I've had—" said with determination, "—no reason to doubt what they teach."

"Evidence here—" Marcus waved his hand at their surroundings. "Sona change. Maybe Om'ray not care and forget," this as if a huge concession, making her frown. "Adepts write record. Maybe they not care and forget. Record—never forget."

Her frown lifted in surprise. But the Human wasn't wrong.

If any Sona Om'ray had come to Yena on Passage, his arrival and Joining would have been recorded by Yena's Adepts.

Had long-ago Adepts recorded Sona's death, too? They would have felt it. Part of the world would have suddenly ceased to exist; every Om'ray would be disoriented, the way she'd been when her father died, then afraid, as she'd been.

So afraid.

Lost.

Marcus leaned back, hands clasped around one knee. "Where these records?" Oh so casual. "In Cloisters?"

Never for strangers!!! But he couldn't feel her sending, could he, no matter how furious or forceful. Marcus Bowman wasn't *real.*

All Om'ray could die and nothing would change for this Human or his kind. They would make their own kind of record and go about their work. They would travel anywhere, not only where they felt existed. They would remember anything they chose, long after an Om'ray would forget.

"Sorry, Aryl," he said quickly, sitting straight. "Not mean harm. Curiosity too much. Sorry."

They were the same outside, Aryl thought, staring at his too-familiar face.

They were not the same within.

She leaped to her feet and ran into the dark.

"Aryl! Please stop!"

She'd do nothing of the sort, Aryl vowed as she staggered forward, hands out to break a fall, if not prevent one. Behind her came the Human, too quickly. He shouldn't be catching up. She tried to hurry and tripped on the uneven ground.

They were both fools. She knew it. Knew it was sheer folly to be out in the dark of truenight, let alone to run over unfamiliar ground. But she couldn't bear it—couldn't bear *him*. All that mattered was getting away. She climbed to her feet to run again.

"Aryl—Ooooffph!" Another gasp and grunt. He fell more often. "Stop!"

How could he be gaining on her? She risked a look back. No light. They'd left the campsite behind. She'd wanted to find the grove, to lose herself among its stalks. Where was it? Sona was behind her . . . so dim she might be dreaming the glow of Om'ray. She was losing her sense of direction . . .

If she went too far this way, she'd fall out of the world. She'd be nowhere . . .

Not if the Human's ideas—not if her new ideas—not if the world was more than Om'ray . . .

. . . then what was she?

Aryl sobbed, wiping blood from her nose, and staggered on. She was too alone. Only the M'hir was close by. If she could lose the Human, she'd be able to stop, to concentrate. Use it to find her mother. Find anyone. Go anywhere but here.

"ARYL!!! Look out! Danger!" His shout was louder than the waterfall's drone.

A trick. She slowed anyway, hands pushing truenight from her face. Slowed, but didn't stop.

Her next step threw her into empty air, down and down to suffocating darkness that pulled and tumbled and bit . . . her scream cost the last breath from her lungs . . . she tried to inhale and ice-cold water poured into her mouth and nose . . . the darkness was like the M'hir, overwhelming and endless . . . she surrendered and fell . . .

"Aryl."

She spasmed awake, then held on as the world tilted around her. Held on . . . ? Aryl looked down to find her hands clenched on Marcus' arms. She let go and pushed herself away with frantic kicks until her back hit something solid and she couldn't move.

"Safe." His voice was strained and hoarse.

There was light. Daylight, not one of his devices. Firstlight. His face was dreadful: gray-tinged and badly scratched, a bruise starting below one eye and a swollen lower lip. His hair and clothes were soaking wet; the color leaked from his pretend-Yena tunic to stain the dirt. Hunched and shivering, he watched her without moving.

She was wet, too, Aryl discovered, dragging her hands up to her face. Wet. Cold. Achingly sore. Her ribs . . . a knee. "What—?" She stopped. She'd been in water before. He'd saved her from it before.

She looked around, blinking to focus. They were beside the waterfall. But its lake had been a dream, a Sona memory. Now its water poured into a deep pit— "Nooo." The terrified moan couldn't be hers. Aryl fought to control herself. "Tell me I didn't fall into—into that."

"Safe," Marcus answered, as if too exhausted to do more than repeat the word. "Both are."

He'd fallen in, too? Then how—

The support behind her back shifted. "Goodgoodgoodgood. Both safe."

Aryl found herself beside the Human before realizing she'd moved, staring up at the Oud.

It wasn't wet, was her first coherent thought. Of course it wasn't, her next. It didn't like water. If this was the same Oud. "How?" she blurted.

"*Filtrationsystem,*" Marcus babbled. *"Auto."*

"Make sense!"

The Oud remained reared, but silent. The Human sighed. "Metal screen below. Catch what fall in. Keep out big objects. Understand? Catch us. Rise. Dump us here."

Too much sense. Aryl pressed against him, suddenly finding the Human less frightening. The Oud had diverted the river from Sona. Put their machines in it. Had they destroyed this place to take its water? Why?

The Oud's limbs waved in unison. "Alive now? Goodgoodgood."

Incomprehensible creature. "Of course I'm alive," she began.

"You no breathe," Marcus whispered urgently in her ear. "Stupid Oud. Thought you dead. I stop it take you underground. Make it let me fix."

Fix? Aryl turned to look at him. "I wasn't breathing?" she asked uncertainly.

His lips trembled, blue with cold, but his eyes were fierce. "Aryl fine now. Stupid Oud not know *humanoid physio—*"

"Alive! Goodgoodgood!" the Oud interrupted. Its limbs moved with dazzling speed, conveying a small dark object from under its body. "Take take. Hurry!"

Afraid to disobey, Aryl rose to her feet. Marcus came with her, his arm firm around her shoulders. She wasn't sure which of them supported the other, but she was grateful.

"Take!"

She held out both hands, and it dropped the object, a dusty cloth pouch, into them.

"Open!"

Hard to glare at something without a face, but she did her best. "Tell me what's inside first."

"Us!"

Which made no sense, other than suggest this was yesterday's Oud.

"Curious," Marcus whispered.

Aryl knew her body, knew it close to failing, knew she couldn't—not for her people's sake. Transferring the pouch to one hand, she slipped the fingers of the other between the Human's and pressed their palms together, taking comfort and warmth when she dared take nothing more. Not so close to the Oud. But even through her shields, she could *taste* Marcus' emotions. *Determination. Courage. Loyalty.* A healthy dose of *fear.*

She wasn't alone.

Aryl smiled her mother's smile at the Oud. "I'll open it if you promise to give water back to Sona's river."

The limbs stopped their constant fidgeting. "Open first."

Fair enough. She freed her hand—Marcus resisting for an instant—and flipped open the pouch. And stared.

"Us," the Oud insisted.

"What is?" Marcus whispered.

Aryl eased the Speaker's Pendant from the fabric. It looked the same as the one Taisal wore; it should, they were all the same, whether Om'ray, Oud, or Tikitik. Dirt-encrusted. Buried among bones, perhaps, until Sona echoed with Om'ray voices once more and the Oud—by the Agreement—required a Speaker.

If she put this around her neck, would that make Sona a Clan again?

If she didn't, the Oud would be within their rights to ignore their very existence. They could reshape this valley at whim. And probably would. Her people could never outrun the destruction.

Aryl put it over her head. The metal links were cold on her neck and the pendant left streaks of brown dirt on her sodden stranger-coat. She stood as tall as she could without shaking. "Send your Speaker to Sona," she told the Oud. "We have much to discuss."

"Yesyesyesyes." With each exuberant word, it backed itself into the ground, spraying them both with dirt and pebbles. "GoodGoodGoodGood! Soon."

Then it was gone.

"Marcus," she said—or thought she said. Everything was growing dim. "Marcus?"

"Here." A shoulder pushed under her arm. "Here. Need rest, Aryl. Come."

He wasn't wrong. Left to herself, she would have gladly curled into a ball on the stony ground and slept right there, but he insisted on moving.

Aryl did her best to stay upright and move her feet. He staggered when she did, making her chuckle. "Silly Human."

"Aryl fell first."

"Don't tell anyone," she pleaded, her cheeks warm. Then, with dreadful suspicion. "Don't take me to other Om'ray. Don't talk to them. Promise me, Marcus. Please."

"Too far," he said grimly. Practical, if not a promise. "My camp. Secret."

Secret. She didn't want any more secrets. About anything.

But as she stumbled between nekis that were too short, too thin, thrifty with bud, the M'hir swooped close. All she had to do was close her eyes to see what had been here before . . .

Blankets on the stone . . . cushions scattered overtop like leaves . . . children nestled like bright summer flowers . . . they used fine-tipped brushes to write their names on polished flats of wood . . . to write words that made each other laugh . . . to write whatever they wanted . . .

Words . . . or were they only lines and curves and dots on wood . . .

Aryl *pushed* herself out of the dream, letting herself sag into arms that didn't let her fall.

Interlude

ENRIS GROANED AND BROUGHT HIS arm up to shield his eyes. He squinted. How did the sun get up there so fast? It should be truenight. There should be . . . rocks? He sat so quickly his head spun. "I'm not dead!" he proclaimed.

"Were you expecting to be?"

Enris twisted to face the voice, one hand supporting himself on the pebbles. Ditch. He remembered. He'd fallen into one of Sona's ditches.

And he was facing the last being he'd expect to find here.

The Tikitik squatted comfortably, its knees above its head—which was easy, since its head hung below its shoulders on a long curved neck. All four of the creature's eyes were on him, the tiny front pair on their movable cones, as well as the large pair near the back of what passed for its face. The wormlike protuberances where its mouth should be writhed slowly. Cloth marked with symbols circled both wrists and ankles.

Gray wrists and ankles, the color of the pebbles. Its skin of overlapping bony plates was gray, too. Only the short spines running up the outside of each arm and the eyes were the black he remembered. A different kind of Tikitik? He'd never heard of such a thing. Enris found a more dignified position. "Being dead was a reasonable outcome of last 'night," he observed.

"Because of them?" A long, too-thin arm gestured toward Vyna.

Enris looked, then stared.

There had to be thirty rocks of various sizes, piled on one another, all too close. He scooted backward quickly, bumping into his pack.

"They cannot come nearer, Om'ray." The Tikitik barked its laugh. "I thought you knew you slept in a safe place."

"Safe . . . how is this safe?"

"The Sona built well."

Sona? The only thing "built" here was the remains of this ditch. Could that be what it meant? The rock hunters had indeed stopped before touching the bed of same-sized pebbles. If so, he'd avoided being crushed and consumed by a couple of steps, no more.

And a fall. Enris took stock, the Tikitik seeming content to sit and watch. His head hurt. He dragged fingers over his forehead and found a lump, but no wound. One elbow twanged painfully, but it moved freely. Nothing broken.

He'd had the kind of good fortune that came once in a lifetime, if he didn't count present company. What was the Tikitik doing here—and why with him? They couldn't be trusted; to his inner sense, it wasn't *there* at all. He'd learned to ignore that particular discomfort.

Perhaps the creature could be useful. Enris made himself lean back comfortably. "Why would an empty ditch stop them?"

Its head bobbed sharply, twice. An indication of some strong emotion, he thought. "Hard Ones have an instinct for self-preservation. The courseways were not always empty. The risk of encountering water?" It turned a hand downward. "They drown. That is why they rest on one another if they can, for fear of rain. Those on the bottom rarely survive. Do you think that cruel?"

Enris glanced at the pile of living rock, then beyond it. He frowned at the Tikitik. "I think they're a problem. I'm on Passage." Make it official, lest the creature interfere. "I don't see any—" what had it called the ditch? "—courseways between here and the mountain." Or streams, for that matter. Which raised an interesting question. "How did you get past them?"

A bark. "It is the Hard Ones who fear me." The Tikitik rose to its feet. Its concave torso was wrapped in paired bands of cloth, the same pale dull color as its skin. The bands supported bags on what would be waist and hips for an Om'ray, as well as a sheath. From that, the creature drew a long—familiar—blade, which it attached with a twist to a staff. "Are you hungry, Om'ray?"

Without waiting for his answer, the Tikitik strode over to the rock hunters. Enris was astonished to see the entire pile start to quiver. The movement was slow and halting, more an indecisive landslide than purposeful flight. The greatest speed was attained by those falling off the top, who managed to roll and bounce a fair distance from the rest. Once on flat ground, they leaned until they tumbled over, stopped to become rocks again—as if to fool any watcher—then leaned and tumbled once more.

By day, he decided in disgust, the things posed no conceivable threat to anyone or thing able to walk. By truenight, asleep or trapped—that was another matter. Could there be a defense? Despite his aching head, he stood to get a better view.

The Tikitik used no stealth. It selected a rock the size of Enris' pack and turned it over using the butt of its staff. The rest kept rolling away. For some reason unsatisfied—or to torment the rock—the Tikitik pushed it over again, then held it in place with its foot. "Come," it ordered, bobbing its head twice. "See."

Keeping a wary eye on the retreating rocks, Enris joined the gray Tikitik. Up close, the creature smelled like unwashed clothes and sweetpie. It tapped a spot on the rock with the blade of its weapon. "There. Hard Ones have formidable armor, but everything breathes."

Enris had to lean close to see what the Tikitik had found. It was a deep crevice, the width of his little finger. Unlike a natural crack in rock, this curved in a sinuous line twice the length of his hand, never changing in size.

"Find the midpoint," the Tikitik said, doing so with another tap. He held the blade tips up. The metal was plain, but otherwise the tool was identical to the one currently inside Enris' coat, with one hooked tip longer than the other. "This severs the organ that controls breathing. Thus."

The "Hard One" struggled, but as its effort consisted of a grinding push against the ground, easily countered by the pressure of the Tikitik's foot, it appeared helpless. Reversing the blade, the Tikitik plunged it deep into the crevice at an angle, then brought it straight with a quick powerful motion. There was a loud whistle— Enris couldn't tell if the Hard One screamed in pain or if this was its final exhalation—then the "rock" sagged into itself.

In death, the Hard One appeared more alive, a bag made to look like a rock, rather than stone itself. He dared touch it. The "skin" felt like the sand sacs he and his father used for fine polishing, rough and cold.

The Tikitik barked. "What waits inside is of greater value to one on Passage." It levered the blade sideways and the "bag" split open. "Especially a hungry one."

There was nothing remotely appetizing in the mass of green, black, and glistening yellow that spilled out on the ground. And the smell! Enris covered his nose with his sleeve and stared at the Tikitik. "You'd eat that?"

It poked and stirred the remains, adding considerably to the smell and mess. Enris was about to protest when the Tikitik withdrew the blade, a fist-sized lump of blue caught on the hooked tip. "I'd eat this. A delicacy, foolish Om'ray. Only found in the young ones." It thrust the lump at Enris and wiggled it suggestively.

"Thank you, but I've food of my own," the Tuana said hastily. Tikitik had taken Aryl prisoner and force-fed her. She'd described the experience vividly; they hadn't used their hands.

"As you wish." The Tikitik shook the "delicacy" from its blade. It landed with a sodden thud among the oozing remains. "You should move," it advised, walking back across the shallow line of ditch and sitting exactly where it had sat before. "The Hard Ones find their own impossible to resist."

It was true. Their almost imperceptible roll to escape had become an almost imperceptible roll to return. Because of their greater size, each roll moved the larger of the Hard Ones farther, so they soon outdistanced the rest.

Soon? Metal, Enris judged, cooled faster. Being thirsty as well as hungry—if not for a blue lump—he left the rocks to their business and returned to his pack. The Tikitik's small eyes roved about on their cones; its large pair followed Enris, an unwelcome attention the Tuana chose to ignore.

After a cautious drink from his dwindling supply, he undid the ties holding the waterproofed flap, then opened the top to rummage through his supplies. His eyebrows rose as he pulled out a tight coil of rope, rope he hadn't packed. The lengths were few enough. He'd taken nothing the exiles might need.

Except himself.

His fingers found something small and soft attached to the rope. A lock of brown hair, cleverly tied in the shape of an Om'ray. Keeping his back to the Tikitik, Enris unhooked it with care, then tucked it safely inside the pouch hanging around his neck, with the old firebox and odd wafer.

No mystery who'd done this for him, who'd given him Passage gifts as a family should.

There was more: Grona travel bread—a large bite of which promptly went in his mouth; one of the Sona blankets; other Sona supplies: rokly, swimmer meat; last, but not least, a Yena longknife.

He recognized the nicks along its fine edge; not that Aryl would give him anyone's but her own. It was an admirable tool—and weapon. At that thought, Enris put away the longknife, grabbed the bag of rokly, and turned to face his companion. He sat, then reached into his coat for the blade he'd found with the bones. He balanced it on one knee. "Rokly?" he offered.

The small eyes snapped forward so all four could stare. At the blade, he noticed with satisfaction, not the morsel he held out.

The Tikitik bobbed its head upward, twice. "A shame Om'ray have forgotten how to read," it said finally.

Forgotten? Nothing this creature said was by accident. It must know Om'ray Adepts read in the Cloisters. Heart racing, Enris ran his finger over the symbols. "Is that why the Oud destroyed Sona? Because that Clan let everyone, not just Adepts, learn to read and write?"

A too-thin arm lifted languidly, two fingers pointed where the dead Hard One had been. Had been, Enris saw with a lurch of his stomach, because the remains were now beneath a slowly shoving pile of its own kind. "The Oud are equally tasteless and unsophisticated," pronounced the Tikitik, lowering its arm. "They don't care about those who read. They don't themselves. They claim their flesh remembers."

Enris pressed. "The Sona are gone because the Oud reshaped this valley. Why?"

A bark and a sly dip of its head. "The Sona are not gone."

He knew this feeling: it was the one watching Aryl and other Yena gambol across the beams of roofs and up vertical cliffs gave him. A dizzy, fingerbreadth from disaster, about-to-fall-into-an-abyss, dry-mouthed, disbelieving terror. With a sincere dollop of frustration. They never listened to him. Stay on the ground. Stay away from the Oud. Don't stay here.

"Are they in danger?" Enris didn't recognize his own voice in the raw, ragged demand. "Are they?! Answer me!"

The mouth appendages writhed as if tasting the air. "An unusual concern for one on Passage. What are you called, Om'ray?"

His hands itched to tie a knot in that long neck, to strangle its smug superiority. He clenched them around the blade instead. "Enris Mendolar," he ground out between his teeth. "Are they in danger?"

"A Tuana . . . so far from home. Curious. I enjoy curious things." The gray Tikitik touched its fingertips to the wrapping on its wrist. "You may call me Thought Traveler. As for Sona's risk?" Its head stretched forward, eyes swiveled to stare. "They are safer than you, Enris Mendolar."

Chapter 9

"ENRIS?"

His name died on her lips. Aryl sat up and pushed free of the softness that covered her body. He wasn't here. She shook her head. The remnant of a dream, she decided. Not the useful kind.

As for here . . . where was she?

Oh, she knew where she was relative to Sona and Grona, although their remoteness made her inner sense uneasy. She had only the haziest memory of their final steps, but Marcus hadn't brought her far from the Cloisters. Aryl swung her legs over the side of what was a bed, solid and raised on a platform, moving in silence despite the snores from the other side of the room. Room?

Daylight streamed through an abundance of too-small windows: narrow rectangles set head-high in the walls that angled into the smooth domed ceiling, a pair on one of two closed doors. Everything else—walls, ceiling, doors, and furnishings—was of a dull white material. She'd seen such before. The strangers used it in their more permanent structures.

The place was a mess. Every possible wall space supported shelves cluttered with devices, tools, and clear jars of what appeared to be dirt. Counters ran beneath, crowded with boxes. The boxes had buttons and controls; some had screens displaying patterns of flickering light. The floor was a maze of the white crates the strangers used to carry supplies in their aircar, most empty and on their sides. Either the Human had been here a long while, or he'd had help who unpacked in a hurry.

Here for a rest, was he? Hardly.

The Human—a lump under fluffy blankets—slept on a second bed platform. There was a third suspended above it. She looked up. Another above hers. Two more farther along, these folded against the wall.

Alone, was he? For now, perhaps.

Aryl stood, finding herself in her still-damp tunic and leg wraps. Her boots and belt—and the Human's—lay on the floor with his coat, carelessly dropped. Her knife . . . there it was. On one of the counters, sharp point to the wall. Not so careless.

She went to the door with windows and looked out, relieved to see stunted nekis stalks and a too-neat path between them. The Cloisters was that way.

The other door led to another pleasant surprise. It opened into a 'fresher—the one stranger technology she'd gladly add to her life.

Sorely tempted, Aryl looked back at the Human. What she could see appeared asleep. Besides—when would she have another chance?

She stepped inside the stall and fastened the door, shedding her filthy clothes with relief. Her hairnet came apart as she tugged it from her hair, hair thoroughly tangled and, from the feel, mud-encrusted. Shouldn't it have been cleaned by the waterfall? Water . . . her pockets! Aryl grabbed her tunic to check. Her Grona fire starter was gone, but the headdress was still safely tucked in its pocket, if filthy. The rokly had swollen into an unappetizing mass, coated with dirt. She scooped it out and dropped it on the floor.

The Speaker's Pendant thudded against her chest, cold and

heavy, as she straightened. So it hadn't been a dream. She left it around her neck.

Aryl tapped a square in the wall, and warm, fragrant foam sprayed her from every side, head to toe. She gathered hand-fuls and rubbed it on her clothing. It couldn't hurt. Foam col-lected on the lump of swollen rokly, but didn't wash it away. The device wasn't perfect, she thought, amused.

The soft wind of heated air dispersed the foam from her skin and hair, and most, if not all, from her clothes.

Refreshed and alert, Aryl dressed, picking clumps of dried foam from her tunic. Her leg wraps had fared best, being al-most white again.

She lifted the pendant in both hands to examine it, clean hair brushing her cheekbones. It gleamed like a leaf after the rains, markings no longer obscured by dirt. They weren't like those on Sona's wooden beams, or on Enris' blade. They weren't like any other writing or drawing she'd seen—or dreamed—here. As she'd expected, Sona's pendant was the same as those worn by her mother and Grona's Speaker, as the one fastened to the cloth band of the Tikitik's Speaker. That was the point of the pendants. They identified the wearer as a Speaker.

What was she, an unChosen, doing with such a thing?

Only a Clan's appointed Speaker was, by the Agreement, al-lowed to talk to his or her counterpart from either of the other races. Aryl had no idea how other races chose theirs. For Om'ray, few could converse comfortably with what they sensed as an object, not a person. Of those who could, fewer were will-ing to accept the risk. The Speaker assumed responsibility for whatever was understood or not. Speakers sometimes died for his, her, or its mistakes. That was the Agreement, too.

Although, Aryl thought with some impatience, the other races persisted in talking to her, without a pendant or her con-sent, as if rules didn't apply to them.

Was that why the Oud had given her this? Did it know she'd talked to Tikitik? To the strangers? Was this to get her out of trouble—or into more?

More, she decided, and tucked the pendant inside her tunic before leaving the 'fresher.

Snores greeted her. Aryl almost envied the Human his trust in walls. Almost. She collected her knife and belt—hair falling in her eyes—slipped on her damp boots—hair in her mouth—and put on the Human's pretend-Grona coat. It was dirty but dry, as the real garment wouldn't have been. As for her hair? A quick search of a countertop supplied a length of threadlike metal. She twisted it around the annoying locks and pulled them into a painfully tight knot at the base of her neck. There. Out of the way.

A length fell back into her eye. Aryl ignored it.

Stranger-doors could be locked. When she pressed her palm flat against the square plate beside the door, she was relieved to have it open, sliding to one side instead of turning around its center. Too wide, but she supposed the gap was necessary. Strangers came in a variety of races; she'd met one much larger than a Human.

Aryl stepped out, closing the door behind her. As she did, its surface transformed from white to . . . she lifted her hand, astonished to find herself facing the pale gray-streaked stalk of a nekis, one of several. There were more in the distance.

Image or drawing?

She brushed her fingertips over the door and couldn't tell.

Aryl turned to face an oval clearing of packed dirt, free of stone if not footprints. They appeared all the same: the Human's. The clearing and path were free of roots or cut stalks. Impressive, given how densely nekis grew all around, their roots writhing up through the ground.

Broken cloud overlaid the mist, but the sun's light came through. Midmorning, she guessed, displeased to have slept so much of the day. On the thought, she tied another knot along her rope. The interior of the building had been warm. The outside air had a bite to it; she was glad of the Human's coat. As she walked away from the building, she held out her hands. Despite feeling foolish, she had no desire to walk into another illusion.

The thought made her look back. From here, the image was almost perfect. A hasty glance would miss the building entirely, despite its size. Marcus didn't rely on his Om'ray-like clothing alone. More "policy"?

Aryl spotted a second area of not-quite-right nekis. Another building. When she investigated, she was disappointed to find its door locked.

Secrets.

Enough. Anything the strangers would lock away wasn't for Om'ray. Time she was gone. She could reach Sona before first-night, if she moved quickly. She wanted her own kind.

Something made Aryl look back before she entered the shadow of the path. Strange. From here, the buildings—their illusions—met. For no reason . . . or to hide something behind them from anyone approaching from the Cloisters?

She hesitated. What did it matter? This was the strangers' camp—Triad business. She should leave, now. Before Marcus woke up.

She'd never know . . .

"One look," she promised herself.

Putting the locked—and hopefully empty—building be-tween herself and the one where the Human—also hopefully—still snored, Aryl traced its disguised wall with her fingertips, keeping close. The waterfall's background drone, the wind rustling the twig tips of the nekis made more sound than her steps.

She came around the back and gasped, flattening herself against the wall.

The Oud paid no attention.

Too far away to detect her—or didn't they care? Nothing hid her. Nothing grew between—it had been removed, she real-ized with dismay, along with any growth on the towering rock above. Plumes of spray from the waterfall filled the sky toward the Cloisters, hiding the mountain. To the other side of the Oud, the cliff folded inward, as if to hide itself. This was the valley's end.

And the Oud had been busy here.

Beginning only steps in front of her—and the strangers' buildings—the dirt was churned and treacherously soft. No, not all. Her eyes narrowed. Oud ground vehicles had left paired tracks; where they'd been, they packed the dirt into hard lines. Most paralleled the cliff, leading from where the Oud worked to the mouth of their tunnel. She'd seen its like at Grona: an immense slanted opening framed in wood. This one had been thrust up through the edge of the living grove, leaving stalks splintered and dead to either side.

Aryl counted five of the creatures at the base of the cliff. What were they after? There were dark pits—holes—in the cliff face above the Oud. Were they Watchers, like Yena's, whose immense pipes were blown by the M'hir Wind each year to sound a warning? She couldn't be sure.

Below, the bulky Oud and their machines kicked up so much debris she couldn't see past them, creating a roar and rumble like the waterfall's.

They were moving rock. A great deal of rock. Digging into the cliff itself.

She hadn't realized Oud could do that.

It didn't matter. The cliff was above ground. Above ground belonged to Sona's Om'ray, not the Oud. She was their Speaker—appointed by the Oud, at any rate.

Aryl pulled the pendant out and made sure it was in plain sight—not that Oud had eyes. She would go to the creatures and demand to know what they were doing out of their tunnel. It was her duty.

She took a deep breath . . .

Pounding feet made her spin about, knife out and ready. The Human almost collided with her. Only her quickness saved him from impaling himself.

"Fool," she exclaimed, shaking as she put the knife away.

Marcus flinched but didn't retreat. His eyelids were swollen and purpled, as was most of his face; his eyes were wild. He hadn't stopped to put on his boots. "Aryl—"

"You're too late," she interrupted. "I've seen what's going on here." She jerked her head toward the Oud.

He glanced toward the cliff, then back to her, looking confused. "Aryl not run away again?"

Is that what he'd thought? Aryl flushed. Not her finest moment, dashing off into truenight. No credit to her they weren't both dead. She owed him her life.

She didn't owe him any part of Sona.

"You told me you came here for a rest, Marcus Bowman," she accused. "You lied!"

His expression darkened. "Not lie. Not! Oud already here. Invite us many time. Push. Rude. Want full Triad *assess* site." He shook his head violently. "No proof. No *surveyindicators*. We not come. Oud ask again. This time different. I can't do my work. So I say yes. I come. Curious. Unhappy. Understand? Me only, set up *survey* camp, determine if real find or empty hole. Make Oud happy. Me, away from others. Peace. Truth, Aryl," this with a heavy sigh, as if he didn't expect her belief. "Oud want explore ruins. They interest in Hoveny Concentrix. This place no Tikitik stop them."

Oh, she believed him. Aryl instinctively tightened her shields to keep in her reaction. The Tikitik kept the Oud from exploring? The Oud went to the strangers for help to do just that?

Was the Human trying to terrify her?

"Have they found something?" she managed to ask, surprised her voice sounded normal.

"Oud think so." Marcus leaned on the wall of not-nekis and rubbed the bottom of one foot, grimacing as he did. She guessed he didn't run barefoot often. "Not let me look yet," he said with a resigned shrug.

Which helped explain, she realized, why the too-curious Human had been poking around the Sona Cloisters. He'd been bored.

He peered at her through his swollen eyelids. "Aryl want breakfast? Sombay?" From his hoarse tone, he did.

"I have to go. My people are waiting—" For what? Answers? *Who appointed you Speaker for Sona Clan? Who said there was a Sona Clan? What if we want to leave? What if the Oud refuse to share water? What if the Tikitik object to the Oud's "explorations" and blame us? How dare strangers make camp in Sona? What do they want? Didn't you promise Marcus Bowman would never come near us again?*

"Aryl not eat first?"

"Maybe I should," she sighed.

Aryl sat on the ground and crossed her legs. Being low kept her out of the damp, chill breeze that swayed the nekis, but she wasn't about to admit that. "We can eat here," she suggested.

"Here?" Marcus looked horrified. "Aryl come inside," he insisted, leaning against the side of the door's opening. "Please. Don't sit on dirt."

Not her first choice, to go inside his building, surrounded by all that gave the Human an advantage, but the bruises on his face were her fault. He'd saved her life again. How he'd followed her through the darkness was a mystery; she assumed some gadget or device gave him an advantage. What mattered was that he'd jumped into the waterfall after her, risking his own life. Ridiculous.

Heartwarming.

The waterfall may have spat them both out, but Marcus, battered and scared, had protected her from the Oud. He'd made her breathe again, a trick she'd like to learn. She could no longer doubt him.

Everyone else. Them she doubted. What he was here to do. That she doubted.

Aryl sighed again and stood. "Inside," she agreed.

Once through the door, Marcus shoved and tossed crates aside until he cleared the area of floor between their beds. "Wait," he told her when she tried to help. "I do." He pressed a control that folded both beds against the wall—their blankets stuck out as if trapped—then grabbed a handle she hadn't noticed in the floor. A pull, and up rose a table, complete with attached seats. "There," he beamed at her. "Not sit on dirt. Sit."

She sat with a certain amount of caution. Furniture that came out of a floor could, in her opinion, sink back into it without warning.

In short order the Human filled self-heating cups, gave one to her with a box of "supplements," found soft, useless-looking boots to put on his sore feet, and sat down across the table with a groan of pleasure. "There. Better."

Aryl smiled into her cup.

"Aryl happy?"

As Speaker for Sona Clan, she had every right and obligation to talk to the not-*real*.

She probably wasn't supposed to like the not-*real* individual in question.

"You think hard." Marcus scrunched his face. "Like this."

She pretended affront. "I don't look like that."

"Yes. Laugh is better." They sipped in companionable silence for a moment, then Marcus gestured toward her. "See what Oud gave you? Scan. Find how old?" With that too-innocent look.

The Human had accepted that the Cloisters were off-limits as far as she was concerned—or he'd stopped asking, which suited her. Aryl found herself equally reluctant to share the pendant. To divert him, she pulled the wet and still-grimy headdress from her pocket and laid it on the table. "You could scan this. It's from Sona," she added when he didn't reach for it. "I found it with Om'ray bones."

"Went through 'fresher." Complaint or observation? "Not good."

Complaint.

She should have guessed from what lined his shelves that he'd prefer things covered in dirt. Aryl nudged it toward him anyway. "It stayed in a pocket."

"Hmm."

Collecting what he needed, Marcus returned to the table. He handled the metal links with greater care than she'd shown them, holding a length gently against one end of a palm-sized device, before he pressed a series of buttons. Small lights flickered and she could have sworn the device gave a satisfied hum. The Human's eyebrows rose. "Old, is."

"How old?"

He pressed more buttons. "Two times get. One wrong."

"Two?" Aryl reached for the headdress.

Marcus laid his hand over it. "How long *exposed to elements*? 'Fresher," he said, shaking his head dolefully. She almost gestured an apology. Then, "How long since *manufacture*? Different times."

"What are you saying?"

He blushed easily. "Sorry. Excited. This," he raised the hand over the headdress, "was made over 240 *standard*—sorry. Your year, close to same, good enough. Little more." At her impatient nod, "This made to this shape 240 years ago." He held up the headdress and peered through its links at her. "What is it?"

This time, he relinquished it at her gesture. Aryl laid it over her hair, shivering as the decorative piece crossed her forehead. "A headdress—to keep hair quiet and well behaved. Only a Chosen would wear one."

A grin. "Mother give daughter, yes?"

She took off the headdress and put it back in her pocket, more carefully than before. Enris' Clan traded for such ornaments. She had no idea what Sona would have done. Still, something so difficult to make, yet lovely and useful—in Yena, such would stay within a family, to be treasured. "Or to the First Chosen," she hazarded.

"Then this could be gift many many—"

Trill! Loud, from a box on the counter behind Marcus. Flashing lights accompanied the sound. Muttering impatiently, he slapped a control and turned back to her.

Trillll! With more lights. Then a deep male voice uttered incomprehensible words, sounding none too pleased.

"Tyler," Marcus announced with a shrug. "Triad First, Site Two. I better answer." He held a finger in front of his lips. "Aryl, no sound please." A gesture to his abused face and a crooked smile. "No vid, sure."

Having seen him use a comlink before, Aryl understood. She sat quietly, enjoying the warm drink, while Marcus exchanged strings of stranger-words with this Tyler. Site Two was where they'd uncovered large structures, inexplicably whole, from the side of a mountain—a discovery important enough to make Marcus take her with him to join the others.

From his tone, this "Tyler, Triad First, Site Two" wasn't a friend. They exchanged short bursts of words, like scouts reporting. Whatever it was about, Marcus remained calm and assured. By the end, Tyler's voice went from argumentative to resigned, as if Marcus had made some point.

The Human switched off the comlink and sighed. "Sorry, Aryl. Missed last night's *check in*. I tell them I all right."

So many words for that? She decided not to press for an explanation. The less she knew about the strangers' doings on Cersi, the better.

Though she wondered what they'd found . . . how they'd entered the buildings, if they had . . . and why . . . ?

Before she could ask—or to forestall any questions—Marcus tapped the table with a finger. "Need to know how many times that be gift. How many First Chosen. How many mothers to daughters."

Her surviving great-grandparents could remember one of their great-grandparents—injury took the lives of most Yena before they grew old, and Ele Sarc had lived a remarkably long life—so she'd grown up hearing the stories of more ancestors than other Yena families. Of course, whomever had lived before that was no longer *real* and didn't matter. They might never have existed at all. She'd certainly never given them thought, until now. "I don't know."

"We can *estimate*. For Om'ray, how long *per generation*?" Marcus immediately rephrased his question. "Sorry. *Generation* is how long for Om'ray from born, grow up to be mother, have own child. How many years for that?"

What an odd thing to ask—a Clan always had Om'ray of every stage in life. Maybe Humans were different there, too. As for his question? Those Chosen pairs who could have children became pregnant soon after Joining. After that, some might have more children or not; everyone hoped. A Clan needed children. There were never enough Om'ray. Yena had diminished in number long before the disastrous Harvest.

"Sixteen years," Aryl said cautiously. "For most." The coming M'hir would be her eighteenth. Surely she would be a Chooser by then. What was it like to Choose . . . to Join . . . to have a Chosen's body . . . to carry new life inside? She wasn't supposed to wonder. After Choice, a new Chosen stayed with her mother, to learn, to be cared for as she matured.

Hers might as well be on one of the Tikitik's fabled moons, Aryl thought with a bitterness that startled her. She took a sip of her sombay.

For some reason, the Human appeared distracted, too. He fussed with the device in his hands until it made a buzz of complaint, then tossed it aside with a grumble in his language. "How old your elders?" he asked after a moment.

The Human had a gift for asking what she'd never considered before. For most of their lives, Om'ray paid no attention to age, only accomplishments. "Old."

That drew a laugh. "My son say same." But something bothered him. Aryl didn't need to seek out his emotions to know. She waited, sure some of their mutual confusion came from haste. Marcus rubbed one hand over his face, then looked at her, determination in his eyes. "Quick generations," he said at last. "Aryl say Om'ray have only living past." A frown, as if this continued to be difficult for the Human. He drew a circle on the tabletop with his finger, over and over again. "Means quick forget. Quick generations means change quick, too. Om'ray not remember. Change inside. Change outside. Om'ray now, not like Om'ray many many generations past."

About to protest, to explain why this couldn't be, Aryl closed her mouth and stared at Marcus. He gazed back, his expression solemn. Hadn't the Om'ray changed? Wasn't she proof? Those with her proof? New Talents, new strength. Enris and his ability to resist a Chooser. Her Clan's Adepts had purged their population of those new Talents to prevent more change—but hadn't that changed Yena, too?

"Change normal. Many generations, population *adapts*," Marcus said gently, as if sensing her distress. "Change not bad."

Maybe to a Human, she thought, grappling with ideas as strange as his disguised building and a box that sensed time. Maybe to someone from another world. On Cersi, change was deadly. It had destroyed Sona. It would destroy Yena, if there was no Harvest this M'hir. Another Clan lost.

How long then before all Om'ray forgot Yena had existed?

"When did Sona die?" she demanded. "Tell me."

"This?" A vague gesture at the outside world. "Happen eighty-three years ago. Headdress could be outside, in dirt and water and air, same time. Not know. 'Fresher." He could be as annoying as Enris. "Most five generations Om'ray." That keen look. "How forget?"

"I don't know," she said for the second time, her heart pounding. Those on Yena's Council would have been alive then. Cetto and Morla should remember that day, as should their Chosen, Husni and Lendin.

But by all she'd sensed, they'd been as surprised by Sona's existence as everyone else.

"Maybe Sona different kind of Om'ray? Not-*real* as you say for me?"

"They were real." Aryl had no doubt at all.

"Sometime, those who live want a different history remembered. Tell lie. My job, look for truth, not what living want."

Implying conflict. The possibility twitched nerves used to the canopy; it was all she could do not to check her knife. "Do those who lie try to stop you?"

"We take care. *Clearancechecks*. Vid records." A too-casual shrug. "Here? Aryl not worry. Nothing *contentious* here. No lie to fight."

Still, she didn't care for the sound of it. "The Oud want to find their own Hoveny ruins—to look for some truth of their past or to bury it?"

"Good question, Aryl. Very good. I not—I don't know." He laid his hand on his chest. "My thought only, for you. Oud not care truth or past. They care things. Things of use, of value. But that is my idea, not certain." He shrugged. "Not easy, talk to Oud."

The strangers had been talking to the Oud for years. If she was the Speaker, how could she do any better?

Tomorrow's problem.

Marcus gave her a considering look. "Why you run away last night? What I do? What I say?"

"What you are," she admitted, feeling her cheeks warm. "We're different, Human. It's worse sometimes, because you look so much like us. But I know you aren't."

"I understand. To me, you could be Human," he said. "Basic shape, *humanoid*, common. Some *assembler* species look same, too. Need bioscanner to know Om'ray, not Human. Aryl—any Om'ray—could walk on my world. No one know difference, outside."

Aryl shuddered. It was one thing to accept Marcus Bowman as *real* enough to be a person, quite another to accept his entire race. Let alone more not-Om'ray mimics. Her head hurt. "I'll stay on my world, thank you."

He turned his cup around slowly, looked into it rather than at her. "You need a place, safe place, stay here."

The Human didn't know, she realized with a start. He believed she was alone. That she'd left her people, or they'd left her. "Thank you." She dared touch his hand with hers, stopping the cup. If he'd been Om'ray, she would have *sent* her gratitude through that contact. "You're a good friend," she said instead, when his eyes lifted to hers. "I have a place, Marcus. The people you helped escape the swarm? They've come with me. We're making a home in Sona. I'm here looking for water. We have everything else we need."

"Haxel, too? And the big one. Enris?"

The other Om'ray who'd seen the Human—in person. She'd shared his image with the rest, but hadn't dared let them meet, afraid they wouldn't be able to deal with the confusion between sight and inner sense. "Haxel, too," Aryl agreed. "Enris—" For some reason, her voice caught.

Marcus let go of the cup and gripped her hand. *Dread. Anxiety.* "Enris dead?"

"Why would you—of course not! No," she went on more calmly. "Enris left. He's on Passage to Vyna. He travels to another Clan," felt his *confusion*. Mentioning the Tuana's true quest would be like dangling food scraps over the Lay. "It's what our unChosen do when they seek a Chooser—a lifepartner, like your Kelly."

Anger. "Enris stupid." He scowled. "You best lifepartner."

Aryl gently freed her hand, not that the Human could sense her feelings in return. "I'm not ready for Choice. Enris couldn't wait for me." Why was she explaining this to a stranger?

Because he wasn't, not anymore, not to her. The person sitting across the table, bruised and worn, with kind green-brown eyes, was her friend—however unusual his origins. He wanted her to be happy as well as safe. A teardrop hit the table; she wiped the second from her cheek, then said what she hadn't to anyone else. "I did want Enris to stay. He might have, if I'd asked, for me. But I couldn't, Marcus. He had to go."

"You not go?" Before she had to answer, he gave a quick nod. "No, you not leave your people. Your family. I know that, Aryl. Sorry. Sorry."

"My family," she whispered, feeling the pull of that too-distant glow. Louder, "I have to leave, Marcus."

As she rose to her feet, the Human did, too. "You come back, want find me, knock on door." He drummed a pattern on the table. "I not talk to other Om'ray. Promise. I give *au-tolock* your *palmprint*. I not here, door open for you, anytime. No one else. Aryl use 'fresher, anytime." This with that dimpled grin, distorted by his swollen lip.

She considered what he offered. Access to him, to his amazing technology, whenever she wanted—on her terms. "What if I don't come back at all?"

The grin widened. "You come. Aryl curious."

That word.

Aryl found herself smiling back.

The valley was different now. Familiar. Smaller. Defined. It contained a friend and comfort. Not to mention something that hoped to eat her, making this a more normal place. Aryl studied the rock hunters she passed. Once aware of them, she found it simple to pick them out from ordinary stone, even if dusted by snow. A little too smooth. A little too symmetrical. Large and small, the same basic shape. If she'd had time, she would have examined one. Anything could be killed. It was only a matter of finding its vulnerability.

"Maybe you're good eating," she told a pile in the shadows and imagined a quiver of fear.

Threatening rocks was probably not the sort of thing a Clan Speaker should do. She couldn't imagine Taisal doing it. Then again, once made an Adept, Taisal di Sarc had no longer hunted or climbed—or lived at home.

She'd been without a mother, Aryl thought wistfully, longer than she'd realized.

Costa had been there instead. Her kind and funny brother. Not a hunter or a climber—but he'd let her do as she wanted. He'd lived at home until being Chosen by Leri Teerac.

Who'd become Lost at his death. Leri was in the Cloisters now, a mindless pair of hands in service to the Adepts and others.

Sona had no Lost. And no Adepts. Aryl sincerely hoped it would stay that way.

She climbed the arch of the second bridge and stopped to consult her *geoscanner*, a gift from Marcus. Hand-sized, with a flat base and a clear dome over an intimidating array of small glowing parts, she'd refused the thing at first. It wouldn't fit in a pocket. She'd break it. After the Human gleefully hammered and stomped on the device, she could hardly use that excuse. And it was well worth having, though she'd have to find a better way to carry it than down her tunic. For the Human had *preset* the geoscanner to hunt for tunnels. It would display a symbol on its dome if it detected any, a symbol that would flash red if the tunnels *radiatedenergy*.

All Aryl needed to know was that red meant Oud, nearby and active.

No symbol. Nothing below the surface but rock.

She carefully tucked her treasure away, sucking air through her teeth as its cold touched bare skin. Sona had its own Watcher now, unlike any on Cersi. With this, maybe they could find all the tunnels—watch for any reshaping. With this, the Oud couldn't surprise them.

The Human had given her a less welcome gift: a puzzle. Sona had been destroyed within the lifetime of living Om'ray, but those who should remember, didn't.

She wasn't sure what to do about that.

Aryl started moving again, running in an easy lope. The effort kept her warm; she'd left the Human's coat and hadn't bothered to collect her sodden Grona one from the grove.

She wasn't sure what to tell the rest about Marcus Bowman either. There was already the stolen river. Two of them, if she counted the one missing farther down the valley. The Cloisters. The Oud and its gift. The potential for negotiation.

Speaker for Sona. That alone should get everyone talking, she thought with an inner wince.

Maybe she'd leave the Human out of the discussion, for now.

The shadows were dark and noisy by the time Aryl came to the final turn of the valley before Sona. The noise was the grind and clatter of rock hunters, apparently willing to risk her attention now that she was leaving their hunting ground. They didn't move quickly, unless tumbling from on top of a neighbor, but their numbers were unsettling. When she glanced over her shoulder, it was like being followed by a sluggish landslide.

Maybe they hoped she'd stop and conveniently fall too deeply asleep to hear them. Or trip and knock herself out. Not that a self-respecting Om'ray would panic and run like a fool from a bunch of rocks.

From a Human?

Mistakes you survived were lessons, Aryl told herself firmly.

The glow of Om'ray ahead lengthened her stride. Not just ahead, but someone coming toward her. She *tasted* a name. Haxel.

Impatient for a report, no doubt. Hopefully, the First Scout would settle for words. Haxel couldn't read her memories against her will—no one here had the Power to penetrate her shields—but there was something wrong about deliberately hiding part of a memory. Neglecting to volunteer a minor detail or two, like meeting a Human, wasn't the same at all.

Though Haxel wouldn't miss what she could see. With reluctance, Aryl unwound the length of stranger-metal from her hair and tucked it deep in a pocket. Errant strands flew in her eyes at once and snagged on her chapped lips. Annoying stuff.

What would it be like if more than the wind moved it?

More than annoying, she decided.

Her head turned, drawn by another solitary warmth. *Enris.* He hadn't left the valley floor yet, but moved away at a steady pace. Easy to imagine his long strides. She didn't try to send to him. Wouldn't. Talking to the Human had, in an odd way, helped. Marcus understood and sympathized with her decision—if not the Tuana's. Her lips curved.

Aryl focused on the glow of her people, *reached* for their names, but kept the touch feather soft. Everyone was where they should be.

More than everyone.

She drew back to herself with dismay.

Slow they might be, but the Grona would be here before firstnight.

Haxel turned and matched strides with her rather than stop, her hood down. Her white hair strained against its net— agitation, not the wind. "Traveling light?"

The missing pack and coat. "Rock hunters." True enough. "They like shadows." Aryl nodded at the far wall, black to within a third of its top. So the return trip, admittedly at a good pace, had taken her less than two tenths. Yena's Cloisters had been almost as far from its village.

"Hunters, are they?" The First Scout gave the oh-so-still-now stones a considering look. "Threat or meal?"

On the snow that by rights should cover them, they were easier to spot than ever. As if that wasn't enough, each had pressed a trail of white as it rolled. "Nuisance," Aryl decided. "Though I didn't take the time to find out for sure."

"You've news, then."

"I found water—the source of the river. It's no closer than where we're getting water now," she warned, "but will be faster. This goes all the way." She scuffed her toe against the flat stone of the road.

"What else?"

"The river's dry because of the Oud."

The First Scout stopped. Aryl, resisting the urge to lean toward Sona, so close, did the same. "The Oud?"

"They made a hole to take the water below ground. And they haven't left. One confronted me—gave me this." She pulled out the Speaker's Pendant.

Haxel raised a curious brow. "You have been busy."

If only she knew—or better still, didn't. Aryl put away the pendant and chose her next words with all the care she'd use climbing an unknown rastis. "I think it understood me. That we need the water back. They'll negotiate."

"To put the water back." They both looked toward the empty riverbed. "I suppose if they can dig a hole . . ." As if to dispense with the chancy topic of rivers empty or otherwise, Haxel took off her coat and tossed it to Aryl, who pulled it on without argument. Whatever warmth running had given her was long gone; she had to clench her teeth together to keep them still. The First Scout began walking again, and Aryl hurried to keep up. "You found the Cloisters?"

"Yes. Empty, but whole."

Satisfaction. "I don't suppose they left the doors open."

"No." Aryl hugged the coat close. "I found bones, too. Most of Sona died there, not here."

"Locked out, were they?" None of them would forget their own exile.

"Or taken by surprise. The Oud dig as fast as we climb."

The First Scout glared at the ground. "How can we watch the dirt?"

About to tell her, Aryl hesitated, unsure why. If Enris had been here, she'd have already pulled out the geoscanner, boasted of its power, let him try it. Haxel knew Marcus Bowman, too—she'd met the Human, seen some of the strangers' technology. The First Scout wouldn't flinch at anything that offered an advantage for their people, regardless of source.

Threat or meal . . .

If Haxel believed Marcus had anything more to offer, she'd want it.

If he refused? There was no Yena more ruthless; none more dangerous.

"There might be a way," Aryl said as casually as she could, her shields firm. "I thought I *sensed* the Oud who approached me. I can't be sure, but if that's so . . ." she let her voice trail suggestively.

Haxel took the bait. "If that's so, Aryl, we've an advantage." Cheerfully. "Just remember what the Tuana said." Her lip curled. "The stronger your Power, the more you'll suffer if you use it near an Oud. And you are the strongest we have. I'd rather not have you incapacitated when we're about to have our first guest. Or is it guests?" All innocence.

"Guests." Typical of the First Scout to thoroughly embrace every Talent she deemed useful, Forbidden or not, dangerous or not. Aryl sighed inwardly. She hadn't wanted to think about the Grona, but that was foolish. Haxel should know. "Six. Bern and his Chosen, Oran di Caraat. The rest are family. Her brother and a cousin. Her uncle and aunt."

"Coming for you." A hand dropped, not casually, to the hilt of her longknife. "I expected it."

"You did?" The words came out as a squeak, and Aryl closed her mouth hastily.

Haxel chuckled. "What did you think I'd miss, young Sarc? Bern's lack of gratitude for being saved at the Harvest or your reappearance at Yena the instant we needed you most? I'll take what I sense over any explanation, thank you, no matter how convincing. You've a Talent like Fon's, that lets you move from place to place, or move someone else."

The forlorn and stunted grove of nekis followed alongside the road. Equally humbled, Aryl asked, "Why didn't you say anything?"

"You can't control it yet, or you'd have used it to save us instead of calling your stranger." The First Scout laid a hand on her shoulder. *Pride* blended with *sympathy*. "Taisal knew, didn't she? That's why the Adepts exiled you."

"That's why they exiled all of us," Aryl replied bitterly. "It's my fault—"

The hand gave her a friendly shove. "It's their loss."

Futile to warn her, but Aryl had to try. "This isn't like other Talents, Haxel," she began. "It's dangerous. I need time to learn it, find where the traps lie. It may never be controllable."

"Don't worry." Calm and sure. "Until you're ready, no one else need know. As for our guests?" A rude noise. "They won't announce what they've come for, unless they're thorough fools. If they are? They won't eat before we send them home again, truenight or not. You've my word on that."

The warmth she felt was more than the coat.

Aryl climbed up the riverbank beside Haxel, and stood, transfixed.

"We've been busy, too." *Pride.*

Deserved. A true village had sprung from the ruins since she'd left yesterday morning. Their original shelter and second building not only had roofs and doors, but were faced by two more structures under construction. All were square-edged and sturdy, well-suited to the weather. Paths had been tramped through the small field between, narrow and leading to openings in the low wall that, when intact, must have tied the original buildings together. The Sona design was revealed: four sturdy homes had backed onto each open space, with roofs that overhung sheltered areas along their outer walls, those areas connecting their doors one to the other, like Yena bridges. Add water and growing things?

This would be a place she could live.

The wind snickered through dead plants, raising dust.

"We'll have a home for every family by spring," Aryl replied in defiance.

Haxel smiled. "Sooner."

There. They'd said it, both of them. Aryl could *feel* the realization in Haxel's thoughts, a peaceful drawing close, like the moment when glows were lit and ladders pulled to protect Yena through truenight. "We're staying, then." The First Scout sounded amused. "Didn't even take a Council vote."

They didn't have a Council. If they did? Took the eldest of each family? Aryl grinned. Then Seru would serve with Morla and Cetto. The last time she'd seen her cousin, she'd been staggering alongside the elderly weaver, using her chin to keep a massive stack of coats together. He and Husni were going to teach her how to alter the Sona coats, which were warm but overlong, with too much material that hampered movement.

They walked past the pile of beams and stone that had been Sona's meeting hall. Aryl blinked in surprise. When she'd left, the narrow road that went behind the buildings had been blocked by huge slabs of stone. Now it was a clear passage, if dirt. She turned to Haxel. "How?"

"Fon," the other explained smugly. "Cetto's notion."

A greater change than the road, then. In Yena's Council, Aryl had listened as Cetto sud Teerac spoke passionately against the use of Power to move objects. He'd warned it would lead to taking, instead of sharing, that Om'ray would become divided by their abilities instead of brought closer. His was the one voice she'd believed would be raised against using what she could do.

Did he no longer fear those consequences? Or had Cetto realized it was too late to do anything but ride the storm and hope to survive?

Maybe Haxel had convinced him. Aryl felt a certain sympathy. She shivered despite the coat. The First Scout—who didn't appear to notice the mountain cold any more than the wilting heat of the canopy—could ask the rest of her questions somewhere warm. With food.

"Think I'm in time for a meal?" she asked hopefully as she lengthened her stride.

"There'll be some in the pots. Rorn sees to that."

"Wonderful." Maybe she'd get a chance to ask Cetto or better yet, Husni, about those memories they should have. It would have to be carefully done. They couldn't learn what she knew or how . . .

"Looks like your cousin can't wait to see you."

Seru?

There, without any coats, running flat out toward them between the rebuilt homes, hair loose and streaming. Alarmed, Aryl *reached* to her cousin.

Desperation. Her heart lurched in her chest. "Something's wrong."

Haxel broke into a run, Aryl right beside her. The three met, hands outstretched to clasp one another.

It's Myris! Fear gave Seru's sending new strength. *Hurry!*

A real door had replaced the blanket at the entrance to the second shelter. There was no center pivot to allow it to turn, but an arrangement of slats and rope held it in place or moved it aside, like the mechanism the scouts used each night to pull up ladders, to protect Yena. Had used.

Haxel threw it open, leading the way inside. "Ael—"

Stay away!

"I brought help, Uncle." Seru closed the door behind them, fumbling with the ropes.

The room inside was now twin to their original shelter, embers aglow on a stone hearth and oillights on the walls, except for ranks of shoulder-high jars and baskets from the mound. The floor stones tilted this way and that, packed dirt used to level the result.

The musty scent of long-stored blankets and woodsmoke couldn't hide that of sickness.

Myris lay on a platform of blankets. Before they could take another step toward her, Ael blocked their path. "Stay away, Haxel!" Aloud, this time, and hoarse. His face was terrible to see, tear-streaked and pale; his lips struggled to shape words. "All of you! Go!"

"Hush, little brother." The First Scout's voice was unusually gentle. "I'm here. What's wrong?"

Aryl had forgotten their relationship. Though Ael had been

born Kessa'at, not Vendan, he'd been raised by Haxel's parents after his own fell to their deaths in the Lay, victims of a rotted span of bridge. The two had never seemed close.

Not that she'd cared about the past of any Chosen, she thought with a twinge. Before the Harvest, she'd considered adults—other than Costa—boring, opinionated, and against anything a lively unChosen might want to do instead of work.

After? They weren't what had changed.

"Wrong? Nothing you can fix." Ael waved his arms, as if they were biters to be shooed away. "Go. Please, Haxel. Take them with you. Get away, now! It's not—safe. She's not."

Chaun, who should have been here, was gone. Moved to the other shelter, despite his injuries. There was no one to help Ael or Myris.

A desertion with only one explanation. Aryl swallowed, hard, and *listened*.

Sure enough, to her inner sense, Myris was unshielded chaos: emotions, memories, words tumbling in purposeless frenzy. Locked within her mind for now, but that could change in a heartbeat. If it did, her madness would engulf other Om'ray who were too close, taking first those who shared any connection. Like kinship.

Aryl turned to Seru while the other pair argued. "You can't be here. Go. Keep everyone in the shelter."

Comprehension widened those green eyes. "But you—"

"Go."

To her relief, Seru didn't argue.

Ael hadn't stopped pleading. "—Haxel, listen to me for once," he begged. "There's nothing you can do. I don't want you here."

"I'm not leaving—"

"Why?" From pleading to rage. "Tell me that. What good are you? What's our mighty First Scout going to do about this? Comfort me when my Chosen dies? I won't care. I won't hear a word, will I? I won't know who you are—who I am." As she tried to answer, he raised his voice to a shout. "I've a better idea. Kill my husk, so it won't waste food. That's what you're good for!"

Aryl had never seen her cheerful uncle enraged; she'd never imagined Haxel speechless with hurt.

Myris needed help, not this.

She pushed between the two, facing the First Scout. "The Grona are coming, Haxel. Go."

Their eyes locked. Aryl didn't dare lower her shields to reinforce the command, but Haxel had to obey. Whatever her outer strength, she couldn't protect herself from Myris. They'd lose her, too.

But whatever the other read on her face was enough. The First Scout spun on her heel and walked out.

"Aryl . . ."

"Uncle." She made herself smile as she turned. "What have you done to my poor aunt while I was gone?"

Everywhere else, *anticipation* ran mind-to-mind. The newcomers were on the road to Sona. They'd made good time despite having chosen to walk the maze of abrupt hills left by the Oud. The weather had held for them: clear, if windy and chill. If the Yena had delayed their own departure from Grona by a day, they'd have missed the storm.

If they'd missed the storm, Aryl thought, she wouldn't be sitting here, in the relative gloom of Sona's second shelter, desperately wondering what to do. A broken bone was a simple matter.

A broken mind was not.

Myris was so still. Her eyelashes brushed shadows on ashen cheeks and the gash over her temple had grown a dark, ugly bruise. Her thick golden hair lay flaccid, without life.

Ael kept his eyes fixed on his Chosen's face. "I thought at first she'd fallen asleep. Sleep would be . . ." his voice trailed away, then firmed. "Don't worry about Haxel. We always end up shouting. I was never good at doing what I was told. Didn't know or care if there was a difference between daring and stupid." To himself as much as to her, Aryl decided. "She looked out for me, brought me home, patched me up. Did you know she wouldn't let me take Passage? Oh, I was wild to go. She said the waters were too high that season . . . too many stitler traps even for her. When I refused to listen, she threatened to tie me to a chair. And she would have. She would." A wan smile. "Haxel thought I was good enough for a Sarc, you see. Because of her, when Myris was ready, I was there." His fingertips hovered just above the golden hair, traced the length of it as if inviting touch. But it didn't lift from the blanket. "My life—my life began that moment."

Ael radiated *fear* and *misery,* his shields barely coping with the strength of his emotions. "Now it ends."

"Not yet." Aryl laid her hand over her aunt's.

"Careful!"

"It's all right," she assured him, fervently hoping it was. Despite her shields, being this close to a mind out of control affected every sense. Hard to be confident when the room tipped at whim, the lights flared until she squinted or was blind, and why did she smell overripe sweetberries? "Let me try."

Through the touch, she *sent* strength, what little she had left to spare. Enris would have been furious, but if it could help Myris' struggle to hold on to herself, at least she'd gain time to find an answer.

The floor steadied. The lights behaved. Not everything was normal. Aryl sniffed, recognizing the soap used to soak dresel wings. She sat back with a sigh.

"Thank you."

Startled, she looked at her uncle. Ael looked deathly ill, his usually bright eyes dull and fighting to focus on her. But he managed a smile. "I felt it, too. Your—gift. I'm sure it helped."

He felt it because the Chosen were one. An unnecessary reminder that if Myris died, she'd lose them both.

"I don't know what else to do, Ael," Aryl admitted. "You must be sorry you followed me."

"Daughter of our hearts. No." His slim callused hand covered hers. *We're family. We belong together. She wants to be with you when you commence your Chosen life. It's only . . . now . . . so much . . . confusion . . . so much pain . . .*

PAIN . . .

Shuddering, Ael pulled away. "Forgive me." Harsh and low. "Go. You need to eat. Talk to the others. She's a Sarc, don't forget. Strong. Stubborn. She'll hold on. You've helped. We'll be fine. Some rest. That's all."

"I'll be back, Uncle," Aryl promised, shaken. "As soon as I can."

Ael didn't answer. He rocked in place, back and forth. His fingertips hovered just above his Chosen's hair, traced the lifeless length of it.

Over and over again.

Haxel stood outside, coatless. "We go up the valley. Tonight."

Aryl's hand dropped from the door fastener. "What?"

"Get Myris ready. I'll tell the rest."

Just in time, Aryl stopped herself from shaking her head in the Human's gesture. "We can't leave," she protested. "What about our supplies? The Oud—the rock hunters!" The creatures hadn't crossed the dry riverbed to follow them, to her relief and the First Scout's intense interest.

Haxel seized her arms, powerful fingers digging through the coat to bruise, hair breaking free of its net like something alive. "Don't argue with me! We take her to the Cloisters. Tonight!"

"Haxel, we can't." Aryl's lips felt numb, her mind thick and slow. She'd felt alone when Enris left, but she hadn't been afraid. Not like this. First Scout Haxel Vendan wasn't like ordinary Om'ray. She was beyond emotion, incapable of rash judgment, always their wise and calm protector. Wasn't she? "It's locked. I told you—"

"We'll find a way in. There'll be something inside. Something to help them." Hair lashed Aryl's cheeks, left a sting near one eye. "Don't you understand? I have to do something. I have to fix this!" *Fury!* "I won't lose them!" Suddenly, she was supporting most of Haxel's weight. "I can't lose him." Almost a whisper. "Aryl. I can't. Not after . . . not after losing everything else . . ."

How could they be safe, if Haxel failed?

Aryl's heart hammered in her chest. It hurt to breathe.

There'd never been safety. She'd let herself use Haxel the way a young child would the tether tied to her waist as she learned to climb. Like a child, she'd believed she'd never be allowed to fall.

But she was no child. Haxel was extraordinary, not invincible. She owed her better—didn't they all? Cut the tether, Aryl told herself.

"They aren't going to die, Haxel." This with all the confidence she'd ever heard in her mother's voice, having none of her own. "Listen to me. Myris is probably in retreat, like I was once. If so, she can be called back. I'll try. Like this." She let strength *flow* through that contact until it left her dizzy and the other's eyes dilated in shock. "I've given her what I can for now. She's—she's resting. I need to eat, warm up. I need you to help me tell the others what I found, what it means. Prepare them for the Oud. I don't want anyone afraid."

She was, Aryl thought glumly, scared enough for everyone already.

"The Cloisters," she made herself add, "can wait."

The First Scout inclined her head, hair subsiding. "Speaker." She straightened. Her hands eased open, lingered on Aryl's arms, then busied themselves in a futile effort to shove her hair inside what remained of its net.

"The others should hear your report." Brisk, assured, the old Haxel. She glared down the road. "We've Grona on our bridge. If they expect us to waste food in one of their feasts, they're in for a surprise. Let's go."

They walked together to the shelter, as if nothing had changed between them.

As if the world had boundaries and certainty and shape.

As if, Aryl thought wistfully, they were safe.

Chapter 10

A FEW TENTHS MORE THAN a day. Aryl couldn't imagine what kind of welcome a longer absence would create.
Upon word that Myris was resting, everyone began to bustle
around her at once. Haxel's coat was whisked away, a blanket
draped over her shoulders. A special place was readied for her
by the hearth, on what had to be a first for Yena, a bench con-
sisting of a blanket-covered wooden plank supported by large
stones at each end. A bowl of something remarkably tasty was
pressed into her hands.

A few brushed their fingers across her cheek, as if they
needed touch to be sure she was back, as if she'd gone too far
for them to sense, and they'd believed her lost.

Best of all, the sense of *home*. *Goodwill* and *relief* flowed mind-
to-mind, through each touch, until she ducked her head to
hide her tears. These were her people.

"Tell them what you found, Aryl." Haxel's order silenced the
hum of quiet voices. Everyone paid attention. Everyone was
here.

Except Myris and Ael.

First things first. Aryl rested the warm bowl on her lap, her
fingers pressed to its curve so they wouldn't tremble. She pre-

pared an image of the waterfall and *sent* it to them all. As they reacted, some with dismay, others with astonishment, she continued aloud. "The Oud have stopped the water from going down the river for now, but there's a good road. Easy to make it there and back in daylight."

"A good road? Then what we need is a flatlander's cart," Morla offered. "Enris showed me the design." She touched her bandaged wrist. "Veca and Tilip can build it."

"Before or after finishing the next home?" This from Veca. "People need space."

"The cart first!" Kayd paled as he realized his elders were all looking at him—most with surprise—but didn't back down. "Water's more important."

"And heavy." This from someone in the crowd drew *amusement* from everyone but Fon and Cader, who'd also spent yesterday carrying bags of water on their backs.

Haxel had been leaning against one wall, arms crossed, her eyes on Aryl. She stirred. "Tell them the rest of it. What you mean by 'for now.' "

Aryl passed her bowl to Seru, who sat cross-legged and patient nearby, then brought out the pendant.

It sent reflections skittering across the dark beams and blanketed walls, flashed in startled eyes. "The Oud are willing to discuss restoring the river."

She let them absorb the shock, feeling the race of inner conversation—some cautious and private, the rest she politely ignored. *Telepathy*, Marcus had called this ability. Until he'd named it, described it, she hadn't realized all races didn't communicate this way. How did they connect to one another? How could they trust what was said, if all they had were words?

"May I see that?" Cetto held out his hand, broad and callused.

She gave him the pendant and waited.

The former Councillor turned it this way and that, as if searching for a reason to dispute what it was, then passed it back to her. "Some might call it unfair, Aryl, to give someone so young such responsibility," he stated in his deep, loud voice. "I call it rare good sense by the Oud."

Startled laughter eased the *feel* of every mind. Aryl sent a flash of *gratitude* to Cetto, who smiled kindly.

Lendin sud Kessa'at, sitting by his tiny Chosen, spoke up. "What about the Oud?"

"What about them?" Husni looked around the room. "A Clan's supposed to have neighbors."

Agreement. Aryl sensed it coursing through the others. However unwarranted, many were relieved by this return to the proper order of things. A Clan had neighbors, Tikitik or Oud. A Clan conducted civilized dealings with those neighbors through a Speaker. Until now, they'd been uncertain of their status.

From Aryl's point of view, that hadn't changed. She wouldn't argue. Let them be comforted.

Except for Chaun, resting on a blanket platform, and Myris—her people looked better, she thought. Rested. Fed. And more. They'd begun to settle into this place, to make it their own.

She'd been right. Whether they'd intended to become a Clan or not, they had.

Sona lived.

Aryl slipped out, leaving the others in the midst of discussing what they'd do with plentiful water. None had ever planted or grown food; there was, nonetheless, optimism. Plants, after all, wanted to grow. In the canopy—as Taen pointed out—they'd struggled to keep greenery from taking over rooftops and bridges. Should growing food prove difficult to learn, there were the rest of the storage mounds. If half contained supplies similar to the first, Sona could support ten times their number for years. Though by then, Ziba had proclaimed, she'd be sick of dried rokly.

Haxel watched her leave. The others, too obviously, did not.

Aryl understood. They wanted to believe she could help Myris. Wanted, but couldn't. She was no Healer.

Maybe not, but she was the only Om'ray here who dared approach Myris in this state. Fon's mind was strong enough, but his parents would never let him take that risk. Risky it was, Aryl thought, feeling as if she ventured over an untried branch. But Ael shouldn't be left alone, that at the very least.

Cloud coated the sky, tattered in dark strips against the top edge of the ridge closest to Grona. Aryl shivered inside her warm coat. Something unpleasant fell up there. Snow or ice-rain. Their visitors pushed on for good reason. If they kept their pace, they'd be here well before truenight. Only Sona's fourth, she realized. How quickly life could change.

Aryl opened the door and stifled a gasp of dismay. The interior of the second shelter had changed as well. The room ballooned at its far end, the jars wider than tall. The oillights were small suns on the walls, painfully bright. The wind outside, always present, always rustling and moaning, whistled shrill around her legs until she closed the door to keep it out.

Her senses lied for one reason—Myris was worse.

Resolutely, she walked forward and put her tray—a short plank—near the hearth. A container of water. Bowls of Rorn's latest. Ael, beside Myris, flinched. One hand sketched gratitude. Aryl doubted he could eat; Rorn had insisted.

Much of this, and she'd lose her own supper. She averted her eyes from a basket determined first to be a ball, then a waving stalk, trying not to breathe through her nose. None of the odors vying for attention were pleasant.

"Aryl?" Her uncle's dark head lifted, turned in a vague search. Could he not see her?

Fighting back pity, she touched his shoulder, letting him *sense* her presence. "Told you I'd be back, Uncle." Confusion spilled from Myris, this close. Careful to shield herself, Aryl adjusted her aunt's blankets, then went to touch her hand.

Ael grabbed her wrist. "No!"

She didn't resist, allowing her renewed strength to flow

through that contact instead, to him. Gradually, his fingers loosened and something saner showed in his reddened eyes. "Aryl." Convinced, now. "You're here." Glad, if weary to the bone. "Thank you."

She patted the makeshift bed beside Myris. "Why don't you lie down? Rest a moment." The suggestion alone made him yawn. "You'll do her no good exhausted."

"I won't sleep," Ael vowed.

"Of course not. But I'm here now. I'll keep watch."

With a final, doubtful look, Ael laid down, taking great care not to disturb his Chosen, though he had to know nothing so simple would arouse her. Like someone old and stiff, he shuddered with relief as he stretched out.

Suddenly, he looked younger, too young. Aryl blinked as what she should have seen—the mismatch of Yena tunic, Grona leggings, Sona coat they all wore—was replaced by a handsome white shirt, worked with threads, a new tunic, and leg wraps. Her uncle as he'd been the day of Choice.

The vision distorted, then was replaced by reality. The room spun around its axis, spun and tipped. Aryl swallowed bile. If her mind was assailed by chaos from Myris', how much worse was it for Ael?

Aryl pushed aside her pity. They lived.

She laid her hand on that of her mother's sister, and gave what she could of herself.

Heart-kin.

Faded, that bond.

Horribly familiar.

Aryl rose to her feet, moving without sound, hand seeking the hilt of her knife. Ael slept, muscles atwitch as if beset by nightmares. Myris didn't move, hadn't moved. Her battle was deeper and the strength Aryl had given could only help her wage it, not win. The room, for now, was real.

Heart-kin.

That recognition had never made her feel this way before, cold inside. Afraid.

Bern Teerac, once her dearest friend, was here. Bern, now Bern sud Caraat. He wouldn't be alone. He couldn't be. *She* was here as well.

His Chosen. Oran di Caraat. Adept and trouble. The others, Oran's kin.

She had to know why they'd come.

With a final look at Ael and Myris, Aryl went to find out.

The wood platform Tilip had rebuilt along the front of what had just become their meeting hall was jammed with packs. Aryl's lip curled as she looked at them. Overloaded, too heavy, with trailing ropes and hanging bags to snag the carrier at every step. Unless, she reminded herself, the carrier made sure to stay on clear, open, and very flat roads. Grona, if she hadn't already known.

Her hand was almost on the latch when she felt it again. *Heart-kin.*

Aryl opened the door.

Wet fabric. Smoke. Sweat. The less definable odor of whatever cooked in the communal pots. Dust—always that bitterness on the tongue, reminder of time passed and disaster.

What had been life-saving shelter against their first winter storm had four walls and a complete roof in time for the next. If blankets covered gaps packed with splinters and dirt; if the roof took a steep dip at one end so Rorn, their tallest without Enris, had to duck; and if the floor was no more level than any one rough stone? It was a safe place, it was their place, and it was blissfully warm.

The warmth lured her in, but Aryl delayed after she pulled the door back in place and secured its rope, letting her eyes adjust from daylight to the shadow of lamp and fire.

The newcomers, a tight little group, stood beside the cook fire. They hadn't removed their coats; dirty snowmelt puddled around their boots.

They held steaming cups, Sona-made, doubtless more of Rorn's soup. Her people didn't fail in hospitality.

Or in caution. No matter how Om'ray felt drawn together, there was a statement made by who stood closest to these strangers. Haxel, of course, but also Syb and Veca. Did the Grona have the faintest idea how quickly those three could draw knives? Om'ray didn't attack one another. When everything else changed, so could that. As for Cetto and Morla. Experience, diplomacy, dignity. Could the Grona sense their deep abiding anger, their well-learned distrust?

Something tight eased inside her chest. Enris and Haxel might be the only ones to know why she'd left Grona in haste; her people stood by her nonetheless.

Aryl slipped among those who stood against the walls to watch, looking for Seru. No one took their eyes from the Grona as she passed, but hands, held low and inconspicuous, turned to meet hers. *Welcome. Warmth. Caution.* Stranger names: *Gethen. Hoyon. Oswa and Yao. Caraat. Kran and Oran.* One who hadn't been a stranger until now. *Bern.* What little else they'd learned before her arrival. *Adepts. Oran di Caraat. Hoyon d'sud Gethen. A mother, Oswa Gethen. Her child, Yao. A brother, Kran. Oran's and unChosen.*

From a few: *hope.*

From the rest: *distrust.*

Aryl replied in kind, giving a little *strength* through each contact, keeping her *dread* to herself. *Seru?* she asked one. Juo.

Sulking. The other was amused. *He's not ready.* The Chosen were rarely sympathetic to those less fortunate.

There. She spotted Seru where folded blankets made a comfortable bench in their most windproof corner. Her cousin sat, feet together, hands folded on her knees, the image of polite disinterest. Husni and Ziba sat to either side, Taen beside her daughter. Weth was there as well, Chaun supported against her shoulder. Her blindfold hung loose around her neck; she suffered the changes in Sona best when she could see them happen.

Change, this was. Aryl planted herself by Tilip, using his shoulder and arm as a shield past which to see the Grona and not, she hoped, be seen. Not yet.

Kran Caraat was a younger, male copy of his sister. Tall and slender for Grona. Pale of skin and hair, dark eyes. The same facial structure, beautiful and austere, though Oran's bore fine lines at the eyes and mouth. Concentration and effort could have put them there; Aryl was inclined to believe it was temper. Certainly Oran's hair—free, save for a loose cap in the Grona fashion, to express itself—twitched its ends constantly, as if impatient.

The other Adept was heavyset and red-faced. He stood as if about to fall. Unused to exertion, Aryl judged. Or maybe it was the clothing he'd yet to shed. The Grona had come dressed in the kind of cold weather gear they hadn't, for some reason, bothered to give the Yena who'd passed through their village. Thick coats, stuffed round through the sleeves and chest. High boots, also thick with extra lining. Looked hard to move in, impossible to bend—perhaps why she hadn't seen a Grona bow yet. She'd have thought it ridiculous, if she hadn't experienced a winter storm.

Hoyon's daughter Yao was a waist-high shadow behind her mother, a shadow herself. Aryl frowned. The child was too young to travel away from safety; not that any of them should be here. Oswa Gethen silently sipped from her cup as the others murmured pleasantries; her brown hair shifted slowly over her shoulders. Exhausted, at a guess. She'd have the added burden of shielding the unfettered emotions of so young an Om'ray, though to be honest, of them all, only one looked able to walk another step.

And was the most relaxed of them here, by face and voice. Why not? Cetto and Husni were his grandparents. Weth—who squinted uncomfortably at him as much as smiled—an aunt.

He who'd been Bern Teerac stood among friends as well as family, a homecoming the likes of which no unChosen who'd left on Passage could expect.

Did he also expect a welcome?

Bern turned his head to stare right at her, as if somehow hearing his name in her thoughts. He hadn't. He couldn't. No matter the bond they'd forged as heart-kin, hers was the stronger Power. He could never see into her mind without permission, a permission she'd never again give. Not when his was Joined for life with Oran di Caraat's.

Could he see her heart, *feel* what she kept from the others?

Let him. Aryl made herself smile.

"We came," he said, as if to her alone, "because I knew you'd need help."

"What kind of help, Grandson?" Cetto's deep voice drew Bern back around.

"Yena don't know the mountains—"

"Ah." A warning in that tone, to those who knew Haxel. "You came to give us good Grona advice."

Bern, who did, gestured a hasty apology. "Of course not." He quelled a scowling Hoyon with a look. "Oran and Hoyon are Adepts—"

"Troublemakers, you mean." This from Veca. Tilip stirred beside Aryl, echoing his Chosen's anger. "We've no need for Adepts."

"Peace, Veca." Barely taller than Ziba, Morla's soft voice nonetheless commanded attention. "These are our guests. They may have more to offer. Something useful. Can you grow food, Adept?" to Hoyon, who looked as if a small biter had attached itself to his nose. "Can you tile a roof?" to Oran, whose hair twitched its outrage. Morla shrugged. "If you can't, well, no offense, younglings, but you should go back where others will provide for you. We will not."

"You need me," Oran replied with total conviction. "You've injuries."

"This?" the former Councillor lifted her bandaged wrist and

flexed the fingers of that hand. "Doesn't slow me at all." Veca grinned.

"Oran is a Healer," said Bern stiffly. "Her Talent drew us to your need." He pointed to Chaun and Weth, the latter looking up with abrupt hope. "How could we not dare this difficult journey? We're family. Om'ray. Nothing else matters."

A stir throughout the room. Healers were rare. Valued. Oran hadn't, Aryl realized with a chill, been wrong to expect a welcome here.

She did wonder what Grona's Council thought of their own people roaming the slopes after a pack of exiled, ungrateful Yena.

"We don't ask to stay. We brought our own supplies." Oran's glance into her cup was less than appreciative. "Give me a tenth, no more, to rest from the journey, and I'll do what I can for your people before we leave. We'll be gone by truenight."

"We can't go so soon!" Oswa spoke for the first time, a hand fumbling for her daughter. "We can't! Hoyon, tell them. There's a storm coming—Yao's too small. She's already exhausted."

An instinctive swell of *care* and *reassurance* answered. Oswa quieted in response, her lips trembling, eyes wide as she looked from face to face. Strangers to her, Aryl reminded herself.

Haxel made a brusque gesture. "No one goes out in truenight or bad weather."

Hoyon managed to bow despite the coat. "Thank you."

The First Scout's smile twisted her scar. "As for you, Oran di Caraat? If you're a Healer, prove it now."

Aryl watched Bern walk out in the road past the coals of the watch fire, make a bold show of scouting for threat. No self-respecting Yena would swing his head from side to side when a subtle flick of eyes covered the same range without shifting balance. A display for Oran's benefit, no doubt. Was he aware of his surroundings . . . did he see what they were building here?

From Haxel's sour expression, she wasn't the only one to judge him. The First Scout went to the door of the second shelter, but didn't open it. "In here." When Bern went to enter, she snapped, "Not you."

Oran hesitated, her yellow hair moving in heavy, unsettled waves, ends plucking at the weave of her scarf.

"I'll come with you," Aryl said quickly. If the Grona Adept was a Healer, the sooner she saw Myris the better. "It's my aunt."

"Myris?" Bern gave her a startled look. "What happened? Is Ael all right?"

So now he cared?

Her own scorn made her ashamed. He'd known them all his life, too. "She was struck by falling ice, like Chaun. Ael's with her."

"Where you should be." Haxel looked set to grab Oran and throw her through the door.

Before that disaster of manners could occur—inciting a justified rebellion in their hoped-for Healer, not to mention her Chosen's likely regrettable response—Aryl pulled the door aside. Oran pressed close, in a hurry to see Myris or avoid Haxel. Or both.

The door closed behind them.

Aryl was relieved to see the room appeared itself. Ael looked up, surprise on his face. "Who's this?"

"The Healer," Oran announced, sweeping forward. She couldn't quite manage warmth in her voice, but bowed graciously in the Grona fashion as she removed her scarf and opened her coat. Both garments were thrust at Aryl. "I'm Oran di Caraat. I've come to aid your Chosen."

"You're too young to be an Adept."

Aryl managed not to smile.

"Do you want my help or not?"

As "not" wasn't an option, either for Myris or the grim First Scout waiting outside, Aryl spoke up. "Uncle, let her try."

Oran's hair gave an annoyed flick. At her use of the word "try," no doubt. Confidence was important, Aryl reminded herself. She put the Adept's outerwear on a basket—mercifully square and solid—and found a place to stand she hoped would be out of Oran's way.

Ael knelt by Myris, brushed limp hair from her forehead, then took her hand. "Go ahead," he said at last.

The Adept frowned at them. "I require privacy. A Healer is left alone—"

"No."

Only the word. Ael didn't look away from Myris to say it, but Oran knew better than to argue. She went to her knees beside the platform of blankets, the fingers of both hands touching as if to net a ball of air. She closed her eyes and moved her hands, still fingertip to fingertip, over Myris. Side to side, across her waist. Lower down. Then, up to her head. Aryl could detect the stir of Power; she didn't dare *taste* it and risk the other's concentration.

The movement of Oran's hands ended above Myris' forehead. Aryl didn't know what to expect. She focused on breathing very quietly.

The ugly bruise began to fade, from purple-black to brown to yellow, hopefully not another trick by her senses.

The gash itself knitted from both ends at once, until it became a smooth seam, nothing more than a scar.

This was beyond what Yena's Healers could do, Aryl was sure. Their best could speed healing by days, not cause it to occur before your eyes. Was this what Yorl sud Sarc, her mother's great-uncle, had done for his own ailing body? He'd needed her strength. Did Oran?

Aryl looked at the Adept. Her eyelids were half-closed, revealing only the whites of her eyes. Her face, chapped and reddened by days in the cold, had a new, sickly pallor. A sign of the effort she expended, to use her Power this way? Whatever else she felt about the Grona, this she respected. Should she offer—

Oran muttered under her breath, then screamed! The air filled with the miasma of rot, wet and cloying. The Adept's terrified face stretched until her chin touched the bed and ran below it. The world began to slip sideways, as if they clung to a great rastis as it fell . . .

"My-ris!" Her voice or Ael's?

Oran—the blur of color that was Oran to Aryl's distorted sight—continued to flow away. No, she fell! Aryl threw herself forward to catch the Adept, ease her to the floor. She heard a shout that turned itself to birdsong. Bern, she guessed.

Haxel would keep him out. Had to keep him out. It wasn't safe here.

For anyone.

Words walked by and shouted themselves at her. "Don't! Leave! Stay! Stay! Hold!"

Ael.

Leave?

Aryl fastened on the word, remembering what had happened with Enris, what she suspected about the Lost.

Was Myris—her mind—caught in the M'hir?

Without hesitation, without fear for herself, Aryl dove into that inner darkness.

MYRIS!

She *reached* for her aunt with all her strength, summoned an image of her well, of those wide gray eyes—so like her own—sparkling with mirth, her cheery smile . . .

. . . *Aryl* . . . ?

Faint, frightened.

. . . *where . . . am I Lost?*

NO! Aryl's denial coursed down that tenuous connection, Power forging a deeper, stronger pathway—like the Sona river, cutting through rock itself.

Amazement.

Ael?

Aryl refused to be distracted by his presence, or what it meant. She *reached* for her aunt, as she would when trying to contact her in the real world. *Myris. Listen to me. Hold on.*

. . . Aryl . . . ? Stronger. Still frightened. *Confusion* threatened their link. *Where is this place? Where are we?*

We're riding the M'hir, Aryl sent, adding *encouragement* and *calm* to the words. *Follow me home.*

As she had with Enris, Aryl *gathered* what was Myris close to her. Even as she held herself within the M'hir, she sensed Ael's presence as an echo of brightness, steady and sure.

And more.

Suddenly, she realized she could see—*sense*—all of the exiles. Not *where* they were, but *what* they were. Their Power, their vitality. They might have been her little fiches, aglow, dancing within that unseen wind. So much more than she'd ever felt before.

Enris, too. She *reached* for him, stopping just in time, fought to focus. Almost free. *Stay with me, Aunt,* she urged, holding on with all her strength.

There . . . at the edge of this strange vision. Another presence she *knew.*

Not aware but as clear to her as if she saw him standing before her. What was Yorl doing in the M'hir?

Yet another. Taisal? Her mother. Unlike the rest, she watched, somehow. Was aware, somehow. Suddenly . . . she was closer . . . she was . . .

Here. The connection between them locked in place.

Help or leave! Aryl sent fiercely as she concentrated on Myris, on keeping Myris with her . . . on escape . . .

You can't save her. An upwelling of *grief* threw the M'hir into chaos. *She is Lost.*

No! Not while I have her . . . Aryl tried to pull free of Taisal, who resisted. Insisted.

Save yourself!

As they struggled, tangled in the M'hir, in themselves . . . memory blurred. Did she see Taisal's tears at their parting, or feel her own? Did her heart pound with a mother's despair, or a daughter's rage? Which of them disobeyed, which of them punished, which of them would take a step to save the other, if it risked the rest . . .

Neither . . . they were Sarc, of a kind, and there would never be doubt. Their people came first.

The link strengthened, raw Power coursing between them. The M'hir steadied, grew almost calm.

Daughter.

Mother.

Myris . . . Aryl struggled to hold that dim, frightened presence . . . began to fail . . . *MOTHER!*

We have her. Go.

A *flood* of Power, as if the M'hir itself threw them clear.

Hesitantly, Aryl opened her eyes.

The room was real.

Myris lay motionless. As before.

Then, without warning, a lock of hair stirred on the blanket. It slipped up and around Ael's wrist and with a glad cry, he bent over his Chosen. Dark hair blended with gold. His shields were nonexistent.

Aryl quickly tightened hers. "Ael. Uncle? Is she all right?"

He eased back, looked at her. Tears streaked his face. "Aryl. Yes. Thank you. Thank you. You did it."

Aryl didn't correct him. But she hadn't done it alone. Taisal had risked herself in the M'hir to save them.

Why?

After condemning her for traveling the M'hir to save others. After helping exile—condemn—those the Adepts judged a threat to Yena.

Why?

With Yena protected, was that it? Was Taisal di Sarc willing to help her daughter and sister then?

Had she wanted to before?

Did it change anything?

"You'd better help the Healer."

Aryl was aghast to see Oran sprawled on the dirt-and-stone floor as if her bones were missing. Her eyelids fluttered and jerked open as she fought to stay awake. Her eyes, when they showed, were shot through with blood, their expression alternately vague and alert. They found Aryl, seemed to ask a question.

"Ael says Myris is better—" a scowl dismissed that answer. What else? The rising commotion at the door? "I'll let Bern in," she assured the Adept, but as she rose to do just that, Oran's hand clawed at her wrist.

"How—" she had to lean down to catch the broken whisper— neither of them had lowered shields, "—how dare you— should have—warned me—"

Remorseful, Aryl gestured apology. She hadn't considered any risk to Oran. Weren't Healers able to protect themselves? Maybe one older, with more experience, could have—not an observation to make Oran feel better. Instead, she bowed her head, Grona-fashion. "You saved them both." That, to ease her pain. "Thank you."

Oran finally put a sentence together. "Get me off this filthy floor."

Myris woke with a smile. She looked bemused to find Aryl by her bed. "You're back already? How was your journey? What did you find?"

She'd found a river emptied of the water Sona needed. She'd found a Cloisters surrounded by the dead.

Aryl smiled and did her best to radiate *confidence*. "Haxel's going to make me one of her scouts if I'm not careful. Let me tell you all about it." She settled, cross-legged, and gave her haggard uncle a meaningful look. "How would you like some of Rorn's latest?"

Myris lifted one hand, sketched a fitful apology. "I couldn't . . ."

She could. Success was measured in spoons of soup, what kind none of them knew. It was warm and savory and Ael sud Sarc willingly emptied his own bowl as he listened, too.

Aryl described her adventures up the valley, taking shameless advantage of her aunt's attention to trickle spoonfuls between her dry lips. Four. Five. A talent she'd never expected.

The soup's virtue showed in her uncle's relaxed smile and the faint color on her aunt's cheeks, although she was sure Ael responded more to his Chosen conscious and eating than to his own full stomach.

They'd had no visitors. Oran had hurried out, presumably to her solicitous Chosen; Haxel hadn't come in.

She, Aryl decided, wasn't leaving her aunt. The outer wound had healed, any visible sign of injury was gone, but Myris remained dangerously close to the M'hir. She could *sense* it. Like the edge of the glows in Yena, where the dark of truenight began, where the swarms fed. It was all she could do to hold her shields and smile, talk about rock hunters and crazed Oud.

When she came to the part about the pending Visitation, Ael's spoon stopped in midair. "The Oud are coming?" Dismay. On both faces.

If they weren't here now—a notion Aryl kept to herself. "They're willing to discuss restoring water to the river," she pointed out. "I think that's worth a visit."

"Listen to her, Ael. Our little Aryl, the Speaker. Taisal would be—" she faltered, her eyes swimming with tears. "I'm sorry."

"Don't be," Aryl said gently. She stroked her aunt's hand, sending *reassurance* and strength through the touch. "I wish she was here, too. Better her talking to the not-*real* than me."

"Why?" Ael bristled. "Yena's had no dealings with Oud. You've done more . . . with them . . . with the Tikitik." He waved his spoon in the air. "Those strangers, too."

Not a reminder she wanted, but she managed to smile. "I suppose."

"I must get out of this bed. Meet our strangers." Myris

changed the subject with her usual perception. "You said there was an unChosen, didn't you?"

Ael looked down at his Chosen, their eyes meeting for a moment, then glanced up at Aryl. He had the oddest expression on his face. She couldn't tell if it was surprise or hope. "Yes," he said. "You go, Aryl. Get to know him."

Get to know Kran Caraat? "You, Uncle, could use a nap," she retorted. "I'll stay here, thanks. Seru can get to know him, if she wants. She's the Chooser."

Myris smiled gently. "As you will be soon, daughter of our hearts."

She would? Aryl closed her mouth and stared at her aunt.

"Myris is never wrong," Ael asserted. "Don't waste more time with us. We're fine, thanks to you. See who's going to be available. No need to let Seru pick the best!"

Pick the . . . she couldn't utter a word. Instead, Aryl filled the spoon with soup. "Three more," she challenged.

After that . . . she refused to imagine.

Aryl blinked when she stepped out of the shelter. Blinked and shivered. The wind had become a capricious howl, chill and promising worse to come. Despite the cold, someone waited, little more than a taut shadow. She smiled. "Myris will be fine, Haxel. They both will. You can go in if you—"

"Healer looked worse than Chaun. Sent her and Bern to rest. What about you? Can you scout for the Oud now?"

If the words were hoarse, and the First Scout's tightest shields couldn't hide a tumult sof *gladness/guilt/relief/shame*, Aryl wasn't about to show she noticed. "Of course. I need to—"

"Get it done. I don't want any more surprises." With that, Haxel headed for the other building.

No rest yet, then. Aryl gave a contented sigh. Some things— some Om'ray—should never change.

She'd wanted a chance to use the geoscanner. Had it only

been this morning she'd received it from Marcus? She shook her head. The sun was on its way behind the mountains, going wherever it went before returning to Amna tomorrow. Their fourth truenight at Sona.

They wouldn't, she judged, see this sunset. Cloud already coated the sky, tattered in dark strips against the top edge of the ridge toward Grona. Something unpleasant fell up there. Snow or ice-rain. Oran had pushed her little flock for good reason.

Unlikely Haxel would tell the rest why she was wandering the ruins. Aryl grimaced. Some would think she'd avoided the Grona.

Would that she could.

None of the exiles believed they'd followed only to offer help, but they'd be willing to leave it at that. Om'ray manners. Tradition.

By that same tradition, Kran should have a token, but brought his sister instead. Why? Adepts never left their Clan, yet these two had. Why? The child, Yao, was hardly old enough to walk, to judge by her size. Too young to risk outside her village, let alone traveling through the mountains in winter. Why?

The exiles had rushed to have Oran care for their injured. What of the Grona? Did they truly plan to go home after offering their "help"?

Tonight, Aryl vowed, there would be answers.

After she checked Sona for the Oud.

She activated the device.

Nothing . . .

Aryl walked as Marcus had instructed, the device held discreetly in her hand, hand near her waist so a downward glance sufficed. No need to lay it directly on the ground, if her steps were smooth and even. He'd smiled as if this was funny, and told her he'd didn't think she could move any other way.

The Human said the oddest things.

She kept her shields tight, her sense of the others no more than *there* and *here*, the inner comfort of *close*. A relief to be

among Om'ray again. She pushed away thoughts of Enris, who
was not.

The *range* of the geoscanner was narrow—a compromise to
allow it to look more deeply underground, he'd told her. Good
enough for her purpose. She'd start with the roads that bordered the reconstruction, then cut through the path between
the buildings. Haxel was right—they needed to be sure they
were safe where they slept.

Nothing . . .

Their visitors were there. In the "meeting hall" with the remaining exiles. Emotions—*gratitude/curiosity/caution*—were
barely perceptible now, politely tucked behind shields.

Her sleeves were too long; her Sona coat needed altering.
The net she'd repaired was no better fit. Hair whipped against
her cheek and she shoved it behind one ear. "Pick the best?"
Aryl muttered under her breath. She'd blame Myris' troubling
pronouncement on her aunt's head wound, but . . . Ael was
right. Myris infallibly predicted the next Choosers.

Part of her Talent, she supposed.

She didn't feel any different. Other than being so off-
balance she wouldn't trust herself crossing a bridge.

Enris. He'd have known this about her. Wouldn't he? Her
heart pounded. He would have known and stayed for her.
Wouldn't he? She had to believe it.

So it wasn't her time, Aryl told herself firmly. No matter
what Myris sensed. Not yet.

The wind buffeted her as she left the taller ruins. She ignored it. Nothing . . . nothing. When the first snowdrops
began, she blinked them from her eyelashes and used her other
hand to shield the glow of the device. Her fingers numbed.

Nothing . . .

Aryl eased through the path between the meeting hall and
shelter, heading back where she'd started. Despite the inner
warmth of being surrounded by Om'ray, she was beyond cold.
The snowdrops, thick and wet, were already a nuisance.

Not the only one. Bern. Out of the shelter, alone.

Sensing his approach, she casually pulled her hands into the too-long sleeves of her undercoat, turning the one with the geoscanner so he wouldn't see its faint glow. She should, Aryl told herself in disgust, have expected him.

He climbed the wall to wait, a silhouette of unknown intention. She stopped short. "What do you want, Bern?"

Bern jumped down, crushing dead stalks beneath his boots as he approached. "We can't leave tonight. Oran's barely conscious. She needs to recover."

Explaining why he was here, Aryl wondered, or how? She couldn't imagine Oran di Caraat in favor of a private meeting between her Chosen and an old friend. Still. "I'm sorry. I didn't know she couldn't protect herself—"

"Oh, Oran's quite convinced you made her suffer because of me. She'll never trust you." A hint of pride in his voice, as if this pleased him. He came closer, too close, but Aryl refused to step back. "I do. I know you better than that, Aryl. Better than anyone." Beneath the words, he sent, *Heart-kin. You could never hurt someone, no matter how provoked.* With entirely unwelcome *affection.* Aloud, "We need to talk, now, before she—"

"Before she shuts you up," Aryl supplied helpfully, shielding her *disgust.*

When Bern Teerac had come to her before leaving Yena on Passage, he'd worn his favorite heavy tunic, woven from supple braid, lovingly inlaid with slices of bleached and polished dresel pod by his father. Protection from claw and tooth, camouflage from other hunters.

Bern sud Caraat stood before her now buried inside a too-fat Grona coat, his powerful legs trapped in too-fat boots. Useless clothing. Was that what happened to those who left their Clan? Did they abandon all that was good from their past and accept the shape of their future without question?

Not Enris.

"Yes," Bern admitted easily. "Oran, though wonderful and wise, detests you. I suppose it's my fault—my best memories have you in them." *Heart-kin.*

Aryl gritted her teeth. "My feet are cold, Bern. Get to the point."

Snowdrops slid down his coat, clung to his eyelashes. "Oran's too proud to ask for help. I'm not—not from you. I convinced her you'd listen—"

"Not if this is about—"

"It's not." He dared reach for her arm. This time she moved to put space between them. "This is about Passage. Our Passage. We—I need you to speak to the rest. For us. We want to stay. To become part of your Clan, of Sona."

Aryl found herself colder inside than out. The words made no sense at all. If she'd dared, she'd have lowered her shields and *felt* the truth mind-to-mind. "Part of Sona," she echoed in disbelief. "Why?"

Bern did know her. Too well. His mindvoice, once so familiar, flooded her thoughts. *The Grona aren't like us, Heart-kin. They interfere. They tell me what to do, how to behave, where to sleep. They keep Oran in their Cloisters . . . to keep us . . . to—*a wild flash of *despair* and *need—we've never touched! They won't allow a baby while she's in training. I'm dying inside, Aryl. You'll help me, won't you? Let us live here, as Chosen should!*

So Ael had been right, Aryl thought with pity. Oran was too young to be an Adept. Grona couldn't stop her Choice—but they could control her Joining. "You want me to believe Oran di Caraat's willing to give up her home and Cloisters to live here, in Sona's mud. With us."

"I told her. Promised her. If she came, proved her worth, you might change your mind. I know—" Aryl opened her mouth to protest. "—I know you'll give her a chance." *Heart-kin . . . for me.*

A trade. Bern tried to trade her Talent for their Joining bed. *Heart-kin . . . please . . .*

Was it Bern's fault—any incomplete Chosen would be desperate—or Grona's? Which, she sighed to herself, was worse? "What about Hoyon and the rest?"

"Their soft-headed Council agreed to let us come tend your injured. They have other Healers. The Adepts," a snarl to the word, "weren't so sure. They sent Hoyon and Oswa with us to make sure we came back."

"And to keep you apart," she hazarded.

"Yes. But Oran persuaded Hoyon to stay."

She could guess the argument. Her secret had spread before she'd found a chance to tell those who deserved it. Aryl found her mother's smile. "Here's an idea for you, Bern. Get her pregnant, then go back. They can hardly close the screens once the biters are inside."

Bern's handsome face turned sullen.

Aryl winced. Oh, she knew that look. It meant he'd tried exactly that and been rebuffed. Oran protected her future. If they had to return, she wouldn't risk the Adepts refusing to train her. She wouldn't accept being anything less among her own people.

As for what she could be here? "What do you want me to do, Bern?" If they were children again, she thought wistfully, she could kick his shin. Hard.

"Speak for us. That's all. Your people don't trust Adepts—for good reason, I know—but you could vouch for us. They'll listen to you. They trust you." *As I trust you, Heart-kin.*

The *affection* repulsed her, but she couldn't shield against it. "They trust me not to make mistakes."

"What mistake? You need a Healer."

"Not anymore."

"You need unChosen. Oran brought her own brother for your Choice—"

Aryl was speechless.

"You need me, Aryl." Bern came closer still, until she couldn't see past him. "You blame yourself for all of it—how Yena sent us, her unChosen, away, the Tikitik attack, the exile of those here. You're torn between guilt and responsibility, with no one else to talk to, no one else who understands you, who remembers the joy you used to take in life." *Heart-kin. Let me stay. Let me be your friend again, share your burden, remind you how to laugh.*

The wind and falling snow blurred their surroundings, turned the world into a small space, trapped them inside. As intimate as the canopy, vistas behind curtains of vine or rain, havens within the shadow of a frond. Aryl lifted her hand, touched his chest. *We were good friends.*

They'd been more. She'd loved him once, wanted nothing more than to be together, always, had saved his life instead of Costa's for that love.

We can be again, Heart-kin. Help me have my Chosen. His *lust* was like a slap. *I can't wait much longer. Please.*

She pushed him away. "You always did talk too much, Bern." And she'd been a fool once already. Love. Her lips twisted. The word she'd given Marcus counted for so little, in the end, to an Om'ray. Snowdrops melted on her eyelashes; they could have been tears. Bern deluded himself if he thought Oran would let him be her friend in any way.

But he was right—they had been heart-kin. She couldn't forget that.

"I can't make any promises," Aryl said at last. "I don't know yet if I can move through the M'hir safely—let alone if I should teach anyone else. We've been busy staying alive. You can't make promises either," she cautioned when he made to speak. "You don't control the Adepts."

"But you'll speak for us. You'll let us stay." With *triumph.*

He did know her, too well. Aryl tightened her shields. "It's up to Oran and Hoyon. Sona needs more Om'ray, not more problems. If they'll stay—and work—under our terms?" However unlikely that seemed. "I'll do my best."

Heart-kin.

"Don't make me sorry, Bern," she warned.

Heart-kin. With that cloying *affection.*

"Once. Not now."

Another warning, if he was wise.

Aryl had done harder things than enter the crowded meeting hall and smile, but those had involved imminent death and pain at the hands—or claws—of the not-*real*. This was a room full of her people, her family. If she couldn't accept the Grona in the same spirit, she owed Bern her best effort not to see them as intruders.

Which wasn't easy when Oran, sitting wrapped in a blanket in pride of place on the new bench, gave her a look of pure fury.

So much for peace in that family.

Her outer clothing dripping wet, she stayed near the wall by the door, using the moment to tuck the geoscanner securely away, then hung her coat and scarf on wooden pegs hammered between wall beams. Bern, who'd come through the door behind her, did the same. She felt his stare on her leg and arm wraps, her tunic. She was still Yena, as he was not.

Before she could work her way to a quiet seat near a back corner, Haxel beckoned her to her side, near the fire. Those seated between lifted their hands to hers. Without hesitation, Aryl brushed her fingertips across them, receiving their *welcome,* sending back *warmth.* How it looked to the Grona, she didn't know or care.

Bern, used to how things had been, was probably scandalized.

A comforting order had developed. Their eldest, Husni and Cetto, Morla and Lendin, sat on stacks of folded blankets, in the warmest part of the room by the fire, safe from the worst drafts. Their largest families had their spots, the Kessa'ats here, the Uruus with Seru, there. Myris and Ael, looking worn but happy, sat with Juo Vendan. Of Juo's kin, Haxel rarely stayed in one place, and either Rorn or Gijs were on watch. The unChosen, Kayd, Cader, and Fon, were together—usually as near to where the food was as was polite.

They had not, Aryl noticed, added Kran Caraat to their ranks. He sat with Hoyon and Oswa, off to one side. Hard to tell they were close kin.

Yao wasn't with her parents, though she had to be here, somewhere. Aryl sensed no glow in Sona beyond Gijs on guard outside the door. She looked around the room; with the improvements to the roof and smoke vent, the air was clear. Was the child with Ziba? She spotted Ziba curled between Seru and her mother, as if for protection. Which, now that Aryl thought about it, was a very good idea. Ziba's shields were not yet mature. They confined most of her emotions, allowed her to roam from her mother without disturbing the minds of other Om'ray, but they were less than trustworthy around an upset younger Om'ray.

The last thing they needed right now would be the two of them expressing their personal reactions and needs with all the strength of instinct.

Aryl took a place beside Haxel, every tenth of this day expressed in the relief of being off her feet. She took the bowl passed to her by the Kessa'ats, gesturing gratitude to all involved with her free hand. "No Oud."

"What did he want?"

"Bern?" She blew steam from a spoonful she was too tired to want. "Freedom from Grona's rules. Rules concerning their Adept."

"That's the way of it?" The scar twisted along the First Scout's cheek. "No wonder he looks to be sitting on a thickle. Wouldn't let anyone interfere with mine." *Fondness.* Across the room, Rorn sud Vendan glanced their way and broke into one of his rare smiles.

The unChosen, among themselves, chafed at the connection between Joined pairs, felt excluded from what they envied and longed for—their own completion. Hadn't she complained about Chosen secrets and their silly, besotted looks? But lately, what she noticed wasn't what was the same about the Chosen, but what was different. Each pair was unique. Haxel and Rorn went their separate ways and showed no obvious affection, yet Aryl couldn't imagine one without the other. Ael and Myris were miserable on their own. Tilip and Veca might argue every waking moment, but they worked shoulder-to-shoulder whenever they could.

Costa and Leri? They'd stay apart for tenths for no reason than the joy of reuniting again. There had been a time she'd thought them fools.

Bern and Oran. Those were the fools. The connection between them should have brought them joy. It should have Joined the best of each. From all she could tell, so far it had brought out the worst.

Or maybe it was Grona. Hoyon and Oswa didn't appear too happy with each other either.

"Think they'd stay?"

Aryl startled back to herself. "I don't know. Do we want them?"

"That may not be up to us. Look." Haxel nodded to where Chaun lay, Weth supporting his shoulders.

Oran knelt beside them, on a folded blanket. Her hair rose around her head as she passed her coupled hands over Chaun's chest. She had the rapt attention of every Om'ray in the low-ceiling hall.

Chaun coughed, then took a deep, free breath. He looked up in wonder. "Nothing hurts." Weth, though her eyes were closed, smiled tremulously. Both gestured gratitude as Oran rose.

The Healer staggered and would have fallen if Bern and Husni hadn't hurried to support her. Whether planned or necessary, it left the right impression. Smiles, more gestures, murmurs of appreciation, followed as Bern escorted her back to her bench seat.

"Nicely done," Haxel commented.

Aryl concentrated on her stew.

A moment later, Ael and Myris approached. Aryl stood quickly, and lifted her hands to her aunt, assessing how she looked. Weary, yes, but the wound looked months healed and her smile was every bit as bright as it used to be. When their fingers touched, the M'hir was its normal, distant roar to her inner sense. "You're better," she said, relieved.

Ael gestured gratitude with one hand, his other arm firmly around his Chosen. "Thanks to you as much as our new Healer."

"No need for that," Aryl said, hoping he took her meaning. She wanted no questions from Oran about her own ability.

"Of course," he agreed, a twinkle in his eye. "Now, we're off to bed."

"Ael insists I need more rest." Myris' smile acquired a mischievous dimple. "I haven't heard that excuse for years."

Definitely better. Aryl let them feel her *joy*.

Around them, things had settled to a quiet buzz of conversation. Impolite, to speak mind-to-mind in front of others. The topics were carefully neutral: projects underway, projects to be tackled, the not-unpleasant but different flavor of tonight's stew. Sona's Om'ray, carefully avoiding their visitors.

Not Grona's way. Aryl was sure every exile remembered— not happily—the questioning they'd faced before Grona's full Council. Everyone but Ziba had had to give their version of the events that led them from Yena to the mountains.

They'd all lied, of course. They'd kept the secret of the stranger's aircar, claiming Oud had brought them. They'd omitted being exiled for their new and Forbidden Talents, for their willingness to change, claiming instead the Tikitik's attack on Yena meant some had to leave, to preserve enough supplies for the rest.

Maybe that was why no one asked an accounting from these new arrivals. They feared lies in return.

When had Om'ray come to this? Wrong. Wrong.

Aryl found herself on her feet. Voices hushed as all turned to look at her.

Haxel radiated *satisfaction*.

What would Taisal do? Civil behavior. Aryl combined a bow that wasn't quite Grona with the sweeping two-handed gesture of gratitude that was pure Yena, directed at Oran. The adult Grona gave halting bows in return. "Welcome to Sona, Oran. Bern—" beside his Chosen on the bench, "—Hoyon and Oswa.

Kran and—" the tiny child was impossible to see among the rest "—Yao." When in doubt, be formal. "We are Sona Clan, and we are pleased to offer you shelter from the storm." Which cooperatively moaned and hammered against their newly stout walls.

As everyone reacted to the thought of being outside those walls—Oswa with wide eyes and a grab for a blanket—Aryl continued, gaining confidence. "Thank you, Oran, for putting your duty as Healer and Adept ahead of your own well-deserved rest." She paused to let the exiles once more gesture their thanks. Chaun and Weth cuddled against the wall, Husni close by.

Oran managed to bow her head graciously. Her shields, to Aryl's perception, were flawless.

As were her own. Aryl smiled. "I believe I speak for every-one when I invite you to stay, if that's your wish. Sona will need strong hands and backs for the work ahead."

The quiet laughter wasn't altogether kind. Of the Grona, only Bern had calluses, and those weren't fresh. Oran? Likely never sweated a day in her life.

Sona had no room for idlers.

Or lies. "You didn't come because we needed a Healer. You came to Sona on Passage, hoping to stay. I'm sure everyone is curious . . . why." The hush following her statement was tangi-ble. Aryl could see Hoyon gathering himself to be first to speak. Oran's face turned sickly pale; Bern gathered her in his arms.

Aryl sensed threads of *anxiety* drawing the exiles close. Most wanted to put the past behind them. Was she proposing to re-veal their truth in turn?

There was nothing to gain either way, she decided. The ex-iles were ready to forget Yena. As for the Grona? If she re-vealed Bern's plight, she'd humiliate him and Oran in front of everyone. If she told the truth about what the Adepts sought—to trade their help and unChosen for knowledge of her ability in the M'hir—she'd be forced to make that potentially danger-ous decision here and now.

Leaving her one choice.

"We've come for the same reason," she stated. "To shelter from a storm. Sona has given us that and more—a new Clan, a new life. Does it matter why any of us started the journey? We're here. Only what we do together, from this moment, is important.

"I say anyone who comes to Sona for shelter should leave their past on the road. I say we should accept you for who you are and what you do here." *DO YOU AGREE, SONA?* She sent to every mind, with all her strength, unintentionally dipping into the M'hir to reinforce her question.

The answer came back in an outpouring of *warmth* and *welcome*. The exiles surged to their feet and—rare for Om'ray—clustered around the startled Grona, offering their hands, patting shoulders. There were tears in not a few eyes.

Aryl stood apart with Haxel, watching. She'd done what she could for Bern: silenced the Grona before they could lie or expose themselves, and given them a way to become part of Sona.

"Hoyon looks ready to choke," the First Scout commented.

Aryl shrugged. "He didn't plan to stay. He may not. Depends how persuasive Oran can be."

"They'll leave when they get what they want."

Watching Oswa smile shyly at Taen, Yao chase Ziba through a grove of adult legs, Aryl shrugged again. "Maybe they'll find more here than they expected."

Haxel snorted. "More work, that's for sure. We'd best keep watch on them."

"I couldn't refuse," she admitted, now worried. Likely the older Chosen's intention. "He's still—well, I couldn't."

"Think they didn't know?" Haxel laughed at whatever showed on Aryl's face. "Take it as a compliment. You look for the best. I prepare for the worst."

Which had she just done?

Interlude

PASSAGE WAS DANGEROUS. Other unChosen, Enris assured himself, suffered and often died trying to reach their one true Choice. Or the Chooser easiest to reach. He'd never been fully clear on that part. They suffered and often died, with dignity. Alone.

While his fate was to be inflicted with unasked, unwelcome company. First that perverse Oud had dragged him through its tunnels, and now this . . .

"You don't have to come," he said wearily.

Thought Traveler barked its laugh. "But you are such a curiosity, Enris Mendolar. How can I leave before seeing how you end?"

The Tikitik had matched him stride for stride all day. At first, Enris had tried to ignore it. Then argue with it. Finally, he'd given up.

The creature had its use. Hard Ones shuddered and rolled aside well ahead of their approach, clearing an uncanny path. Thought Traveler claimed to regularly hunt them in this area. If so, it wasn't particularly effective. Or the Hard Ones bred quickly. There was no end to them in sight.

The mountainside was in sight, too. His other problem. With every step closer, its slope looked worse: cliffs steeper than those on the other side of the valley—the ones he'd avoided climbing; the few ravines choked with loose stone. Presumably, at least some of them alive.

"I may end here," he muttered.

The Tikitik had unfortunately good hearing, for a creature without obvious ears. "Any Yena could climb it."

He didn't bother to argue with it. Firstnight was here. The weather was turning colder, windier—warning of another storm on the way, to make life perfect. Enris tightened the straps on his pack. Down the valley it would have to be, a difficult but not impossible path. The ground was disturbed right to the rock, heaved into loose mounds higher than his head. He'd have to find a way between them.

"Why go that way?" Thought Traveler bounded ahead and stopped, forcing Enris to do the same. Facing it put him too close for comfort to the cluster of worms that covered its mouth, and he took an involuntary step back. "I thought you were on Passage to Vyna."

"As you've noticed, I'm not Yena," Enris said dryly. "I'll go around, thank you. You don't have to come." He tried to pass the creature.

Its hand shot out, fastening on his arm like a metal clamp before he could avoid it. "Do you seek death? The ground is not what it seems, Tuana. Look carefully."

The first line of heaved dirt rose within a few steps. Enris obliged the Tikitik by studying it, since he couldn't shake its grip. Dirt. With the occasional wisp of dead plant. Stones. More dirt. The whole zigged and zagged at angles to the mountain, like a giant furrow in a field. Weathered, solid, and altogether unremarkable.

Except for its origins. Enris stiffened. "Is that what you meant—when you said Sona was in more danger than I was? Are the Oud about to reshape this again?"

The Tikitik released him. Enris didn't bother glaring at the creature—in his experience, the not-real didn't care about his opinion of their actions. "I'm impressed, Tuana. You know your neighbors."

He had to warn her—to urge Aryl and the exiles to run—but even as Enris formed a sending, his concentration was broken by a hideous scream.

"Ah," said Thought Traveler calmly. "Here is a neighbor you do not know."

Another scream. Ears ringing, half crouched, Enris desperately looked for its source. Finally looked up . . .

. . . into a red mouth gaping wide enough to swallow him whole.

"Remain still, Om'ray."

Oh, he was doing that. Running wouldn't accomplish anything.

Wings like storm clouds thrashed the air as the beast descended, stirring up dust until he had to throw up an arm to protect his eyes. It landed on six long, clawed feet, knees—it had knees!—bent to take the force. The wings—there were two pairs, clear and veined in black—remained outstretched and rigid. The body was thin, tapered, covered with fine brown hair. Its head swung low, regarding him—now that its enormous mouth was closed—with two pairs of large eyes. The neck was elongated, like the Tikitik's, but sagged with wrinkled skin, as if usually swollen.

Enris lowered his arm and rose to his full height. Around that neck, behind the head, was a band of cloth, marked in symbols. "Yours?"

The head shook violently, spittle flying from the edges of its mouth to pock the ground and Enris' boots. He didn't move. Thought Traveler barked. "Impressive again, Tuana. Most do not take their first sight of an *esan* well." Another bark. "Likely because they know it will be their last."

"If you'd wanted something to eat me," Enris countered, "you'd have left me to the Hard Ones."

The esan flapped its head again, as if aggravated by his voice.

"It's true, you are a rare entertainment. More so if you survive your Passage. I would enjoy a familiar face among the Vyna." For some reason, it barked amusement.

"I'll survive."

It wasn't Thought Traveler he promised, but the creature regarded him with all its eyes. "Then listen as I will tell you, Enris Mendolar of Tuana Om'ray, what may increase your chances. Leave your pack. Take only what you can carry on your body."

The Tikitik was insane. "My supplies—"

"Of no use if you are dead. Hurry or not. It is your choice."

Hurry? What did it know? Enris shook off his pack, furiously concentrating, striving to *reach* Aryl. She was distant . . . too distant. He dumped the contents on the dirt, grabbing what he had to have. *ARYL!!!* No answer. Her rope went around his waist, her longknife through that makeshift belt. What food he could ram into pockets. He already had his pouch, with the firebox and wafer. Her knot of hair. *ARYL!!!!!! BEWARE THE OUD!!* Enris trembled inside with effort and didn't know if she'd heard.

The M'hir sang to him, its ripples of black behind his eyes, its surges of power so close, too close. He dared let it come . . .

A rush of wind, real wind full of fresh dust, knocked him flat. Before he could do more than sputter, another rush and a scream . . .

And claws clenched around his body, pinning one arm, pulling him off the ground. Enris fought to free himself . . .

"Don't jump yet, Tuana," he heard. "You'll know when."

Another rush of wind, this time free of dust. They were airborne and rising!

The esan's wings gave one final full beat, then began to vibrate rapidly, chattering his teeth. It climbed with bewildering speed. A fall now, Enris judged, would break every bone in his body— although landing on the Tikitik would have made that worthwhile. And still it climbed.

He hooked his free arm around the leg that held him and did his best not to look down.

Had Aryl heard him? Would the Oud attack Sona again—or had that been part of Thought Traveler's "amusement"?

Was he being carried over the mountain or to the esan's nest, like a stolen trinket clutched by a loper? Trinket or meal?

"Where are you taking me?" Enris shouted angrily.

The esan shook its head. One of its rearward legs stretched

past him to scratch vigorously at its neck, causing the creature to slip alarmingly toward the rock face before it recovered.

Don't talk to the flying monster, he told himself.

＊ ✳ ＊

Enris had flown before. Twice. Once in an Oud aircar. Once in the strangers'. Since he'd been unable to see out during either flight, he remembered only stomach-wrenching sensations and the fear of not-knowing. Though the strangers' had a comfortable bench.

Now that he had an unimpeded view, he preferred the not-knowing fear.

The claws' grip wasn't too painful. There were three, none constricting his breathing. The obvious answer, that the creature was accustomed to carrying something alive, wasn't as reassuring as it might be. Tuana might not have Yena's wild abundance, but the fields contained a small, nasty hunter that carried its living prey below ground. Croptenders liked it. Being in the prey's position, Enris felt differently.

If he'd had both arms free, he would have used the rope to secure himself to the leg, not to mention had the longknife ready to use.

Probably as well he didn't, Enris decided. Thought Traveler had warned him to be ready to jump. And the esan wouldn't notice a blade five times longer than his.

Jump. He swallowed bile. Not now.

The esan hadn't flown over the mountain. No, after flying high enough to make him ill, it had elected to fly into it, choosing one of the ravines carved into the stone for its road. A winding, jagged, water-rock-ice-filled cavity with shadows and teethlike protrusions and—he closed his eyes hastily—the occasional very sharp going-to-die bend. Wind whistled and moaned. The sun barely touched this place; his feet were numb, although his boots had stayed on. At times, the esan's wings brushed both sides. Rock tumbled free—those wings weren't as delicate as they looked.

Or the mountain was about to crumble. Enris swallowed again.

It was taking him toward Vyna. His kind were somewhere ahead, their combined glow closer and warmer with each miserable moment. He clung to that comfort as tightly as he clung to the esan.

His kind were behind as well, one isolated, most together, others on the move. Beyond them was the solid glow of Grona. Below—so far below.

Enris grinned. What did they think of him, so far above?

His grin faded. Would Aryl think he'd abandoned her and her people for the strangers or the Oud? That his avowed purpose had been nothing more than an excuse to leave without argument? That he'd found something to trade for a flight in one of their aircars?

"I wish," he said fervently. The esan shuddered, but didn't scratch. Perhaps this journey through rock was something it considered dangerous, too.

Also not reassuring.

* * *

Enris found it harder and harder to stay conscious. It wasn't sleep, though he was exhausted to his core. The air had chilled until it hurt to breathe; he shivered constantly now. His mind felt slow and thick. Most terrifying of all, he found himself confused by where he was and why, and fought to hold his shields.

Through it all, the valiant esan flew, wings quivering. He no longer feared it would eat him. Why carry a burden this far it could simply swallow? Its exertion made it a companion, a friend, a brother—or maybe sister, since he couldn't tell its sex.

Had his token come loose? He should have put it in a pocket, not left it on his coat. Without it, the esan might as well eat him, or drop him. Vyna would be within their rights to refuse him entry. Refuse him their secrets.

If they had any . . .

Enris shook his head, hard. He couldn't afford maudlin worries. Thought Traveler had warned him to jump—that he'd know when.

The joke would be on him if he jumped at the wrong moment and died, after flying through a mountain.

He couldn't *touch* Aryl's mind. He'd tried. Too far. A fine time to learn his limits; the worst imaginable time to attempt a connection through the M'hir. He could hardly think past the vibration of the esan's wings, the noise of the wind. Impossible to concentrate and hold himself together.

Sona was on its own, for now.

* * *

Enris roused, feeling a change. Warmth, that was it. The air was warmer and moist, like a summer afternoon after a shower. Thicker. He opened his eyes, surprised he'd closed them, and gasped.

No more mountains or jagged ridges. Instead, they were descending beside a wall of black stone, smooth and sheer. Above was heavy cloud, dark and stormy. The wall disappeared into it, as if it went through the sky. To either side, it curved like the sides of a bowl into the distance. Below was featureless gray, more cloud, the kind that formed against the ground.

Drawn by an irresistible pull, his head turned away from the wall to face an otherwise identical section of the lowermost cloud. A Chooser's Call . . . sweet, rich. More . . . Om'ray! Vyna! The esan had brought him where he had to be. Enris laughed and thumped its leg in gratitude.

As if this had been an expected signal, the claws loosened.

Desperately, Enris grabbed hold, his no-longer pinned arm hanging numb and useless from his shoulder. His feet scrabbled until they found purchase at the claw joints. There. Safe.

Stupid creature!

Thought Traveler would have enjoyed this, too, he grumbled to himself.

Hard to stay grim when every slip downward brought him closer to Vyna. What did they think of an Om'ray drifting down from the clouds? Enris grinned. Nothing like making a spectacular entrance.

The esan flexed its thin body, sucked in a deep breath, and let out one of its hideous screams.

Enris winced. Not going to impress the new Clan.

The new Clan . . . his new Clan, if they were what he hoped.

First he had to arrive in one piece. He searched the cloud below for any hint of what lay beneath. Nothing. The gray was impenetrable. The esan continued to descend. Its wings stilled abruptly, then began to beat in long, powerful strokes instead of quivering. He hadn't realized how bone-shaking the vibration had been until it stopped, and resisted the urge to pat the creature again.

The gray swallowed them. Tiny droplets caught on his eyelashes, the esan's hair, the threads of his coat. Enris licked them from the scales near his face. Not a drink, but the moisture relieved the dryness of his mouth and cracked lips. The mist pressed closer, until he could only see the rest of the esan during the down stroke of its front wings, when the mist swirled and parted for an instant.

Then, they were clear.

Black rock loomed out of nowhere. They were too close to the ground!

Enris let go and threw himself in a frantic roll to the side as the esan's leading wing struck. It screamed again and again, claws scratching as it fought to stay upright. A final heave from all six limbs, a crack like thunder of wing against rock, and it disappeared into the mist.

He was still alive.

Waiting for the spinning in his head to subside, Enris lay on his back, stretched out his arms and legs, and laughed.

From this vantage point, he could see that the mist started about waist height. He was lying—he rolled on his side to see better—on a long stretch of perfectly flat and smooth black rock. He'd have thought it metal from a distance. A road, he decided.

What was that?

Discovering that he couldn't see his outstretched fingers if he stood, Enris dropped to his hands and knees to follow the gentle sound. Knee . . . hand. Knee . . . his hand found nothing and he jerked back in reflex before exploring more carefully.

Ah. He'd found the edge of the road, as sharp and clean as the side of his cart. He extended his arm as far as he could. Nothing. The sound came from below and suddenly, he knew what it was.

Water. Lapping against the rock.

Carefully, Enris turned and moved in the opposite direction. Knee . . . hand. Knee . . . hand. Twice more. Then, another edge. Water. Lapping against the rock.

How close had the esan come to missing this sliver of dry land? What if he'd stood and blundered around in the mist?

Swimming was not a Tuana skill.

He found the middle of the road and lay down, his heart racing. Om'ray were coming toward him. He could sense them.

He'd just wait here.

Chapter 11

OUTSIDE, THE STORM PROWLED, testing each repair with icy claws, piling snow on roofs made of planks and coats until planks creaked and coats bulged downward. By so little was it kept at bay, but it was enough. Inside, the oillights were dimmed, fires aglow. Bodies lay together, warmed by each other as much as the flame. They were all weary, especially the Grona. Hoping for a useful dream—or none—Aryl closed her eyes, listened to the steady music of breathing, and made herself relax.

Tried.

Failed.

How had Enris traveled so far—so fast? How had he managed to be higher than other Om'ray? They'd all felt their world expand upward for part of a tenth, then regain its proper shape. Husni, dizzy, had sat abruptly on the floor.

Only she'd known for sure it was Enris, though doubtless several of the exiles guessed. They probably also guessed, as she did, that he'd been carried over the mountains in an aircar by the Oud or the strangers. She'd only Marcus' word he wouldn't approach other Om'ray; to the impulsive Human, Enris was almost a friend. As for the Oud? They'd shown unusual interest in the Tuana before. Had he been in trouble—been rescued? Not that help would be free of risk from either source.

Didn't matter, she told herself. However he'd managed to fly, Enris was in Vyna.

Was it of stone or wood? Were there towering stalks of rastis and nekis, or the flat dreary—which Enris professed to love—land of the Tuana? Or was it more like Grona, stuck on the side of a mountain?

He'd have met his new Clan by now.

Were they welcoming? They'd be surprised, she thought. How many went there? They had to need new Om'ray. Someone of the Tuana's quality had to be rare. He was skilled, accomplished, strong . . .

Annoying.

Aryl snuggled deeper into her nest of blankets. If they wanted to impress Enris, they'd best set a full table.

Were there Choosers?

Not what Enris sought, but she wished it for him. Someone bright and fun, who was interested in how things worked, who cared about other Om'ray. Someone who would laugh with him.

She missed his laugh . . .

Someone tugged the cover from her shoulder. "You have your share, Seru," Aryl grumbled, pulling it back.

A touch. *Help me.*

Oswa? Aryl rolled over, instantly alert. The Chosen knelt beside her, hair lashing with distress. "It's Yao." So quietly she had to strain to hear.

The dreaming? With a pang of guilt, Aryl sat up. "I'm sorry, Oswa," she whispered. "I meant to talk to—"

"She's gone."

How could a child be gone?

Instinctively, Aryl lowered her shields to *reach*. What she felt brought her rushing to her feet, running for her coat, Oswa stumbling alongside.

Yao was outside.

Not only outside, but moving away from Sona—from her mother. Too young to be farther than any Highknot climb Aryl knew. Too small and helpless to be out in truenight, let alone in a storm.

How could a child do that?

No wonder Oswa was distraught. Their bond, the tightest of all between Om'ray, must be a torment. She was amazed the mother had been able to make a sensible plan, to get help. "You did the right thing to wake me," she praised. Boots, coat. "You shouldn't go out in truenight alone."

Others were throwing off blankets and called questions. "The little one's playing a trick," Aryl answered, afraid it was nothing of the kind. "I need a light."

"Here." A snap and flare as one was lit in front of her. Aryl squinted through the brightness at Haxel. "Rorn. Syb!" More lights were lit. Everyone was moving.

"Hurry!" Oswa grabbed the nearest coat; she didn't bother with boots as she ran for the door. Her hair whipped its desperation; it carved red streaks across her face and neck, barely missed her eyes.

No point trying to stop her. Taking the light from Haxel, Aryl looked for the only one who could. She was shocked to find Hoyon seated on the bench, his back to them.

A question for later.

Rorn and Syb thundered mere steps behind as Aryl followed Oswa out the door and into truenight.

The storm she'd mocked to Bern had become a thick swirl of snowdrops, pushed this way and that by the bitter wind. They caught and stopped the light, making it impossible to see more than a few steps ahead. That didn't slow Oswa Gethen. She wasn't Yena, but her desperate need to reach her daughter kept her moving at a reckless pace. Aryl matched it. Rorn and

Syb had drawn their longknives, the blades glinting in the lights they carried. What good they'd be against rock hunters, if any were out in the snow, she didn't know. But she didn't suggest they put them away.

"Why isn't Yao coming back?"

Rorn was right. The child kept moving away. Aryl *reached*, lowering her shields.

CONFUSION/FEAR . . . MOTHERWHEREAREYOU! . . . WHEREAREYOUWHERE . . .

Wincing, she quickly raised them again.

How could the child not know where her mother was?

Over the wind and the muffled pound of feet through snow, she could hear the choked moan Oswa made with every breath. No matter her will, the weaker Om'ray was failing. Aryl tossed the light to the ground and took her arm as she staggered and slowed, sending *strength* through that contact. "Let us find Yao," she pleaded. In answer, Oswa sagged heavily against her, mute and gasping. "Syb, go!"

Rorn stayed with them; Syb, freed to move at full speed, disappeared beyond the wall of snow with his light.

Rock hunters were the least of their fears now, Aryl knew. Unlikely the child had a light. If she made it through the ruins and treacherous footing, she would walk off the river's bank.

If Yao stopped? The cold had grown deadly. In a warm coat and boots, every lungful made her shiver inside.

Boots.

"Rorn. Take her." He came at once, holding Oswa with one arm, the other lifting the oillight.

"I have to find Yao . . ." the mother gasped, but couldn't break his grip.

Oswa hadn't stopped for boots. Aryl knelt. The thin cloth Grona wore on their feet was little more than shreds, the flesh beneath bloody and torn. Too much skin showed, all of it mottled with white. She sucked in a breath between her teeth. What would Yao's feet be like?

They could only help one at a time. She took off her boot—

too narrow. Rorn grunted and lifted his foot. "Use mine." Oswa didn't argue again, her *relief* muted by *pain* as her feet warmed.

Snow filled the air, collected on their heads and shoulders, softened the stone. They didn't try to follow Syb; they couldn't take Oswa back. As it was, the Grona mother sobbed quietly, her hair straining against her hood. Aryl couldn't imagine the agony of being forced to wait, apart.

Surely Yao felt the same?

Oswa straightened in Rorn's hold, snow sliding from her coat. "She's coming!"

A heartbeat later, Aryl felt it, too. Yao, moving in their direction. Considerably faster, she thought with relief, than those little legs could travel in daylight, let alone the dark.

Syb carried her.

With a sigh of relief, she retrieved her light from the snow and relit its flame. "Go back. I'll wait with Oswa," she told Rorn. Though his feet were wrapped in a tough double layer of Yena gauze, they had to be numb by now. He didn't argue, gesturing gratitude as he limped away.

Oswa stood on her own, now, as if her relief was a Power as potent as any Healer's. Aryl could feel her *joy*—and something else. *Apprehension.*

Why? "What's wrong?"

"Wrong? Why do you say that?" The Chosen's voice came out thin and harsh. "There's nothing wrong."

Hardly the way to convince her, Aryl thought, but let it go. It wasn't her place to question a mother, after all.

They stood together in the circle of light, eyes half shut against the sting of snowdrops that, in her opinion, aimed themselves at faces, and waited in silence.

The wall of snow brightened, revealed Syb, the child wrapped in his coat and held against his chest. She squirmed as they approached, her head popping out from its covering.

HEREHEREHEREHERE!!!

Syb exclaimed in pain. Aryl's head pounded. The blissful

sending dampened to bearable as Oswa's shields extended around her daughter.

Confusion as Yao bellowed—nothing wrong with her lungs—for her mother to carry her, while Aryl and Syb made it clear to both mother and child that this wasn't about to happen. Between Oswa's abused feet within Rorn's big boots, and the terrain? They might have to carry both. Then an exhausted calm.

"Let's get home," Syb suggested, his teeth chattering. He'd refused her offer to take the child. At least, Aryl thought, she made a warm bundle in his coat.

Yao's eyes were bright and curious. "Which way?"

"Hush," Oswa said quickly, tucking the coat around the child's head. "None of your silly talk, Yao. You know you shouldn't go outside without me. Be grateful these fine Om'ray were willing to come out in the cold just for you."

Her father hadn't. Why? Something was wrong. Aryl stared at the child, then her mother. Syb shifted from foot to foot, looking uneasy as well as cold. "Where is Vyna, Yao?" she asked abruptly.

Haggard and worn, Oswa nonetheless gave her a defiant glare. "Hush!" she ordered her daughter.

Not to be denied, Aryl *reached*. Yao's mind lay protected by Oswa's powerful shields, but that wasn't what she sought. The connection between Om'ray went beyond the mind; even the Lost remained tied to all others of their kind. She'd never tried to trace it before, to extend her inner sense to follow it between minds. She'd never had to.

There. Strong, steady. A bond between Syb and Oswa, from both to herself and back, from all three, reaching outward to every other Om'ray and back.

From Yao to them all. That as well. She was sure.

But to Yao?

Nothing.

The child existed, severed from everyone else, even from her mother. Blind to the glow of her kind.

Like Marcus, Aryl realized with horror. Like the Humans. But not.

On impulse, she dipped into the M'hir.

Hello.

Yao?

The child was a tiny light, calm and assured, as if floating in the wild *darkness* was perfectly normal.

Who are you?

There—there was the connection. Aryl could *see* it, burned through the dark between Yao and her mother.

How is this possible? What are you, Aryl Sarc? from Oswa, creating whorls of fear and worry.

Before she could think of a response, Syb's plaintive "Roof and a fire, Aryl?" brought her back to the real truenight.

He was right. Whatever was going on here, no reason to stay in the cold to find out.

"This way, Yao," she told the child, pointing to the warm glow of their kind.

A reassurance no Om'ray should need.

By the next morning, Sona had been carpeted in a smooth, glistening layer of fresh snow. It clung to every surface and showed no signs of melting, despite the brilliant sunlight. Haxel, ever practical, put the unChosen to work packing snow into empty jars. Hoyon suggested they make piles on the sunless side of upheaved stone, then pile wood on top. While Grona used such for a means of keeping certain foods cold, Sona's need was for water. This would work as well.

Not that everyone worked. There was laughter in the sharp cold air. Yao was showing Seru and Ziba the Grona game of shapes in the snow. It involved a great deal of snow being tossed at one another, as well as lying in the stuff.

As she helped Veca roof their next building, Aryl watched them. By day, the youngest addition to Sona proved to be an ordinary child, delicate of feature and build, with the brown hair and eyes of her mother. At most, six years old. Her true-night ordeal had been washed away by good sleep and food. Yao had been remarkably sensible and dressed properly before leaving on her adventure, however she'd managed that without notice amid the busy Om'ray. She'd told Seru this morning that she'd gone outside to look for her Grona playmates. When Seru related this to Aryl, she'd laughed at the cleverness of the child, to make up such a story.

Not clever, Aryl thought. The truth and tragic.

Oswa had begged them not to tell Yao's secret, to let her do it. Which had to wait. The mother hadn't fared as well as the child. She was with Oran in what was being called the Cloisters by some; true, it was their place of healing, complete, Aryl grimaced, with Adepts. According to those experts, the cold was more than unpleasant—the Grona insisted in dire tones that toes and fingers could be damaged by short exposure, that Om'ray could die of it.

Which made the cold, Aryl decided with some amusement, a threat like biters—dealt with by the right clothes and common sense.

"Need another plank?"

She eyed the dark gap in front of her. "Do I?" Her job this morning was to stuff dried vegetation into cracks. They hurried to finish the fourth building in the square, as well as improve the roofs. Coats, as they'd discovered overnight, couldn't hold much snow without support. On the ground, Tilip and others had begun laying down stone for a walkway to connect this home to the others—an innovation Hoyon claimed would keep feet out of the mud that came with the melting of snow in the spring.

Mud she hoped would grow plants.

With a chuckle, Veca spanned the distance with her hand. "I'd say so. Unless you want someone's bed to be wet."

"A youth misspent climbing," Aryl explained. She put down the bag of twisted leaves and picked the top plank from the stack beside her, though "plank" was an optimistic word to describe the ragged pieces scrounged from the wreckage of hundreds of other homes. "I should have helped Costa with the roof tiles."

"Feels good to teach the skills again." Veca helped her fit the wood in place. "Fon has less interest these days." She grinned at Aryl's wary look. "Don't worry. You won't be working wood forever. Haxel has other plans for you."

Not a statement an unChosen could dispute. If she hammered the fastening hook with excessive force, the other Om'ray paid no attention. Instead, Veca asked casually, "Have you shown Hoyon the headdress you found?"

Aryl missed the hook. "No. Why?"

"He knows about old things."

She'd shown the object to Marcus Bowman, who'd revealed more about Sona from his brief inspection than any Grona Adept could. Or would—if Hoyon kept secrets the way she suspected. "I'll think about it," she replied tactfully.

Veca wasn't done. "Do you believe him?"

Aryl looked up. "About what?"

"About the mountains. That their shaking damaged Sona, not the Oud." Veca shifted, her rugged features displaying an unusual unease. "Doesn't that make more sense? Look at this place. What race could do such a thing?"

To every side, the valley floor was heaved and torn, buildings tipped and knocked apart. What they'd accomplished, the restoration of these four homes, made as much difference to the devastation as the finger-sized hole a stinger chewed into a giant rastis.

It was a start, Aryl assured herself. They didn't need more than that.

"I don't know about shaking mountains, Veca, but I've seen Oud for myself. Trust me. Oud could do this." She remembered how the creature had moved through the ground as easily as she'd walk a branch, how they tore rock from the cliff. "Does Hoyon explain how a mountain could destroy the village but spare the nekis grove, stop up the river and take its water, but leave the road between alone? The Oud did do this. To think otherwise is to dangerously underestimate our neighbors."

Something Aryl was abruptly sure the Grona did. It explained why they slept so well. They pretended—or truly believed—the Oud were harmless. Enris must have realized it, too. Was that another reason he'd never intended to stay there—being all too aware his hosts were fools?

"You're the Speaker," Veca said cheerfully, as if assigning her to deal with Oud was safer than arguing with a mountain.

She might be right. Or not.

"Right now," Aryl reminded her, "I'm a woodworker. A not very good one. What's next?"

She paid attention, but it was hard. Her mind kept wandering.

How many other exiles were listening to the Grona Adept?

And why did that make her afraid?

Veca was right. Haxel Vendan, First Scout and Sona's distributor of work, did indeed have other plans for her. Aryl sharpened her new longknife—it wasn't a proper one, a Yena one, but served the same purpose—with hard, straight strokes and considered the potential for disaster in Haxel's latest one.

She had plenty of time. They were late.

She sat on a beam, that beam the only one left on this roof, this roof over a home no one wanted yet, and sharpened her longknife.

She hadn't argued either. How could she? When Haxel called her down from the roof to tell her she was to lead Oran and Hoyon to the Cloisters, to see if the Adepts could open its doors, what could she say but yes?

The wind tore at her coat and teased hair from its net.

The perfect use of resources. The Adepts weren't helping to

rebuild, Oran's healing Talent was no longer critical, and, as Haxel smugly put it, the Oud hadn't shown up, so they didn't need a Speaker either at the moment.

Perfect.

Stroke . . . stroke.

If they ever started. Not that she planned to rush whatever preparations had the two former Adepts delayed. More time to think of how to hide any sign Marcus might have left at the Cloisters, to hope the Human would see them coming and hide himself as well, and to think of what to tell the Oud, if it showed up and wanted to go inside, too.

Perfect.

Aryl paused. Someone had stopped below. She *reached* and relaxed. "Took you long enough."

"Hah!" Seru scrambled up beside her. "You'll have to try harder if you want to hide from Rorn's cooking. It'll be ready soon. Blue—whatever it is. " As she settled, she puffed, admiring the resulting cloud of breath. A glance sideways. "You're going to ruin that."

Aryl tested the blade on her thumbnail. "It's Grona."

A moment's silence. Then, "We needed a Healer."

She found a section marginally less sharp and spat on it. "We needed a Healer," Aryl conceded. Myris and Chaun—thus Ael and Weth—would live. For that alone, she'd endure a fist of Orans. She rubbed the offending edge against the stone. "Should make everyone happy."

"Juo," with relish, "won't let Oran anywhere near her. Said no upstart Grona Adept whelp was to fool with her unborn. Morla was less polite about it."

Not a surprise. Morla Kessa'at had been the Councillor most betrayed by Yena's Adepts, Aryl thought to herself, remembering that day and moment very well. Besides, a broken bone didn't need Power to cure. Time and a splint would do. Juo? Hopefully she wouldn't need a Healer when her time came.

But the rest? "Some must be pleased to have Adepts again." Gijs for one.

Exasperation. With elbow. "No one forgets who tossed us off the bridge. We won't trust Adepts again. From any Clan." Seru drew her knees up under her coat, fitting herself on the narrow beam. The wind tugged at her scarf; its chill reddened her cheeks. "As ordinary Om'ray, they're welcome. That's all."

All? "How do you know—" Aryl hesitated.

"About Kran?" Her cousin gave an exaggerated sigh of relief. "I know. Trust me. He's not ready. Just as well. I'd rather not have an Adept against me." She lowered her voice to a reasonable imitation of Oran's. "My brother would be an Adept already, but Grona's Adepts were jealous of his Talent. Kran deserves a Chooser of equal or greater Power, not a mere Parth."

The sharpening stone slipped; Aryl caught it before it fell. "She said that?"

"She didn't have to." A grin. "Haven't you noticed? She won't let him so much as look my way."

Aryl nudged Seru with her shoulder. "I see no reason you'd want him to."

"It doesn't matter what any of us want," Seru admitted. "What I need is to Choose someone. Anyone." Another sigh. "Soon."

"Fon is nice—" Aryl began cautiously.

"I helped at his birth."

She lifted a skeptical eyebrow. "You were four."

"And helped. You know my Talent."

True. Seru might not be strong, but like her mother she was a gifted Birth Watcher, the one assistance Juo would need. Om'ray unborn were reluctant to leave the womb, to let their inner bond to their mother thin with distance. Without the baby's courage and cooperation, birth was a grave risk to both. A Birth Watcher could not only *sense* when a baby should be born, but would contact that young mind to offer reassurance and encouragement.

"Mother took me with her. All the time." *Sadness* leaked through Seru's shields; she gestured apology.

"Fine." Aryl put her arm around her cousin. "Not Fon. Cersi's a big place, Cousin. There'll be Choice—the someone you've wished for."

"Wish?" Seru's right hand moved restlessly. "It's not like that, you know. What I feel. What a Chooser feels. UnChosen—we don't have any idea what's to come." She laid her head on Aryl's shoulder. Almost a whisper. "They should tell us the truth."

What had her aunt said . . . you can't know what it's like for Seru?

Feeling awkward, she sent *compassion*. "I'm sorry—"

It's not grief or longing. Seru's mindvoice was distant, as if she *listened* to herself too. *My family's gone, and I miss them every moment. But I can remember good things.* Images came and went: parties, chases along a glow-lit bridge, games. Sensations: laughter, the squeeze of baby fingers, warm rain on skin. *There's nothing good in how a Chooser feels.*

She could pull away, close her mind to Seru's. Be ignorant. Instead, curious, Aryl drew Seru closer. *Show me, Cousin.*

. . . *emptiness*

. . . *need*

. . . *weary despair*

Aryl slammed down her shields. Too late. Tears froze on her cheeks; words in her throat.

Seru eased away, dangling her feet over air as if a child again. "When there wasn't enough dresel," she offered, "I'd dream about my favorite ways to eat it. Dresel cakes. The sweets my uncles made. I'd imagine the taste—that smell. When I got my ration of powder each day, I'd pretend it was fresh and try to enjoy every mouthful. But after a while, I didn't care. I needed it so badly, I'd have chewed the spoon and bowl if I thought there was more left.

"That's being a Chooser," flat and sure. "The longer I stay empty, the less I care who fills me." A shudder. "Even if means I'll be changed, like Bern—or Joined to someone who despises me, like Oswa. I have to offer Choice."

Choice wasn't supposed to dry your mouth and send a thrill

of fear down every nerve, like hearing the footsteps of a predator at your back when there was nowhere safe to jump. It was supposed to be the joyous start of the rest of your life.

Maybe it was, for most. But wasn't this also the truth? Aryl asked herself, refusing to flinch. That unChosen took Passage alone, in fear. That Choosers waited in an agony of need and uncertainty. That their union was beyond any control or reason, though it changed both forever.

Like riding the M'hir.

"Don't listen to me," Seru ordered shakily. "You're a Sarc. It won't be like this for you." She managed to laugh. "You watch—you'll Call handsome unChosen from every Clan, including Vyna. They'll arrive all at once and beg for the touch of your hand. And bring sweets. I expect you—" archly, "—to share, Cousin."

Aryl chuckled. "The unChosen or the sweets?"

"Both!"

"I promise."

If the words were less than steady, Seru pretended not to notice. "Good," she replied. "I'd better get back. Hoyon claims it'll be a bad storm. The undercoats, you know."

"The undercoats," Aryl agreed fervently.

Sona's light, mobile clothing cut the wind, but did little to keep out the deeper cold. Seru had dreamed again last 'night, more productively than Ziba, who recalled only dreams with sweets. The loose white coats they'd guessed were for indoors or spring were meant to go under the windproof outer one. The combination was warmer by far, while easy to move.

Doubling the number of alterations needed. Sona, Aryl decided, seemed to do that to its new inhabitants. She glanced up the valley, coated in fresh snow. "A shame you don't have them ready. Haxel's sending me off again."

"I heard. With the Grona. Enjoy yourself."

Aryl gave her cousin a shove. "Go."

About to drop to the ground, Seru paused. "What do you think of Hoyon?"

That the most dangerous fools were those who believed themselves right? That if he wasn't a fool, he was something worse? Aryl settled for, "I think he should talk less."

"He doesn't talk to Oswa at all. Or Yao. Have you noticed?"

Chosen varied, but to ignore his own daughter? "That's—" It was more than strange, as was his failure to help search for her. Om'ray parents, Adept or not, were close to their young children, whose maturing minds depended on theirs. "Yao's different—" she began.

This gained her a fierce "Aryl Sarc!" A reaction she should have expected, Seru having been forced to leave her beloved baby brother in the care of the Uruus family. "Hoyon's the one to blame here."

"She is different."

Deep offense. "A Tikitik is 'different.' Yao's a wonderful child. Any family would be glad of her. You wait till you've one of your own." Seru swung down and landed lightly, then walked away.

Yao was different, Aryl reminded herself. Perhaps enough to cost her bond to her father, if not her mother.

Another change, she thought, troubled. This one at the heart of what they were.

Chapter 12

"**M**UST YOU WALK SO quickly?"

Aryl didn't bother to answer. If the Grona couldn't keep up, they could follow behind. It wasn't as if she could lose them.

"Is there a reason you have us running?"

Because they'd wasted the entire morning?

Aryl eased her pace, slightly, and glanced over her shoulder. "Recognize those?" she said, pointing at the snow-cloaked lumps to either side.

Hoyon, red-faced and panting, gave her a sour look. "Rocks."

"That's what they'd like you believe."

His eyes widened.

"We're safe in daylight—as long as we keep moving."

Oran, head bundled in bright Grona scarves so only her eyes showed, merely lengthened her strides.

Just the three of them. Bern, who had been Yena and—however reluctantly—a skilled maker of rope and ladders, had, in Haxel's unarguable opinion, use. The trip itself was, also in her opinion, safe. After all, if there were Oud, who else could talk to them but their Speaker?

If she'd looked a little too pleased with herself, not even the Adepts had dared protest.

Aryl had been tempted.

They were already at the second arched bridge. The sun was overhead, turning shadows an impenetrable black, reflecting from snow piles with painful intensity. Exposed stone sparkled like the wings of the flitters that flew highest in the canopy. Stark. Beautiful.

Sona's valley was never the same twice. A lesson, Aryl decided, to be remembered.

"Are you taking us to the end of the world?"

Not far enough, she thought. "We're close. Feel the waterfall?" She could, drumming through her thinner boots. They looked puzzled. "We're close."

"And you're sure the Cloisters is intact?" Every word from Oran had been variations on that theme. "You should show us."

Lower her shields to these two? "You'll see for yourselves soon." Aryl turned away and resumed walking, faster than before.

As if she could outrun them.

Snow could lie. It coated the hill of bone and shattered homes, blurring its shape, hiding its source. The Grona thumped and scrambled up the slope on their too-big boots, oblivious to what lay beneath, their labored breaths puffing in the cold air. Aryl didn't bother to tell them they climbed on Sona's first Om'ray. They wouldn't care if they knew. What Om'ray would?

She'd become strange, she thought without regret, and made her steps soft.

The waterfall was even more impressive under a clear sky, its vast weave of plumes distinct and white against the spray-dark cliff. Aryl tilted her head but couldn't see its upper reach through the mist at the top. The sun, she decided, must pass through it.

Straight ahead, she spotted the arrangement of ropes and wood Rorn's group had constructed—while she waited for Oran and Hoyon—to take advantage of the nekis stalks leaning into the pit. They could suspend containers out in the falling feathers of water, catch what they could, then haul them back to empty into waterproof bags. They'd passed them, Rorn and Syb, the three unChosen, on the way back, bent under their loads. The five reported seeing no other life. She'd trusted Marcus to stay out of sight.

Veca and Tilip were working on a cart. Once finished, it would help only if they could get it close to the water. Aryl tucked her lower lip between her teeth as she considered the problem. Impossible to haul anything with wheels, as Enris had shown them, over this loose, rubble-strewn hill.

It would be possible if they went around the hill, to the side of the waterfall beyond the Cloisters, where the nekis had never grown along that edge, or had been removed by the Oud. Easier access to the water itself as well. Aryl flushed. Too easy, for a fool running in the dark.

The grove was in the way. She grinned. They could copy the Human. Cut their own path around the hill.

Cut down nekis?

When had she started thinking like those who lived on the ground?

When it became their new home, she told herself sternly.

Hoyon stopped, shading his eyes with one hand. "I don't see the Cloisters. We've come too far." There was a tremor in his voice Aryl understood. Hadn't she felt the pull of other Om'ray fading as she moved farther and farther away?

It no longer bothered her.

Perhaps, despite all appearances, he missed his Chosen and daughter. "Don't worry," she said, finding it odd to reassure an Adept. "The world doesn't end. Not yet. There are mountains beyond this. The waterfall comes from them."

"Were you taught nothing at Yena? The waterfall comes from the Village of the Moons," Oran stated, as if to a child, "where the Sun rests its fire in its hearth by night. There are no more mountains. The world—" her eyes narrowed, "—ends at that village. Hoyon's right. There's no Cloisters here. Take us back."

Some things weren't safe to argue. "We're close now," Aryl replied calmly. "Beyond the nekis."

That drew a frown. "These can't be what you climbed."

"Yena's are taller." The Chosen of Bern Teerac. What other memories did she have? Doing her best not to wonder, Aryl led the way down the hill to where the grove began.

The growth, though stunted and bare, warmed her heart. Her fingers lingered on snow-dappled buds, the promise of leaves to come. No path here between the tight-growing stalks. She slipped out of her coat and hung it beside the one she'd left two days ago, offering not a word of explanation.

She glanced at her companions, waiting. Neither Hoyon nor Oran were heavy by Grona standards; they weren't Yena-slim. Those stuffed coats made them twice as wide. As for the scarves?

Realizing what she expected, neither Adept appeared happy.

She hid a smile while fine spray from the waterfall collected on her face and crossed arms.

"Take off your coat, Hoyon," Oran snapped, throwing back her hood. Her thick blonde hair flooded over her shoulders as if offended by its brief captivity. Aryl had no idea what kept the small, loose cap in place on the top of her head.

"But—" He looked appalled. "You can't be serious."

"Is there another way, unChosen?"

Only if she was willing to take them along the cliff face, past the section where the Oud hunted Hoveny secrets from the rock itself. "No," Aryl replied, doing her best to sound regretful. "We could go back—you can try again once there's a path cut."

At this, Oran threw her coat to the ground; her scarves followed, red and yellow and blue, writhing like something alive
as they fell. Beneath she wore not the sensible warm tunic or
woven vest she'd arrived in, but a very different garment.

Adepts appearing at Council or in their official capacity
wore this white robe, so densely sewn with thread of the same
color that its surface shimmered with shapes and its pleats fell
stiff and heavy to the ground. Her mother wore one as
Speaker, though her role as Adept also gave her the right.
Councillors would don them, too, but only for formal occa-
sions.

Hoyon removed his coat and hung it over a branch. He
wore a robe as well.

No wonder they'd been slow to get ready.

Both Adepts had folded their hems through their belts and
wore pants underneath, stuffed into high thick boots. Practical,
Aryl supposed, if lacking respect. To protect the precious garments from the weather, or from curious eyes?

Not that it mattered. They were the ones, she thought with
amusement, forced to move in the almost solid material.
Though against snow, the white had advantages. She'd have to
tell Haxel. Yena preferred to blend with their surroundings;
wise in a place where what you didn't hunt, hunted you. Difficult, so far, to match the bleak gray-browns of stone and dirt.
Sona's white undercoats had promise against snow.

"This way," she said, stepping into the grove.

Now to hope Marcus was watching.

And that the Oud weren't.

For once, the two Adepts didn't move slowly or complain,
though their faces bore angry red marks—they had to learn to
raise their arms to protect themselves from twigs—and both
were thoroughly winded from struggling through tight spaces
before Aryl led them to the edge of the grove.

"Wait," she admonished, when they would have plunged forward into the cleared space. "The Oud—"

"We know the Oud, unChosen." Hoyon shoved her out of his way, a shocking rudeness for any Om'ray. "Look, Oran! The Cloisters!"

"I see it." With quiet triumph.

Aryl pulled herself straight, rubbing her elbow where it had met a branch with decided force. No choice but to let them go ahead. She followed, watching for Marcus and his flying "eye." Their footsteps sank through the thin layer of snow into the still-loose dirt left by the Oud. Hard going. The Adepts didn't care, possessed by fresh energy in sight of their goal.

She cared. Aryl scanned the snow for any tracks, any disturbance. Only the Adepts' prints marred the white surface. As for the path the strangers had blazed through the nekis?

It had been there. Right there. Aryl tried not to be obvious as she stared at a section of compact stalks where none had been before. More stranger-illusion, she decided, growing cheerful. Marcus did know they were here. He was keeping himself—and his camp—out of sight.

As for the Oud . . . she had the geoscanner, but all it would tell her was yes, there were Oud here, and likely everywhere.

The Adepts were half running now, working their way across the shallow depression Aryl's dreams told her had been water. Hoyon freed his robe from his belt, its pleated length flapping as he ran. He looked ridiculous, dressed like that, out here.

Or magnificent.

Suddenly, she wasn't sure. These were Adepts, the most powerful and Talented of their Clan. They belonged inside a Cloisters. Wasn't it right and fitting they were here, now? That she'd brought them?

What she'd said to her people, to her Clan last night— hadn't it meant this as well, that she must accept Oran and Hoyon as Sona's first Adepts?

When they promised to stay, Aryl told herself, feeling cold inside. When they proved themselves worth having.

Then, and not a moment before.

The Oud ramp remained. Oran climbed it without pausing to look for another entry; she disappeared down the other side, Hoyon right behind. Aryl hurried to catch up.

When she jumped down behind them on the platform, Hoyon started and whirled around, one hand up as if to push her again.

Aryl kept her distance. "Can you open it?"

There was a door centered on every arch. These, in her limited experience, weren't normally locked. A Cloisters wasn't normally empty of life and half buried by curious Oud either.

Oran stood, palms pressed to one side of the nearest door, her head bent in an attitude of concentration.

Concentration . . . or frustration.

Her hair thrashed uneasily down her back. Her knuckles whitened, fingers pressing hard. Adepts didn't use force to open the doors. They were taught a technique, given a secret passed down within their order.

Aryl remained quiet and still. Perhaps the Oud had somehow damaged the door, pushed dirt into its mechanism. It was possible.

No sign of Marcus. Snow had filled in his tracks, blurred his ladder of rock into something that might have been another, very small, ramp.

No sign, she saw with relief, of the Oud.

Oran stayed where she was. Hoyon went to the next door, hands flat, eyes closed as if he communed with the metal.

Aryl eased her weight from one foot to the other. The sun reflected from the upper portion of the Cloisters, it didn't reach here. Their robes were heavier than her tunic, but she wasn't worried about the cold. The movement of the sun was the concern. They were running out of time. She had to get the Adepts back to Sona before truenight and they couldn't run the distance, as she had. There were oillights in the small pack she carried. Would they keep away the rock hunters? Not something Aryl planned to test with only these two for help.

Oran joined Hoyon at his door. If they *sent* to one another, it was nothing she sensed.

She waited until she was sure.

They couldn't do it.

"Oran. Hoyon." Neither looked up or acknowledged her. "We should leave now."

"No!" This from Hoyon, hoarse and angry. At her or the door's failure to obey?

Stupid Grona.

"We'll come back," she said reasonably. "Bring help to clean away the dirt. If you want, we'll dig out the main doors. But we have to leave. It'll take three tenths—" if they kept a good pace, "—to get back to Sona. That's pushing firstnight if we go now." She wasn't the one, Aryl reminded herself, who'd caused the slow start.

Oran glanced over her shoulder, lips curled with disdain. "How could I forget? You Yena fear the dark."

Poor Bern.

Aryl didn't bother reacting. "We came to see if you could open the Cloisters," she pointed out. "You can't. It's time to leave."

Both Adepts turned to face her. "You think that's the only reason we came?" Oran said, her voice smooth and sure. Her hair lifted like a cloud.

Hoyon laughed.

Power *pressed* against her from not one, but two minds. Aryl staggered back, her hands over her head as if it could help. Hammer blows of *force* and *demand* and *OBEY!*

Once before, she'd been attacked like this. Her mother had ripped apart her shields to take the memory she wanted. By comparison, that assault had been gentle. Those who wanted entry into her thoughts now cared nothing for the damage they caused.

PAIN!!!!

She was on the ground, writhing in the snow. Someone screamed.

NO!

She wasn't a child anymore and they weren't as powerful as Taisal. But they were two—and winning. Aryl tried to resist. She poured all she had into her shields, but layer upon layer shredded away.

She drew up her most horrifying memories to throw like knives: the osst being eaten alive in the Lake of Fire, the swarm, Yena burning . . .

FEAR!!! Her sense of Hoyon faded.

Oran kept coming.

Let her come. Aryl slipped into the M'hir, embraced its chaos . . .

And waited.

Oran followed, her presence tasting of *triumph* and *greed* . . .

. . . only to falter as she realized where they were.

Welcome to the M'hir.

Like a stitler springing its ambush, Aryl launched herself at her enemy. She didn't know if she rode the M'hir Wind or was that wind . . . all she knew was *RAGE.*

She tore at Oran, tossing parts away, letting them go in the *darkness* . . .

AGONY . . .

She didn't stop . . . stripping away more . . . and more . . . until what was left of Oran di Caraat sobbed and gibbered and flickered at the edge of existence.

Aryl?

Bern?

He flickered, too, tossed by storm and turmoil, desperately holding to what remained of his Chosen.

Aryl . . .

Her rage winked out, replaced by sick dread. What had she almost done?

She *gathered* Oran together and drew them both to safety.

Aryl spat snow, dirt, and bile from her mouth. She raised herself on arms she wouldn't allow to shake, collected herself. In one smooth motion, she was on her feet, confronting her attackers, longknife out and ready in her hand.

Hoyon cowered against a window. Oran was on hands and knees in the snow and dirt, vomiting.

Not good.

Aryl put away the knife and wiped her face with the back of her hand. Her stomach lurched, and she fought the urge to spew as well.

She hadn't defended herself. She'd tried to kill Oran—and Bern.

Self-control was the first, most important lesson of all.

"You didn't need to attack me," she told them wearily. "Once I learn to control it, I'll share the ability to move through the M'hir with anyone who wants it—starting with my Clan." Hoyon gave her an incredulous look. Oran lifted her head, her hair flat and soiled, eyes shot with blood.

"You didn't believe Bern, did you? Or want his new life, here." Aryl stressed the word. "You decided to take what you wanted and go. To be greater than all of Grona's other Adepts. You'd trade your healing Talent for it—your brother. But destroying me to take it was even better, wasn't it? Then I couldn't teach anyone else. It would be yours alone."

Oran used a handful of snow to wash her face, then spat to one side. Her eyes never left Aryl's. She didn't answer.

She didn't need to.

Aryl sighed. "You don't see it, do you?" she said reluctantly, remembering a mug shattered on a floor. "Too much Power, held by too few, will destroy us. The Agreement keeps the peace not just between races, but between us, our Clans. You're right. Moving through the M'hir could be the most valuable Talent of all. But if we dare change, if we throw this at the Oud and Tikitik, we threaten the balance that holds Cersi together. We'll fall." The world could end. She knew it, deep inside. She'd proved it. Hadn't she almost killed another?

"There's only one way. Once this ability is safe, every Om'ray must have it. Including you."

"Why?" Hoyon straightened. "After— Why would you do that?"

Because they were all Om'ray, a race disappearing from the world?

Because they were surrounded by those with more technology and real power than they could imagine, who didn't care about them?

Because some good had to come from her mistake . . . from Costa's death?

He'd had to ask, which meant he'd understand none of those answers.

"Twenty-two Om'ray are not enough to sustain and build a Clan," Aryl told him instead, which was also the truth. "Sona needs you and your families. You've seen what we've accomplished in our first fist of days. Shelter, food, and now water. But it's not enough."

Oran sat, drawing her robe away from the soiled ground. "You Yena have no idea what it's like here in the cold." A peace offering?

"No, we don't," Aryl agreed. Not the time to mention the dreams. "We're not ready for winter, let alone what will happen afterward. We could use what you know about living in the mountains, about growing food. We need your Talents and training. If you stay and help—when I'm ready, I'll share what I can do with you as well as the others."

"You tried to leave me *there*. Tried to kill me." Oran's hair came back to life, lashing the air around her head. "You expect me to trust anything you say?"

Aryl gazed at the Adept. This was no friend. The best she could hope for was the kind of truce that existed in the canopy, when two predators avoided each other during their hunts.

I expect you, she sent, just to Oran, through the M'hir that now so readily connected them, *to be afraid of the dark.*

Nothing troubled their return journey. It was much like their first, Aryl thought. The Grona Adepts hadn't talked to her then either. They'd collected their coats—she both of hers—and the Adepts had tucked up their robes, however filthy. The rock hunters were piled closer to the line where shadow conquered light, a line moving steadily inward from both sides as the sun left the sky, but she didn't bother to mention it. They were adults, after all, Chosen and powerful and Adepts.

If they were blind to danger, it suited her. They were blind to other things as well. Like the occasional glint from overhead, a reflection from what followed them, something cautious and discreet.

A comfort, to know a friend was watching. Aryl would have given anything to look up and smile at Marcus, but not even Grona were that blind.

They also didn't see—or care to mention—the lines of compressed dirt here and there on the paving stones. She'd seen such paired tracks before. An Oud machine. It must have taken this road while they were at the Cloisters.

Since they hadn't encountered it, the Oud traveled away from them, down the valley. Aryl kept them to the fastest pace Hoyon could manage, but the machine didn't come in sight.

Stupid Oud. If it wanted to talk to the Sona Speaker, it should have waited here.

The only Om'ray who knew more about Oud were with her. Aryl chewed her lower lip a moment, then decided. "There's an Oud ahead of us, " she informed them. "Going to the village."

"Oud go where they will," Hoyon said in a patronizing tone. "There's no way to know where they—"

"What makes you say that?" Oran interrupted.

She'd learned there were things to fear. Aryl wasn't proud to be the reason, but it was useful. "These tracks." She pointed. "They go down the valley. There are no others. Plus . . . there's this." She pulled the pendant from its place under her tunic. "They promised to come and talk to me."

Hoyon burst out laughing. "An unChosen?"

"I asked them to release water into the river," Aryl said evenly. "We need it for the fields."

He ducked his head deeper into his coat, for all the world like a offended flitter, but didn't slow his pace.

"If this is to be an official Visitation," Oran offered after a moment, "the Oud will ask for lists."

"Lists. Of what?"

"Of everything." Hoyon snorted. "Not that you have anything."

"We have you," Aryl countered. "Lists are records, are they not? Written down? That's what you do."

"You know something of our work. Were you training as an Adept?" There was a new eagerness in her tone, as if Aryl being of their kind mattered to Oran.

"No," she replied evenly. "But I've seen lists." There had been lists made by Yena's Adepts. Lists of their diminished supplies. Lists of what could be spared for the ten unChosen sent on Passage—including Bern Teerac and Yuhas Parth, who'd made it to Tuana Clan. Two had died. The other six? Aryl wished she'd disobeyed custom and law and *reached* to follow them. There were so few Yena left. "Why do the Oud want them?"

"No one knows."

And no one cared, Aryl corrected to herself. Until now. "Do you trade with them?"

"What would we trade with Oud?"

This was different. Yena had always given dresel and seeds to the Tikitik who came after the Harvest, receiving in turn the glows and power cells, the metal and oils they needed for the coming year. Enris told her how the Tuana grew large numbers of a plant the Oud wanted, how the creatures took that harvest when ripe. In turn, the Oud left glows and other supplies at the mouth of their tunnel. "Provide food the Oud want. Receive glows and power cells in return. Metal."

"We go in the tunnels and take what we need. The Oud don't care. They just want their lists. Crops. How much food we were able to grow," she clarified at Aryl's puzzled look. "They don't want any of it. Whatever we built or used. How many of us there are, who died and how, who was born. Lists. Our Speaker—" with emphasis "—reads them out."

Aryl doubted that. The Grona Speaker was not, like her mother, an Adept, and no other Om'ray in a Clan were taught to read or write. But she didn't doubt the rest. For whatever reason, the mountain Oud treated their Clan differently.

Had it been the same for Sona?

Would it be?

Firstnight and the Oud made it to the village before they did. Aryl had worried her way through several scenarios during the final tenth of their journey—during the worst, she'd forced the Adepts into the best run they could manage, only to have Hoyon collapse on the road, wasting valuable time. The Oud, however, waited on this side of the dry river. It lay on its machine, shrouded in brown, dusty fabric. Her people lined the other bank to watch it, those who weren't perched on a roof for a better view.

They'd have sensed Aryl and the Adepts returning. She could only imagine how they'd felt before. The Oud here. Their Speaker not.

Not every day the First Scout was wrong.

To be fair, the Oud were the least predictable beings Aryl had met. They made the Human seem normal.

His tiny airborne eye had left them before the final turn of the valley. She'd been sad to see it go. Not that Marcus could or should have helped—but it had been nice to have a companion who didn't hate or fear her. Or want something.

About to *send* reassurance to the others, Aryl stopped herself.

Don't use Power near Oud unless you must. Enris' advice—which she trusted more than anything the Grona might say.

Instead, she waved her hand as they approached, made sure to smile. The Speaker's Pendant glittered against her coat. She hoped the creature recognized it clean.

Hoyon and Oran walked past the Oud, barely glancing at the creature, and clambered awkwardly down the river's bank. Their heavy clothing didn't help. Hoyon fell again; Oran didn't wait for him. He stumbled to catch up to her.

That figures detached from those waiting, prepared to help them up the other side, wasn't a compliment.

Aryl walked to the dusty dome she assumed covered the head of the Oud. Small biters scurried away from her, but stayed near the machine as if they belonged. So long as they bit Oud hide and not Om'ray, she didn't care.

Only the biters appeared to notice her.

Was the Oud asleep? Dead?

It would be dark soon. She'd rather not be on this side of the river then. Behind the Oud, the far side of the road was edged in hopeful rocks, some daring enough to roll into the lingering sunlight. Not that they moved when she looked.

Aryl drew herself tall and straight. "I see you," she said. Loudly, in case the Oud was asleep.

No reaction.

It was the right creature. A Speaker's Pendant was attached to the fabric below the dome.

She fingered hers, frowning, then leaned forward and rapped her knuckles on that smooth surface.

"Whatwhatwhatwhat!" The creature reared violently upright, clattering limbs and words, then fell off the machine to one side. Disturbed biters whirred and clicked into the air, then subsided around its limp form.

Had she killed it?

Aryl didn't glance over her shoulder. Not the time to seem as if she didn't know what was going on. "Get up!" she urged.

Black limbs, some disturbingly like hooks, waved weakly.

Not dead.

She wrinkled her nose at a musty odor but stepped closer. "Are you—" The word "hurt" died in her mouth as she saw the green stain spreading across the dirt and stone.

Ready to leap back at the slightest excuse, Aryl lifted the heavy fabric draped above the stain. It took both hands and all her strength to raise it high enough to look underneath.

The flaccid, pale body was slashed open along three lines. The cuts were precise and too straight. Powerful strokes, she judged. Skilled. Possibly using a weapon made for this purpose.

Another Oud?

She'd tried to kill her own, Aryl thought grimly. She eased the fabric down. "Who did this? Why?"

"Let it die in peace, Speaker for Sona."

She spun, knife out.

The Tikitik rose from its crouch, hands empty at its sides.

She hadn't seen it, Aryl thought numbly. How could that be?

It wasn't like the Tikitik she knew. This was gray on gray, its skin and cloth a perfect match for the stone. The same body shape, the same intent four-eyed stare.

The same threat. She kept her knife ready. "What are you doing here? This is Oud land."

"Is it?" The Tikitik bobbed its head, as if amused. "Forgive my trespass, then. I was . . . curious."

A familiar symbol on its wristband caught her eye. "You're a Thought Traveler," she guessed.

"That is part of my name. Curious indeed." It sounded pleased, as if a puzzle was what it sought. "Do you know what it means?"

"It means you go between factions—" Tikitik, she'd learned, didn't count themselves as part of a place or village, but grouped themselves by belief. Thought Travelers were something else, individuals outside any one faction, yet in service to them all. "—and share whatever you've learned."

"If I think it wise," the Tikitik qualified, its mouth protuberances stirring. "Knowledge can be dangerous, can it not, little Speaker? Our unfortunate companion discovered that."

They loved word games. She remembered that, too.

"This is Sona," Aryl said carefully. "Our neighbors are the Oud. Tikitik don't belong here."

"New Om'ray," it mused, its smaller eyes flexing on their cones to aim at those on the other side of the river. Who must, Aryl thought worriedly, be trying to decide whether to come to her aid or not. Not, she wished desperately, but didn't lower her shields. "New ideas. Do you change the Agreement?"

"Change . . . ?" The pit that swallowed the river was nothing compared to this. Aryl stared at the Tikitik, then at the Oud. "I don't know what you—"

A clatter of limbs. A faint rasp of voice. "Om'ray. GoodGood-GoodGood. Sona Oud."

"Precipitous being." The Tikitik rose to its full height and focused all its eyes on the dying Oud. "Look where misjudgment and haste has brought you."

Hanging from a belt around its narrow hips was a double-tipped blade, like the one Enris had found but plain. The metal shone, from frequent or recent use.

She had to know. "Did you attack it?"

The small eyes swiveled toward her. "That would certainly change the Agreement."

Not yes or no. The consequence.

Aryl felt cold. She shouldn't be hearing this, shouldn't be stuck between the other races. It wasn't right or fair.

Which didn't change the fact that she was the one standing here, responsible for the safety of those on the other side of the empty river. Or that she had a dying Oud and its machine to deal with, and truenight approaching rapidly. She eyed the Tikitik dubiously. "Is there something we can do—some way to contact its kind? Help it?"

The Tikitik barked its laugh. "The Hard Ones come to help it."

"Hard Ones" had to mean the rock hunters rolling closer

with the dusk. When she looked up the road, they pretended to be random piles of stone. Except for a small one that tumbled along until it ran into a larger and bounced back.

The Oud twitched. Because she discussed its fate with its murderer? She shuddered.

Thought Traveler kicked dirt at the Oud's vehicle, scattering a cloud of whirr/clicks. "This will be retrieved. They value their machines more than their flesh. Remember that, little Speaker."

Something in its tone reminded her of the other Tikitik she'd met—it had seemed to enjoy enlightening her. "What else should I know about the Oud?" she dared ask.

Disconcerting attention from four eyes, then another bark. "You amuse me, little Speaker. For that, I will tell you something more. A gift." Its mouth protuberances writhed as if it relished the words. "The Oud cannot comprehend your fragility. They expect Om'ray to be here. That there was a time without Om'ray confounded them. You are, to them, the beings whose bones decorate the ground."

With that, the gray Tikitik turned and ran into the shadows, its long toes soundless on the stone and snow, its longer legs covering ground with terrifying speed. Rock hunters in its path tried to roll aside with almost comic haste. She didn't blame them.

The Oud's limbs moved, passed a small object up the length of its body from one set to the next with agonizing slowness. Aryl thought about helping, but stayed still.

At last, the object—another small bag—was clutched in the limbs closest to those it used for speaking. "Sona . . . Sona . . ." It paused between each word as though the effort to speak was too much for it. "Take . . ."

Aryl took a step back.

No one would see her refuse. The rock hunters—the Tikitik's "Hard Ones"—would crush whatever it meant her to have.

Gifts from other races brought nothing but trouble.

"Take . . . goodgood . . . go—" The limbs relaxed their hold. The little bag tumbled free, landing in unstained snow.

What was inside?

Her own curiosity, Aryl fumed to herself, was worse than the Tikitik's. She bent and picked up the bag.

"Good." A last shudder of limbs. "Here . . . Soon."

The Oud's body sagged beneath the weight of its fabric cloak, its limbs folding neatly together.

It was dead. Aryl tightened her fingers around the small bag. She glared past the corpse at the line of Hard Ones waiting not too far away.

So something was coming, here.

Soon—whatever that meant to an Oud.

Aryl hopped down to the riverbed, resolutely turning her back.

Behind her, the slow grind of rock.

Interlude

ENRIS STOOD IN THE TALL arched window, gazing out at Vyna, and wondered about many things.

Chief among them, his future.

The Tikitik had helped him get here. Why, he didn't know, unless it was the creature's cruel nature.

There was no soil here to farm, no giant stalks to climb or bear fruit. Only black rock shaped into this island and the enclosing wall that towered on all sides—or was this the hollowed inside of a mountain? When the sun penetrated the haze overhead, the black absorbed its light and cast even darker shadows into the water that lay between island and wall. Water like nothing he'd ever seen. It was warm, warm enough to produce the mist that hung above its surface most of the day and all truenight. Its smooth surface glistened with the colors of congealing metal: purples, reds, flares of iridescent blue. He wasn't sure if he'd have drowned falling into it, or been poisoned.

It held life. Life the Vyna hunted from wide-bottomed craft able to float on the water. There was no obvious control or mechanism pushing the craft, yet they moved with precision and sometimes speed, leaving a froth of lingering yellow bubbles behind. Platforms along the island's shore received them when they returned; steps carved in the black rock led upward, for the sides of the island were sheer, its people perched every bit as precariously as the Yena in their canopy.

He half smiled, thinking of Yena. Aryl wouldn't call the Vyna's technique hunting. From what he could see, what they pulled wriggling from the water was as eager to be caught as the Vyna were to catch them.

Do you understand what you see?

His mother's uncle, Clor sud Mendolar, had come on Passage from Amna, with fascinating stories of life on the shore of the bitter water. Though, from what he remembered, those swimmers weren't so easily caught. "They're catching swimmers," he answered out loud.

Fikryya came to stand beside him and covered her ears. *Hush, Enris.*

"It's you I don't understand," he whispered.

Vyna didn't speak. The ones he'd met understood what he said. None replied in kind. They wanted him to use mindspeech, an intimacy he wasn't prepared for—not without more answers.

I'm here to answer your questions.

No emotion. Fikryya's shields were perfect. Better, he was sure, than his own. Another reason for caution.

The Vyna was his height, though so slender he could have spanned her waist with his hands. Her hair was hidden beneath a tight red-and-gold cap; its curled ends framed her face. Twists of sparkling blue fell from small knots on the cap: an illusion of hair to brush her back and shoulders.

Her face—she was Om'ray, his inner sense knew it—her face wasn't right. Her eyes were too deeply set; the bones of her jaw too pronounced, chin thrust forward. Her skin was so pale he could see blood vessels; her lips were almost blue. The color of her shadowed eyes eluded him. Her eyebrows had been replaced by a doubled line of glittering red dots.

She wore a robe from shoulder to toe as revealing as her skin, a flow of symbols in red and gold the only disguise to parts of her body he found remarkably distracting.

As was the second thumb on each elegant hand, opposed to the first.

A Chooser. Something deep inside responded to her presence in a way he couldn't ignore. Not that he'd rush to take her hand, if offered. She was intriguing, but . . . no. Not for him.

His heart thudded in his chest. Had he just proved Aryl's belief? That he'd been exiled not because he was unable to Join, but because he could refuse?

Not that the Vyna Chooser Called to him. He supposed he was as strange to her as she was to him.

Enris coughed. "Why are you keeping me here?" "Here" being the room to which they'd brought him, in such haste he'd caught only tantalizing glimpses of his surroundings. Black rock, metal doors, windows open to the air, without covering or shutters, long boxes of stone filled with green, growing things. Vines heavy with fruit. Glows where there would be shadows.

Something about his arrival had upset them. He wasn't surprised, but he was tired of this room, with its over-thick cushions and deep carpets. He was tired of being dirty.

Not to mention of being hungry.

"Well?"

He hadn't moved toward her, but Fikryya flinched away, the fabric of her robe so fine it took an instant to settle against her body again. Her hands covered her ears.

Enris gestured apology. "Forgive me," he whispered, giving her his best smile. "But I've come a long way. This isn't the welcome I expected."

Council must decide what to do.

That didn't sound good. He kept his voice down. "With me?" A startled flash from those hidden eyes. Worse. "You can sense what I am, Fikryya," Enris coaxed. "An unChosen. Eligible. On Passage. My mother thinks I'm good-looking."

Her blush was spectacular. *You are not Vyna.*

Enris leaned against the wall and crossed his arms. *I could be,* he sent, adding overtones of *friendliness* and a warm hint of *interest.* Didn't hurt to show good intentions.

NO! You are not Vyna! A lash of outraged *fury.* Her shields, he winced, weren't perfect after all. *You are a lesser Om'ray. Choice between Vyna and lesser Om'ray is Forbidden! Council decides if our Adepts should waste their time scouring your mind before you are fed to the* rumn, *that is all.*

With that, and a whirl of fabric that left nothing remaining to his imagination, the Vyna Chooser left the room. The metal door spun closed with a thud.

"I'll take that as a no," Enris said mildly.

Not good at all.

* ✳ *

They weren't interested in his belongings either, leaving him the clothes he wore and whatever he'd shoved into his pockets at the Tikitik's suggestion. For that small favor, he should be grateful, Enris thought grimly as he chewed his last morsel of food, using his tongue to find pieces of lint and swallowing those, too.

On second thought, he'd like to introduce Thought Traveler to Vyna's strange lake. No wonder the creature had been entertained. He'd demanded to go to the one Clan Forbidden to accept those on Passage.

Why?

More importantly, how was he going to change their minds?

Enris laughed. He sounded like a certain Yena.

Still, these were Om'ray with secrets. He had a few. A trade might be possible.

He needed to know more about them first. From the window, all he could see was what surrounded the island: water, mist, and a soaring wall of rock. The narrow bridge where the esan dropped him wasn't in sight.

What else? They might be isolated, but Vyna didn't lack power. There were six glows attached to the walls of this room alone; others in use along the walkways. Their style was peculiar, with outer casings shaped like swimmers and leaves.

A people with time for aesthetics.

He tried taking one of the glows down, but it was inset into the rock wall as if there would never be need to remove it. Another mystery. In Tuana and Yena, glows had to be replaced regularly, along with the sealed cells that powered them. The Oud used a similar arrangement in their tunnels. He supposed the Tikitik did as well.

The lighting within a Cloisters had its own, apparently endless supply of power. Cloisters. Something he hadn't seen while being hustled to this room. Perhaps Vyna had found a way to extend that power to where they lived.

An exciting thought. To not depend on the technology of others.

As for the strangers . . . power for their devices had been among the hundreds of questions he would have asked Marcus Bowman, if it hadn't been too dangerous for all concerned. Aryl had been wise to resist temptation. They were having trouble enough with the Oud and Tikitik . . .

And now with their own.

Despite Fikryya's vehement denial, there was only one kind of Om'ray. Vyna were the same as everyone else to his inner sense. What else mattered?

Manners, for one. Enris swallowed his last, very well-chewed mouthful and listened to his stomach complain about its emptiness. Surely they'd feed him before . . .

Before what? Before they fed him to whatever she'd said?

Om'ray kill Om'ray? He'd never heard of such a thing. That didn't make him less afraid. Too easy to summon the memory of those kicks and blows in the dark, his own desperate realization that while these were his people, his Clan, their anger was about to send them across an unimaginable line.

Anger, he could understand. A cold decision to end another life? Why?

He fingered his token. When they'd left it untouched, he'd assumed there would be a grand ceremony—with feast—to welcome him. But other than Sona, Vyna was the smallest Clan. How could they not need unChosen, especially—no point being modest—one of his strength, skill, and Power?

And ability to annoy. Enris smiled, remembering the outrage in Aryl's gray eyes when she suspected he made fun of her.

He'd tied her knot of hair to the thong holding his neck pouch, where his fingers could easily find it. Now he touched that tiny softness.

She'd believed in him.

He hadn't come this far to fail.

Enris straightened his tunic and checked his boots. He'd been welcomed by the Grona. Sona, too, had he stayed. He'd make these Vyna appreciate him.

Thoughtful of them to leave his things.

The glows might be unfamiliar, but the spindle on which the door turned was as normal as could be. The rings holding it in position would be of softer metal than the back of his knife. A moment's effort to pry them open and off, then he tugged the door down and toward him, freeing the spindle's tip from its hole. The door, now turning on the lock rod, tipped inward. With a grin, Enris crouched and crawled underneath.

There was no one outside. He'd have known. Yena's First Scout might mock his inability to move quietly—something their children could do—but no one had to teach him to be aware of those around him. While working on the Om'ray device, he'd always been careful to check that he was alone.

Not to mention it had helped him avoid Naryn S'udlaat. For a while.

For the first time, he wondered about her reaction. Shocked out of her skin, he imagined, grinning with satisfaction. Hadn't the spoiled daughter of Adepts had her way from birth, doted on by aging parents, worshiped by her gang of useless friends? He'd been one of the few unimpressed by her Power or beauty. When she'd *pushed* a hammer at his head in a fit of temper, he'd refused to support her claim to that Talent. The only reason, he supposed, she'd wanted him at all was because he didn't want her.

Served her right he could refuse.

Though he didn't envy whomever Naryn had finally claimed. He hoped not one of his cheerful cousins.

And not, he thought, his grin fading, Mauro Lorimar. Lorimar had led the attack against him. Dangerous, indeed, Joining such unnatural violence to Naryn's selfish Power.

Enris shrugged. He'd only know if another Tuana came to Vyna on Passage. This was his Clan now.

If he wasn't eaten.

Beyond his room was a short straight hall with arched openings to the outside at either end. No biters, he guessed, the first thing about Vyna he liked. He'd take that as a promising start.

No need to keep out the cold either. The water surrounding the island was warm, the air still. If that was the sum of their seasons, he supposed he could get used to gloom and mist, though the abundance of glows hinted the Vyna themselves didn't care for it.

The arch he chose led to a walkway, too narrow to call a road, neat, straight, and flat. Its black rock was inlaid with bands of white. The inlay caught the light from the glows, giving the darkness between the illusion of depth. He found himself reluctant to trust his footing.

To his inner sense, the Vyna were scattered throughout their island—all below this level—and on its water. None nearby.

Enris paused, startled. Many—too many—were Choosers. He could *taste* them, like a sweetness on the roof of his mouth. Everywhere. Yet none were Calling. That he'd feel.

They didn't seek a Choice? How could that be?

Without knowing the capabilities of these Om'ray, he wasn't about to lower his shields and *reach* for any one mind to ask. Nor was he going to let any Adept "scour" his. Whatever that meant.

The being-eaten part was, in any case, completely unreasonable. Whatever a "rumn" was.

All he had to do was find a way to impress the Vyna with his quality.

* ✳ *

Tuana's shops and homes were works of beauty. Intricate brickwork inlaid with precious wood, carved and polished. Metal bands, treated to bring out rainbow hues, at curves and angles.

Light welcomed through sheets of clear surry. And what light. Until experiencing Yena's canopy, Enris had taken for granted that huge arch of sky, with its star-laced dome at truenight. Until stumbling across mountain slopes, he'd given no thought to Tuana's level roadway: how it connected buildings and fields, made easy the path to the meeting hall or Cloisters, and kept the Oud from driving where they shouldn't. Usually.

Vyna differed in every way. The island thrust from the water like a jagged shard of metal protruding from a bin. Rooms had been cut from it, or rather into it—how, he couldn't imagine, unless the Vyna worked rock the way other Om'ray worked wood. The result wasn't a village but a single building, little more than a room's width at its narrowest, but tens of levels high. He'd been housed close to the top. Walkways stepped and staggered around its girth, sometimes meeting platforms overhung by arches, at others taking abrupt turns to end at blank walls as if waiting for a forgotten door.

No dirt. No dust. Mist curled in corners, scattered beneath glows, blunted sharp edges. Vines trailed from irregular openings high overhead, self-conscious against the black rock, withered at their tips.

If there were differences between homes, storerooms, or shops, none showed from outside. He could pick any door, go inside . . . Enris snorted, hearing his mother's voice in his head. 'Poor manners make a poor guest.' "

His father wasn't the only one with sayings.

Still . . . it could be time for supper. Maybe that was why he'd seen no one. Surely even a stranger under a death sentence being ignored by an entire Clan could walk in and share a family's meal.

Despite not sensing any Om'ray here, Enris paused and sniffed hopefully near one of the always-open arches. Not food, but . . . he sniffed again and coughed. Musty. Damp. Like the back corner of a storehouse in spring. Old.

The whole place was musty and old, he decided with a grimace. It didn't matter how clean it appeared, how perfect. There was rot somewhere.

Up was—he leaned back to see—an appalling number of steps without any change.

Enris picked down.

* ✳ *

Down meant around as well. By the time he reached the lowest level, Enris had circled Vyna twice. His feet hurt and he was unhappy, being, as Aryl would doubtless point out, too easily ruled by his stomach. His shrinking stomach. Fine for Yena to starve themselves, he grumbled to himself. None of them were his size.

From above, he'd spotted three bridges connecting the island and wall, each a stretch of black rock barely wide enough for a child. That he'd needed to be led by the hand on his arrival—and almost fallen off every other step—was proof. The mist obscured most of their length, but two ended in tunnel-like openings into the mountainside, lit by glows. The third didn't come out of the mist. Perhaps it wasn't finished.

The last step. Enris greeted the platform at the water's edge with a groan of relief. It stretched to either side, matched to the sharp, irregular lines of the island itself. Beside him, the upraised tips of floating craft pretended to be a forest. Instead of being tossed by a breeze, they rose, leaned, and settled with the water's movement. Not that he could see the water through the mist. It fingered its way up the sides of the craft, pooled against the black edge of the platform. Steps disappeared into it, as well as the light from the glows.

Plenty of Om'ray here, shadows without voice. They looked at him as they passed with hooks and mesh over their shoulders, sidelong looks without welcome or curiosity. As if to see where he stood, so they could avoid him.

Which only worked if he let it, Enris thought, amused. He planted himself in the path of the next burdened Vyna and smiled widely. "Need help with that?"

This didn't get the reaction he'd hoped. Every Vyna in earshot stopped what they were doing to glare at him. *HUSH!* The sending was from more than one.

With an undertone of *fear*.

Of him? Not judging by the disdain on the face of the Om'ray he'd interrupted.

A familiar face. Deep-set eyes, a prominent chin and heavy cheekbones, skin so pale it reflected the light from the nearest glow. Tall, bone-thin. Like Fikryya, his hair was hidden beneath a tight cap, this one green and blue, with tassels of blue hanging to his shoulders and down his back. Unlike the Chooser, he wore a snug-fitting yellow tunic, overwritten with black symbols, that went to his knees and left his arms bare. Scrawny arms, like a child's. No, that was an insult to young Ziba, whose arms were ribboned with muscle.

Enris felt thick.

Though he had no idea why his voice upset them, he gestured apology. *May I help?* he sent, careful to maintain his shields.

The Vyna shrugged the mesh from his shoulder to the platform. *Bring that.* Once Enris moved aside, he walked to the nearest step and disappeared into the mist. *This way.*

If there was *anticipation* and a not-pleasant *amusement* in the sending, the Tuana chose to ignore them.

He picked up the mesh and put it over his shoulder.

It was a start.

*　❋　*

The craft of the Vyna were metal, not wood as he'd expected, and extraordinarily simple. The shape, like a curled leaf, was hammered from a single thin sheet. Enris ran his hand along the side, imagining how it would have been poured and cooled to retain its strength. Folds reinforced the top edge and midline. Wide, lengthwise bars created a floor; he had to be careful not to wedge his boot in their gap. There were two narrower bars across the width. After climbing over the side—in his case, a graceless struggle made worse by the damp footing of the steps—the two Vyna leaned back against one of those bars, mesh bundled beside them, their expressions impassive.

He leaned on the other and smiled. *I'm Enris Mendolar.*

The silence, inner and outer, was almost painful. Then, *Dar-youch.* The older Vyna, who'd given him the mesh to carry.

Etleka. The other Vyna. UnChosen. A son, he guessed. The similarity between the two, and to Fikryya, must mean close kin.

Of the same family?

Of Vyna. This from Daryouch, with a *snap* of impatience, as if Enris asked a stupid question. *Make no sound once the float begins to move.*

Move how? Enris couldn't see any mechanism or device to—

Power. He *sensed* it, felt it. But—

The float, as Daryouch named it, slipped away from the steps, mist parting as if to let it through, then closing in behind.

The Tuana almost laughed in amazement. They were using Power to move their float—and themselves—across the water. The control required outstripped anything he'd imagined. He had to learn this. He'd been right to come.

The only sound was their breathing and the slide of water along the metal sides. Mist poured into the float, swirling and damp. At times, it obscured everything below their waists, so they might have been sitting in a cloud. The sky above was masked as well. Nothing to see in any direction. If it hadn't been for his *sense* of other Om'ray, Enris would have been lost.

That and the smell. The must of old rot was stronger out here.

The float came to a stop.

Ready the net.

Etleka held out one side of the mesh. The Tuana took it, watching carefully as the other Om'ray demonstrated, with his two-thumbed hands, how to grip a thicker edge rope in one and take a handful of the fine mesh in the other. *Raise it like this.*

In the air? From the glint in Daryouch's eye, he knew better than to ask. Dutifully, Enris copied Etleka's position.

Hold. No matter what.

Enris braced himself within the metal leaf, boots against a floor bar, his back to the one that crossed the width.

Power. This time not to move anything, but to summon.

It was like the Call of a Chooser, but immeasurably stronger. And, like so much of Vyna, Enris realized it was not . . . quite . . . . . . right.

Even as he grasped that the summons wasn't meant for him, a small shape appeared in the mist, flinging itself toward them. It collided with the net, and Etleka grinned. *Denos,* he sent. *Supper!*

Then the mist was full of flying shapes. The denos seemed oblivious to the net, quickly becoming entangled in such numbers that Enris copied Etleka and fastened his rope to the bar. The two plucked the swimmers free and dropped them to the floor where they fell through the gaps, a writhing harvest of silver and black that soon spilled over the bars and flopped around their feet.

The summons ended. With a final splash, the last denos dropped into the water on the other side of the float, safe for the time being.

Etleka clapped Enris on the shoulder then began folding up the net.

"Let me help," the Tuana said without thinking.

HUSH!

No missing the *fear*. The Vyna looked horrified; Daryouch furious as well. Both froze in place, staring into the mist.

Something was there.

Enris wasn't sure how he knew, but he stared as well.

The float rocked once, gently.

Something approached.

His inner sense. That was it. But how? How could he *sense* something *in* the water?

Not with his inner sense, he realized with a shudder, but with what connected him to the M'hir. That was where he felt that cold, strange touch. It wasn't Om'ray. But *real*. Alive.

The Vyna had summoned something from the depths, something to terrify the denos into their net.

And now it hunted his voice.

He pulled his knife, gripped the bar with his other hand, and readied himself.

Put that away. For once Daryouch didn't *feel* angry. *A* rumn *can swallow three floats with one gulp. Stay still and make no more sound. It should leave.*

That was a rumn?

No wonder the tiny swimmers thought leaping into the air was safer.

Enris wanted to join them.

✳ ✱ ✳

Two days in a row and he hadn't been eaten.

Enris decided he was pleased. He also decided to avoid extremely large hungry creatures on the premise a third encounter could be his last.

After an endless tenth waiting for the rumn, whatever that was, to choose not to eat them, they returned to the platform. He helped Etleka unload their catch, now fully understanding why the Vyna didn't care to speak out loud—particularly by the water.

How do you eat them? he asked Daryouch, eyeing the still-flapping denos with ravenous intent. If they said raw, he'd take that plump one first.

Flatcakes. This from Etleka, with an *image* of white flesh, shredded and spiced, shaped into disks and fried a crisp brown.

Stomach growling, Enris licked his lips. *I'll take a few of those.*

Stranger! A harsh summons. The Tuana glanced up at the grim-faced pair on the platform. They could have been Daryouch's brothers and were dressed like the denos-catcher, except for the green metal rod each carried, about the length of an arm. Tool or badge of office?

An escort, that he knew. Enris gave the dying denos a wistful look, shrugged at his companions—who turned away to become too-obviously busy with their catch—and climbed out of the float. *Supper?* he asked.

In answer, they pointed the rods left.

Not up? Enris shrugged again and started walking. The pair set themselves one to each side, as if to make sure he didn't elude them by diving into the mist-covered, rumn-infested water or choose to walk into a rock wall. As he had no intention of harm-ing himself, he projected a mild *amusement*.

They didn't respond. He hadn't expected they would.

The platform met another that turned a sharp corner. One of the bridges loomed ahead, a black tongue tasting the mist. Enris lengthened his stride to get past the dangerous thing. To his dis-may, his escort stepped in his way, rods pointing where he least wanted to go. Enris stopped dead. "You—" before they could ob-ject, he switched to a sending, a most emphatic one. *You can't ex-pect me to walk on—*"OOF!" The sound whooshed out as a rod poked him firmly in the stomach.

Hush!

Enris braced himself to grab the next bit of metal aimed his way, but the two merely waited.

If you plan to feed me to the rumn, he sent, keeping his feelings— which were intense on the subject—firmly behind his shields, *you'll have to pick me up and throw me in.* If they tried, he vowed, they'd go in first.

The pair exchanged looks. *You've been summoned to Council, stranger. We're to make sure you arrive safely.*

He stood a better chance with Vyna's elders than their odd Choosers, Enris assured himself, feeling more cheerful. He had the right smile, according to his grandmother. Resisting the urge to rub his abused middle, he gave a little bow. *Lead the way.*

One did. The other motioned him ahead. Enris took a deep breath and followed, taking the smallest possible steps once on the bridge. It was worse than climbing a branch in the canopy. At least there, he could hold on to something. Here he felt as though he tipped from side to side. Not to mention the mist obscured the footing. He slowed. Despite that care, one foot slipped. He stopped.

Take hold.

Of what? His escort? These Vyna, however, were better pre-pared than those who'd met him on his arrival. Rather than offer-ing a hand, the one in front swung his rod back, taking hold of the rod from his partner.

Railings.

Enris stifled a laugh sure to attract the wrong kind of attention. *Clever.*

Take hold.

Trust them, or knock them all into whatever lay hidden in mist. Enris locked his right hand around the rod to that side, his left to the left.

Whether their confidence came through that contact, or it was their matter-of-fact strides, Enris soon found himself able to ignore what was—or wasn't—under his boots. Mostly. But just as he estimated they'd passed the halfway point, his escort slowed, then stopped.

Why? There was nothing here. Just as Enris was about to point this out, and suggest a return to ground wider than his shoulders, he realized they weren't alone.

Om'ray.

Not ahead . . .

Below.

The mist ahead blazed yellow, then parted, sliding from the bridge with palpable reluctance. Enris found himself staring down at a familiar pair of metal doors, slowly turning open. Their movement pushed aside the mist, let light from within touch his face.

Vyna's Cloisters.

The bridge ended here, with these doors. Between them, a set of stairs carved from black rock led down, steeply down. Enris couldn't see the end of them. Water lapped, unseen. Mist began to slink back around his legs, explored the opening.

The rods in his hands twisted, he let go and their owners reclaimed them. *Go. You will be met.*

He gestured gratitude. *I thank you for your care.*

Both Vyna stared at him, their heavy lids half closed. Then, *Do not expect a welcome.*

✳ ✳ ✳

He'd expected walls, at least. But the stairs led to more doors. Beyond those had been . . . this. Windows. Tall arched windows just

like those that graced Yena's Council Chamber. After his first astonished stare, Enris did his best to keep his eyes on anything else.
The darkness pressing inward wasn't the sky. It had no right being
populated by stars. Stars that moved with disturbing suppleness or
would abruptly gather and still, as if watching.

"Anything else" was only slightly less disturbing. If he thought
Vyna's Cloisters strange, what could he call its Council? No one
outside Vyna, Enris thought wryly, was going to believe this.

Instead of the eldest of each family—something he supposed
was unreasonable if they all considered themselves members of
one—he stood before six pregnant Chosen.

Very pregnant. When his mother had been this large with
Worin, he and Kiric had teased her about moving out of the house
until she gave birth.

All were dressed in the next-to-transparent fabric Fikryya had
worn, as if it was important to flaunt their swollen abdomens and
breasts.

He couldn't have told them apart. This went beyond the resemblance of kin to kin. Any one of them, if not pregnant, could
have been older Fikryyas.

As well as the Councillors, there were nine Adepts, attended
not by Lost, but by nine unChosen males. Vyna's Adepts were
the oldest Om'ray he'd ever seen, frail and confined to chairs. For-
tunately, a judgment he kept to himself, they were wrapped in layers of fine white blankets. He couldn't have told their sex. He
couldn't tell if the two in the middle were still alive, but assumed
the rest knew.

All wore brightly colored caps over their hair; all had tassels of
fake hair hanging to their shoulders. The colors varied, but not the
style. It was as if they wanted to look alike.

He brushed his straying black locks from his forehead self-
consciously.

Enris Tuana.

Disconcerting, not being able to tell the source of the words.
Though not as disconcerting, Enris thought, as the tone of *bore-
dom*. He smiled politely at the Council, quite sure his smile would

have no impact on the Vyna Adepts. *I have come on Passage and hope for your welcome.*

Strange, how that part he'd never doubted until now.

Tuana bears the stain of Ground Dwellers.

Another mindvoice. *And of the Meddlers. An esan dropped him here.*

Meddler—that suited the Tikitik. Ground Dwellers? Had to be Oud. He felt a fierce rush of hope. Had he been right? Was Vyna free of the Agreement, safe from the demands of other races?

Does Vyna not have such neighbors? he sent, allowing a tinge of envy.

We are not lesser *Om'ray.*

The emphasis stung, as the sender no doubt intended. The third Councillor, he decided. The one closest to the Adepts' row of chairs. There was something in her posture that matched the overbearing pride of the sending, a hint of greater strength. Or ruthlessness.

Careful of that one, he told himself.

I come in search of Om'ray technology. Enris delicately offered his memory of the device the Oud had given him, just its shape, nothing more, not yet. *Is this of Vyna?*

One of the Adepts slumped forward. The attendant unChosen immediately placed one hand on his or her shoulder. Enris *sensed* a flow of Power, a giving of strength from the younger Om'ray. The ancient Adept wheezed and sat up again; the attendant, now gasping, removed his hand.

The rest ignored this lapse, their wizened faces intent on him, lipless mouths working eagerly as if he'd offered them a sweet morsel.

These would "scour" his mind? Shaken, he checked his shields.

Show us. Noncommittal, but he sensed *interest*.

Which was a problem. The device was still in the Mendolar shop, unless the Oud had reclaimed it. If only he'd taken it . . .

Wait. Enris pulled the pouch from his neck and opened it. *I have this,* he sent, holding the clear wafer on the palm of his hand. It was old, strange, and Om'ray. He'd meant to leave it with Aryl; a

small curiosity of Sona, a bauble of no possible use to an unChosen on Passage.

Of definite use, if it bought him his life.

The wafer rose from his hand and flew to that of the third
Councillor. Enris let out the breath he hadn't realized he'd held.
More than interest.

He wasn't prepared for her to press the wafer over the swell of
her unborn and exclaim—out loud—in rapture, "Take her, Glorious Dead! Take her and be born again!"

The other Councillors took up the chant, the Adepts gumming
the words. "Take her! Be born again!"

The clear wafer turned milky white and began to glow, pulsing
in time with the chant.

It wasn't the only light to play over the rapt faces of the Vyna.
Enris looked at the windows. The stars-that-weren't swarmed in
greater and greater numbers. They pulsed, too, but faster, as if excited.

He rubbed his hand against his tunic. What had he been carrying?

Take him. No telling who gave the order, but Enris stepped back
quickly, ready to defend himself. He didn't want to hurt anyone,
but he'd be willing to throw a few.

You'll live, Tuana. Too cold to be reassuring. *Take him to those already contaminated.*

Chapter 13

"THOUGHT TRAVELER SAID THE OUD would come for their machine."

Haxel raised an eyebrow. "And they needed this?"

"This" being the surprise that greeted them at dawn. An Oud tunnel mouth had opened on the other side of the river, complete with support beams and a ramp leading into the depths. Aryl shrugged. "The machine's gone."

Along with the corpse. No Hard Ones in sight, but she didn't doubt they'd been the first to arrive. As for the tunnel? "Before it died, the Oud told me something was coming here," she reminded the First Scout. "This could be what it meant. Maybe this is how the Oud establish their presence. A—door. There's one at Grona."

"Theirs is tucked under a bridge. Discreet. This is in our way."

Aryl's lips quirked. Haxel gave her a sidelong look, then chuckled. "You're going to tell me to be grateful they didn't put it through one of our homes."

"Not in so many words, but yes."

"Glad you're the Speaker, Aryl Sarc."

With that less than comforting statement, the First Scout headed back to the village.

Aryl lingered, trying to see down the tunnel, but the contrast between daylight and the faint glow within was too great to reveal detail. It went down, that was all she knew for sure. She tried the geoscanner. Its red symbol told her what she could see for herself: Oud, here, and active.

A mere five days after Om'ray stumbled on its ruins—ruins they'd caused in the first place—Sona's Oud were ready, even eager, to resume official relations. Had the creatures been waiting all this time or had they watched them leave Grona? Would any Om'ray have done, or was there something about the exiles they approved?

Disturbing thoughts.

Aryl pulled the small bag from her belt and stared at it. The dying Oud's "gift." Probably should open it, she told herself. They might show up at any moment, and ask for it back. Or not. Who could predict what they'd do?

The pendant. The headdress from the ridge. The blade Enris found. Sona itself. Things from the past had an unsettling way of changing the present.

The wonder, she decided, wasn't that the strangers were interested in what happened long ago, it was that they dared look.

Were they braver than an Om'ray? Aryl pressed her lips together, then untied the bag's fastener, shaking its contents out on her open palm.

A circle of green metal.

A familiar circle. Her fingers trembled as she brushed dirt from its inner curve.

There. A small square. Inside, six tiny dots. His stars. His name.

Aryl slipped her hand through, pushing the band up her wrist until it was covered by her sleeve. The chill of the metal warmed to her skin. Enris had made this. He'd shown her the memory.

She could guess how the Oud came to have it. An Oud—possibly the same one—had stolen the Tuana's token and pack, before dragging him for days through their tunnels. But why bring this to her? Why now? There was a message in both timing and gift.

Aryl *tasted* change, bitter and ominous.

Something was coming.

Despite what she'd said to Haxel, the Oud hadn't meant this tunnel.

Whatever it was took its time. Their second fist passed, marked by clear skies and bitter cold. Hoyon professed this to be more typical weather. The exiles took full advantage, working outside from firstlight to truenight, using large fires to stretch the day. The Grona might be unused to heavy work, but even they seemed swept up by the enthusiasm to rebuild Sona. It helped that each new structure meant more space and privacy.

Hoyon preferred to work with Gijs sud Vendan, who seemed flattered by the older Chosen's attention. Juo was not, and continued to avoid both Adepts. Oran and her Chosen took their ease—when they had it—with Chaun and Weth. Kran, not yet accepted by the Sona unChosen, hovered near his sister.

When he wasn't, Aryl thought uneasily, staring at her.

On the surface, Sona was a unit, working to the betterment of all.

But the Adepts would stop talking when she walked by, and neither volunteered a word to her. Bern barely spoke at all, perhaps because Oran made a point of sleeping with others— to the blunt-spoken dismay of his great-grandmother. Husni, in no uncertain terms, expected babies. Sona needed them. What was Oran thinking?

Oran, Aryl knew, was thinking about being a proper Adept in a real Cloisters, trained and valued. She'd do nothing, yet, to risk her chance of a return to that life.

Nervous, quiet Oswa, little Yao her shadow, went from useless at cooking to useless at mending. Taen, normally the most patient of Om'ray, declared the older Chosen an inept menace following a too-close call pouring hot oil.

There was, however, something Oswa did very well. Aryl discovered it when she entered the meeting hall looking for Veca. The woodworker wasn't there, but the Grona sat at one end of a long table—the hall now boasted two—Yao beside her paying rapt attention to what her mother's hands were doing.

Oswa was writing.

She used a splinter and a liquid from a small pot to draw symbols on a length of white fabric. A child's undercoat, Aryl realized.

"This is me?" Yao asked, pointing at a double curve.

"This," Oswa replied, touching the ink-free end of the splinter to a series of circles and lines. "See? There is the road. The river. This is where you mustn't go. This is the way—Aryl. I didn't hear you." She laid her hands flat on her work, not to hide it, but hold it, as if she thought it would be taken away.

Perhaps it would, in Grona. Oswa was no Adept. If she knew how to read and write, it was knowledge gleaned through her Joining to Hoyon. Also Forbidden.

This wasn't Grona. "May I see?" Aryl asked. A way to represent the world that didn't rely on their inner sense? She'd never heard of such a thing, but she wasn't the one with a crippled daughter.

Yao climbed into her lap when she sat beside Oswa, snuggling into place with a contented sigh. Aryl put her arms around her, *feeling* the mother's shields. "It's Sona," the child said proudly. She was a warm little thing, happiest when touching others. The exiles believed it made her feel less alone; even Haxel would put aside her work to ruffle Yao's fluff of brown hair and smile.

Aryl, who knew Yao could sense them all through the M'hir, thought it just the child's sweet nature, blossoming under the exiles' attention.

Young as she was, Yao knew better than to climb in her father's lap or touch any of the Caraats. Hoyon and the rest treated her as if she was not-*real*, at best uncomfortable when she was near. Aryl had to believe he'd been willing to risk his daughter's life to reach Sona because he hadn't felt there was a life to risk.

If he or Oran knew Yao existed partly in what Yena's Adepts called the *Dark*, it would be worse.

Aryl pressed her cheek to Yao's head. "How does it work?"

"I can't bear her to be lost again," Oswa said defensively, her hair lashing. "I can't."

None of us could, Aryl sent, putting *commitment* beneath the words. "Show me. I'm truly interested, Oswa," she persisted at the other's look of doubt.

The Chosen spread the undercoat. "This is here." A symbol like two sticks braced against one another. Her finger went to one side of the 'coat, indicated a line from which three others rose. "This is where we see the sun in the morning." To the other side, a line alone. "This is where it sets. The empty river." Two wavy lines. "The mounds." Dots of black.

Sona. Defined not by the Clans around it, but by its relationship to other places. Aryl's eyes shot up to Oswa's. "Remarkable."

"I wrote her name—she knows it—here, with mine. So we're together." A line of symbols beneath. Painstaking, detailed work. The Grona sighed. "Foolish, I know."

"It's clever," Aryl said sincerely. "Like looking down from the sky." Was this how Marcus saw his surroundings? Was this how he found his way from place to place—world to world? She felt dizzy trying to imagine it. "Would you teach me?"

"Why?"

Freeing one arm from Yao, now half asleep, Aryl touched the mark that was Sona, then drew her finger across the empty white and pressed where she thought would be the waterfall and Cloisters. "Yao will go here, one day. She'll need to know the way. I'd like to draw it for her."

"She can't go out on her own," Oswa objected, reaching for her daughter. Unconcerned—or familiar—with the talk of adults, Yao stirred only to settle in her mother's lap, promptly closing her eyes. "She never will," the Grona continued. "You know she's—" a whisper, "—she's not like other Om'ray. The world isn't there to her."

Aryl regarded the now-sleeping child. Before meeting Marcus, she would have shared her mother's grief. Now, she found herself smiling. "The world is there—and more than the world, Oswa. Yao may be the first Om'ray able to walk beyond the end of the world, to see what's there."

"Om'ray are the world," as if Aryl was the child. "There's nothing more."

She didn't argue. "So, how should I draw a mountain?"

A tenth later—and Aryl's attempts at drawing the valley— Oswa relaxed enough to laugh. She had a lovely smile, belied by the lines on her face. With Yao asleep, the burden on her Power lessened, though she continued to shield against any dreams. Sleeping children didn't confine themselves to their own minds.

Dreams. Maybe, Aryl thought, it was time. She put down her splinter and wiped her fingertips on a scrap. "Has Yao had any unusual dreams, Oswa? I don't want to concern you, but Seru, Ziba, and I—" she decided not to mention Juo's unborn "—we've each had one or more since coming to Sona. Dreams about what this place was like. That's how we found the supplies hidden in the mounds."

The Grona didn't look surprised, though her cheeks paled and she held Yao a little tighter. "Teaching dreams."

Aryl blinked. "You know what they are?"

"Adepts use them. That's how they learn." A flash of *bitterness,* quickly stilled. "Memories are stored in the Cloisters, I don't know how. But certain skills and knowledge—whatever must be known by those who come after—those are kept. To learn from them, an Adept dreams."

Aryl's heart pounded. "Why are we—why would Choosers dream?"

The other bent her head, rubbing her cheek against Yao's soft curls. Her own hair moved restlessly, but didn't disturb the child. "I don't know. But . . . A few years ago," she said so quietly Aryl had to strain to hear, "a sickness came. It weakened the eldest first, and the children. The Adepts stayed in the Cloisters, searching the records—" while a young mother waited outside, alone, and in fear, Aryl thought with pity.

"One truenight," Oswa went on, "our Choosers, all of them, dreamed the same memory. A teaching dream, sent out of the Cloisters as well as to the Adepts within. The sickness came from one of our plants. Because of the rain and cold during harvest, it had a growth inside that made a poison. We had only to stop eating it. The Adepts rushed from the Cloisters to save us—" a note of triumph "—but we had already saved ourselves."

The Sona Cloisters, sealed and abandoned. Could it have been sending dreams all this time, Aryl wondered, trying to save a people who no longer existed?

"I dreamed," she said, picking up the splinter and reinking it from Oswa's little pot, "that everyone in Sona learned to read and write. Even unChosen."

When Aryl looked up, Oswa Gethen was smiling.

"I don't trust either of them."

Aryl traded looks with Seru, who gave a pained lift of her eyebrows. Cetto sud Teerac had been a Councillor for Yena, confident of his authority and purpose until handed a token of exile with the rest. Husni had taken the Adepts' betrayal of her Chosen and family personally indeed.

"We've seen it," she said now, driving a needle through fabric with unnecessary force. "Adepts have their own schemes and plans. None for the good of ordinary Om'ray. You saw that, young Aryl."

Since her own mother had been one of those Adepts, there wasn't much Aryl could do besides gesture agreement.

"Oran healed Myris and Chaun," her cousin spoke up.

"That one?" Husni made a rude noise. "Smaller stitches, Seru," she ordered, "or the cold will find its way in."

Aryl slipped to the floor beside Seru, crossing her legs comfortably. Much as it pained her—and much as she inwardly agreed—there was nothing to be gained if Husni continued to speak against the Adepts. "I'm not suggesting you trust them," she began, sending *sincerity* through her shields.

Another jab of the needle. "Never will. Never!"

"But Sona is a fresh start for all of us. Including Oran and Hoyon." Who, despite being worked as never before, showed no signs of leaving. "We should give them a chance to prove themselves."

Husni, who had no hesitation expressing herself when away from her larger-than-life, outspoken Chosen, made a rude noise. "They talk about you, too, young Aryl, and not words you'd like to hear. 'Forward.' 'Doesn't know her place.' 'Just an unChosen, barely more than a child.' 'Who does she think she is, ordering everyone?' 'Haxel's favorite doesn't have to do real work.' "

Aryl's lips twitched. "Here I thought that's what you said about me."

Wrinkles creased in a wicked smile. "Of course. But to your face. Though you haven't done badly for a Sarc." The smile disappeared. Husni laid her hands on the pile of clothing in her lap. "Mark what I say. The two from Grona mean you no good and they've found fools to listen. If Sona is a fresh start, is that what we want? Secrets? Spite behind shields? You should do something."

She had. It had only made things worse. Secrets indeed. Aryl wished she could believe all would be well once she could offer her people the ability to move through the M'hir. If she should. She'd give anything to have someone she trusted to talk to about it.

If only Enris had stayed . . .

The other two were watching her, Seru with a slight frown. Aryl rose to her feet. "What I have to do is catch up to Haxel. She's waiting for me."

"Don't trust her either," Husni grumbled, picking up her needle and giving the sleeve in her other hand a dire look. "Upstart Vendan with her notions."

Aryl smiled sympathetically at Seru as she left.

The First Scout's notion of a meeting place would have raised Husni's hackles even more, Aryl thought with amusement as she climbed the rope ladder. Haxel, wanting a better vantage point to watch the valley, had built her own—a platform rising the height of three Om'ray from the top of the nearest mound. That this exposed whomever she assigned to watch to the full brunt of the ceaseless winter wind didn't appear to bother her.

On second thought, Husni probably approved. Anything that smacked of their life in the canopy brought a gleam to her washed-out eyes. Climb a swinging rope to a perch that, to be honest, shook with every gust of wind?

Just like home.

Aryl swung herself up and onto the platform. Haxel waved at their surroundings from her perch on one edge. An invitation.

From here, she could see the Oud tunnel, the dead grove of nekis, and follow the road and river to the first bend in the valley. The snow that fell no longer melted by day, although the wind scoured it from any rise. The result erased shadows, leveled the landscape. Did snow keep the Oud underground?

Looking across the valley, the snow emphasized the pattern of pebble-filled ditches that led from the empty riverbed, a pretense of water.

Beyond that?

Aryl squinted at the formidable cliff on the other side. Beyond that was Vyna.

Deliberately, she turned. Looking down the valley, she found it easy to tell where the destruction of the Oud stopped and started. Not random. The village, the road from it, the wide open fields. Anywhere a Sona might have run to escape.

"Any sign of our little friends?" she asked. Haxel had become, as she succinctly put it, "familiar" with the Hard Ones. Hammer, ax, or burning fuel oil only made them roll away. Nothing daunted, Haxel had stayed with a group for the better part of two days, finally baiting them close with her rations. Hard Ones, she discovered, exposed a soft body part underneath to feed—what she called their "sweet spot."

As well as triumph, she nursed broken toes. An unusually large Hard One had managed to pin her foot—an event Haxel dismissed as an excellent opportunity to test if jabbing a knife point up through the sweet spot was how they could be killed. It was.

But she wouldn't eat one.

"They don't cross the river," the First Scout observed. "Or the ditches. My guess is the Sona knew how to keep them away. Have you dreamed anything about it?"

"I haven't dreamed since coming back." The others hadn't either. It would have been helpful to know how to unlock the mound doors—or the Cloisters.

"Our Adepts claim it's because we have what we need. That these 'teaching dreams' are for emergencies." An undertone of *frustration*. The First Scout never enjoyed relying on the Power or knowledge of others.

Oran had had a difficult time believing in the dreams; after all, she'd had none. Aryl refused to argue the point. It hadn't been necessary. Little Ziba had dismissed the Adept as "silly" in front of the entire Clan, then proceeded to demonstrate how to dismantle and clean one of the Sona oillights—a skill she'd never been taught.

Oran had believed then.

"What we need is water." Aryl gazed up the valley again, feeling the wind redden her cheeks. So far, the road had been passable, though the cart had yet to roll. Morla refused to admit defeat, though the mechanism to let the round wheels turn smoothly remained a mystery. Veca built one design after another; Tilip busied himself with tables and benches, avoiding his wife's mother as much as possible.

The road was passable—but only until another ice storm, or much more snow on the ground. At least that could be melted for water. "If I knew how to call the Oud," Aryl said with her own frustration, "I would."

"Taisal used to say the same about the Tikitik."

Aryl's thoughts scattered like biters tapped from a window gauze, settling in a new pattern. She hadn't *tasted* Taisal's presence in the M'hir since that day. It didn't mean she wasn't there; Taisal's control in the *other* had advanced, too, and she had an Adept's trained discipline. She might be able to hide among its currents.

As a comfort or threat? It would, Aryl decided, feeling as old as the ruins below, depend on whether they were on the same side or opposed.

"Did she find a way? To contact them?" She tried to sound vaguely uninterested and doubted it worked.

"No. We tried following them once, she and I." Haxel stretched like a predator. "Before she was Speaker and Adept. I, First Scout. They lost us within a tenth." As if that long-ago failure still rankled.

Aryl couldn't wrap her mind around the image. Her mother . . . racing through the canopy after Tikitik on a whim? Taisal di Sarc had never been that young, or foolish.

Had she?

"Don't worry, youngling," Haxel went on. "I happen to agree with Cetto. The Oud showed some sense there, making you Speaker. You've already talked to strangers—which is more than Taisal or any Clan Speaker can say." A too-innocent pause. "I wonder how our Marcus is doing?"

Aryl checked her shields, but it was only habit. Haxel couldn't read her thoughts without her permission. The gibe was dangerously accurate, though; she hoped her face hadn't shown anything. "All he wanted was to dig for the past in some hole." The truth was always safer. "I'm sure that's what he's doing."

"If it had been up to me . . ." The First Scout didn't bother completing that sentence. Instead, she went off on another topic. "You're right. We need the Oud back here. Get them to put water back in the river. Hoyon tells me going down their tunnel is out of the question—"

Only Haxel would consider such a thing. For once, Aryl was in complete agreement with the Grona Adept. Go beneath the ground, where the sun couldn't reach?

Enris had barely hinted what it had been like. He hadn't wanted to think about it. And he was Tuana—used to spending truenight under the pathetic glow of stars.

"—so what we should do is backtrack the one who did come. Either find more Oud, or find out what happened to that one. Have a story to tell its relatives, if need be."

"You want me to go back up the valley." Aryl paused, suspicious. "Alone?"

"The rest are busy." That scar-twisting grin was a challenge. "You can practice that new Talent of yours without an audience."

Other than Taisal, Aryl thought with an inward wince.

So much for the First Scout's unusual patience over the last few days. She managed to gesture gratitude. If her gloves made it less than gracious, Haxel could take it as she wished. "While I appreciate the thought—" not much, "—I don't need practice. I need—" She hesitated.

An esask would quail under the anticipation in those eyes. "Need what?"

To be desperate . . . ?

The First Scout would gladly supply such a situation, Aryl knew. "Among other things, a peaceful, clear mind—" this, sincerely, "—which I won't have until we've a water supply."

Haxel settled back, again the image of patience. "You're the Speaker."

Patient only to a point. "I'd better get going." Aryl tried not to climb down in haste. It might feel like an escape; unwise to make it look like one.

Husni had been right to warn her about Haxel's "notions."

Marcus Bowman lifted the lid from the first pot and waved his bioscanner over its contents.

"That's no way to treat a gift," Aryl complained from her perch on his table. She'd come straight here, reasoning it was the best place from which to launch her search for Oud—given there were some busy at work in the distance.

Besides, Marcus needed real food.

The Human grinned at her. "This is the right way. You don't want me to be green and die. I don't want that, too." He went to her next offering, a fragrant loaf baked with pieces of rokly. The 'scanner shrilled a protest and he showed her its agitated display, for all the good that did. "See? You can eat this. I can't."

"Fine. You can have all of Lendin's swimmer stew. I'll eat the treat." As she helped set out a pair of dishes, she glanced at him curiously. "You're speaking much better."

"I practiced." He looked suddenly uncomfortable. "Would you like sombay?"

"Yes, please." She'd never had to learn a language, but this seemed exceptional progress for a single fist, when he'd told her they'd studied words from the Oud for years. "I'm impressed."

Instead of getting cups, the Human sat on his bed with a thud. "Geoscanner," he said with a heavy sigh.

"Do you need it?" She hoped not, but it was his. She drew the device from its pocket and held it out. "If you don't, I'd like to keep it."

Instead of taking it, he tapped the side with one finger. "Comlink."

The device he used to talk at a distance. Aryl opened her mouth, closing it as she understood. No wonder he looked like Costa when she'd caught him sneaking the last dresel cake. "You've been listening to me."

"No. Not listening. Not. Collecting. Words. Phrases. Sentences. How Om'ray put words together. Syntax. When I had enough data, I ran through *sleepteach*." A hint of pleading in his voice. "I don't want to sound like an Oud."

After sorting all this out, Aryl held up the geoscanner. "Show me how to make this so you can't listen—collect—" when he tried to protest, "—any more words without my permission."

He leaned forward and pressed a depression on one side. "This is off. Press again," which he demonstrated, "and it is on."

"And 'on' means you can hear me." Satisfied, Aryl pressed the depression once more. "Off," she asserted, putting the valuable device back in her pocket. "Now, how about that sombay?"

As Marcus moved to get their cups, Aryl considered him. They weren't the same; there was, nonetheless, a tantalizing possibility. "You called it 'sleepteach,' " she began. "Does that mean Humans dream to learn?"

"What is 'dream'?"

"When you sleep, sometimes you feel awake. You can see things. Hear things. Dream. Don't Humans?"

"Ah!" Marcus looked pleased. "Yes. Humans dream. Good dreams." He feigned a shudder. "Bad dreams. *Sleepteach* is different." Putting down the cups, the Human went to one of the many crates stacked on the counters, returning with a clear bag filled with metal threads and disks. "This *sleepteach* device." He pulled out the contents and showed her how the disks fit against the sides of his forehead. "I sleep, this teaches what I want to learn. When I wake up, I remember new things."

So it was the same, only under his control. "It gives you dreams," Aryl concluded.

Marcus grimaced. "It gives me a *headache*. Pain here." He

pressed his fingers into his temples where the disks would go. "But works." After a moment's hesitation, as if debating with himself, he thrust the device at her. "You could use it to learn *Comspeak,* the language of the Trade Pact."

Silly Human. Aryl chuckled. "Why would I want your words? I have my own."

"With Comspeak, you could talk to any visitor, from any world, and be understood."

"You understand me." She had no intention of being drawn into more. "This is the world that matters to me."

He shoved the sleepteach back in its bag, tossed that on his bed. Made unnecessary clatter getting the sombay into the cups and adding water. Bumped into the table and muttered in his own language. Put the cups down so hard they sloshed.

Something bothered him. She waited.

Sure enough, Marcus sighed and stopped, his eyes troubled. "If we prove we've found Hoveny ruins, Aryl, your world will matter to many others. There are rules, not to talk to *indigenous remnants,* not to interfere. But no promise it won't happen."

It had happened. She looked away, her fingers toying with a fold of her tunic. "If you don't find them, will you leave?"

"Is that what you want?" Another, heavier sigh. "It's not something I control, Aryl. I'm Triad First, but there are other Triads, other seekers. What we have found on Cersi looks already good. I can't give a *falsenegative.* Do you understand? I can't hide the truth. They won't believe me. I can't stop them."

He'd thought to do that for her, for Om'ray?

Aryl's heart pounded. Her fingers gripped the fold. Her right hand, she noticed, momentarily distracted. "What I want . . ." What did she want?

He was the only one to ask her. The only friend she had left. She didn't want Marcus to leave, ever.

She hadn't wanted Enris to leave.

Or Bern.

"What I want," she said finally, "doesn't matter."

The Human had learned it was impolite to touch without invitation, but he lifted her chin gently, a contact Aryl could have avoided, but didn't. His eyes searched her face. "Something's wrong. Is it what happened at the Cloisters, when you and the other Om'ray—when you fell to the ground, when the other *woman* was sick? I couldn't help, then, I knew that. Maybe I can help now."

Was that how it looked to him? She laid her hand on his wrist, telling herself it was to move his arm, finding it impossible to do any more than leave it there, pressed to the warmth of his skin. "Yena don't fall," she said obliquely.

"My mistake." A lopsided smile. When Marcus released her chin and drew back, she let go. He sat on the seat attached to the table, looked up at her. "I went over the place afterward. There's nothing *emanating* from that building. No unique *bioticsignatures* or disease organisms. I'm not a scantech, but I'm sure."

So no stranger device could detect what passed between Om'ray minds, or between those minds and whatever the Cloisters might be sending to Sona. Their astonishing technology had its limits.

Let Marcus capture her words from a distance, take images from the air; he remained safely deaf and blind to what made Om'ray *real*.

Aryl tore off a piece of the sweet loaf, finding herself in a much better mood. "The Grona," she improvised, "brought a stomach illness with them. Impolite and a nuisance." Which tidily described the two Adepts, in her opinion. "We've recovered."

Marcus appeared doubtful. "I can help," he repeated. "I have *medicalsupplies*—I can help make sick Om'ray better. Stop spread of illness. Your people are vulnerable."

The Human excelled at being difficult. Offer to heal? She didn't doubt he could, but this was a notion she had to end, here and now, or how could she keep Haxel—or any Om'ray— from tearing that knowledge from his mind? Hating herself,

Aryl forced an edge to her voice. "Break your own rule? Interfere with the 'indigenous remnants?' "

Instead of the offense she expected, he took one of the neglected cups, passed her the other, then took a sip, gazing at her consideringly over the rim. "No one would know. You take a bioscanner, put close to sick Om'ray. It sends me data, here. I would make a *medicine* or tell you what could help. Not perfect," with a shrug and a bright-eyed look. "Better than no help."

She was beginning to fear Marcus liked to run on thin branches, too, a daring that had led him to explore a world far from his family and kind, to befriend her.

It could get him killed here. Or worse.

She should never have accepted the geoscanner. She'd encouraged this.

Another sip. A shy smile. "Our secret?"

Secrets upon secrets. Her fingers explored the shape of the handle, the cool smooth exterior of the cup.

Without warning, touch became the most intense sensation. Distracting. Consuming.

Important.

The room was too warm. She was. But she wasn't . . .

"Aryl?"

"Yes. No! Let me think about it."

Think? How could she? She'd never *felt* everything like this before. The lines of shadow and light through the windows were knife sharp. The air—it was full of scents, some strange, some pleasant. Her own breathing . . . his . . . they blended like songs in the canopy at firstnight.

"What's wrong?" Words that meant nothing. "Are you sick?"

There was nothing. She was nothing. She was utterly empty . . . Aryl bent over, hearing her cup drop, hearing the Human's alarmed outcry, with all that mattered in the world to hold her hollow, empty self together with all her strength.

Abruptly, the world was normal again. She sat up, cheeks flaming with embarrassment. "I'm all right." When Marcus would have waved his bioscanner over her, she held up her hand to keep him away. "No. I'm fine."

But she wasn't.

She was becoming a Chooser.

Secrets upon secrets . . . the Chosen had no secrets from one another. Someone else was going to know about Marcus, about his devices, about her, about . . .

"Aryl—"

"I'm not sick. Leave me be!"

Was there a worse time her body could have picked? She wasn't sure if she wanted to cry or pull her hair.

What would it be like, to have a Chooser's willful hair?

Trouble, she decided. It was all trouble. Starting with how soon the sensations overruled her self-control. Sarcs were not known for being quiet, polite Choosers. Seru Parth's tantrums would be nothing compared to hers.

"You should reheat the soup," Aryl said desperately. "It will taste better."

The Human, perhaps because he was Chosen and a father, grasped when to allow himself to be distracted. He helped clean the floor, then settled them both at the table. Among the marvels of his kitchen—a kitchen she'd yet to see Marcus actually use for anything but storage—was a spoon that warmed what it stirred. While she pretended to enjoy the sweet loaf— and a fresh cup—he heated his soup, giving a startled look of pleasure at the first mouthful.

No wonder. Nothing could taste worse than those e-rations of his.

"Thank you," he said, then pointed the spoon at her. "You are not sick—?" A pause while he waited for her to mimic his head shake of denial. "Good." Another pause, then that innocent look. "You didn't come to bring me swimmer soup and talk about dreams."

He wasn't slow. Aryl half smiled. "The Oud built a tunnel entrance near Sona, but we haven't seen one since the day I visited you. Haxel's impatient. She sent me looking." Her smile faded. There was worse to tell him. Where to start? "The Tikitik have been around, too."

"Tikitik?" Marcus' forehead creased. "Where!? Here? Close?"

She wasn't sure what qualified as "close" to the Human, so settled for, "It was with the Oud. I haven't seen one at this end of the valley, but they're hard to see against the stone. It was different from the Tikitik in the canopy. Gray, not black."

"*Chromatophores,*" he replied, one of his words. "Their skin change—changes—color. What did it want?"

Interesting. Slow-moving and tasty, an aspird could hide against any part of a rastis, changing its patterned back to match fronds crossed with shadow or the feathered texture of the stalk. Making the Tikitik more dangerous than ever.

"I don't know. It said the Oud were 'precipitous.' Accused it of 'misjudgment and haste.' And—" She hesitated. Marcus had learned to fear Tikitik. They'd attacked his aircar; his escape had left an uncounted number of them dead. And he'd seen what they'd done to Yena. The Oud, however? He had to work with them—was here alone with them. Maybe he needed the confidence of not-knowing.

"What else?"

She could hear Enris now. When had she believed ignorance was of any use? "Thought Traveler—the Tikitik—told me the Oud don't understand how fragile we are. That they think we're the same Om'ray who lived here, long ago."

Marcus gave another of his nods, remarkably unconcerned. "Could be. Different *lifecycles.*" At her frown, he clarified, "Every *species* has its own way of living, of growing. Common problem in the Trade Pact. Confusion always. Rude to one, not to another. It can make for good jokes."

She'd forgotten. He was accustomed to other races. More than she could imagine existed—or wanted to know about. Cersi's three were enough.

And there was nothing funny about this misunderstanding. "The Oud was attacked. Three deep cuts, here." She indicated the slashes against her own side. "It died, Marcus, to come to us."

"An *emmisarymurdered*?" She'd seen many expressions on the Human's face, so like an Om'ray's. She'd never seen outraged fury before. "The Tikitik?"

"I don't know. That's why I'm here. Your machine watched us leave and I—" She stopped. He was already in motion, tripping over a boot in his rush to one of the consoles.

Once there, his hands flew over the controls of the device. Aryl went to stand by his shoulder, silent as he worked. An image of the valley appeared on the screen, from above. A perspective she usually enjoyed; now all she felt was impatience. Had it seen the attack?

The display soared over the barren nekis, over the hill of debris, swooped lower as it found and followed the road to Sona. And three figures, two staggering.

"I watched this *narrowfield*. To see you." A tap of the control and the view expanded to the full width of the valley, as well as before and behind. The pace became quicker. The figures, much smaller, now moved their legs and arms at a ridiculous speed. Rock hunters appeared and rolled in pursuit with ominous—and unreal—haste, using the arched bridges, which she hadn't realized. Shadows slid past, as if Marcus hurried the sun as well. She swallowed, dizzy.

The Oud would have been ahead of them. This was where she'd picked up its track for the first time.

A bulge of dark at the rock face caught her eye, moving differently from the shadows cast by the sun. "Wait. There!" Aryl pointed and he pressed a control, stopping the image. "Can you look closer?"

It was like falling, the way he took them diving to the ground. She kept her eyes fixed on what she'd seen—or thought she'd seen. Larger, clearer, still confusing.

Marcus grunted. "Good. Watch." The fall stopped. The bulge of dark was set in motion again, this time slowly.

It was the Oud, on its flat vehicle, emerging from the rock.

"There's no tunnel," she protested. Impossible she could have missed it—she'd been by that very spot five times now.

"Clever." Marcus did something to the image and a doubled line appeared. "The opening is hidden from the road. Like this." He leaned back and put his palms together, sliding them apart to leave a gap between. "The Oud came out behind a wall of rock. From the side, can't be seen."

He let the vid play, but the vehicle and its passenger disappeared around the next bend. "Sorry I stopped recording," the Human commented grimly.

Aryl gestured apology. "It's not your fault. I should have seen it." She'd let herself pay more attention to Hoyon's complaints than to their surroundings, been too confident the only threat was what rolled and tumbled behind. Haxel would never have made that mistake. In the canopy, she wouldn't have.

Walking on the ground wasn't only boring; it dulled the senses. She'd be more careful from now on.

"We should—"

The lighting in the room flashed red, then blue, then back to normal.

"What was that?"

"Company." Marcus tapped once more. The image on the screen was replaced by a view she recognized, behind the stranger encampment, over the tracks made by the Oud.

A pair of their vehicles were approaching.

"Good!" The Human swept their dishes into an empty she hoped—crate and lowered the table and seats into the floor, as if he expected to entertain the enormous creatures here. An Oud couldn't possibly fit through his door, but Aryl didn't bother pointing this out. Marcus babbled at her as he gathered equipment and clothes, an excited flood of his words and hers. "They must have found something. I thought maybe yesterday, when they *penetratedthenextstratum*, but they didn't come then. I told Tyler—the other Triad First—when he *checkedin*. He thinks I'm wasting my time here, wants to send P'tr sit 'Nix to *retaskthestation*. I told him we should give the Oud a good chance to prove or—"

"Marcus," Aryl interrupted.

He stopped, one arm in his coat, and gave her an abashed look. "Sorry. I've been here too many days, waiting for access to their site—"

Passion, if no common sense. "That may not be why they're coming," she said gently. "Remember the dead Oud?"

Offense. "I had nothing to do with that."

"No, but they could have seen me arrive." She hadn't, Aryl thought with disgust, used any stealth in her approach. She'd been more concerned with soup.

Not that she knew how to hide from what lived underground. Haxel, who assumed the worst as a habit, thought the Oud could feel footsteps over their heads, the way an Om'ray heard footsteps or rain on a roof.

"If true . . . Aryl, you should leave. Now." Pulling on his coat, Marcus went to the door and threw it open, gesturing wildly. "Hurry!"

"Not a good idea," Aryl told him, pulling out the pendant.

Through the open door, she could see what the Human hadn't.

Coming through the nekis grove were five Tikitik.

Chapter 14

Marcus closed the door, fingers flying over a panel beside it. *"Securityfield. Autodefense,"* he explained as he sagged, his back to the wall. "Safe."

She shouldn't have told him about the dead Oud. "Safe doesn't accomplish much. I'll talk to them." Aryl held up her pendant again. "I'm Sona's Speaker, permitted to converse with other races." By the Agreement.

"Open the door?" She might have asked him to jump back into the waterfall. "No. Follow protocol. Make sure they have peaceful—are peaceful first. Talk over comlink."

Which might work if just the Human was involved. Aryl didn't think the Oud or Tikitik would expect manners from the strangers. But they had to know she was here—it was too much of a coincidence. Interesting, that the stranger illusion hadn't fooled them.

She gestured apology, but took a step toward the door. "Trust me to know my own world. You can wait here. I'll be safe."

"Saw that on Oud." Marcus pointed at the pendant. "Not protect it."

He had her there.

"You can leave," she insisted. "These are my neighbors. I have to live with them. Let me outside."

"Stubborn."

She shrugged. "Please, Marcus."

"I'm coming with you."

With that, he straightened his pretend-Om'ray clothing though, having sensibly abandoned his Yena leg wraps for stranger-trousers, she doubted the result would fool even an eyeless Oud. A couple of devices she didn't recognize went into the pockets of his Grona-like coat; his stony expression didn't invite argument. "This is not a good idea," was all he said as he turned off whatever he'd done to the door and opened it.

It wasn't as though she had a choice.

They stepped out, Marcus turning to lock the door behind him. Protecting his secrets, she thought, and approved.

Tiny snowdrops sparkled in the air, though the sun shone down. The waterfall's spray, she realized with a shock. It glistened on the nekis. Closer to the pit, it was likely forming ice. A new and serious problem for those assigned to bring water to the village.

One thing at a time. Aryl walked forward to the center of the open space. She stopped, Marcus beside her. "We see you," she told the Tikitik.

The snapping of stalks announced the arrival of the Oud vehicles. They drove between one of the stranger-buildings and the edge of the grove, lurching from side to side, knocking flat whatever was in their way. One scraped a corner as it turned to join them; the illusion on that section of wall flickered, then turned white. The Tikitik gave their guttural bark, clearly entertained.

Marcus tensed, ready to protest. She dug an elbow into his ribs and whispered. "Fix it later."

Five Tikitik—none with familiar symbols on their wrist cloths. They were gray, as Thought Traveler had been, but there the resemblance ended. Instead of a band of fabric about their narrow hips, these wore a tunic-like garment, white and inked in black with straight lines that came together at angles. If she stared at the pattern for long, it hurt her eyes. They'd inked or painted their faces as well. Circles of black around the base of their eye cones. Dots of the same color made a line from their mouths, along the side of their long faces, and continued up the curved necks to the shoulders.

The centermost bore a Speaker's Pendant affixed to a band of cloth. The others were armed with the hooked blades, this time on the ends of long wooden staffs. No sacks or bags. Not, she decided, here to trade.

The Oud, one per vehicle, stopped side by side. They might have been the two she'd already met, for all the differences between them. Whirr/clicks settled to the stone, some on snow.

"We see you," Aryl repeated, though sure they'd all heard.

"Sona." An acknowledgment from the Tikitik Speaker, who took a quick step ahead of its fellows. "We have come with a serious complaint against these Oud."

The Oud closest to the building reared on its platform, dust and snow slipping from the fabric of its cloak. Limbs moved in a wave, bringing forth a Speaker's Pendant. "Decide other."

Was this a request or order? To her or at the Tikitik?

"They defile the Makers!" Its mouth protuberances writhed, and one hand clawed the air toward the cliff. She was glad to have it out of sight, Aryl thought. "They do not belong here. Sona is Tikitik! Tell them so, Speaker."

The Oud held its ground. "Decide other."

Aryl looked from one to the other. "What is going on here?" she demanded.

"These intrude where they are not welcome." The Tikitik lowered its head, smaller eyes on the Oud, larger on her. "They disturb the remains of the Makers, seeking what was never meant for us. It is Forbidden by the Agreement—"

"NOTNOTNOT!" The Oud reared higher in emphasis, lashing from side to side. The vehicle tilted and groaned beneath. "Agreement, keep us! Goodgoodgood. Tikitik bad. Tikitik leave!"

"We will not. Sona is ours, you stupid lump of flesh!" The Speaker's fellows hissed and raised their weapons over their heads. The second Oud reared, limbs flailing violently.

This wasn't good.

Marcus touched the back of her hand. She turned hers, wove her fingers with his. Steady, she wanted to *send* to him. Trust me. Wait. All she could do was hope he understood her tight grip.

"The Agreement demands clarity in all conversation between the races on Cersi," Aryl said loudly, in her best imitation of her mother's stern tone. "What do you mean, Sona is yours?"

The Tikitik Speaker bobbed its head twice. "Before the Oud took interest in what they shouldn't, this valley was home to Tikitik as well as Om'ray. But they are insatiable, Sona Speaker. First metal from the ground. Water. Now this unlawful search. It is our duty to protect the Makers' Rest!"

"Makers, not! Tikitik fool."

She winced inwardly. The Oud wasn't helping, especially if the painted Tikitik were of a faction who believed Cersi and all upon it had been created for their benefit by powerful beings. In the version she'd heard, the Makers lived in the Moons, to this day toiling to repair their mistakes—which happened to be the Om'ray and Oud.

At least in this one, the Makers didn't appear to be active participants.

The Tikitik had been Sona's neighbors? That explained the wood construction, as well as the nekis and a water system to nurture a variety of plants unfamiliar to the Grona.

She didn't want them now. "The Agreement is to keep our world at peace and in balance." If only Taisal could hear her, spouting what she'd overheard during those long and boring night conversations.

The Oud settled. "Peace. Goodgoodgood." The Speaker waggled its pendant with each "good."

A pendant that had come from a corpse.

As had hers, Aryl reminded herself. What mattered was now and here.

The Tikitik had lowered their weapons; all eyes but two were on the Oud. "Where's the balance?" demanded their Speaker, staring at her. "Do you speak for a Clan?" Its barking laugh. "Those pitiful few Om'ray? This valley is ours."

"We are a Clan." She bristled, pulling her hand from Marcus'. "And this is our home, not yours, Tikitik."

"Decide other," the Oud concluded in a smug clatter of limbs. "Few. Less. More soon."

More what? More Om'ray? "What do you—"

"No!" the Tikitik shouted. "This is unacceptable. We will tolerate no more change. We stand by the Agreement. The Oud must go. This—" with a disdainful eye flick at Marcus, "—must go."

Aryl stepped in front of the Human, sweeping him back with one strong arm as he tried to stay beside her. "You are not welcome here," she said firmly.

"Tikitik, bad!"

Weapons flashed in the sun. As Aryl grabbed for her own knife, the ground erupted. She lost her footing and fell with Marcus, twisting to see.

The Tikitik had time to do nothing but scream. Aryl wasn't sure if they were pulled down or if the ground became a liquid and they sank below its surface.

Her legs . . . they were sinking, too! "No! Stop!" The Oud didn't know how fragile they were. Sona Om'ray had died like this. She flung out her arms, tried to stay above ground. Dirt entered her mouth and she spat, fighting to breathe.

"Aryl!" Marcus tried to pull her free. He plunged suddenly to his waist in the moving stone and dirt, dropped with a second jerk to his shoulders. She held his hands. Looked into his desperate eyes . . .

. . . and concentrated. The swirling madness of the M'hir felt comforting by comparison . . . she *pushed* . . .

. . . and collapsed on the floor with the Human, surrounded by crates.

"Teleportation."

They'd almost died, Aryl thought wryly, and Marcus was grinning so widely it had to hurt his jaw.

"Teleportation!"

His language had a word for what she could do. Somehow, that wasn't a comfort. She leaned against the door, peering through one of its rectangular windows. The Oud were laying on their vehicles; in front of them an oval of dirt, slightly sunken and too level, to mark where the Tikitik had been.

Where they'd been.

She supposed the Oud might have stopped in time, might have realized they were about to kill the two beings they wanted. "Might" being the word. She hadn't been willing to risk their lives. To be buried alive? She didn't wish that on any-one, even the Tikitik.

She'd *tasted* no one. She hadn't tried, too busy surviving. Desperation indeed.

Could Taisal still know what she'd done? Did such a quick—was trip the word?—through the M'hir leave a trail, like tracks in snow? Or was it more like stepping through water, where the current washed away any trace?

And what about the Human . . . did he leave a *taste*? Her mind shied away from that disaster.

Though so much for all the warnings about using Power near the Oud. Unless the M'hir was something different . . .

"Aryl. We have to talk about this. Before others come."

She turned from the window, brushing dust from her clothes.

His eyes were fever bright. "Can all Om'ray do it? *'Port* your-selves?"

Haxel would slit his throat.

She should.

Instead, Aryl sat beside the Human on his pulled-out bed, both of them filthy and shedding half-frozen grit, and sighed.

"Just me. I don't know if anyone else can learn how. I've only done it three times. No one else knows. Except you and Enris." And Haxel, a name she wasn't going to mention.

"And the Grona." Anger deepened his voice. "That was what I saw. They tried to make you show them."

She almost smiled. Never underestimate him. "That's why they came," she admitted. "Don't worry," she said with a companionable lean into his shoulder, "they can't make me do anything. I'm stronger."

"And telepath. All Om'ray telepathic." With total conviction.

"Yes."

"I thought so. Geoscanner. Om'ray don't say enough words out loud, not like Human." When concerned about her reaction to something, Marcus had a way of ducking his head, then turning it to gaze up at her. "A feeling, too. I feel I know you always. Been friends always. Did you do this to me, Aryl Sarc? Make me feel your friend? Use influence?"

She stared at him, realized her mouth was open and closed it. Myris could affect the emotion of a moment, but not the underlying feeling. Not for long. The mere idea was sickening. Tamper with another's mind? Violate who and what they were? From childhood, Om'ray were taught to protect the privacy of their innermost thoughts, not from fear of those being controlled by someone else, but to be an individual within the whole.

If this "influence" was something telepaths in the Trade Pact did to those unable to shield their minds, how could they be trusted? How could anyone?

Her stunned silence apparently reassured him. "Had to ask," he said cryptically, then patted her knee. "Now. We must hurry." He drew in a deep breath, then let it out, rising to his feet. "Listen to me, Aryl. No one else in the Trade Pact can know what you do. No one. I'll take care of the vid record. You be careful. Don't show this to anyone else. Don't do it where 'eyes' could record. I'll never tell. Promise!"

"What about Kelly, your Chosen?" Her own nightmare.

Choice couldn't be denied—and her selection of eligible un-Chosen included Kran Caraat. If he learned about Marcus now . . .

His head gave an emphatic shake. "Never. She can't know. Too dangerous. *Interrogation. Mindcrawlers.*" This last with a troubled look. "Are my thoughts easy to see? Can you see them? Any Om'ray?"

"You aren't *real*—" Before he took that as reassurance, Aryl went on, owing him the truth. "You don't *send* beyond yourself. Your thoughts don't leave your mind," she explained. "Some Om'ray are like that. To talk mind to mind, they must touch." Only the less powerful, but she didn't think he needed to know that.

"If you touch me?" he asked quickly, perhaps remembering how she'd taken his hand. "Then you see my thoughts?"

"I can sense how you feel. That's how I knew you meant me no harm the first time you wanted to use the bioscanner." As he considered that, from the rosy glow on his cheeks wondering what else she might have detected, she smiled. "But you think in your words, Marcus. None of us understand those."

If she went into his memories, there were images she could understand. That was the danger. She'd sensed his growing discomfort at her *search* and stopped at once. But if Haxel or another with Power wanted his secrets?

They wouldn't hesitate, no matter the damage it caused him or pain.

Unaware of the dark turn of her thoughts, the Human looked relieved. "That's good," he replied. "*Offworld* problem for later. For now, Om'ray safe."

"Safe from what?" Why was he was more worried about keeping her ability secret than she was? "What are you talking about? I hope more Om'ray will learn how to '*port.*" She liked the short, strange word. "One day, all of us." Then let the Oud try to dig the ground from under their feet.

"Aryl—" Marcus went to his knees in front of her, putting his somber gaze level with hers. "Listen to me. If we discover the best possible Hoveny find . . . a *functional installation* . . . Cersi would be safe. Om'ray would be safe. Seekers would come, but careful. Respectful. If anyone discovers what you can do?" Despite knowing she could sense his emotions—or because of it—he touched her cheek. Through the contact, she felt *sorrow* and *dread*. As well as *determination*. "Aryl. Every *government, criminalorganization,* every species in Trade Pact would come here. No respect. No protection. They would take you away. They would destroy your Clans, your life. For this power, they could *gotowar.* Worlds fighting worlds."

The *taste* of change.

What could she tell the others? If she taught them, if she now should, what could she say to keep them cautious? That there were mysterious invisible watchers?

It would be true.

She should use the knife, Aryl thought numbly. Not on the Human's throat . . .

On her own. End this.

The lights flashed red, then blue . . .

"The Oud!" she warned, following Marcus as he lunged for the console.

It wasn't.

A lone Tikitik stood at the edge of the grove, feet pointedly not on the churned dirt. It was shouting something. The Human hit a control and a voice filled the room.

"Little Speaker. Come out and talk to me."

Thought Traveler.

It should have been familiar, Aryl decided, being unable to trust her footing. But what the Oud had done wasn't like a rain-slicked branch or ice-coated stone. They upset all expectation. They made the ground itself unsafe.

A power never to be discounted, she thought.

Neither were the Tikitik. Thought Traveler squatted comfortably near where its kind had died moments before, its small eyes riveted on Marcus, larger ones on her. "Greetings, little Speaker. And who might this be, this ally of the precipitous Oud? What is your name, stranger?"

"Stranger will do," she told it before Marcus could reply. This Tikitik was an entirely different problem from those before. Give it information and there'd be no stopping its spread.

As if to confirm her fears, it barked its laugh. "An Om'ray who stands with a stranger. That gives me your name, little Speaker. 'Apart-from-All.' Aryl Sarc, discard of Yena Clan. I knew you would be entertaining."

The Oud Speaker, subdued to this point, reared. "Decided other!" Its limbs clattered against one another. "Sona Oud. Goodgoodgoodgood. Tikitik go."

"Oh, I will," Thought Traveler said easily. Its eyes fixed on her. "Entertaining indeed," it murmured. "Remember this day, Apart-from-All. Remember how you triumphed."

Triumphed? "We only want to live in peace—"

"Under the Agreement, of course."

Something wasn't right. Aryl found herself afraid to say another word. What was going on?

Thought Traveler stood and looked at the Oud. "Unlike the fools you dispossessed here, I don't care what you do. Dig up the past. Haul it to your pits. Trade it to strangers. But by the Agreement, you must address the balance."

The Oud waved its pendant. "Balance, yes. Comply. Good-GoodGoodGood."

"What do you mean?" Aryl demanded.

"Enjoy your peace, Apart-from-All," the Tikitik advised, then slipped away into the grove.

It couldn't be this easy. Before she could do more than glance at Marcus—the confusion on his face a perfect match to her own, the Oud spoke again. "Peace goodgoodgoodgood. Come, Triad First. Authenticate. Now. Come."

Not a word about what had happened, the dead Oud, the

dead Tikitik, what she'd done. Did they not care? Or not notice? Different *lifecycles* Marcus called it.

Different minds, that above all.

"I have to go." The Human looked grim. "If I don't, my people will wonder why."

He'd been so happy before, tripping over himself in his eagerness to see what the Oud had found.

"Comecomecome!"

"I'll get my equipment." Calmly, as if he dealt with creatures capable of killing another every day. To her, "Stay here, inside *securityfield*."

"Marcus—" Her protest died unspoken. They each had to do what they must. "I have to go back. They need to know what happened." As much as she could say of it. "Be careful."

"You, too." A wistful smile cracked lines through the dust on his face. "It was good soup."

"I'll bring more," she promised.

They were, Aryl decided as she walked away through the too-soft ground, thorough fools.

As for triumph?

They were still breathing.

The Oud hadn't asked about their dead, but as Aryl jogged the road to Sona, she watched for the place in the rock wall shown by Marcus' machine. They might not care; she did. A threat to something as large as an Oud was surely a threat to an Om'ray.

And if it had been the Tikitik, she might stop thinking about those she'd watched die.

Nothing helped her stop thinking about the rest. She ran, wishing every beat of foot to stone could turn back time. She'd left this morning, worried only about Oran and Hoyon, when to try her ability again, what to say to the Oud the next time they met. She'd looked forward to surprising Marcus, to learn more about him. Instead . . .

Instead her footsteps were reminders. *Beat beat . . .* dying Tikitik . . . *beat beat . . .* Oud risking the Agreement . . . *beat beat . . .* revealing her ability not to those who deserved it, who needed it, but to a stranger from another world . . . *beat beat . . .* becoming a Chooser?

Aryl misstepped and almost stumbled. Not fair, she told herself. None of it.

She could almost hear her mother's voice. One handhold at a time. Be sure of your grip.

Be sure? Her laugh echoed, as if the towering rock shared the joke.

The rock could tell her one thing, she remembered, and starting paying closer attention to where she was.

There. Spotting the section of cliff, she left the road. Hard Ones lay everywhere, only a few larger than her doubled fist. She kicked the smallest from her path. After a couple clattered and pinged, the rest began rolling out of her way.

They observed what was around them and reacted to avoid trouble. Or they'd met Haxel and learned to feared all Om'ray.

Aryl slowed as she neared the rock face. Under the bright sun, the shadows at its base were intensely dark, if narrow. She would have avoided such in the canopy, wary of ambush. Stitlers were particularly fond of shadow, since it allowed them to stay close to their traps.

She'd forgotten to be properly cautious on the ground. No more.

Something buzzed by her ear. A biter? It was too cold, too dry.

Another. This time she caught a glimpse of it. A whirr/click.

There were more. They clung to the rock in neat rows, evenly spaced. Every so often, one would shift position. Those nearest would do the same until all had adjusted. Then they were still again.

Weren't they always with Oud?

Aryl eased forward, a step at a time, checking where she would put each foot before she moved it.

Another step, her hand on the cold rock face, and there. She could see the opening. The cliff was split here, a separate wall of rock standing in front of the ridge itself. It looked weathered and old. Perhaps the Oud had many such doors to their underground world. Or had this one been made when they'd destroyed Sona?

Neighbors now, she reminded herself. Neighbors were always perilous. That was an Om'ray's life.

The passage between could fit an Oud vehicle. She'd need a light to see tracks.

More buzzing around her ears. Whirr/clicks lined the inside walls. She waved a couple from her face. Biters, crawlers. Even the ones that didn't like the taste of Om'ray were a nuisance.

Were they waiting for the next Oud?

Aryl trembled and listened. Nothing but faint *whirrr/clicks*. Nothing but her breathing. Her heart pounding.

She hadn't asked about water.

The Tikitik—the Hoveny—none of that should have mattered. She'd been there, talking to the Oud's new Speaker, and hadn't said a word for her people.

Why?

Her mouth twisted. She'd been afraid. Afraid of what the Oud could do. Afraid to risk it. Like she was now. Willing to leave Marcus to them, while she ran.

Her mother never flinched from her duty. Even when it meant condemning her daughter for the good of Yena.

One handhold at a time. The Oud were in Sona to stay. So was she.

Her toe sank deeper than it should.

Aryl threw herself back and away as the ground in front of her shot upward. Enormous hooklike claws cut through the air, scraped against the rock wall. Pebbles rained down. The whirr/clicks abandoned their perches for the safety of anywhere else.

The hook-claws—there were six, taller and wider than she

was—grabbed at nothing one last time, then plunged back under the ground.

She stood up, selected a good-sized Hard One, and heaved it where the hook-claws had disappeared.

The ground shot upward. The hook-claws cut and scraped, one connecting with the Hard One which shattered in a spray of green, black, and glistening yellow. The rest turned in mid-strike to plunge into the mess, then sank out of sight again.

Aryl walked very carefully back to the stone road—a construction material that suggested the Sona had known very well what could lurk beneath looser ground. The Oud Speaker must have been shielded, in part, by its vehicle—otherwise, it wouldn't have left this spot.

So . . . a natural predator or a cunning trap left by the Tikitik, who used living things as their tools?

At least the hook-claw appeared fixed in place and none-too-bright. The canopy had innumerable such hazards. Once the rest knew, they'd be watchful.

At the thought, Aryl *reached,* seeking that comfort. There. Her people. After the Oud and Tikitik, even Oran was a welcome *taste*.

She could be with them before taking another step. All she had to do was picture the warmth and comfort of the meeting hall and *'port* herself there.

Who might be watching? A stranger-device, far overhead? A Tikitik, skin matched to stone? What about the Oud . . . they hadn't reacted to her use of the M'hir. That didn't mean they wouldn't.

Marcus had been right to warn her.

She began to run again.

Interlude

ETLEKA EYED ENRIS.
Putting his hands behind his head, Enris eyed him right back.

Five days of his best behavior. His parents wouldn't have believed it. For his trouble, his hands bore new calluses from five mornings of catching the hapless denos, as well as cuts from five afternoons of hauling that catch to be cleaned and cleaning it. He'd endured flatcakes at every meal, by now almost inured to the Vyna's mouth-burning spice. He wore the clothes they gave him: the tunic and pants were cool and comfortable, if snug. No shirt. From the Vyna he'd seen, there wasn't a size to fit his shoulders.

Five days of doing whatever he was told, without argument or complaint. Of giving the Vyna time to grow used to his presence. Hopefully, time enough so they wouldn't feed him to the denos' unseen nightmare.

Any stranger had to prove his worth. But what Etleka held in his hand?

There was, Enris thought cheerfully, always the moment best behavior ended. "You can't make me wear it."

Stop talking out loud. Etleka held out the cap, a sparkling confection of blue and green, complete with yellow tassels. *Everyone stares at your head when we go out. It's embarrassing.*

"Doesn't bother me." Enris deliberately ran his fingers through his thick hair and added to his list of having behaved very well five days of talking—not talking—to no one but the two denos-catchers, neither of whom communicated a thought that wasn't about either denos or catching them. Unless it was to complain about his strangeness and having to put up with him.

He tried not to think of the five truenights he'd been left alone in this windowless bedroom. Every 'night, once asleep—he could only stay awake so long no matter how he tried—once asleep, he would hear the chant of Vyna's Council and Adepts echoing through the corridors of the Cloisters, an incoherent howl like something with teeth and terrible appetite, watched by bodiless eyes that pressed against the windows.

"You have no idea, my friend," Enris said peacefully, leaning back in the chair and crossing his long legs, "how long I can talk out loud. Let me start with my grandmother. Did I tell you she had a—"

You're impossible. Etleka placed the rejected cap on the table and flopped gracelessly into the other chair. Those furnishings and a narrow bed competed for what space there was. The other two rooms were no larger.

The Vyna had done more than cut into the island, they'd tunneled completely through it, like Oud. Enris had discovered the massive shard of rock was hollow, as if rotted from within. Where the rock narrowed—at its peak and ends, a single room might have doors to the outside piercing three of its walls. At its thickest, like here, along the lower levels, rooms opened only to other rooms. Vyna had no hallways inside its rock. Workrooms, including the one where he'd gutted denos were on the outside, with windows. Anyone going home had to walk through them first, then continue through whatever other rooms were in the way.

Many of those rooms were empty. Vyna had been more populous once.

I'm not impossible, he sent, inclined to peace now. *I work hard. I'm pleasant.*

You think that matters? Etleka replied scornfully. *You're lesser Om'ray. That you made it here past the mountains and water doesn't change anything. You can't be here, and you can't leave. You have to die.*

Enris grinned. *Haven't yet.*

Even a Vyna's laugh was soundless, a gaping of the mouth, a shake. *No. You tossed a rumn into Council, that's for sure.* The younger Om'ray's mindvoice was decidedly pleased. *They're still in session, arguing. Until that's settled, you can help with the denos.*

Arguing about what?

I shouldn't talk about such things.

Oh, he knew that look. He'd see it on Worin's face, when his little brother ached to tell a secret to someone. *If they're going to kill me eventually,* Enris sent, with a deliberate hint of amusement, *why not tell me? I'm curious.*

Beyond curious. Desperate.

Patience, he told himself, keeping his body and face relaxed.

Tarerea Vyna, the High Councillor. She claimed the Glorious Dead for her unborn, used it before the others had a chance. There should have been a vote. Disdain. *Not that they'd have agreed on anything.*

What's a "glorious dead"?

Etleka's eyes widened. *You really are lesser, aren't you? Don't you know anything?*

The Tuana imagined a certain Yena's response to this and gave his best smile. *Maybe not. Tell me.*

When an Adept can no longer be kept alive through the gifting—that is my future, the unChosen added with *pride—I am strong. One of their servers will fail soon, and I'll be Called. They won't Call you. I've heard they fear your taste will be sour.*

Remembering the unChosen waiting to give their strength to those too-old bodies, Enris was mutely grateful.

When an Adept is close to death, Etleka continued, *another scours the memories from her mind and puts them in a Vessel. When an unborn is ready, she receives the Glorious Dead. It doesn't always work. The unborn can be willful and refuse the gift. If it does work, a new Adept is born, with the memories and Talents of the one gone before.*

Vile. Horrible. Enris fought the urgent desire of his stomach to express its own opinion, fought to keep his shields tight and to project only *curiosity*. How could they do this to the unborn? What were the minds behind those old eyes?

So the argument is about Tarerea?

Another grin. Etleka had likely never had so eager a "listener." *They argue about you, Enris. You brought a new Vessel to Vyna, the first ever. They want more, badly, but no Vyna would leave and be contaminated by the world beyond. They could send you. You are already ruined. But you can't be trusted to return. You can see their problem. Some want you dead now. The rest argue for a delay, saying you could be neutered, made useful while they try to find a way.*

Neutered? Enris didn't care for the feel of the word—or the *satisfaction* that came with it.

Not that any Vyna Chooser would crave a lesser Om'ray, but if it happened? Nothing can stop Choice and Joining. All that can be done to protect the Chooser from her misjudgment is to remove— Rather than send an image, Etleka spread his legs and pantomimed the slash of a knife. *Those of feeble Power cannot be allowed to breed.*

"You expect me to believe you mutilate Chosen?" The outburst rang against the walls. Enris didn't care. "I may be new to Vyna, my friend, but I'm not stupid."

The other jumped to his feet, pale face flushed with anger. *Ask Daryouch, then.*

"Your father?"

At the door, Etleka gave Enris a scathing look over his shoulder. *I had none.* Not with grief—with *pride*.

Once the incomprehensible Vyna was gone, Enris leaned his head back and closed his eyes. If his future was set, this lesser Om'ray needn't risk his life "helping" catch denos.

What should he do?

The irony didn't escape him. If there was any unChosen on Cersi the Vyna shouldn't worry about contaminating their precious Choosers, it was him. He hadn't come in answer to a Call. To be honest, he found the one Vyna Chooser he'd met as appealing as an Oud and had no higher expectations from the rest. He felt no urge whatsoever to Join any of them.

He fingered the knot of hair at his throat. He'd come here to help all Om'ray and found the only ones who wouldn't. No wonder Thought Traveler had been amused.

If the Vyna thought he was going to sit here while their strange Council and withered Adepts decided his fate . . .

He laughed loud and long.

. . . time to misbehave.

Enris delayed only to change into his own clothes. The Vyna garments, he left lying on the floor.

Now to find something worth taking.

✳ ✱ ✳

Each truenight, sent to his bed, he'd listen to the door being locked. It wasn't now, Enris discovered when he went to break it open. Either he'd angered Etleka to the point of carelessness, or the unChosen had no idea how uncooperative a lesser Om'ray could be. Grinning, the Tuana investigated the main room, where Daryouch prepared and served their meals, but its few cupboards contained nothing but dishes, utensils, and clothing. Perhaps the Vyna had no need for preserved or dried foods, going out daily to catch the hapless denos.

Another excellent reason to leave. A steady diet of the things and he'd become as thin as any Vyna.

He wouldn't be able to leave unobserved. There were four "homes" and a storeroom between here and the outside. Vyna privacy was based on a deliberate turn of the head to not look directly at those already in a room—or those passing through—as if the pretense possibly mattered.

No one home in the first three. Enris opened the door to the next and strode inside. He'd never seen anyone there.

Until now. A smokelike mist, redolent with musk, swirled around the naked Chosen standing inside. She grabbed her cap from the table, fumbled it over her head. No pretense this time. She stared at him as he stared at her.

Who are you?

With a frantic gesture of apology, Enris hurried through, turned the next door, and bolted for the safety of the storeroom.

He slowed, tasting musk at the back of his throat. What had the Chosen been doing? He had a confused memory of . . .

A Call flooded his mind, pulled at his thoughts, twisted his senses. He stopped with his hand about to turn the door to outside. A Call from . . .

. . . the room he'd just left.

No. Impossible. He'd seen her. Too well. The swollen breasts and hips of a Chosen, a body ready to nurture new life. Her exposed hair had been strange, a thin pale fuzz like the coating of a fruit, but it had moved with her emotions.

He'd seen her.

The Call continued, stronger than Fikryya's, than Seru's. Despite his revulsion for all things Vyna, Enris hesitated, surprised by longing.

He had only to turn around. Go back through that door.

To what? What *was* she? A Chooser waiting for completion— or a Chosen half-thing? Or was this another aspect of Vyna, that their Choosers need not wait for Choice to mature?

Etleka claimed no father. Had he meant exactly that? No. Impossible.

Enris licked dry lips. Wasn't it?

Did Vyna need the unChosen at all?

She did. She wanted him. Her urgent desire ached in his bones, fired his blood. *Come back . . . let me offer myself . . . offer you Choice . . .* Sweat stung his eyes as he resisted. Her Call, so close and powerful, weakened his shields, shook his hold on reality. The M'hir surged closer, pulled at his sanity, sang destruction . . .

No! He would not.

Rebuffed, the Call withered and stopped, a triumph of will over passion. He choked back a cry at its loss . . . turned the door and half fell through it . . . found himself . . .

Outside.

And ran.

* ✳ *

Morning could be midday could be firstnight. The mist-laden water and clouded sky diffused light, confused all sense of time. His stomach helped, insisting he'd missed breakfast.

His pounding blood said he'd missed something else.

With an effort, Enris forced his thoughts away from the memory of her Call, of his ability to refuse it. She hadn't sent again, perhaps stung by his rejection—Choosers, he'd noticed, didn't take well to being spurned—perhaps gathering strength to send it again. If she did, could he resist her again?

Whatever she was.

Wrong to refuse, something inside argued. What was he waiting for? Enris suddenly thought of his cousin Ral, who doubted the next sunrise until he saw it for himself. He'd been fond of stories of unChosen who failed to find a Chooser. Their fate, according to these tales, involved a long and romantically miserable life made bearable by incredible feats of daring and accomplishment.

Kiric had lasted a year before walking off a Yena bridge. There, thought Enris bitterly, was the truth.

His own emptiness? He filled it with determination, with anger, with the need to help others. Made himself remember the *pain* Naryn had caused, when she'd tried to force him to answer her Call. With the *terror* of being lost in the M'hir, in that endless insanity of darkness . . . Should he add a new one? That his own ability might keep him from any Choice at all?

Enris broke out laughing. "Now I sound like you, Ral." Who, for all he knew, had already Joined with sweet, if hiccup-ridden, Olalla. Besides, if he believed Etleka, he'd escaped a match that would have cost him dearly. He tugged his pants for reassurance.

Whatever else, he had to leave this place. To his inner sense, the Vyna were spread over more than the island. The denos-catchers were heading out in their floats, Daryouch and Etleka among them. Not that he planned an overwater route. Even if he could use his Talent to move one of the craft, the thought of what swam below?

No. A Tuana belonged on ground. Solid, flat ground.

Which meant a bridge. And he'd complained about Yena's. At least they'd been wide, with rope rails.

Enris paused by one of the Vyna's always-bright glows, gazed at it thoughtfully. "What powers you?" he asked it. No cell. No oil. But what?

The Vyna themselves? They used Power in novel ways.

Determined, if glad no one watched, he put his hand against its cool outer case. The light shone through his flesh, painting his fingertips pink. Cautiously, Enris lowered his shields, *reached* with the part of his mind that understood Power and objects, that could sense another's *touch*.

Nothing.

What are you doing?

He tightened his shields and turned to face the sender, startled to have to look down. The mindvoice hadn't felt childish. The shield he gently explored was as firm as any adult's, yet this was a child too young to be away from her parent's protection.

What are you? A miniature Fikryya, complete with the same haughty tone. She wore a shift, bright yellow, that went to her knees. A cap—also yellow—covered her head, answering his curiosity of whether all Vyna wore the things, although hers was adorned by black knotted fibers bound by wire in a tuft on top. Her slim wrists and ankles were covered in bands, not of metal, but of black thread strung through the eye sockets of white skulls, smaller than her fingertips. They were tied so they wouldn't click against one another.

He went to one knee. *My name is Enris Mendolar. What's yours?*

Tiny eyebrows collided. *That's not a real name.*

Enris sensed her *disapproval,* as if he tried to make fun of her. He carefully didn't smile. *It's not a Vyna name,* he agreed.

A flare of *curiosity,* again with that unnatural control. *You're the one the esan dropped on the bridge.* She eyed him up and down. *You don't look hideously deformed.* This with distinct *disappointment.*

Very young, he decided, with growing concern. *Let me take you to your mother.*

Her eyes widened; he sensed *alarm* mixed with *longing* and a bitter *resignation* no child her age should be able to feel. *I'm a fos-terling. I'm not allowed near my mother.*

Enris couldn't contain his *dismay* at this; he didn't try. *That can't be.* Even as he protested, he *reached.*

The bond was there, between the child and her mother. It wasn't the one he'd known, or what he'd felt between his new brother and Ridersel. Instead of that fierce, protective closeness, this burned with Power, as if ignited by the tension of distance, or as if both minds fed it strength to keep it alive.

And it felt like the connection Aryl had forged between them, in the M'hir.

Wrong. Like everything else here. *You should be together,* he sent desperately. *Let me take you home.*

A hand, light and cool as mist, rested on his. *It's not for long. She slips from me if I'm not careful. Soon I'll be of no use. Then I can go home.*

Enris stared into the child's patient, weary eyes. *I don't under-stand.*

You're lesser Om'ray. As if he should accept this.

As if he could. Mist curled over stone, muffled even their breath-ing. *You shouldn't be here alone.* It was all he could find to send.

A shy smile. *I think you're nice, Enris Mendolar. And I'm not alone. Look, here comes Jenemir. Jenemir Vyna,* she added formally. *My name is Nabrialan Vyna. He can't send very far.* With *pity.*

Enris rose to his feet and turned to face the oncoming Om'ray. Like the Adepts, Jenemir was older than any Om'ray he'd met outside Vyna. He shuffled more than strode, one hand locked around a staff pressed with care to the pavement, its well-wrapped end preventing any sound.

Much longer here, Enris told himself, and he'd long for Olalla's hiccups.

The child rushed to the old Om'ray's side, looked up adoringly as she grasped his free hand. It took Enris a moment to realize the ferocious creasing of Jenemir's face was a smile. *This is Enris, Jen-emir.* Nabrialan's sending was powerful enough. *He's nice. For a lesser Om'ray.*

Eyes that were slits beneath thick lids gazed at him. A puckered hand wedged the staff under an arm, then was offered.

Enris didn't dare hesitate, taking Jenemir's cold and twisted fingers in his. *The child is without her mother,* he sent immediately, with undertones of *urgency* and *concern. We must take her home.*

Nabrialan lives with me. The sending was labored as well as faint. Had too many years sapped Jenemir's Power as well as his body? *It is Vyna's way. Why are you here?* His fingers twitched; Enris could feel the other's mind fumble at his shields. *Strong. Very strong. Shame you are lesser Om'ray.*

The corner of Enris' mouth quirked up, and he restrained a laugh. The Vyna were consistent, he'd give them that. *Which is why I'm leaving,* he informed the other, *once I understand what powers your glows.*

Nabrialan looked at the nearest fixture, then back at the Tuana. *Powers the glows?* Her sending was perplexed, as if Enris had asked why the sun bothered to shine above the mist. *They light Vyna.*

Jenemir's face creased into its smile again. *And well they do, little one, or we'd have rumn crawling the streets at night.*

He hadn't wanted to know that.

There'd been *pride* in the other's sending to the child. *You know how they work,* he sent to Jenemir.

Definitely pride. *Of course. Those who cannot gift the worthy or offer Choice still have their place in Vyna. I worked for many years on the fire below. Important work. Valued work.*

You can't be still unChosen. Enris hadn't meant to share the thought, but Jenemir's creases only tightened.

Of course, the Vyna sent again. *Only the weak can survive alone. The Power's need—it eats the powerful from inside. You can feel it, can't you. A mercy to let them spend themselves to maintain the lives of their betters. The most powerful . . .* He stopped there.

What about them?

If they are Vyna, they are Chosen. Our Choosers refuse any less. A hint of *apprehension* beneath his mindvoice; the gnarled hand trembled in Enris'. *You shouldn't be here. Your Power will tempt them. It's Forbidden to Choose a lesser Om'ray. You must go.*

Enris forced a smile. *I'll be gone as soon as you tell me about these glows. What is the fire below?*

The other thought to refuse, but his shields were thinner than the gauze of Yena's windows. Memories surged through his mind, memories of a lifetime spent working within an immense cavern, sensations so vivid Enris could feel the searing heat from its floor of molten rock on his skin, imagine his legs cramped with the effort of climbing stairs, his throat rasped by fumes.

A cavern. *The Oud,* he concluded with disappointment.

We have nothing to do with lesser races. Ground Dwellers dare not enter our cavern. Meddlers dare not cross our lake. The Vyna—this with overwhelming conviction—*are not part of the outside world.*

Molten rock explained the too-warm lake water, and the mist above it. It didn't, as far as Enris was concerned, explain glows with no power cells. There had to be more. Something he could learn or take with him. *What makes the glows work?* he insisted, careful not to tighten his larger hand. Those old bones would break.

Why do you care? Nabrialan broke in, *impatience* under the words. *Come, Jenemir. I'm hungry. Let's go home.*

The old unChosen looked down at the child. *Go ahead, little one. I will make sure this lesser Om'ray goes where he belongs, then cook you a fine supper.*

Enris watched the tiny figure in yellow skip down the roadway, the only life and color to be seen, her footsteps smothered by the mist. *What will happen to her?* he asked.

Nabrialan? She will sit on Council one day. Her unborn may even receive a Glorious One. She has great Power. As if this mattered most of all.

To the Vyna, maybe it did. If it led to this? A Council that squabbled over the memories of the dead, their greatest ambition for their children to bring those memories back to life? Om'ray who died were supposed to stay that way.

Vyna was as foul as its air.

The glows? Enris sent gently but firmly. *In my Clan, I'm a metalworker. There are many things I can do with fire, Jenemir, but powering light from glows isn't one of them. Tell me about them, please.*

Vyna's Heart. Instead of more words, another memory, this time deliberately shared. Enris *was* Jenemir as he stood before a machine larger than a Cloisters. Its lower surfaces took their color from the molten rock lapping against its base, reds and oranges, swirls and eddies of searing white against the black. There were moving parts, none of which made sense, most larger than an Om'ray. Some spun, some turned, others came and went through openings he couldn't see.

What didn't move was just as incomprehensible. Five massive "arms" had been driven up and into the ceiling of stone, or the stone had formed around them. Curls of pipe entered the molten pool, unaffected by its heat or seeking it. Openings that couldn't be reached without wings.

And Om'ray, stripped to the waist, carrying cubes of black rock on their bent backs down long, narrow staircases. Cubes that were stacked by other Om'ray atop a wall of other cubes that ran along the near border of the molten pool, holding it back. From the height and breadth of that wall, the Vyna had been doing this longer than Enris dared imagine.

Not all the Vyna, he realized. Those without Power to give an Adept, or attract a Chooser. Their weakest unChosen.

Their expendable fools.

The glows? he sent, somehow keeping his disgust from Jenemir, though he no longer hoped for an answer. Even if he could understand the workings of this machine, even if he could build another—where else on Cersi was a cavern that melted rock itself?

Jenemir's tongue worried at a solitary, yellowed tooth. *They shine as long as the machine floats on the molten lake. So was made the Promise.*

Adept prattle, Enris judged it, to make the carrying of rocks important. *Glows can be powered by other means,* he offered, unsure why.

We need nothing from the outside world. Where you belong, lesser Om'ray. The Vyna pulled his hand free, moved his staff, moved his feet, and made his slow way after the child.

Enris made the gesture of gratitude. Jenemir was right.

He didn't belong here.

* ✳ *

Mist butted the black stone like a mattress of lies. Layers of it were above him, obscuring the sky, cutting the light until the glows to either side were the brightest source. When he kicked out with one foot, the mist shied away, then curled back, as if enjoying the game.

The bridge had to be here. Somewhere.

Enris stood at the edge of the platform, *reached* with care. There were no Om'ray ahead—or below. This wasn't the bridge to their Cloisters.

Nor was it a game.

There were stairs to the water here. Somewhere. This might be where they'd brought him, the first day. He vaguely remembered doing more congratulating than paying attention, grateful to have been saved.

Saved. Enris would have laughed, but the mist covered the water, and the water held what he especially didn't want noticing him.

Especially when he had to walk out on the bridge, surrounded by water.

The bridge he couldn't see for mist.

Enris sat down, his legs hanging over the platform. His fingers toyed with the knot of hair as he considered the problem. The mist swallowed his feet and ankles, tasted his knees. He reached down with his foot. Nothing. A shift to one side, a reach. Nothing. Shift, reach. Shift, reach. Shift . . . there. Just as he felt a thorough fool, the side of his boot struck what he couldn't see—a solid surface. The bridge, or a stair to it.

When would they try to stop him? He *reached*. No one nearby. Enris frowned thoughtfully. Were they letting him go?

Or did they know something about his planned escape route he didn't?

Not that it mattered. He was leaving and now.

Enris cautiously descended what proved to be stairs, feeling his way. It wasn't slippery, but he loathed the mist even more as he sank into its damp warmth, its stench. He tried not to think about it or the bridge, instead concentrating on the feel of real sunlight and a proper, cleansing wind.

The third step was the last. The bridge. Mist engulfed his body from the waist down. It would rise higher by truenight. Ahead— an appalling distance ahead—rose the smooth black rock that encircled the lake, the opening that led inside. To what?

He'd worry about that if—when—he got there.

Wishing for Aryl's effortless balance, Enris slid one foot ahead of the other, making sure each was on a solid support before shifting his full weight to it.

Water lapped, unseen. Vyna craft moved across it, unseen, unheard.

Nice to have company, he decided, licking sweat from his upper lip. Step, step.

Though Enris tried to move in a straight line, too often his next step would slide off the edge of the bridge and he'd freeze in place to keep his balance. After the fourth close call, he glanced over his shoulder at the island.

What island? Mist had consumed the platforms, slipped under the lights. All he could make out was a rumor of height.

He clung to his sense of other Om'ray—without it, the world had no up, down, or sides. There was nothing but mist.

Time for a different strategy.

He lowered himself to his hands and knees. Mist pressed soft and wet against his face; he closed his eyes. It wasn't as if sight was helping.

Better. He believed what he touched; his movements didn't need grace, only patience.

Enris measured the bridge by the growing soreness of his knees and palms, unused to supporting his bulk. He vowed to eat less, although with a certain self-pity, since he didn't see how that was possible. His last meal of denos seemed a feast in memory. He had nothing in his pockets or pouch but his Oud firebox. And the knife in his belt.

The Vyna weren't used to having captives, he mused as he crawled forward. Just as well. None he'd seen, all modesty aside, would be a match for his big hands and strength. He didn't want to hurt them.

Warn other Clans, yes. He'd find a way. There was no welcome for those on Passage here, despite Vyna's abundance of Choosers. No one else should come here.

Enris paused, shaking his head like a beast. Droplets flew from his hair. Something wasn't right.

He wanted to laugh. Crawling along a thin bridge of stone through impenetrable mist to an end he couldn't be sure existed? What could be right about that?

No, he told himself, rocking back to sit still and listen. It was something else.

Something *within*.

A Call.

As he braced himself to resist, he heard a sound. A little splash, only that. Then another, and another.

Denos.

The Call wasn't from a Chooser—it was the summoning the Vyna used to bring up the rumn!

Enris drew and held his knife, eyes blind in the mist, and began to crawl again, as quickly as he could with only one hand free. As quietly, too. He tried not to breathe.

The Vyna approached the bridge. They made no sound either. Denos began to land on the bridge, silver bodies wriggling and slapping in their struggle to return to water. One thudded into Enris, and he grunted with surprise. More landed in his path, and he swept them aside rather than risk putting a knee on their slippery sides.

The rumn.

It was coming. The denos knew. His inner sense knew.

Enris moved faster. Once beyond the splash and smack of denos, he put away the useless knife and pressed himself flat against the bridge, breathing into a sleeve, wishing his heart to slow. He'd wait it out. Surely a deepwater dweller couldn't stay near the surface for long. It couldn't find him if he was quiet.

A shape loomed from the mist and collided with the bridge beside Enris. *Bang!* One of the Vyna floats—empty. It rocked back with the force of impact, out of sight.

From the other side—a second empty float hurtled toward him. *Bang!*

Simple, Enris thought with disgust. He couldn't see them in time to fend them off with his own Power. And they made enough noise to summon the entire lakeful of rumn.

Time to go.

He crawled as quickly as possible, no longer worried about noise. It followed him, the Vyna precise in their aim. Presumably they'd run out of empty floats soon.

Another shape loomed beside him. Enris braced himself for the sound, but there was none. The shape didn't collide with the bridge—it *turned* and began to slide alongside. A glistening darkness, the curved sweep of a back.

Not entirely dark. There were faint whorls and patterns of light embedded in it, as if the stars had become stuck in the rumn's skin. If it was skin and not a hole in the world . . .

Perverse. Wrong. Like everything here. Enris spat and kept moving. The bridge couldn't go on forever. Once on land, he'd take his chances against anything alive.

The rock bridge shuddered under his hands.

And again.

The rumn was alive, wasn't it? Despite its terrifying extension into the M'hir . . . its feel in his mind . . . it had to be a living thing . . .

He wasn't sure why that was vital, but it was.

Crunch!

From ahead. He knew that sound—a careless foot on loose stone—and launched himself to his feet, desperately running toward it.

His foot lost the bridge, struck what was firm enough to support it, something that *rose*.

Enris didn't look down, didn't dare. He pushed off with all his strength, regained the bridge, ran through the mist . . .

. . . and into another Om'ray, who fell back with a startled "Ooof!" The Tuana kept running, now on pebbles. A soundless *wail* burned through his mind, hungry and enraged. Then a scream from behind, cut short . . .

The mist fell back. He found himself on a ramp, treacherous with loose stones. Ahead, the tunnel mouth he'd seen from the island.

And what he hadn't seen.

Its massive, closed door.

Something *moved* behind him. Something *hungry.*

Enris lifted his hands, concentrated, and *pushed.*

With a shriek of stretched, abused metal, the door gave way.

He ran through the opening and never looked back.

Chapter 15

ARYL WASN'T SURPRISED TO FIND Haxel, who would miss nothing that moved near Sona from her perch, waiting by the empty river. "Here," the First Scout greeted her, holding out a flask.

She gestured gratitude but took only a swallow to clear her throat. Best be blunt. "It's not good news, Haxel. We have a problem."

The scar twisted—not quite a smile. "I guessed as much from your rush to get here. Rorn's cooking's not that great. The Oud?"

"And Tikitik." Aryl dropped down beside the other, twisting on the rock so she could see both tunnel mouth and village. "They confronted the Oud, claimed to be first here, demanded the Oud leave Sona. The Oud killed them."

Haxel stilled.

"Thought Traveler arrived. It didn't seem to care about the deaths or the Oud, only about what it called the balance. The Oud said they would maintain it." She remembered something else. "And that more Om'ray were coming here."

"That we know." Haxel's head dipped toward the Lay Swamp. "Quickly, too. Rorn's put on extra. Mind telling me how many to expect?"

Startled, Aryl *reached* immediately, finding a tight cluster where no Om'ray belonged. "Fifteen." She'd been too focused on herself, on Sona . . . As for their speed . . . "They can't be on foot," she blurted the obvious.

The First Scout gestured agreement. "And too low to be flying in one of your friend's machines. I'm guessing Oud vehicles—at Grona, I saw one move faster on a road than I could run." Had she raced with the Oud, just to find out? "Fifteen. Did the Oud say why they were bringing us guests?"

"Only that it had to do with the Agreement and balance." Aryl shivered. "They almost killed me as well. I'm never sure I understand them, Haxel."

A too-keen look. "No water?"

"Not yet." Her hands sketched apology. "I should have stayed—tried to talk to their Speaker—"

Haxel shrugged. She unwrapped her legs from their comfortable folding and stood, Aryl doing the same. "We've fifteen people on their way here. Possibly injuries—the Oud being unaware of our limits. Confused and terrified—I've no doubt. That's enough to deal with right now."

Aryl turned toward the village. Before she took a step, the First Scout dropped a heavy hand on her shoulder. *So your time's come at last.* There was no joy in the sending, only *concern.*

She didn't look at the other. She couldn't. *I didn't plan it.*

We never do. Aloud, then, as if to avoid emotion. "If you can't control yourself, tell me. I've dealt with a Sarc Chooser before."

Aryl winced. Haxel meant her mother, Taisal. "I'll be fine—"

"It's not you I'm worried about."

She had no answer for that.

"That's it, then."

"Seru—"

Her cousin's stiff back expressed her opinion as she left the shelter. That, and the way she managed to slam home the stick that kept the door closed against the wind.

"You can apologize to her later," Myris said gently.

Aryl transferred her glare to her aunt. "She's the one being unreasonable!" They had Om'ray being dragged here— through tunnels, she very much feared, and undoubtedly against their will. They had Tikitik and Oud killing one another—for whatever reason. Marcus was alone with creatures who'd almost killed them both—not that she could share that bit of worry. And she was to apologize for—for— "It's not as if I want any of them," she grated out.

"Do you think that makes it easier to bear when you could have any?"

Aryl threw her armload of Sona bedding into a corner. Rock for a floor and a roof of blankets. Wind whistled through cracks that could fit her arm. No hearth for a fire. Half a wall on one side. Three oillights gave an illusion of warmth.

She kept on her coat.

This excuse for a building was across not one but two roads of tilted stone, with shattered homes and dead fields between. They'd been using it to store the jars of oil, the Grona having warned of the danger of those too close to sleepers.

Suddenly, without argument or discussion, it was necessary to put her here, even though they had room for the new arrivals in one of the four already restored.

"I don't feel any different," she grumbled. It was true. That episode with Marcus, when she'd been overwhelmed by her senses, had been the only one.

Myris straightened the blankets into something closer to a bed. "You will." Her smile was a shade too cheerful. "You know we're all happy for you. But you're a Sarc." A meaningful shrug. "My own time was—let's say there was a reason I had to stay with our grandparents. Once I started my Call, no one could sleep." Her smile softened; her eyes grew moist. "It wasn't long before Ael came in answer. May you find joy soon."

Given the options of trying to respond to her aunt, or

pound a sliver of wood into a crack to hold her coat, Aryl found a rock and pounded. The wood split under the force, and she stung her fingers on the wall.

Myris sighed. "This is temporary, Aryl. You have exceptional control—you always have had. But a sleeping Chooser tends to—can be disturbing."

"Seru sleeps with the rest." As soon as she'd said it, Aryl gestured a grudging apology. Parths had less Power; their Chooser's Call had almost no impact on others. It was the truth, if unkind to mention.

She envied her cousin. That was the truth, too. "I won't stay here during the day—I've work to do. No one should treat me any differently."

Her aunt came close. Her cool fingers brushed a lock of hair from Aryl's brow, tucked it into its net, rested against her cheek. *You may not feel it yet, little Aryl, but you are different. Since we've come to this cold place, being near you has been like finding a warm spot in the sun. Now, you're like a flame. If I ever doubted what Taisal said about your Power . . .* her sending faded beneath waves of *pride* and *love*.

The wind tested the blanket roof. Aryl searched those gray eyes, a mirror to her own. *I don't want this—I'm not ready.* With a wrench of honesty. *Why am I afraid?*

Because Choice isn't about control or planning or what you desire. Myris seemed much older in that instant, the gulf between Chooser and Chosen wider than the world. *Choice is as inevitable and needful as breathing. When the unChosen who can fulfill you stands where I am now, you will lose yourself. When he takes your outstretched hand, you will be unmade. When your Powers merge and you have Joined minds forever, you will become something new. You will be changed by him, as he will be changed by you.*

This wasn't what unChosen eagerly whispered to one other about Choice. She'd feared exposing her secrets—now did she have to fear she'd no longer care to keep them? Was that what had happened to Bern? *Have I no say in this?*

Only what you are. As a Sarc—an upwelling of *compassion*—

Choice will not come easy. We resist. We fight. We challenge. Only an unChosen able to match his will to ours can succeed.

"You make it sound like a battle," Aryl protested, her breath coming fast and hard.

For those of great Power, it is. Her aunt gestured apology. "You need to know, Aryl. To be prepared. Seru can accept any unChosen, her Choice will be easy. But with you nearby, no one will want her. They'll turn to you instead—they must. They'll respond to your Call, to your greater Power, like wastryls scenting fresh dresel."

"Now I'm a prize?" She didn't want to hear this. She wanted Myris to stop.

No. That wasn't true. Something deep inside her responded to the words, to what she was being told. Something believed.

Something *rejoiced*.

"Choice cannot be forced on a Chooser. You must offer it. But you can't complete your Choice with an unChosen who is less in Power. I may be weak for a Sarc," Myris stroked her cheek again, "but my Power to Choose was not. Ael had to struggle against me at first. I was afraid I'd lose him, that our Joining would fail, that I'd stay incomplete. You can't imagine how that felt."

She could. She'd lost Bern and thought it the worst that could happen.

Until she'd lost Enris.

Aryl paced away, then back. "What am I supposed to do, Myris? Walk up to every unChosen in Sona and try to measure their Power against mine, then pick the one I want?"

"Those of great Power can't plan their Choice, Aryl, or control it. That's what I'm trying to explain. Seru's drive is not as strong as yours will be. It's let her wait. Parths can be patient." Her aunt's hands were restless; she clasped them together. "My sister loved Sian. Did you know? They were heart-kin from childhood. When Taisal became a Chooser, she wanted Sian and he wanted her. But it was Mele who stopped her on that bridge at firstlight, Mele whose Power matched hers, Mele who became sud Sarc."

Myris' lips twitched. "For which we were all grateful, let me tell you. Taisal was making truenight a misery for everyone."

"My parents were happy together," Aryl countered, tight-lipped. Had this been why Sian visited their home so often? Not to debate with a fellow Adept, or not only that, but to be near someone he could never have?

"The Chosen are—" Myris seemed to rethink what she was going to say. "You aren't a child, Aryl, to be told Joining is about love and companionship. Neither of those require Choice. Choice is deeper, wilder. It's the body's need: to claim a mate, to mature, to breed. Yes, the Chosen are obsessed with one another—until the urge to have children ends. After that? Our bond remains; what we do with it depends on us. I will always love Ael and he, me. We are partners. But you've seen how Oran rules Bern, Hoyon's disdain for his Chosen. You need to be strong. Sure of what you want. Rule, if you must. You can't let your Chosen take you from us."

Aryl stared at her aunt. "Haxel sent you to talk to me." The First Scout didn't wait for events to happen, not if she could anticipate them. "Why?" At the ripple of *dismay* she felt, she knew. "The Caraats. Haxel actually believes I'll Choose Oran's brother?" She laughed; she couldn't help it.

Myris looked offended. "He's the most Powerful unChosen in Sona."

"No," Aryl replied, sure of one thing. "I am."

Whatever worries and fears her aunt had managed to increase, not ease, Aryl was relieved when she joined the rest for supper in the meeting hall. No one gave her odd looks or moved aside. As usual, hands lifted to hers as she passed; grateful beyond words, she sent *strength* back through each touch.

Not every hand. Oran and Hoyon sat together against a wall, Bern and Kran nearby. Seru managed to be busy serving soup and didn't look up.

But tiny Yao reached up from Oswa's lap and both returned Aryl's smile.

Anxiety and *anticipation* rilled from mind to mind, as noticeable as the increasing howl of wind outside. They could all sense those approaching. At their rate of travel, the newcomers should arrive tonight.

She should be grateful for that distraction, Aryl decided ruefully. Otherwise, the topic of conversation would doubtless be her apparently obvious-to-everyone-else condition.

Which was on the minds of some regardless. When it was her turn to receive a bowl from Seru, her cousin quickly handed it to Rorn and moved to the far side of the cook fire. Hurt, Aryl stared after her.

"She can't help it." Rorn added a spoon with this matter-of-fact explanation. "Close to you, no one will hear her. Choosers have an instinct."

No longer hungry, Aryl accepted the bowl and hurriedly moved away.

Haxel made room for her at the end of one of the tables. "We'll need to eat in shifts once they're here," she said with no preamble. "Fifteen? You're sure?"

"I'm sure." Aryl watched the steam rise from her soup, toyed with her spoon. She could feel Kran's eyes on her, but he was, as she'd hoped, easy to ignore. Murmurs of conversation filled the room like glows. This was more than they'd hoped— to have numbers so soon, to be a Clan.

At what price? *We need to tell them about the Oud and Tikitik.*

Haxel made a dismissive sound. *Speaker's business.*

The pendant was stored beneath her tunic. Nonetheless, Aryl felt its weight.

It wasn't as heavy as other secrets. She tried a mouthful, made herself swallow. One sending, here and now. She could tell them all about the M'hir, how to move through it. One sending, and she could abdicate responsibility for keeping that ability from the strangers. Make whatever happened willful Ziba's fault, or earnest young Fon's, or power-hungry Oran's.

Aryl put down her spoon.

"No appetite?" Morla, on her other side, leaned in. "I was the same as a Chooser. Ate nothing but fresh baked dresel cake for a fist. Hungry for something else, let me tell you."

"Leave her be." Veca gave Aryl a sympathetic look. "Don't let anyone tell you how you should feel, Aryl. Everyone's different. I couldn't stand company—until I found Tilip." This with a softening of her usually dour features.

"Rorn found me," Haxel volunteered. "Not that I objected." The three Chosen shared a laugh.

Aryl pushed away her bowl and rose to her feet. "I have to check on the Oud."

She didn't run from the meeting hall.

She did, however, manage to be out the door before anyone else could comment on Choosing, Choice, and her future.

Snowdrops played in the wind, the thick fluffy kind Aryl had learned found its way through eyelashes and down necks. Drifts were forming again, white scratches against the dark ground. The fire in front of the meeting hall melted the nearest to black puddles.

"Hello, Aryl." Juo was on watch tonight, a pair of eyes and a nose peering from a bundle of coats, scarves, and blankets. "Come to join me?"

Enris had *sensed* her unborn was a daughter, a Chooser-to-Be. Aryl felt a sudden rush of sympathy.

"Haxel sent me to check on the Oud," she said. Which the First Scout likely would have done, had she not been preoccupied.

"In truenight?" Juo shuddered. None of the Yena had lost their aversion to the dark. "I thought they'd stay in their tunnels. They have glows down there. Enris said so."

Enris. The fire grew brighter, the air colder, the fog of breath from her nostrils detailed and strange. She felt *some-*

thing shift, the M'hir close in, and desperately focused on Juo. "They use glows to work outside with their machines—did you see that at Grona?"

"True. Are you sure you don't want to sit with me? Watch for them from here?"

She didn't know what she wanted.

"I'll be back soon." Lighting her oillight, Aryl took the road toward the empty river and the Oud. Within a few steps, the snow surrounded her in its dance of white and gray.

It made her alone, set her apart. She wasn't sure why that felt a relief.

Short of the river, Aryl stepped off the road and made her way into the mass of tossed and half-buried beams that marked Sona's original hall. There, she ducked beneath a lean of stone, out of the snow, and pulled out the geoscanner. Nothing new showed on its screen. The green symbol when she pointed it toward the tunnel mouth meant all quiet.

Her thumb found the control on the side and pressed. He could hear her now, she thought, or rather his machines could pick up words and sort them into his *database*.

The Human claimed not to listen. Still, she mused, shifting her feet under her long coat, he was curious. That above all.

"I know what happened to the first Oud Speaker," she told it. Talking to a machine was very un-Om'ray. Naughty. Something her mother would scold her for . . .

. . . Taisal hadn't wanted Mele?

Aryl jerked her thoughts back where they belonged. "There was a hunter hidden beneath the dirt—it strikes at whatever touches it. It might have been there by its own will, or a surprise left by the Tikitik. They use living things—make them."

She leaned forward, her hood drooping, her eyes locked on the device in her hand. "There are Om'ray coming to Sona. The Oud are bringing them here through their tunnels. I don't know why. I don't understand them. I don't trust them. You should be more careful." This with a snap of worry.

Aryl listened for a moment, hearing nothing but the kiss and slip of fresh snow on drifts, the frustrated hiss and snarl of the wind beyond the shards overhead.

"I wish you were *real*," she said at last. "Then I'd know you were alive—where you were. That the Oud hadn't hurt you or taken you with them. How can you exist like that—not being able to sense one another?" The images of his Chosen, their children, his sister . . . if the Oud had buried Marcus in the ground, how would they ever know?

She could go there, find out. Her hand clenched on the device. Should she? Was it wise, to continue a friendship that could lead nowhere, that could be dangerous to both of them?

Or was it too late? The Oud and Tikitik had seen them together. Her people had Marcus' image in their minds—she'd given it to them, so they wouldn't fear him or his help. Now, it exposed him. She gestured a futile apology with her free hand.

"Aryl?"

She looked up, startled, then realized the quiet voice had come from the device.

Curious and prone to surprises, her Human.

"Aryl, it's me."

She almost smiled. Who else on Cersi would refer to himself as "me?" "I can hear you," she said. "How—" No, that didn't matter. "Are you all right?"

"Tired. Once they decided to show me what they'd found, they kept at it all day. I recorded all I could, but I'll need more *archivalbugs*. Some will have to be shipped *offworld*, there need to be tests—I'll stop now."

He'd have that abashed expression on his face, she knew. "I'm glad you're enjoying your work." More than glad. Her hands trembled. Moisture chilled on her cheeks. Had she been so afraid for him—or was it the relief of having someone to talk to who couldn't comment on her "condition?"

"How about you? You don't sound right."

Now she did smile. "I'm fine. Just cold."

"You're outside?" A note of alarm. "There's a bad *lowpres-*

surecell on the way. The *forecast's* heavy snow—colder. You shouldn't be out tonight."

The Human knew the weather? Aryl was torn between amusement and annoyance. She'd never thought to ask him something so ordinary. Of course, here was yet another reason Haxel would want access to stranger knowledge and technology. "I'll go inside soon—"

Something caught the attention of her inner sense, a disorientation. The other Om'ray were more than close, they were below! Others were on the move.

"I have to go. The Oud might be—" As if listening to her, the symbol on the geoscanner's screen flashed red. She finished, "The Oud are here. Good-bye, Marcus." The path of the Oud underground, their speed, had surprised her—had surprised them all. She had to get to the tunnel's mouth.

"Be careful, Aryl." Quickly, as if he knew she had her thumb on the control: "Leave comlink active. If you need me, need bioscanner, need big help, say: 'Two. Howard. Five.' I *program* to listen for those words. 'Two. Howard. Five.' Promise! Say now, I set *program* your voice."

Numbers. His son's name. Even as Aryl hesitated, she remembered how she'd felt when Marcus and his aircar had arrived, when Marcus had agreed to save the exiles. He was her ally, powerful and wise, in his way.

"Two. Howard. Five," she repeated carefully, committing the words to memory. "You promise me—don't speak from this device unless I talk first and say I'm alone."

"Understood."

Then silence.

Aryl tucked the device back in its pocket, making sure it was safe. Why had she cautioned him? This was his technology. He'd know its weaknesses.

She pulled the Speaker's Pendant free of her coat and scarf, made sure it was lying flat, and prepared to greet who—and what—was about to arrive.

Not alone. A solitary figure already stood on the bank, staring into the dark across the empty river, hair loose on the wind.

Seru Parth.

"Cousin," Aryl greeted warily as she approached. "What are you doing here?"

"Same as you."

Somehow, she doubted that. "You don't think—I'm not—I mean . . ." Aryl fumbled and fell silent, thoroughly embarrassed.

Fingers on her sleeve. *Two are pregnant. Their unborn are frightened. They may need me.* An undertone of *amusement* then *contrition.* "About before. I didn't mean to make you uncomfortable. It's just . . . We used to laugh about Choosers and their chancy tempers, remember? I never thought I'd be like that. And never with you."

Aryl took her in a one-armed hug, careful of the oillight. *You're my dear silly Seru. Nothing can change that.* "Let's greet our new arrivals." As they began to climb down the bank, "You're sure about the babies?"

Seru laughed. "Trust me. I hear them. Juo's daughter will have playmates."

She'd have to take her cousin's word for it.

All Aryl felt was *change.*

Thought Traveler had said the Oud didn't appreciate how fragile Om'ray were. Aryl's first glimpse of the vehicles hurtling from the tunnel did nothing to disprove that claim.

Each vehicle—there were three—pulled another behind. Glows girdled each flat platform, spilling light in overlapping, moving circles. An Oud reclined on the leading machine, five Om'ray clung desperately to the one that followed. There were no whirr/clicks. Maybe they didn't like snow driven by a bitter wind.

The Oud didn't slow as they left the smooth ramp of the

tunnel mouth for the damaged pavement of Sona's road. They headed for the village, vehicles bouncing and tipping violently. The Oud didn't appear to notice; the Om'ray cried out, sliding from side to side, holding on to one another.

Aryl ran through the snow, trying to intercept the first. Seru followed. Haxel and others were on their way, but there was no time. If the stupid Oud drove their vehicles down the rocky riverbank, they could kill their passengers.

She slipped but didn't fall. "Stop!"

Hard to know if they could hear her above the racket of their machines and the crunch of tread through the hardening drifts, the screams of the terrified Om'ray, but she kept shouting. "Stop! Stop!"

Short of the riverbank, the lead vehicle abruptly turned toward her. The platform it towed slewed to one side and small forms flew off, rolling in the snow.

"Stupid Oud!" she shouted. "Stop!!!"

For a wonder, they did.

For a moment, all that moved were snowdrops, sighing and whirling through the air.

Then the forms on the ground began to stir. One groaned. Aryl ached to go to them, but she had to be sure the Oud wouldn't start their machines again. She marched up to the closest and put herself in its way, her hand on the front of the machine. "I'm the Speaker." Loud and clear. "Wait. Let us look after our people."

The Oud loomed over her, a shadow made indistinct by the snow and down-pointed light. "Speaker," it agreed. Then, "Yours. Goodgoodgood."

Aryl doubted the poor Om'ray, unsteadily climbing from the platforms into the snow, would agree, but she didn't budge. "Wait here while we help them. Don't move. Do you understand?"

"Cold is. Leave. Quickquickquick."

Somehow, she didn't think this was a statement of concern for the Om'ray, though it was interesting to learn the Oud didn't like the cold any more than she did. She sent urgently: *Get away from the vehicles! The Oud are moving.*

Sure enough, the Oud in front of her flung itself back down with every appearance of haste, snow flying from its cloak. She had to dive out of its way as its vehicle swerved and bounced back to the tunnel, the others following as if pursued.

Taking their lights went with them.

For a moment, the only illumination was from Aryl's small oillight. She raised it over her head, *reached* for the others, found them. *Help comes!* she sent, adding *reassurance* and *welcome*.

The Oud were gone. The Om'ray they'd unceremoniously dumped on Sona's road were disoriented and afraid. Aryl hurried to the nearest group, brushed her hand over a shivering shoulder, across a hunched back, *sent* strength through each contact. She rushed to the next, seeing a blur of pale faces and outstretched hands, hearing muted sobs. She didn't bother to speak, merely touched, *gave,* and moved on.

Thankfully, Seru was there, too, a shadow helping others stand, murmuring words of comfort.

Four of the last group, those who'd been thrown, were back on their feet. They parted to let her light through, let her through. Aryl touched hands, arms, a leg, then dropped to her knees, dizzy with effort, to reach the last—an Om'ray crumpled in the snow.

Behind her, Haxel and the others charged up the riverbank, bearing lights and blankets. Voices shouted—orders, greetings, questions.

Aryl found her own. "You're safe." That they needed to know, first and foremost. "This is Sona. We've food for you, shelter. A Healer."

"Sona." From one of those standing. Female. "Who are you?"

Before she could answer, another voice intruded. "The Chooser." Deep, male, and regrettably loud. "I told you, Kor. She Called me here."

She had? Aryl crouched lower, as if the snow would hide her. "I offer you Choice, unChosen."

Aryl twisted around. Seru? "Wait," she began, knowing only that this couldn't happen. Not here, not now. Not like this. These were strangers, moving hulks in the dark only their senses said were Om'ray. Seru hadn't met them. She didn't know who they were, why they'd come. Who was kind . . . "The storm! We have to get to shelter first!"

She didn't exaggerate. The snow now fell in a flood, each 'drop thick and sticky, their sum filling the machine tracks and coating the shivering forms around her. The wind was less, but the air hurt to breathe. Marcus had been right. They couldn't stay out much longer.

An Om'ray who rivaled Enris in size staggered forward, shoved another out of his way. Seru stood waiting, her hand now outstretched.

Stop them!

The mindvoice was unfamiliar; the message set Aryl in motion. "No!" She lunged to intercept him—another Om'ray got in her way. She dodged him—they were all slow—too slow for a Yena. Unworthy! "Wait!"

Stop them!

The stranger grabbed Seru's hand, roughly, pulling her off-balance toward him. One of them cried out. Exultation or despair—she couldn't tell. The rest backed away, leaving the two isolated in the snow, heads bowed.

Too late . . . The figure on the ground, the one who'd protested, struggled to her feet. Numbly, Aryl took her hand to help, *gave* what strength she could spare.

Thank you. The *gratitude* came through impenetrable shields. This was no ordinary Om'ray.

Aryl couldn't take her eyes from Seru, dwarfed by the larger unChosen, both motionless. Whatever occurred between them, it was on a level her inner sense didn't touch. She knew better than to try to find it. She could only hope for the best, for someone Seru would have wanted.

And, more practically, for them to come out of their trance before they froze to death.

You should have stopped them. Almost exhausted. *Who lets a Chooser . . . a Chooser . . .* the mindvoice faded.

"Here." Slipping her shoulder under the other's arm, Aryl took a grip around her waist. The rest were forcing their way through the knee-high snow to the lights and sound; she didn't blame them. "There's a short drop, a climb, then we're home. Don't worry. You'll have help."

Help now arriving. Too slow. Too late. Taen passed her, heading for Seru, urgency in every step.

"Our Chosen know what to do."

Too late . . .

The Om'ray she assisted was taller by a head, though slender. Dressed for warmer weather, Aryl thought unhappily as they labored through the snow drifts. The fabric of her coat was soft and too thin. At least they had Grona-style boots, from what she glimpsed by her light.

Or were they?

The Oud hadn't taken a direct route here. They all been puzzled by the twists and redirections as the others approached, unsure which Clan had lost these members. "Tuana," she guessed abruptly.

"Yes." The hoarse voice broke into a cough. She shifted back to mindspeech. *We believed the Oud took us from the world.* A hint of *terrible fear*, quickly hidden. *Thank you. I am in your debt. We all are.*

Reeling herself, Aryl took more of the other's weight as the footing grew treacherous. Almost to the others now, to more light, to help. She strained to look back. Another group followed. Seru and Taen, with Seru's Chosen. "No debt," she managed to reply. The plight of these poor Tuana could well be her fault, something she wasn't about to explain.

Who are you?

"Aryl Sarc."

I am Naryn S'udlaat. And your friend, Aryl Sarc, from this moment.

Chapter 16

THE STORM SETTLED IN THE VALLEY, laying down snow, packing it into cracks and crannies with fitful pats of wind. The village became so many lumps in the landscape; what was restored indistinguishable from what had been destroyed. No one stirred outside. A curl of smoke was the only argument for life.

As far as Aryl could tell, no one cared. This latest storm was an excuse for the exiles' first prolonged rest and the arrival of the Tuana, whole if battered, had ignited a celebration that showed no signs of ending.

As for Seru's Joining? With a supple adaptation of tradition, Husni and Taen had whisked Seru away to Sona's third building, home to both Uruus and Vendan families, there to spend her first truenight as a Chosen. Receiving, no doubt, a great deal of unsolicited and highly intimate advice.

There, in relative peace, her body would take its mature form—a mysterious change Aryl, for one, wasn't in a hurry to experience. Imagine the impact on balance, she fussed to herself. Let alone clothing.

She hoped Seru was all right.

Seru's Chosen, meanwhile, could wait. His body would also

change over the next hours, but apparently not in ways that required new clothes.

She didn't want to know.

Sona was content.

She was so tired her bones ached.

"You want to know how long we've been here?" Aryl propped her chin on one hand and fingered her thin rope of dayknots. Seru's cleverness. Clever and kind, her cousin. She'd tie the second tassel tonight. "Two fists, tomorrow."

"Only that?" Naryn wrapped her long white fingers around her steaming cup; she still wore a scarf around her head and the coat they'd provided, as if chilled through, but didn't complain. Her eyes, large, blue, and fiercely bright, darted from hooks to oillights to the newly-made tables. Her voice would be lovely, once its hoarse cough eased. "Well done. You've made a home."

"We've made a Clan," Aryl corrected firmly. She wanted no misconceptions about what Sona was, or what they offered.

A dimple appeared. "So you have."

Aryl yawned, her jaw cracking, and gestured apology. No one suggested sleep; the Om'ray in the packed meeting hall were too aware of each other, too curious and unsettled. Without doubt, the Tuana were too rattled by their experience to relax any time soon.

One hand left the cup to rest warm and strong over hers. *Here.*

Strength *flooded* her body from that confident touch, driving back her exhaustion. Aryl blinked in surprise. "I didn't need—"

Naryn clutched her cup again. "You drained yourself for us. A fair trade."

Trade. Enris had explained the disquieting concept. Tuana was a Clan of such abundance they had time to produce more than the essentials, had individuals and families who no longer worked for the survival of the whole, but instead produced ornaments and goods distributed not by need, but by exchange for objects deemed of equal value. The wristband the Oud had given her, now against her skin, was one such item—not that Enris hadn't worked for his entire Clan.

Yena did not trade; they worked hard and they shared what they had. Sona-that-had-been? Her dream-memories were silent on that detail, but their stored wealth suggested they could have. Sona-that-would-be?

"There are no debts or trades here," Aryl said stiffly. A hope, perhaps futile. They had so many Tuana now.

So many and in two neat groups. The first, nine strong, were all members of three families: Serona, Licor, and Annk. Different from one another; similar in manner. They sat close together, spoke quietly and courteously to those around them but listened more. Appreciative but cautious. They—and their sturdy, dark clothing—had suffered the least from the rough handling of the Oud. One, Tai sud Licor, was unusual enough even Aryl caught herself staring at his face, skin dappled like the pattern of sunlight through leaves. He'd come on Passage from Amna, where that coloring was common. His two daughters, shy but beginning to smile at Ziba's fascinated attention, were dappled like their father and startlingly tall, with shoulders to rival any Yena male's.

Not yet Choosers. Aryl was dismayed to be sure, just as she was sure the other unChosen, the Seronas' son, was ready for Choice. He kept his head down as if to be unnoticed, his black hair—which reminded her of Enris—tumbling over his eyes.

A group with sensible boots and gloves, used to heavy work by their hands—little wonder Haxel radiated distinct *satisfaction* whenever she looked at them.

She radiated nothing at all when she looked at the others.

Those five sat closest to the hearth, wearing Sona undercoats over the tattered remnants of what had been not-sensible clothing. The fabric—before being dragged through dirt and snow by the Oud—reminded her of flitter wings, brilliantly colored and smooth. Pretty, Aryl told herself, trying to be charitable. Ridiculous, she decided, giving up the effort.

The clothes—completed by ornate, cold-looking footwear—were only the start. These had never worked a day in their lives, as far as she could tell. No calluses. Their movements were awkward and slow, their faces and bodies plump by Yena standards. They sat in sullen silence, although one, newly Chosen from the way she clung to her Choice, wiped fresh tears from her cheeks every time her face left his sleeve and she saw where they were.

Aryl's inner sense persisted in sorting the new arrivals. Of the sullen five, one was a Chooser, pointedly not looking at her. Beko Serona. Another eligible unChosen. He glared at those around them as if the Sona were to blame.

When he wasn't staring at her. Deran Edut was his name, lean for a Tuana, with a pinched face that made Aryl think of sour fruit.

Last of the five, Mauro Lorimar, was the one who rivaled Enris in size, though he moved like something soft. When he noticed Aryl's attention, his full lips spread in a triumphant smile.

Seru's Chosen. Mauro sud Parth.

Aryl found the tabletop of overwhelming interest.

"Never back down from Mauro," Naryn advised quietly. "He likes it too much. Deran? You needn't worry—he hasn't the Power for you. Ezgi might. The Serona runner."

" 'Runner?' " Aryl managed.

A nod at Haxel's favorites, and the unChosen a little too obviously avoiding her eye. "They scavenge abandoned tunnels—we don't have the wood you do." This with an envious pat on the table. "Running's all they can do if the Oud reshape."

Hence their alert air, Aryl thought. Daring and resourceful. Haxel was going to like them even more once she knew. "The others aren't."

Her companion chuckled. "Their idea of risk is to trade for what runners bring up. After all, that defies Council edict. As if anyone really obeys it. Though Mauro—he takes bigger chances." Her lips closed after that and Aryl sensed her withdrawal behind tightened shields.

Naryn didn't belong to either group, she realized abruptly. Not the only puzzle she posed. The other Om'ray might be close to her age, but she wasn't a Chooser—that she could sense, anyway. Not Chosen, surely, though she didn't attempt to *reach* to find that bond. Powerful, controlled. Trained. That she did know. "You're an Adept," she guessed, frowning.

"No." This with a flash of some emotion, hidden so quickly Aryl couldn't be sure of more than disturbance. Naryn gestured apology. "It's been a difficult—I don't know how long it's been," she admitted. "There's no truenight in the tunnels, no dawn. It's all the same. Suen—my uncle's cousin and heartkin, Suen sud Annk—promised I'd get used to it." Aryl felt her shiver. "The Oud came first."

"You're safe now," she said awkwardly, sending *reassurance*.

"We believed we were being punished," a low strained whisper. "The Oud forbid trespassing. None of us had tokens. Mauro, the fool, tried sending to Tuana for help—my head still hurts from the Oud's reaction to that." A grimace invited Aryl's sympathy.

Which she'd give, if she understood. "What reaction? We've never experienced a—problem—with using Power near the Oud here."

"Imagine running as fast as you can, then stubbing your bare toes on a rock."

Aryl frowned. "I'd jump it."

Naryn's chuckle turned to a cough. She took a sip. "Yena. Of course. Though not-*real,* a few Oud have something like an Om'ray's Power. Like, but different enough, believe me. Put them together? Nausea. Headache. Dizzy—"

"Oud have Power?" Not a pleasant thought. Not pleasant at all.

"Not many. Adepts don't like admitting it, but it's hardly a secret. We call them Torments. Tuana has had more than its share lately."

Making the Oud changeable. Another complication. Aryl gave a resigned sigh. "What do the Oud call them?"

A quizzical look. "Why do you care?"

"I'm Sona's Speaker. I can hardly ask the Oud to keep their 'Torments' away. I need their word. The right word." She sounded like the Human, Aryl thought to herself, suddenly amused.

"You'd ask?"

Tired as she was, Aryl grinned at Naryn's startled expression. "Our First Scout doesn't like surprises."

"She'd best get used to them, then." The other Om'ray traced the top ring of her cup with a long finger. "The Oud don't give warnings. Not ones we understand, anyway. They simply act for whatever twisted reasons. Look at us. We didn't know where they were taking us . . . if they'd drop us down a pit and leave us to die . . . if they'd abandon us past the end of the world where the sun would never shine again." Naryn's finger stopped. "Then you were there. I knew we were safe. Thank you."

"Don't thank me." Was she truly to blame for every ill on Cersi, Aryl thought wearily, or only for those that climbed into her home? "The Oud weren't punishing you. They found and brought you here because—" she braced herself, "—because of us."

"Of you? Why?"

Where did she start? Aryl looked into Naryn's pale, exhausted face and sighed. Stick to what mattered. "The Oud felt we needed more Om'ray to be a proper Clan. They found you and brought you here. Their Speaker told me. In a way." She pulled back the sleeve; the wristband caught the light. "It gave me this two days ago." Before it was killed—something else that didn't matter now. She took it off, reluctantly, and held it out. "It's from—"

"That's mine!" Naryn's eyes fixed on the green metal band. "The Oud surrounded us. Took what we carried. Bags, packs. The others lost more. All I had . . . clothes, water . . . that." Her hand began to reach for the wristband, then stopped in midair. She drew it back, drew within herself until to Aryl's inner sense she was almost invisible. "Keep it. A gift, not a trade."

Enris had shared his memory of making the wristband, not its owner, but Aryl smiled warmly as she replaced it on her arm. "Thank you. Don't worry about clothing or supplies, Naryn. We've enough for all." And ample water lay drifted against the walls, the storm's gift. "Sona takes care—"

A furious shout shattered the peace. "We shouldn't be here!"

"Mannerless *igly*." Deeper, just as angry. "You think it's our fault? We were fine till you came. Uninvited. Unprepared. Fools."

Aryl rose to her feet; Naryn stayed seated, her hands around her cup.

Two Tuana were standing in front of each other, both red-faced with emotion. She wasn't surprised to find the deep voice had come from the runner, Suen sud Annk. The older, much tougher Om'ray glared down at Deran Edut, one of the complainers. He glared defiantly back—between quick glances to Mauro.

While Mauro Lorimar leaned comfortably on his elbows, apparently at ease.

UnChosen games, Aryl judged it. Trick a fool into stirring a stinger nest, while you watched from a safe perch.

The emotions beginning to turn in the room made it no game. The stolen Tuana were justly upset, ready to blame someone for their plight. She noticed Rorn and Syb easing their way toward the two; Haxel's doing. She'd tolerate no disruption, not when they were all so close.

Not when outside was only the storm.

Aryl climbed on the table and held up her pendant. "If you want to go home," she said in her best Speaker voice, "I'll try to explain that to the Oud."

The eldest runner, a craggy-faced Om'ray named Galen sud Serona, stood. Their leader, she judged. "We are grateful to you and to Sona. Including those of us who don't act it—" This with a lash of focused *irritation* that stung even Mauro, by his wince. "But Tuana knows the Oud better than most. There's no explaining that won't make things worse. They start in a direction—" he shrugged broad shoulders, "—and all Om'ray can do is get off the road. If they want us here, here we stay."

The rest of his Clan looked unhappy, but no one disagreed.

Haxel stepped up. "I don't care who brought you. You're welcome, if you're willing to work." The two appraised each other for a moment. They were, Aryl thought, amused, as alike as a thin, scarred Yena scout and a bulky old Tuana runner could possibly be.

Rorn diverted to get another bowl of soup, a move that relaxed all the exiles.

Suen eased back, but the younger Tuana wasn't done. "Welcome where?" Deran shouted, waving his arm at the hall. "The tunnels were better!"

"We can take you back to them," Haxel assured him cheerfully, bringing a smile to more than a few faces.

Not to Oran's. A tingle of apprehension ran down Aryl's spine as she noticed the rapt attention the Grona Adept paid to this exchange.

Kor sud Lorimar, the Chosen from Mauro's group, as Aryl began to call the sulkers to herself, laid his hand on Deran's arm. With so strong a resemblance, they could be brothers. Deran made an abrupt gesture of apology and sat.

His shields weren't as tight as they should be. Aryl wasn't the only one to sense the *bitter anger* he sent, not at Haxel or the runners, but at Naryn. Suen slammed his hand flat on the table. "Enough!"

All the other Tuana looked at him then, resentment on their faces; unhappiness on that of Suen's Chosen, Lymin, heavy with their unborn. All but Naryn, who hadn't turned around once. Tension flared, tension that none of the Sona understood.

What sort of mess had the Oud brought them?

Haxel pursed her lips, then threw a glance at Aryl. No need for a sending.

Aryl jumped down from the table. "Firstlight will be here before we know it," she told Naryn. "Care to share my home?"

It wasn't the kindest invitation. Once outside, Aryl discovered
lights were useless; there was no watchfire. Someone had secured ropes between the buildings early in the storm. Whether
dream-memory or Grona advice, it was the only guide through
the bite and howl of wind-driven snow—unless they went back
to talk Weth into that service.

Aryl pulled her scarf over her mouth. *This way.*

You're sure?

The wry tone made her smile. *Unless the roof's fallen in.*

The roof had bulged down at one end, but still held. Someone—perhaps the same helpful Om'ray who'd tied the rope—
had brought one of the oilburners for heat. Aryl lit it gratefully,
adding its glow to the oillights. Within a few moments, the
shelter, sparse as it was, began to warm.

And drip. Snow had blown into the cracks—helping seal out
the wind, but now melting in the heat. Naryn helped move the
now-larger pile of bedding into the center. There was more
than enough, perhaps in anticipation of their new arrivals.
Who, Aryl wondered, had they thought would want to sleep
with her?

Not any of the unChosen, that was for sure. As for her new
companion? "I should warn you. The reason I sleep away from
the rest—"

"Let me guess." Naryn, having made a nest of blankets, bur-
rowed beneath them still in her snowy coat, scarf, and boots.
She grinned over the top. "You snore."

Did she? Aryl let herself be distracted. "I don't think so. No
one's mentioned it." She hung her coat and took off her boots.
"Toss me yours. I'll put them where they'll dry."

Silence. *Apprehension.*

Aryl turned, careful to make the motion unhurried. Enris

had found Yena movements disturbingly quick; so might Naryn. Instead of seeking her share of the blankets, she crouched by the oilburner, pretended to check its flame. The rough stone was cold on her bootless feet, but she waited. Something was very wrong. Haxel trusted her to find out what, for Sona's sake.

Aryl found herself more worried for Naryn's.

"The Choosers of my family have a reputation for being 'noisy' in their sleep," she explained easily. "This will be my first chance to learn if I'm the same. You have exceptional shields, so I hope I can't disturb your rest. You must be—"

"What are you doing here?" Almost an accusation. "You call yourselves Sona but you had a Parth Chooser—a Yena name. You had a home. You had a Clan. Against all custom and the Agreement, you chose to come here, defining this direction for all Om'ray with your presence, drawing Grona here, us. Why?"

Fair question. Aryl chewed her lower lip for a moment as she considered possible answers. But Naryn S'udlaat wasn't any other Om'ray. Power radiated from her—controlled, trained. More than Oran or Hoyon. Likely more than her own. Naryn could be the first to learn to 'port through the M'hir, to help safely teach the others. She had to believe she was trusted and could trust.

The truth, then. "Yena's Adepts decided to remove those with Forbidden Talent," Aryl said bluntly. "Those who might risk the Agreement by daring to use their Power in a new way."

"Remove? You mean exile?" Disbelief. "But you've children here, a pregnant Chosen—"

"Family didn't matter. My own mother was one of the Adepts who tossed us from Yena." Aryl tightened her shields, holding in the anger and hurt, but her voice was strange to her own ears, old. "They expected us to die. But we survived. We found this place." And they would continue to survive, she vowed. "We're Sona now."

Naryn's presence gained an easier *feel,* as if she'd heard

something that reassured her—though what that could be, Aryl couldn't guess. "The hoarding of knowledge should be Forbidden, not Power or Talent. Adepts keep too much from the rest of us, stop us from being all we could be. They have no right."

Aryl looked up. "They protect their Clan."

Naryn leaned forward, eyes gleaming. "Do they? Or do they try to control us? Let me tell you why the other Tuana shun me, Aryl Sarc, because you and I have something in common. My mother—and father—are Adepts. And it was Tuana's Adepts who made it impossible for me to stay there."

A wet, dirty ball of scarf landed at Aryl's feet, and Naryn's glorious mass of dark red hair seethed with freedom.

Chosen. But not Joined to anyone here. How could that be? Unlike Humans, Chosen couldn't be so far apart, not without agony. Unless—Aryl's breath caught. Was Naryn like Taisal, having survived the loss of her Chosen, wounded to her depths . . . ?

"Our Adepts forbade me to reveal myself." Naryn rose, shedding blankets, her coat, the clothes underneath. "They called me ruined." She stood, naked and perfect against the shattered beams and stone of Sona, her face set, without expression. The glows painted her full breasts and hips in light and shadow, drew a hint of curve between. "They don't warn Choosers that if we try and fail our Choice, our bodies will not care. They don't warn us that if we have no Chosen, our Power will seek elsewhere for its completion. They don't warn us we will grow life within, and Join to that life." Her long white fingers hovered over the faint swell of skin, their shadow partners like a stain. "No Chooser is to know. We would be too afraid . . ." Her brave voice failed and she began to tremble.

They were both outcasts. Aryl went to Naryn, threw a blanket around her shoulders, urged her down to the warmth of the rest, then held her as she shook. "Are you sure?"

Wasn't it too soon? Those pregnant claimed awareness began shortly before their unborn was old enough to affect others unless shielded. In practice, some were a little slow. She wasn't the only Om'ray to have inexplicable urges to change position or eat raw dresel near a mother-to-be.

Seru had said there were two unborn coming with the Oud.

"I thought it was Choice, at first. My body had changed—what else could it be? I told the Adepts to bring him back . . . that it had worked, that they had to let me—let us—be together. I begged them, Aryl, but they refused." Naryn's hair flailed against the blanket and Aryl's arm; her body had grown still, warmed perhaps, or numb. "They already knew. Tuana's Birth Watcher could sense the new life in me, that the bond I felt was a Joining not to another Chosen, but to this part of myself. That I was perverse. Ruined."

Enris. Aryl trembled, suddenly sure. It had been Enris. Naryn was the Chooser desperate for his Choice. The one he'd resisted. The one he'd fled.

Naryn continued, her voice without emotion, her hair settling limp down her back. "The Adepts ordered me kept in the Cloisters, hidden from anyone else. A kindness to other Choosers. They said the birth would end my life, that if the child somehow survived it would doubtless be Lost, so I should hope it died, too."

The sounds of wind and storm outside couldn't touch the silence. He hadn't known this, Aryl told herself. He wouldn't have wanted this. No matter what Naryn had done or tried.

Then, with a hint of pride, "As if I'd let them dictate my fate. I went to the Councillor for his family and said I'd expose the truth—how I was going to die because of their unChosen's failure to Choose—unless she helped me escape the Adepts. The old *joop* was glad to see me go. She brought me clothes, a pack, even gifts for my so-called Passage. That wristband. Neither of us could get a token, but she got me out of the Cloisters and arranged for Suen, my uncle's heart-kin, to take me to the tunnels. Where I'd be now, if not for the Oud." A bitter laugh that became a sigh. "As for the others? Menasel has the Talent to tell one Om'ray from another. The silly fool sensed me underground and convinced her cousin Mauro and the rest of his pack to follow. See where it got them?"

"They came to help you—" Aryl guessed.

"Hardly." Naryn pulled free. "They thought I was sneaking down to make a trade with the runners and wanted to spoil it."

"Why?"

"To punish me for taking up residence in the Cloisters, for being accepted as an Adept when they weren't. For refusing to Choose Mauro—as if I could." A pause. "To hurt me. Maybe that. Mauro has a taste for pain. I—I hope your Parth can handle him."

Aryl couldn't imagine any of it. She wouldn't have believed any of it, except . . . she was a Chooser.

The imperative texture of the blankets beneath her hands . . . the depth of flesh warmed by the oilburner . . . the knife-sharp edge of every shadow . . . the music of their breathing . . .

Without warning, she *felt* everything, including the presence of those eligible unChosen the length of the rope away. Enticing.

Essential.

Her mother had felt this, her grandmothers, their grandmothers, generations stretching back through time she'd once never believed mattered, stretching ahead to create the future. All Choosers felt this . . .

"Aryl! Control yourself. Unless you want Deran and Ezgi breaking through what passes for the door."

The slight rasp, the lilting cadence of the voice meant more than the words, meant less than what was building inside her. What had to be *sent* . . .

"Aryl!" There was pain now. "Show some sense!"

. . . and so she Called for the first time, a glorious outpouring of *desire* and *longing* through the M'hir, through space, across the world . . .

Slap!

Aryl's head jerked back with the openhanded blow. Cheek

stinging, she stared at Naryn. Embarrassment fought with affront.

"Now that was Power." Naryn's eyes were fever-bright. "I
can't believe anyone thought simply putting you out here
would protect their sleep." She laughed. "They felt that all the
way to Vyna, mark my words."

Embarrassment won. "I can't—I can't do that again."

"Oh, you can and you will," the Tuana promised. "But for
all our sakes, not until you're ready for Choice. Didn't your
mother teach you control?"

"There wasn't—no," Aryl finished helplessly. Haxel and the
others wouldn't let the unChosen rush out into the storm—
would she? What would she do if they came? Did she want
them to come? Taisal. Her mother. Should she go to her—did
she dare?

No. There was no welcome in Yena.

"I don't know what to do," she admitted.

"I do." Naryn held out her hand. "Trust me." *And know this,
Aryl Sarc*, she sent. *Yena and Tuana's Adepts will regret every decision that brought us together. We'll make this new Clan greater than
theirs, greater than any other. A Clan of Power.*

Feeling her *determination*, her *passion* was like that first
glimpse of the sky above the canopy, expanding the world beyond its limits, affecting everything she thought she knew.

We'll protect our people, Aryl vowed, reaching eagerly for
Naryn's hand.

. . . dreams were not like this.

*Aryl brushed her hand along the frond, palm tickled by its soft down.
She inhaled, filling her lungs with the spice of fresh dresel. The air
against her naked skin was warm, moist, a caress.*

. . . the canopy wasn't like this. Bare skin was a table set for
biters.

"You can come home. As a Chooser, you would be welcome."

. . . her mother's voice was not this voice. She'd never want her back.

Her feet were on a floor of cut and sealed fronds, revealed by lovingly polished nekis wood, patterned in grays, yellows, and rich browns. A yellow swing chair spun on its rope, an invitation. The light of glows caught on window gauze, stroked across wall panels.

. . . her home wasn't like this. It had burned. The ash had fallen into the Lay.

They were all there, all who'd died or left or abandoned her. All smiled. All shared their welcome and love. She had only to take a step . . . only to reach out her hand . . .

. . . dreams were not like this.

Daughter. A voice without body, a ripple in black water. *Follow me.*

Aryl heard a moan.

This is no dream. This is pointless desire. Longing. Foolishness. Stop, Daughter, before you lose us all in it!

Too hot. Why was she under blankets at this time of year? A cool sheet . . . *the breeze through fronds, laughter, peace . . .*

Hot—but there was snow. Ice and snow. Another moan. Her voice?

ARYL!!!! Please. Stop. You can't be here. I won't be here. You'll drag us with you into the Dark . . .

. . . no dream.

Dark. Who was talking about the Dark? Aryl rubbed her eyes, blinked at the oillight overhead.

"Thank goodness." Naryn sat back with a heavy sigh. Her hair thrashed the air, not as willing to relax. "I thought you'd never wake up. You were right. Sarcs are loud dreamers. Where were we? Yena?"

Aryl shot upright. "What do you mean? What happened . . . I was dreaming?" Her mother's mindvoice. The M'hir. "What did you see?" she asked with sudden, horrible dread. Everything of her life had seemed to flash by, forced into some childish, improbable wish for only the good in it, only what she wanted. Selfish. Foolish. Her mother had been right to chase her from it. "What did you hear?"

"I heard nothing," Naryn said gently. "But I saw?" Her smile was wistful. "The world as it should be."

That didn't sound too embarrassing, Aryl thought. Then she felt the blood drain from her face. "You don't suppose anyone else . . ."

The other tilted her head, as if listening. "Oh, I'm quite sure everyone else saw it too. Here, at any rate. Good night, Aryl Sarc, Chooser of Power. Do try to get some proper sleep, for all our sakes?"

Aryl sank back under the blanket.

Not to sleep.

Absolutely not to sleep again.

Ever.

"We tied their feet together. Suen's idea." Haxel radiated *dissatisfaction*. "Ezgi was sensible enough after that. Deran? You've never heard such whining. I wanted to knock him on the head, but our Healer made herself useful and put him to sleep." A considering pause. "Should have hit him."

Maybe she could go live underground with the Oud. Aryl leaned against the stone slab of the doorway and gestured a mute apology.

"Never hurt an unChosen to suffer. How are you?" A triumphant grin twisted her scar. "Besides louder than Taisal ever was."

Underground wasn't far enough, Aryl decided. Maybe Marcus would take her to his world. That had to be at least beyond the mountains. "Can we not talk about . . ." she waved her hand vaguely.

As well as ask the sun not to rise. Haxel gave a wicked chuckle. "Enjoy it while it lasts, Chooser. You've ruined a 'night's sleep for an entire village. Probably started every un-Chosen in Cersi on Passage here. Next time—"

Chooser, Aryl thought with a pang of guilt. "How's Seru?" she interrupted.

"Seru." Something flickered in those pale eyes. Caution?

"Yes, Seru." She tensed. "Something's wrong. What?"

"Choosers don't get invol—"

"Answer me." Aryl didn't intend the *flick* of Power.

Haxel winced then scowled fiercely. "Listen to me, Aryl. It's none of your—"

Not waiting to hear the rest, Aryl pushed past. She'd find out for herself.

Trails had been forced through the snow between the four homes. Only one led out to where she and Naryn spent true-night. Aryl disregarded it, forcing her way through the stuff in a straight line to where she *knew* Seru was.

The First Scout caught up. "There's nothing you can do. She's Joined to him now. It's too late."

Aryl moved faster.

Husni opened the door, slipping its rope latch onto a hook. She didn't say a word, only backed out of Aryl's way.

Taen rose to her feet, eyes darting between them. Silent.

She ignored them both, going to where her cousin sat on a bench, a blanket around her shoulders, another on her lap. Seru's hair moved fitfully, as if tossed by a dying wind. "I'm here," she said gently.

"You shouldn't be." Her cousin looked at her.

Aryl thought she'd seen every expression of those huge green eyes.

She'd never seen them dead.

Seru held out her hand, turned it, let something small and tangled fall to the floor between them.

Her dayknots. Her waiting. Her wishes.

Aryl went to her knees. "Seru—"

"You shouldn't be here. Mauro—" the name twisted her lips, "—doesn't like you. He doesn't like me. He doesn't like anyone. He won't let me . . ."

Aryl flinched. What had the Oud brought them? "Of course you like me, silly Seru," she coaxed desperately, shields tight. "You just need to show him how to like us—"

"He shows me blood. He likes blood. Likes Om'ray who cry in pain—" Seru's eyes filled with tears that spilled without heed. "He almost killed Enris. Wanted to kill him. Beat him. Kick him. Bones break. Feels good—"

HUSH! If Mauro shared that sending, Aryl thought, blind with fury, she hoped it hurt.

Seru wilted. She caught her, Taen helping. "What did you do, Aryl?" Husni demanded.

He's taken the babies . . . Aryl . . . I can't feel the babies . . . all I feel is HIM.

"Hold her." Aryl rose to her feet and turned to find Haxel, hovering in the doorway. "Restrain Mauro," she ordered, her lips numb. "I don't care how. Bring Ezgi Serona here."

"I don't know what you think—"

"I will not allow this Joining."

The others froze, staring at her. Seru gave a wild laugh. "You? Dirty little Yena animal. Think I care what you will allow or not? You're pathetic. All of you!"

Aryl didn't take her eyes from Haxel. "Go."

"She's mine," said the voice from Seru's lips. "Mine forever. Get out of my way. It's time to rut. Maybe she'll scream. Scream for me, my Chosen."

Grim-faced, the First Scout whirled and left, hand on her knife.

Aryl's mind was already elsewhere. She opened to the M'hir, sought within it for Seru. Drew her close.

Aryl? There . . . wistful . . . so small . . .

Sought Mauro. Drew him, too.

WHAT IS THIS PLACE!??

She ignored his loud gibbering fear, though it set the M'hir into wild motion. She concentrated, searching the chaos for the bond connecting the Tuana to her cousin.

There. As she'd dared hope, it was still forming. Pulses of Power attached themselves one to the other, most being drawn from Seru to Mauro. Nothing peaceful about it, nothing willing. Nothing of joy. He took, causing harm for his own gain, as a Tikitik would drink blood from an osst.

She would not allow it.

GET AWAY FROM US!

He was powerful. Brave, in his way.

Another part of Aryl heard: "We're here." Another part of Aryl stretched out a hand, felt a palm, clammy but strong, took hold.

Most of what she was remained in the *other* and sought the new arrival there.

Ezgi.

A blaze of light, of Power. Solid, afraid but unshaken by his surroundings. A song in the *Dark*. Aryl fought the temptation to go closer.

SERU! As she called, she gathered, tearing what she *tasted* as her cousin free of Mauro. As the M'hir seethed and boiled in protest, she *thrust* Seru toward Ezgi.

Eagerly, they reached for one another. Aryl pulled back, readied herself.

NOOOO!!!

Mauro resisted, grabbed for Seru. Aryl struck, severing each link as he made it. Each time, a new one sprang into life between Ezgi and Seru. Over and over. The two slipped closer and closer.

The two were one.

And all that remained in the M'hir was Mauro Lorimar.

CHOOSER! I AM FREE!

He was a storm within a storm, riding its violence with his own, triumphant. *COME TO ME NOW!*

Links began to form between them, pulsing, potent. She reeled, tried to evade, to escape. Others were helpless. She felt them, their fear for her. All it did was stir the force within the M'hir, weaken her.

She was losing . . . no matter how she fought . . . no matter how he repulsed her . . . she would be his . . .

MINE!!

Then, she was alone, the M'hir almost peaceful.

Aryl opened her eyes and promptly threw up, gesturing an apology to the owner of a too-near pair of boots.

Boots already splattered with blood.

Explaining the peace.

She staggered to her feet, helped by strong hands from behind, and gave Mauro's husk barely a glance. "Seru?"

Haxel, busy cleaning her knife, tipped her head. "There."

Seru stood with Ezgi, right hands clasped, left hands exploring one another's face and hair with a tender preoccupation that answered any question she might have.

Husni's wrinkles creased deeper. "This won't do," she declared. "It won't."

Aryl opened her mouth to argue, but Taen's fingers brushed hers. *Don't worry.*

The elderly Om'ray took Seru by the shoulders and pulled the two apart. "I've never seen such foolishness. There must be time apart, then a proper bathing. Go at once, young sud Parth." Ezgi's shy smile and blush matched Seru's. "Someone find him decent clothes. Haxel, clean up your mess. Hurry now!"

The First Scout carefully didn't smile. "At once, Husni."

Seru looked at Aryl, her eyes dancing. "How can we . . ."

"Tradition!" Husni insisted. "As for you, Aryl Sarc." A summons not to be ignored.

Aryl stepped up to the tiny Chosen, wiping her mouth on a sleeve." Yes, Husni." In her best, most polite tone.

Husni beckoned, and Aryl bent. Cool, crooked fingers stroked her cheek, sending a flood of *gratitude* and *pride,* then snapped smartly under her chin. "Some sleep this truenight, if you don't mind?"

"I'll do my best, Husni," Aryl vowed.

"Impressive."

Aryl shrugged, regretting the motion as it sent a thrill of pain across her forehead. Breakfast might help. Or time. She wouldn't ask Oran. "It shouldn't have been necessary."

"It shouldn't," Naryn pointed out, "have been possible. Tamper with Choice? Switch Chosen in the midst of Joining? How did you know how?"

Aryl didn't want that kind of Power. To meddle in Choice. But seeing Seru herself again, seeing her joy with Ezgi, who was as thoroughly besotted and kind as her cousin had ever wished?

Safe from whatever Mauro Lorimar had been?

She'd do it again.

"It shouldn't have happened at all," she repeated. "We need to protect those who are—who can't protect themselves—before it's too late."

The Tuana hung the next blanket over the line, straightening it with great care. Most had been soaked from below as the dirt thawed during the 'night. They could use, Aryl thought with distraction, a proper floor.

"In Tuana," Naryn said slowly, "an unChosen first seeks the approval of the Chooser's family. We receive more strangers on Passage than most Clans. Pana, often. Amna. Rarely Grona or Yena. A meal together, conversation. Time together, a chance to find a good fit. UnChosen aren't rushed."

Criticism? Aryl bristled. "Seru waited a long time. It's no wonder—"

"It's no wonder," Naryn agreed. A lock of red hair writhed free of its net; the Yena fashion had pleased her, but she would need more than braided thread. "Denied, the urge becomes overwhelming. If you have to wait long enough, you might be tempted by Deran."

Never, Aryl thought grimly.

Haxel would be watching to see how closely Deran had followed his friend. Mauro had been an abomination, however tolerated or ignored by the Tuana.

As for Naryn . . . "Did you have to wait too long? Is that why you tried to force Enris Mendolar?" There, she'd said it.

Long, shapely hands paused on the next blanket, then continued moving, spreading it along the line. "He's here?"

"He was. He took Passage."

Naryn tilted her head, like a flitter studying a biter. "You wanted him, too."

"I never hurt him."

"No," the Tuana said softly, "I don't suppose you did. He left before you were ready."

"What does that—"

"It means that Choosers of exceptional Power, like you, like me, are not comfortable partners." Naryn's smile was bitter as she brought out a flat, wrapped package, small enough to hide on her palm. It was so like a portion of dresel that Aryl's stomach growled. "A gift for your future, Aryl Sarc. What Tuana's Adepts use to ease the Joining of those of greater Power. A quarter, dissolved in water. Share a cup with your Candidate. If I'd known—well, I no longer need it. You may."

"What is it?" Aryl didn't touch the package; she couldn't take her eyes from it.

"Somgelt. We trade with the Oud for it."

Somgelt was found in some rastis pods, a parasite on its seeds. Yena used an extract to coat their stairs and ladders, to keep away the hunters of the Lay Swamp. "Poison."

"Safe," Naryn countered, "if used properly." She tucked it away. "I'll keep it for you."

Aryl ignored this last, worried by something else entirely. The Oud could only obtain somgelt from the Tikitik. Wood for the Oud tunnels, she could understand. Metal for the Tikitik. But this? "Do the Oud know how you use it?"

A puzzled frown. "You ask the oddest questions." At Aryl's look, "No. Why would the not-*real* know or care what happens in a Cloisters?"

"They care," she assured the Tuana. Hadn't an Oud spent days trying to dig into Sona's? Wanted her help to enter?

Curious? Or something more?

Naryn smiled suddenly. "He liked you—all of you. Didn't he?"

"Enris?" Aryl fingered the rope. "He was welcome."

"Of course." Her smile faded. "Enris could have been an Adept—should have been—but he didn't want it. I did, and he thought less of me for it. For wanting to be powerful, to use my Talents. I shouldn't have cared. I should have ignored him. He didn't like me. Or my friends. He would never have come to my family to be my Choice. In front of everyone—he ignored me at Visitation—"

"We should get breakfast," Aryl interrupted.

"You wanted to know why."

Not anymore. "You don't need to explain—"

"I do. I must. There was something about him I couldn't ignore. You've met him—you know. When my time came, there wasn't anyone else. I had to Call Enris. But instead of answering, he—he forced me away." Naryn's hair slithered over her shoulders. Her face, always pale, was like ice. "I hope you never feel pain like that."

"Because he didn't want you," Aryl snapped. "You should have stopped. You should have let him go."

"I couldn't. He was pain and anger—" her voice broke, then steadied,"—he was everything wonderful. I had to hold on or lose him . . . but he was stronger. Too strong. He left me. Ruined me. I lost—"

"So did Enris," Aryl snapped.

"I know." Naryn lowered her shields, until Aryl felt *sorrow* laced with *guilt*, a growing *determination*. Then, *You're right, Aryl Sarc. We who can must protect our Choosers and unChosen, ease their Joining. If we don't, we risk losing those of greatest Power. Like Enris and me. Like you.*

There could be no lies here, mind-to-mind. Aryl knew, beyond any doubt, that Naryn cared about the future of their kind. However she'd come to this moment, whatever she'd done before, she would do anything to ensure no one else suffered as she had.

Could Sona ask more?

She wouldn't.

Tell me about somgelt.

Before she Called again and someone answered.

Interlude

WHEN THE CALL STRUCK, ENRIS Mendolar was doing his best to sleep on top of a wall. Between the rumn and a healthy fear of rocks, he'd decided to wait out truenight where neither could surprise him. Aryl would have approved. His arm and leg dangled over the drop he hadn't been ready to chance while exhausted—though given the mist, firstlight might not reveal much more of what lay below. Still, he hadn't heard water, which meant solid ground. Probably. At firstlight, he'd . . .

The Call wiped every rational thought from his drowsy mind—including where he was and why standing suddenly would be a bad idea. He tipped, slipped, and dropped—not that he cared, his mind still caught by a Chooser's *NEED*.

Unfortunately, the Call ceased before he hit the ground and Enris cared a great deal about the jolt of impact through every bone. He lay still, hoping his every bone wasn't broken, and used the moment to gingerly explore the lingering *taste* in his mind.

Not the Vyna's summoning.

Definitely not a succulent reflection of his mother's cooking. This Call had been nothing so peaceful or welcoming.

It had been sheer demand, backed by extraordinary Power. Blunt, careless, utterly selfish.

Which didn't mean his heart wasn't pounding or that he wasn't drawn to it. *Irresistible.* His right hand curled into a fist, denied.

Enris laughed, stopping when his body protested. Irresistible or not, he wasn't going anywhere fast, for this new Chooser or any other reason.

"Now, where's the door?"

The words bounced from walls to either side. Because he was in a narrow box. A warm, mist-filled, featureless box.

Could be worse. He would, if he walked in the only possible direction, put distance between himself and Vyna.

Could be better. No one chased him.

Ordinarily, Enris would take that as a good sign, but not here. They must have expected their locked door to hold him for the rumn—or for those who'd gladly feed him to the rumn, the result being regrettably the same. When he'd removed the door as an impediment, he'd expected to be chased by rumn-feeders. But not one Om'ray had followed him inside.

The hall had become a downslope tunnel—not a surprise. Of polished black rock, lit by those fire-powered glows—that had been, since there were no doors or intersections. Only a numbingly straight tunnel. He ran past a hundred glows before he slowed to a jog—after fifty more, he walked. After that, he stumbled forward, away from Vyna. Unpursued.

The first breaths of fresh, cooler air had been as good as a meal, a hint of natural light a lure. He'd found the strength for one more run, bursting from the tunnel into a narrow gap, sided in smooth black rock, roofed by a starred sky. Freedom!

Almost.

Too soon, the gap ended at another wall, this of cubes of black rock, providing ample hand- and footholds even for a Tuana. He hadn't hesitated to climb, though it bore an unpleasant resemblance to the wall underground old Jenemir had shown him, the one that kept back molten rock.

At the top, seeing—or rather not seeing—what lay below, he'd wisely decided to take his rest before climbing down the other side.

Only to fall down it.

Still, as escapes went, Enris assured himself, growing more cheerful as he surveyed his new surroundings, he could definitely have done worse.

This was still Vyna. Their lights were embedded in the walls at waist height, a dazzling row reflected over and over in the polished rock. The mist that lipped against the wall behind him hung overhead like a ceiling, hiding any stars. Hiding him, too, he grinned.

Best of all, there were no suspicious rocks, only the solid slabs of black the Vyna felt were the appropriate construction material for everything. There wasn't so much as a speck of dirt.

Enris started walking. The floor sloped downward, gently, no more than the tunnel. A good sign. With luck, he'd come out at the bottom of the mountain ridge, where reasonable Om'ray could walk in safety. Not to mention find a mountain stream with clear, lovely—

Crunchsnap!

He looked down and lost any cheer he'd felt.

It was a bone.

He looked ahead.

More bones.

Om'ray bones.

Scattered here. He kept walking, careful of his feet now, finding more and more until they lay in untidy heaps he had to step around. Most were old, weathered gray and brittle. Some were newer, bound together by wisps of skin and clothing. Was this how the Vyna disposed of their husks?

Something gleamed, and Enris picked it up.

A token.

There were more. Everywhere he looked, more.

These had never been Vyna.

He walked faster.

∗ ✳ ∗

Yuhas, in a rare reminiscence about his life as Yena, had told him about a flower that produced an alluring scent, but when biters came within its petals, they slipped and fell into sticky liquid, to drown and be digested by the plant.

This, Enris decided, had been such a trap. UnChosen, drawn up the mountain by the lure of Vyna's many Choosers, would have lowered themselves into this lighted gap, believing it the way to their desire. Once here, they'd find the walls too smooth to climb out, the door from the tunnel locked, and this.

Enris sighed and squatted on his haunches for a better look. The hole—there was no other word for it—was shorter than he was tall. Wide enough, but there'd be crouching involved.

The bars? He'd *pushed* them aside, fiercely glad to be the one to ruin the Vyna's trap.

The crouching, though.

He hated crouching.

Unless the hole grew smaller. He couldn't tell. The Vyna most uncooperatively hadn't bothered to light their hole. This one led away from them. That was good.

If the hole grew smaller, there'd be crawling.

He hated crawling more than crouching.

Tossing a token into it had produced a distant clink, clatter, and slide. Lined with metal, not stone. A tube? If so, there'd be another open end. The first portion ran straight. With a downslope. Down was fine. He'd had his share of mountains.

How much of a slope?

That interesting question, along with where the other end of the tube opened, were questions he'd only answer by crouching.

Making sure his coat was tightly belted, the contents of his pockets secure, Enris bent to enter the hole.

His first step produced a loud, echoing *boom.* He backed out hastily, then took off his boots, fastening them to his belt. Upon consideration, he took off his foot coverings as well and tucked them into the boots. Yena did it, he told himself. Of course, Yena were crazy.

But bare feet were silent and gave purchase on the metal, both reassuring as he left the lights behind.

Every so often, Enris *reached* for his kind. Vyna faded behind, though not as quickly as he'd have liked. Crouching wasn't quick.

Rayna grew closer, but not directly ahead. Was the tube aimed away from the world?

If so, he'd find out what was there. It wasn't, he laughed inwardly, as if he had a choice.

A tenth went by, or more. Hard to judge time. His legs burned, thigh muscles complaining about the abuse. Ignoring them, Enris kept going, one hand on the cool surface overhead, the other in front. It didn't help that the tube's slope varied without warning, sometimes flat, at others too steep to do more than shuffle, bracing himself with both arms.

With nothing to do but crouch and shuffle, stuck in a tube of unknown length, he let his mind wander, and thought about his life since Naryn and the Oud. If anyone had told him a story like his, he decided, he wouldn't have believed a word.

He did his best not to think of the Call he'd heard. Whoever it had been, surely other unChosen had answered it by now. Saving all others from what would be, he was quite sure, an overbearing, difficult, controlling . . .

. . . What was that?

Nothing. The tiniest sounds echoed and expanded. His breathing, the light brush of fingertips, the padding of his feet. Any moment, his suffering knees would creak, adding to the racket.

Still, Enris moved more carefully, listening. Had there been a sound? Had it come from behind—or ahead?

Maybe he was approaching the end—heard wind across the opening, the trickle of a mountain stream. A pot handle let go.

Enris froze midstep. That's what he'd heard. Metal to metal. Ahead. Not loud, but if there was a sound he knew, it was that one.

The dark smothered and disguised everything else. No, not everything. He sniffed.

He knew that smell, too.

He eased down to sit where he was, holding in a groan as he straightened his back and legs, and waited.

Silence.

Darkness.

Then, "I wouldn't stay there long, Tuana."

Oh, he knew that dry, amused voice. "I'm comfortable," he lied. Thought Traveler. How did the thing keep finding him?

"Then you don't know where you are. Most entertaining."

Cold inside, Enris waited for the echoes of its barking laugh to die. "Enlighten me," he suggested grimly. "Or get out of my way."

"I can do both. This is what you Om'ray call a Watcher, though why you would use that term for what has no eyes has never been satisfactorily explained to—"

"What does it watch for?" Enris interrupted. He should have recognized the construction. He'd seen the mouths of Yena's Watchers: three much larger tubes, set into the side of a mountain. Yuhas, from Yena himself, had explained how the powerful winds of fall, the M'hir, blew through the tubes before striking the forest below. The sound warned the Yena to prepare for their strange harvest.

No wind would blow through this. Only the screams and pleading of those trapped above.

"The Vyna don't care for company. Yours. Mine. Any but their own." The Tikitik was enjoying itself. "They protect their little sore on the world far beyond its worth. If they detect an approach and don't favor it, they release some of the poison they call a lake. Flush any intruders from their mountain. The rumble from this 'watcher' can be heard from a great distance, though usually not in time to avoid the result."

Enris rose to his feet and started moving.

"Ah. A fine idea, Tuana. You really should listen to me. Because if the Vyna feel truly threatened—" no amusement now, "—they can send something much worse."

Busy crouching as quickly as he could, one hand out so he wouldn't collide without warning into the Tikitik—although the thought had its charm—Enris didn't bother to ask.

* ❋ *

The Vyna Watcher opened into a narrow mountain valley, distinguishable from others of Enris' experience only in its disturbing lack of small loose stone. After he climbed out and stood, taking a moment to stretch out his back and legs, he turned to look back.

The metal hole he'd left was one of what could be a hundred more, pocked into an artificial cliff of black rock that sealed the top of the valley. They were like open mouths, ready to vomit forth whatever the Vyna chose.

Were there traps at the top of every one? Were there bones?

"Can't stay here," he said numbly, shoving his feet into his boots, having to stop to pull out his feet coverings, pushing those in a pocket to save time.

Thought Traveler's mouth protuberances writhed. "Where should we go?" From the way it stretched, neck twisting, shoulders bent back, crouching hadn't suited its body either.

"You," Enris informed the creature, "can go where you like. I'm getting out of this valley before the Vyna flood it."

"Sensible Om'ray. They won't be happy if they find us together. They may conclude I sent you, to steal their secrets."

He should strangle the thing, not listen to it. But Enris, already five long strides away, hesitated. He looked back. "Since when do Tikitik care about Om'ray secrets?"

"Since Om'ray began to have them." It bounded forward to stop in front of him. "Like this."

Snap!

The Tikitik had his pouch, broken thong dangling, before Enris could flinch. "That's mine!" he objected, trying to grab it back.

Swaying out of reach, Thought Traveler barked with amusement and threw the pouch, unopened, at him. "As you wish."

The thong, it kept. It brought the thin strap of leather to its mouth, protuberances writhing along its length until they reached the knot of Aryl's hair. There, they appeared transfixed.

"I need that, too." Enris did his best to sound casual.

"Oh, but I think you owe me at least this scrap. Have I not interceded for your life three times now? Unless it means more to you . . ." A meaty sound as all of the Tikitik's eyes swiveled to lock on him. "I do hope not, Om'ray of many Clans." Clear threat. "This would not be a match we favor."

What could it know from mouthing her hair? And, if he understood the maddening creature, why would another race care about an Om'ray Joining?

"You broke it. You keep it." Enris deliberately tucked his pouch in his belt. "I'm leaving."

"Excellent idea, Tuana. We'll be safe when we reach the boundary dam." Thought Traveler turned and began to run with its disquieting speed.

He watched it shrink with distance. "Good," Enris told it. "Go. Be gone. Finally."

One thing for sure. He was not traveling another step with the Tikitik.

There was, however, only one way to go.

He started to run after the Tikitik.

The boundary dam, as Enris expected, was made of the Vyna's black rock. But instead of a wall or structure, the rock looked like a river turned solid, somehow twisted to flow in a thick ribbon across the mountain slope, not down. He couldn't help but notice curves and layering as he climbed it, like eddies in liquid.

Metal, he understood. How could anyone control molten rock? The Vyna he'd met hadn't understood their own technology. There must have been a time when they had, or this wouldn't exist.

If so, how had they forgotten such ability . . . ?

At the top of the dam, the Tikitik—who climbed better than a Yena, and certainly better than he—squatted comfortably. Enris thought of climbing the dam elsewhere, but it was too much work. And would amuse the creature anyway.

As he neared the top, the head swung on its curved neck to regard him past a bent leg, all eyes fixed. "Where will you go now, Tuana?" One clawed hand stretched out and slowly closed, as if to grasp the world. "Show me your path."

Enris stepped up and past it, every breath leaving plumes in the cold clear air, tiny clouds above an abyss.

For that's what he faced.

A landscape that couldn't exist. No matter how he strained, there were no Om'ray before him, yet his eyes showed him an expanse that began far below, a rolling mauve plain scratched by frozen ponds, immense beyond belief. It ended at the sky, or was the sky's end.

Impossibly empty.

He found himself sitting beside the Tikitik, hands braced against the rock, as if another step forward would be his last.

"Will you venture forth, Om'ray?" Thought Traveler asked. "Or will you stay where your perceptions guide you? Do you have a choice? I have always wondered what would happen if one of you went beyond your limit. Would you fall to the ground and whimper, disoriented and lost? Or would you adapt? Could you? I do enjoy a puzzle."

Enris didn't attempt to answer. "Is there more?" His voice sounded strange. "More to the world than this?"

"An excellent question. Are you sure you can bear the answer? You seem upset."

As if it hadn't intended that very result. As if it didn't watch him for every reaction, every flinch, and savor them all.

He'd learned of other worlds, other suns, other races. He'd learned there was a before, that life had been different from now.

Enris managed to laugh. "Been a while since supper," he told the creature. "So tell me, Thought Traveler. I'm curious. What is it you don't think I can bear to know?"

"That the entire universe of the Om'ray is nothing more than a speck upon Cersi. If you flew over it in the grasp of an esan until it fell dead from the sky, you would not reach its end. That if you stood upon one of the Makers and looked down on this world, you would see the mighty works of Tikitik and of Oud, and be sure only two races lived here."

Wrapping his hands around a knee, Enris leaned back and gazed at the Tikitik, who stared back with all four eyes. "If we are so insignificant," he said at last, "why does the Agreement include us?"

It surged to its feet with such abrupt violence Enris reached for his knife. But Thought Traveler only stood still, looking down at him. Its head bobbed twice. "The best question of all," it acknowledged—he thought grudgingly—then barked its laugh. "Stay alive if you can, Enris Mendolar. I enjoy our conversations."

A familiar scream filled the air and Enris ducked as an esan swooped low. Rather than snatch the Tikitik, the huge beast hovered, wing beats pummeling the Tuana with blasts of cold, dust-filled air, while Thought Traveler stepped into a basket suspended between the claws of the midlegs.

The esan dropped below the dam, all four wings rigid. Had it crashed? Enris jumped to his feet, only to stagger back as the creature reappeared, wings now vibrating. As the basket with the Tikitik rose in front of him, the creature leaned out and shouted, the words barely audible over wind and wing.

"Don't go home!"

* ✳ *

If the world of the Om'ray was a mere speck, why did it take so long to get anywhere?

Enris laughed at his own joke, then stopped. Not that his prey appeared to be disturbed by the sound, but it wasn't healthy to laugh too much alone. Not when he'd gone the best part of a day without food or drink. Not when he'd been walking in circles trying to find a path to—

Anywhere. Rayna was closest. Rayna would do. There was the small problem of an unclimbable ridge tall enough to pierce the clouds and the other small problem of the storm those clouds were carrying in his direction. And the other small problem of no shelter or vegetation to burn for heat, but . . .

He did have rocks.

And once he found one that was edible . . . he turned over the next in the pile. No opening. He tossed it aside and picked up another.

Ah. The work of an instant to shove his knife tip into the slender crack and twist it to break the Hard One apart. It wasn't neat or efficient. Enris had to pinch his nose as the creature wheezed and died in a mass of goo.

If Thought Traveler hadn't lied to him, the blue bit was what he should—or was it could?—eat. Enris poked with the knife till he found it. With a resigned shrug, he popped the lump of flesh into his mouth and chewed. Moist. That was good. As for taste? He swallowed quickly, then spat.

If it didn't kill him, he didn't care.

The corpse enticed others from their protective stillness. He waited to gather the smallest, then retreated as a boulder half his size rolled ominously close.

No need to be greedy.

He felt remarkably at peace—after all, what faced him was simply walking, albeit a great deal of it. Walking was easy, mindless. No problems to consider, no great decisions to make. Having found food, he should—

DANGER!!!

Enris dropped the rocks and pressed his hands to his head, half stunned by the power of that sending. "What—?"

DANGER!

PAINPAINPAIN

Tuana.

His family.

Without hesitation, without fear, Enris Mendolar threw himself into the M'hir, knowing only where he had to be . . .

It was like falling, inevitable, powerful, swift—like being caught by a flood and washed down a mountain—it was . . .

. . . home.

✳ ✱ ✳

Enris choked on fumes, strained to see through heavy smoke, moved only to bump into something hard. His hands groped, knew what they found.

Home. His workbench. But why the smoke? Was it the melting vat? "Father?" he shouted, *reached* at the same time. *I'm here!*

"Enris?! Look out!"

The floor split underneath and the bench hurtled away. Enris staggered but stayed on his feet.

UP!!! THIS WAY!

DANGER!

PAIN!

FEARFEAR!!!

The floor continued to move!

Enris . . . this way . . .

Coughing, he fought to *hear* that one sending among many. Everyone in Tuana was terrified, fear and pain flooding over any words. This wasn't just happening under the shop. Not daring to believe what was happening, Enris fumbled his way forward, what he touched made strange, until he found a wall and its shelves. He climbed—anything to get away from the floor.

The ceiling was no longer there. The smoke was less. He made out forms, four, clinging together on what remained of the sway-ing roof. Knew them. Jumped and grabbed and forced his way across the slanted, broken beams and wood to them.

Worin. Sobbing, mind numb. Enris swept his little brother into his arms, felt his body for injury even as he sent *encouragement*.

His father. Jorg gripped his arm, pulled them both close. *Bad time to come home.* But beneath the words, an outpouring of *love* and *relief*.

Yuhas and Caynen. No doubt who'd thought of the roof as an escape route. Enris freed one arm to press his hand to the Yena's wide shoulder. *Thank you.*

We're not safe yet. Fierce and angry. *Why are they attacking!?*

Attacking? Enris looked past Worin's head, aghast at what he saw. Buildings were tipping, sinking into the ground. Om'ray ran into the street, only to sink beneath its surface before they could scream. Wood snapped, brick crumpled, metal screamed. "The Oud—" This was Sona—

"They're reshaping under everything!" his father shouted. "The village! The fields!"

"We should get the device—what the Oud left us—" Enris

looked wildly for a way back down, not that there was any way to know where the cupboard had been. "Give it to them!"

"No. No." Jorg shook him. "The Oud came for it the day you left. That's not why they're doing this. No one knows why. We have to run—" His hurried voice changed, became the gentlest, most terrible sound of all. "Ridersel . . ."

MOTHER! WHERE ARE YOU?!!! Worin struggled in his hold, frantic. *MOTHER!!*

Yuhas moved before Enris could think, catching Jorg before his now-limp body could fall off the roof. He brushed the older Chosen's hair from his forehead, then looked up at Enris, his grim expression saying what Enris could already feel.

There was no mind there. Or life. Jorg had followed his Chosen.

There was, he realized numbly, no life anywhere but here. The sounds continued, but only of wood, brick, and metal. There were no more screams, no more sendings. Building after building was being consumed. Only the Cloisters still stood, bright and gleaming, while the ground slapped at its base and shattered its stair.

Worin gasped for breath.

What had the Adepts done to save Tuana?

Locked their doors.

"Come on," Enris said, rising to his feet, swaying to balance. "We're leaving."

"And go where?" Yuhas had his arm around his Chosen; Caynen's eyes were wide with fear, but she hadn't panicked.

The grief would hit them all later, Enris thought.

"Take hold of me," he told them. "Don't let go."

He didn't allow himself to doubt, not when the roof shuddered, not when they were a heartbeat from death.

Where would be safe?

Nowhere at the mercy of Oud. Not Grona. Not—Sona.

The Yena he knew had been a burned remnant. He couldn't trust that memory to be the same, couldn't trust the Yena themselves to welcome him back.

Not Vyna.

Somewhere they stood a chance.

Enris closed his eyes, calmed his thoughts, and concentrated on the stranger camp. A ramp led to ancient buildings, uncovered from stone. Low white buildings, all the same. He kept building on the image, imagined it in daylight, remembered the smell of that air, the feel of the ground.

Then *pushed* . . .

. . . The M'hir remembered him, sang to him, tried to distract. He clung to the others, held them despite their fear—they were four, they must stay four—as strongly as he clung to the image of *where* they had to be . . .

. . . it wasn't working. The M'hir tossed him aside, toyed with him. He lost sight, if sight was what he had, of the stranger camp. He tried to find another way out, strength bleeding from every pore, his sense of those in his care slipping away . . .

NO!

. . . There. Enris *touched* a path of less resistance, as if *here* the M'hir was tamer, more compliant. Desperate now, he *followed* . . .

. . . and felt the world against his feet again.

Worin was a dead weight in his arms. Yuhas, Caynen. They were all here . . . He shuddered with relief.

But where was here?

Dark. No. Not dark.

Glowing eyes looked back at him from every side, small and red. Some green. One winking blue. Enris gripped his knife, knew Yuhas was ready. Was it the swarm? Had he brought them from one death to another?

But it wasn't truenight . . .

Suddenly, it was bright. He squinted. Something moved, and Yuhas pounced on it. The something squeaked in protest.

Then a familiar voice exclaimed, "Enris!" and Marcus Bowman beamed at him past the arm Yuhas had wrapped around his neck. "You can do it, too?"

Chapter 17

*D*ANGER DANGER . . . DEATH!!!!

"NO!!!" Aryl heard the shout, realizing it was hers only after Naryn and Morla whirled to stare at her.

Horror filled their faces as they *heard* the sendings too. "Aryl—what—who?"

"Tuana." Naryn gripped the table, pulled herself upright. "It's Tuana!"

Carts. They'd been talking about Tuana's carts. Ziba had just gone to find Stryn Licor, whose family built carts. While they'd waited with Morla. While she'd introduced Naryn to Oswa and little Yao. While they'd smiled shy smiles.

DANGER!! cracked that peace. Voices shouted, in the meeting hall, outside; inwardly, their own sendings of shock and apprehension reverberated mind-to-mind. The exiles, through this before, were quickest to react. A bleak undertone of *fear* began to spread.

Something had to be done. Tightening her shields, Aryl concentrated and plunged into the M'hir, driving into every mind nearby. *PEACE!* a command, with all her strength. *You are safe. Sona is safe,* more gently, but not letting any elude her. *The sendings are from Tuana. Peace.*

Even as she felt Sona's fear subside, even as Oswa stared at her with tear-filled eyes, the drumbeats of *DANGERDANGER* ceased.

Oh, no. It couldn't be.

The world *shifted* toward Sona. Her awareness of *place,* her existence relative to every other Om'ray, *shifted* with it.

Everyone cried out, staggered. Someone fell.

Only Yao sat still, unaffected. She steadied her mother.

Unable to credit her sense, Aryl *reached* for Tuana and found its glow of Om'ray all but gone. A few glimmers, clustered together, their combined pull no more than Yena's. To her inner sense, Rayna was Cersi's new center, bounded by Pana, Grona, and Sona to the sun's rest, Amna and Pana to its rise. Vyna, as always, alone and beyond.

Naryn raised her head. Her eyes were huge and confused. "Where did we go? There were over six hundred of us." Morla tried to make her sit; the other pulled away and stood straighter. "Where did we go?"

Into the ground that had tried to swallow her. That had drowned the Tikitik. That had destroyed Sona . . .

"We don't know yet," Aryl said aloud. It was easier to lie with words. "We need to get everyone together." They were all running here, to be together. To be with her.

A grip on her arm. "Go," Haxel ordered grimly. "Find any survivors. I'll look after Sona."

"I've never been there—"

"Find a way. Go!"

She was right. Aryl didn't hesitate. She dove for her boots. Her hands knew what to do with them; her mind didn't have room to wonder why she needed them.

Her hands broke a fastener. Enris. He would have felt this, no matter how far away—

"Enris."

The bizarre echo stopped her cold. Had the others noticed?

"Aryl?" Yao leaned over to tug her coat. "Your pocket's talking."

So much for secrecy. Aryl pulled out the geoscanner, noticing almost in passing that its symbol was green—no Oud active nearby. Enris? Without thought she *reached*. Before she found Tuana, she found four Om'ray where none had been, where none should be. Near Sona's Cloisters.

One, beyond doubt, Enris Mendolar.

With Marcus?

They hadn't, she thought numbly, been there a moment ago. He'd learned to use the M'hir. But why go to the Human?

Marcus had said the word to get her immediate attention. She raised the 'scanner, wondering what she could possibly reply, then thumbed it off and replaced it in her pocket.

"What was that?" Naryn. Who, Aryl realized, didn't know the Strangers existed, or that Cersi was one of many worlds.

That wasn't her problem now.

Everything else was.

Sona poured in, those who had been Grona, Tuana, and Yena gathering in confusion and fear. Bern held Oran, called Aryl's name. Haxel shouted over the din, "Go!"

"Naryn, help your people."

"You're going to the tunnel—" the Tuana guessed, grabbing her own coat. "Take me with you. If this was the Oud—I have to know."

There wasn't time to argue. Aryl threw herself out the door, into the snow. She closed her eyes and cleared her thoughts, entering the M'hir.

Easier, every time.

Easiest of all, to go where she'd been before, to go to who she most wanted to see, needed to see . . .

Aryl concentrated . . .

Someone seized her arm. She tried to pull out of the M'hir, to stop the 'port, but it was too late.

. . . she found herself, with Naryn, standing in the Human's shelter.

"I told you she would come."

Marcus seemed to take Om'ray popping into sight in stride—that, or he was so glad to see her, he didn't care. "I'd been up all night. I was taking a nap." With that odd greeting, he turned to a young Om'ray lying on his bed. The child was unconscious, his leg bent in too many places. The Human began assembling his gear, muttering something in his words.

Trusting he knew what to do, Aryl looked to the others.

Who were staring at Naryn, who stared back, as if she hadn't seen the Human or their surroundings at all.

Yuhas Parth. A welcome surprise. With his Chosen.

And Enris Mendolar.

A storm gathered around him, in him. She could *taste* it, despite his shields. All the Tuana were bloody and covered in soot. The Human's white furnishings and floor were streaked red and black, marks of Om'ray tragedy. Enris stood among it all, larger than life, grimmer than death. "You."

"Enris." Naryn lifted her head. Her net had come loose; locks of hair rose to frame her pale face in red.

"Why aren't you dead?" His tone was almost conversational. Almost. Aryl could envy the Human, deaf and blind to the terrible *hate* Enris allowed to spill from his mind. "Why are you here and not dead?"

The color left Naryn's cheeks but she didn't flinch or look away. "We didn't know," a broken whisper. "The Oud found us in the tunnels—"

"The tunnels?" Yuhas' Chosen choked on the words. "You tres—you did this? You brought the Oud down on us?" She threw herself at Naryn. Yuhas caught her by the shoulders, grabbed her tight; she collapsed, sobbing, in his arms. His hand dropped to his belt, as if hunting a knife that should be there.

"So it was your fault." Enris was too calm. Blood seeped down his neck from deep scratches along his cheek and jaw. Aryl doubted he knew they were there. "So you're to blame, Naryn S'udlaat."

"Stop it," she told him, told them. This wasn't right. They were Om'ray, Tuana. They should have been glad to know they'd all survived, not snarling like scavengers over ripe carrion. There'd be time for accusations and guilt—and grief—once she was sure Sona was safe. "The Oud attacked Tuana?"

Enris frowned as he finally looked at her, as if he didn't remember who she was. "The Oud. A reshaping," he said, cold and flat. "Everything and everyone above ground is gone. Except the Cloisters."

"We should go, bring back any more survivors—"

His mouth twisted. "The Adepts are safe where they are, and those with them. There's no one else."

Bile rose in her throat.

"What do you mean, Enris?" Marcus demanded. He half stood, one hand touching the child as if he couldn't bear to leave him, his expression desperate and afraid. "Oud coming here? Hurt us next?"

Not if she could help it.

Aryl brought out her Speaker's Pendant. "Marcus, can you call them, bring them to talk to me?"

"Yes, but—"

NO!

His sending hurt; she didn't let him see it. Instead, Aryl raised an eyebrow and said coolly, "You've been away, Enris Mendolar. Things have changed."

His look to the Human and back at her was deliberate. The way his eyes then locked on Naryn and his hands became fists was not.

"Call the Oud," Aryl told Marcus.

The child, Worin Mendolar, was awake and struggling to sit before the warning lights flickered red and blue. "You don't move," Marcus told him. "The *regenerationcycle* takes time. Your leg will be fixed soon."

How a machine that looked like a tube with bumps could repair a broken bone, Aryl couldn't imagine, but she had no
trouble believing the Human. Nor did Enris, whose face
showed its first glimmer of normalcy as he knelt by his brother
and held him still. "Listen to Marcus," he said gently. "He's a
friend. You can trust him."

"But—he's not-*real*." Worin cried with an anguished effort
to squirm free.

"Be still, Worin."

"The child's right." Yuhas and his Chosen, Caynen S'udlaat,
had stayed as far from Marcus as the crowded room allowed.
Naryn apparently didn't care. "It's not-Om'ray. Not-*real*!"

Before Aryl realized what Marcus intended, he held out his
hand. "Real inside. See?"

Only good manners to touch an offered Om'ray's hand, to
accept that private contact. For Worin to do it took courage.
Enris immediately laid his over both, receiving a puzzled
glance from the Human that quickly changed to a pained grimace.

"Sorry!" Worin pulled his hand free and gestured apology.
"*Real* inside," he agreed soberly. Almost a smile. "Kind. But
different."

"Should be," Marcus managed to say. His hand was still
within Enris' grasp. He didn't try to pull free, simply waited.
And winced again.

What was Enris doing? Aryl started to object—

Which was when, with admirable timing, the lights went
through their warning change.

Enris let go. "The Oud are here," she said, almost relieved.

Yuhas pushed away from the counter. "I'm going with you."
Caynen blanched but offered no protest.

They'd played hide/seek together in the canopy. She knew
his ability as he knew hers, knew and trusted his Yena reactions. But his life was not his alone to risk. "I need you to stay
with the rest."

Naryn wrapped her scarf around her neck, her hair sliding

back and forth over her shoulders as if impatient. Marcus
stared at it. Oh, he'd have questions about that later, Aryl
thought.

If there was a later.

"Naryn—" she began.

"I want to hear for myself."

Enris was at the door, looking out the window. Muscles
worked along his jaw. Aryl remembered how she'd felt, seeing
a Tikitik for the first time after their attack on Yena. It wasn't
Om'ray to want to kill another being.

She wouldn't have minded the chance to watch one die.
Then.

Now? The Agreement was about keeping the peace. There
was no place for Om'ray to live, if that peace ended. They all
knew the hard truth. Whatever had happened to Tuana, to
Yena, to Sona mattered less than survival.

Maybe, Aryl thought wearily, this was why normal Om'ray
only remembered those whose lives and memories they could
still touch. To carry the dead into the future—how could peace
endure their weight?

"I'm ready." Marcus brushed at dirt on one sleeve. Dirt
brought through the M'hir from Tuana, in a heartbeat. Was
that more remarkable than dirt from this world, clinging to
clothing from another? He caught her gaze and smiled. It
wasn't a good smile. The Human was afraid, but would come
with her. He could call for his people and leave this world and
its troubles behind, but chose to come with her. Aryl found she
could smile after all.

Until she realized Enris had watched this small exchange,
watched and judged it, and now frowned at her.

Aryl found she liked that frown. UnChosen should pay attention. Should notice—

A hand brushed hers. *Control,* Naryn stressed. *Remember what
I showed you. Now's not the time—unless you want to risk him refusing you, too.*

Startled, she concentrated and strengthened the guard

she'd learned, suppressing the desire she hadn't felt rising closer to her surface thoughts. Too close. The last thing she needed right now was to lose herself, be a Chooser.

It was, Aryl decided firmly, the very last thing Enris would want.

Three Oud on their vehicles. Three Om'ray.

One Human.

And a great deal of snow.

The storm was over, its clouds shredded by the mountain ridges. The sun, though low, transformed the landscape. Drifts pillowed every rise; glittering white blanketed the clearing. Unlikely rounds topped nekis stalks and the towering cliff might have been hung with gauze. At any other time, or company, the sight would have taken her breath away.

At least it covered where the Oud had killed the Tikitik. Enris didn't need to see it.

The snow, however, was its own challenge. The door opened easily enough, sliding to one side, but Aryl's first step sank until snow covered her knee. She sighed inwardly and thrust her other foot into the stuff, lurching ahead to take the next step.

So much for a bold, confident stride.

The Oud vehicles, predictably, had forced their way through, leaving dark trails of exposed ground behind them. Their fabric coverings bore a thick layer of white, as if they'd sat outside during the storm, though the clear domes over their front ends had been wiped clean.

Preparing for company?

Don't trust them.

Hearing Enris again she quite liked. Thinking her a fool? Surely he remembered better than that. *I'm the Speaker.*

And would have fallen face first in the next instant if he hadn't grabbed her belt. She pulled her foot free—it had broken through some icy crust beneath the snow—and freed herself from his grip.

Annoying Tuana.

She shouldn't think of him as Tuana any more. She shouldn't think of herself as Yena. Those places, those Clans and families, their homes and shops, glows and tables and carpets and silly bits of nothing that filled cupboards and drawers until you tidied them only to find a reason to keep some of them still—all were gone from the world; to be forgotten, once no living memories remained.

As Sona would be, if she failed.

Tired of fighting the snow and her emotions, Aryl stopped short. "We see you," she said, her voice carrying in the cold.

The centermost Oud reared up, creating a plume of snow, and produced its pendant. "Sona Speaker. Here is."

The other two Oud lifted on their platforms and began tossing objects from beneath their bodies at them. Packs. Bulky Tuana-style packs. Nine large ones, well used. A small one, torn along a side. A hail of blades and tools followed, most burying themselves in the snow. The gear taken from Naryn and the others?

As if it mattered.

"That's not why I want to talk to you."

"What is? Water want? Other?"

The Oud being reasonable. The Oud being considerate, if a little late. Did these not know what had happened less than a tenth ago? Dare she ask?

Enris shifted beside her, snow creaking under his big feet. Like thunder from the sky, building to an explosion of light and fire.

She'd ask. "What happened at Tuana today?"

"Why did you destroy it and kill everyone?" Enris roared, stepping forward.

The Oud reared higher. "Whowhowho?"

Aryl drove her shoulder into him, hard enough to throw him off-balance. *Stop!* she sent desperately. *Give me a chance.*

Please, Enris, more softly. *Trust me.*

He subsided. Slightly.

"Tuana was—" she stumbled over their term, "—reshaped. Why?"

Naryn stood with Marcus. Aryl waited for the Oud to answer, hoping for a reason that wouldn't crush her new friend with the kind of guilt she carried. Hoping for a reason they could understand.

Cold. She was always cold these days. Could see the clouds from her breath meet and mingle with Enris'. The Oud spoke without breath, its limbs rubbing together to produce words. It didn't matter, Aryl told herself. They were still words.

"Balance," the Oud said finally. "Balance goodgoodgood-good. Peace."

A child without a mother lay broken in Marcus' bed. Enris stood beside her, so consumed by rage and grief it felt like her own. An entire Clan, lost. "It's not good!" she denied, her voice rising. "Oud killed Tuana's Om'ray. What could that possibly balance? It's not good. Not good!"

It hesitated, as if surprised by her anger. "Decided other. Sona Oud."

What did it mean?

"Exactly." The snow shifted as the Tikitik stood, its skin as white as its surroundings, save for the short black barbs on the outside of its arms and gleaming black orbs that were its four eyes. "I see you didn't die, Enris Mendolar."

"Day's not over," that worthy replied.

They knew one another?

Aryl glared at it. Thought Traveler was attracted to trouble like a biter to blood. "Do you know why the Oud destroyed Tuana?"

"We were in their tunnels." Naryn was at Aryl's shoulder, hair a wild cloud. "Was that why? Was it my fault?"

Thought Traveler barked his laugh. "Tuana has been reborn because of you, Apart-from-All. Did you not realize the Agreement holds the lands of Oud and Tikitik in balance?

That when you resettled Sona and welcomed the Oud—who, it must be said, had pushed rudely into these mountains before your time, but still—that the Tikitik were owed a replacement?"

It toyed with her—with them all. Like Mauro, it took pleasure from their pain and suffering. "You're lying. Why would the Oud kill so many Om'ray because a few of us came here?"

The Tikitik dipped its head, like a sly child. "Why do you think they like lists? They can't count."

The Oud Speaker flung itself from side to side, crashing into its companions. With each movement, it spoke, loudly. "Oud calculate." Thud! "More than." An Oud was tumbled from its vehicle and humped back on top, crouching low. "Less than. Extrapolate." A final thud, then it settled. "Tikitik stupid!"

"I meant no insult, Esteemed Speaker," Thought Traveler said smoothly. Its larger pair of eyes never left Aryl. "I merely educate your counterpart."

"Don't listen to it," Enris urged.

She didn't want to.

She had to.

Was it her doing?

"How did killing the Tuana—" the words were slivers of wood in her mouth, "—restore the balance?"

Thought Traveler's long toes lifted it on the snow. It pranced, more than walked, toward her. "Tuana is again Tikitik. The Lay Swamp already spreads. We have begun our planting. There will be rastis once more on the plains, homes for our mothers. Dresel for our dear Om'ray."

"What Om'ray?" Enris said harshly.

"The strongest." That sly head tilt. "The best."

Hush, she sent to Enris. "What do you mean, 'again'?"

It came close to her, fingers scooping the air. She could smell it: stale dresel, old clothes. "Did you think this the first time, Apart-from-All, that Oud and Tikitik have exchanged Clans for the sake of balance? Do you think it the last?"

"Balance good!" the Oud agreed.

Aryl's hand clenched over the pendant.

It had been her fault. All of it.

She'd stepped on a branch that couldn't hold her, led her people there, gathered the innocent Grona and Tuana to her folly. Believed she was a Speaker, a leader, that she could save everyone.

All she'd accomplished was death. "Why kill them?" Numbly. "Why kill Sona?"

"I did warn you, Apart-from-All. The Oud do not appreciate your fragile nature. They came seeking their metal, water for their industry, and found secrets from the past. Their desire made them impetuous. They reshaped to supplant us and killed Sona's Om'ray instead."

Abruptly, its face thrust at hers—she refused to pull away, even when the writhing protuberances around its mouth patted her lips and chin, tasted the tears from her eyes.

"Delicate, your flesh." This so quietly she doubted anyone else heard. "Dangerous, what lies within. I will tell you another truth, Apart-from-All. The Oud cherish what could destroy them. We are not such fools."

Then it was gone, running on top of the snow.

Aryl lifted the pendant from her neck, over her head, yanked it free of her scarf. Raised her hand and drew back her arm to throw it away.

The Oud Speaker lowered itself until its speaking limbs were barely free of the platform. "Sona Oud? Goodgoodgoodgood? Water want?"

She hesitated, her arm shaking.

Starvation. Flood. Storm.

The Tikitik stole Yena's defenses, invited what climbed in truenight to eat their flesh . . . *watched* and laughed.

The Oud dug the ground from beneath Tuana's feet . . . and seemed surprised they were upset.

The Oud "cherished" them?

"Marcus."

He pushed between her and Enris, slipped in the snow. The Tuana caught his arm to steady him. "I'm here."

"Triad First," the Oud agreed, whether in greeting or identification Aryl wasn't sure.

But it was right. The Human was the only one used to the confusion of many kinds of being, of thought. He'd said the Oud's lifecycle was different.

She lowered her voice, though no one knew how well Oud could hear. "Marcus, could they have destroyed Tuana without realizing it would kill its people? Could they make that kind of—mistake?" Enris flinched at the word. She didn't blame him.

Marcus gave her his troubled look. "We saw them kill Tikitik. I don't think by mistake. Might be," he glanced uneasily at the creatures, "might be they don't value life as we do. *Colonialsociety*—"

"Our words."

"The Oud may be less individual, more group-minded. If some Oud die, it doesn't matter to them so long as the group continues."

"They have individuals," Enris countered harshly. "They know who we are, who you are."

"Other Oud not." In his urgency to be understood, Marcus struggled to put words together. "I've see—seen Oud who work and never talk. Seen Oud who talk and decide—make decisions. There could be more kinds. *Castes*. Or some stage of lifecycle when an Oud could be an individual, at other part of life, not. Complicated life—I don't know, we didn't ask. Do you understand? But nothing like Om'ray or Human. Actions are not like Om'ray or Human. You can't think of them that way."

Aryl chewed her lower lip. If she understood him—something she hoped but couldn't be sure—then the Oud might not feel remorse or guilt. Or any other emotion she could grasp. "What can I do?" she asked hopelessly.

Marcus put his back to the Oud, faced her and the other Om'ray. "Let me talk to them."

"No! I don't know what you are," Naryn objected hotly, "but you don't speak for us. Aryl—you can't let it."

Aryl looked at Enris. His face was pale where he'd wiped away soot. Pale and hard and desperate. Anything, that expression told her. *Anything that keeps us alive.*

Marcus waited in the snow, shivering, in his not-quite-Om'ray clothes. He should have seemed the weakest here, out of place. Instead, suddenly she saw him as she thought others of his kind must: a leader of exceptional skill, confident of his abilities, experienced and brave.

Frightened, yes. But no fool.

She nodded, and the Human turned to the Oud. "Speaker. What happens to Oud who die?"

Not what she'd expected, nor, from Enris' expression, had he. Who cared about those already dead? Or the Oud's dead?

The Oud Speaker reared to answer. "Dead reshaped."

"Reshaped to what?"

The Oud rose higher, its pendant dangling from a limb. "Tikitik."

Aryl blinked. Naryn choked.

Marcus didn't appear surprised. "What do Tikitik become when they are reshaped?"

"Om'ray. Better is."

Aryl opened her mouth to protest. The Human, perceptive as always, reached back and signed her to stop. "And Om'ray?" he asked.

The Speaker rocked gently.

"What do Om'ray become, when reshaped?" Marcus persisted.

She'd been wrong to let him speak. This was madness.

"Oud. Best is."

Did he expect her—expect anyone—to listen to such nonsense? That the Oud believed the bodies of each race somehow became the other?

"Did you destroy the Tuana Om'ray to make more Oud?"

How could he ask that?

What if it were true? They'd never be safe. The Oud would surely kill them all . . .

"Oud less," the Speaker denied. "Tuana reshaped. Tikitik more."

Marcus shook his head. "I don't understand," he objected, sounding shaken for the first time. Aryl agreed. "Where are the Tuana Oud?"

"Oud reshaped." The Speaker shook its pendant vigorously. "Tikitik more. Balance."

The Oud had died, too? Some mass suicide, required to remove themselves from land that was now Tikitik?

If they expected her to feel guilt for Oud deaths, Aryl thought darkly, they should have let the Om'ray escape first.

Before the Human could ask another question, the Speaker spoke again, quickly. "Om'ray live, best is. Om'ray more, Oud more. Goodgoodgoodgood."

Ever-curious, Marcus asked, "How?"

In answer, all three Oud reared, their limbs clenched together.

And all three Om'ray cried out.

Aryl fought to keep her focus as *SOMETHING* twisted inside. Her Power, her inner sense, all that connected her to other Om'ray was being disturbed, pulled and pushed away, taken and replaced . . . until she retreated into the comfort of the M'hir and could find herself again.

Enris. She summoned him there, felt the link between them form and grow strong, Power reaching to Power. *Naryn,* she called.

No!

She ignored his objection. They were Om'ray. They had to survive.

Naryn. Clinging to her at first, then, gaining confidence. Naryn extended a link to Enris.

The M'hir churned with his *hate.* His *revulsion*!

No. Aryl refused to allow it. *The others! Worin!* Had they been—what had the Oud done?

These are Oud Torments. We're taught not to use Power near them.
Naryn's mindvoice, clear and sure. *This . . . this is why. I told you.*
They have their own Power, too different from ours. But it doesn't af-
fect us here . . . with wonder.

She could feel Enris *reaching* for his brother, for Yuhas and
Caynen, felt the three minds drawn into the M'hir, how he
held them there, safe from the Oud.

Away from her. From Naryn.

Aryl didn't waste time feeling hurt. Safe from the Oud didn't
mean safe from the M'hir. And they'd left Marcus, their own
bodies . . .

She eased herself from the M'hir, regaining cold feet and a
foul taste in her mouth.

The twisted sensation was gone. All the Oud were lying on
their vehicles.

Marcus had her by the shoulders. He gave her a shake.
"Aryl! Aryl!"

She grunted something, busy recalling the rest. "That
was—"

"Painful," Naryn supplied. "Stupid not-Om'ray."

Enris was already halfway to the shelter. Checking on his
brother or abandoning her?

Both, Aryl decided.

"Aryl!"

"I'm fine, Marcus. The Oud—" None of the words he'd
given her fit what she'd sensed from the creatures. "They did
something we could feel. Not telepathy. Not words or commu-
nication. Their presence. It was—unpleasant."

"Better now?"

"Yes."

"Good." A dismissal; the Human, unaffected, had no idea
how devastating the moment had been for the Om'ray. Something to remember, Aryl thought. "Listen to me. The reshaping. The Oud aren't talking about bodies. Not flesh. The Oud
talk about—" he waved his gloved hands around his head,
"—telepathy, parts of mind, what we not see/touch, what you

feel. They believe all connected. Om'ray. Tikitik. Oud. Same inside. *Continuum.* I need more words. *Spirit. Reincarnation. Soul. Religiousbeliefs.*" He sputtered along, frustrated. "Important to understand—"

Reading her expression, or guessing, Marcus squeezed her shoulders and gave her another, very gentle, shake. "Not important. Sorry, Aryl. What matters is what it means. The Oud need you. Value you. It's a place to start. Let me try again. Please. I want to help you. Help Enris. Help Sona."

She still held the pendant. Aryl stared down at it, then, slowly, put it back around her neck. "You've already helped, Marcus, more than you know. Stay with Naryn." She walked around him. "Speaker!"

The centermost Oud reared ever so slightly, then swayed in place. Had the disturbance affected them, too? "What is? Water want?"

Consistent creature.

Om'ray more, Oud more. She didn't understand why or how; she didn't care. Her heart began to pound. Why would it negotiate for the future of Sona, unless it needed one, too?

"We want water in the river," Aryl said firmly. "Can you do that?"

"Can. Not all. Oud some."

"Sona to have more than Oud." That, for its ability to calculate. In case it thought she didn't know about the second emptied river.

The Oud rose a little more. "Yesyesyesyes. Oud some. Sona more than."

Now for what was important. Aryl brought out the Human's geoscanner, the device that carried voices, too. The Oud stilled. "Sona is not like other Clans," she told it. "We have friends who see into your tunnels. Friends who will warn us if you start to reshape beneath our feet." Not that she knew Marcus could, but neither did the Oud. They had to respect the Strangers' more advanced technology. "If you do, we will leave."

"Not go! Not go!" The Speaker flailed its pendant. "Agreement stands. Oud not reshape village. Oud not reshape fields. Om'ray grow. Om'ray more than. Oud more than. Goodgoodgoodgood!"

Not good enough. "You will not tunnel under us," Aryl insisted. "You'll remove the tunnels you put there. Without—" she added hastily, "—damaging the surface."

A considering pause. "Oud stay. Fix bridge."

It was negotiating.

Keeping her voice calm, Aryl made her own offer. "We don't need the bridge. You can stay here. Hunt for the Hoveny. The Makers." She gestured toward the cliff excavation, then to her feet. "You will not tunnel under us."

"Oud stay here. Sona Speaker stay here."

About to object, forcefully, Aryl swallowed. By the Agreement, the two Speakers had to meet and talk.

She smiled her mother's smile. "I stay with my people." She held up the geoscanner. "The Triad First can contact me for you. I'll come here."

"Goodgoodgoodgood." The Oud dropped flat. The three vehicles backed and bounced away, retracing the scar they'd left in the snow.

Aryl held her breath until they were out of sight, then let it out in a ragged sigh. "No bridge." But so much more, if she was right. Safety. The Oud out from underneath. A chance to recover. Water.

Life.

Marcus patted her shoulder. "Did your best. Fine job. I'll check on the child. Get warm." His exaggerated shiver turned into a real one.

She watched him stagger through the snow, trying to use Enris' deeper footprints though his stride wasn't long enough. "You should go inside, Naryn," she suggested, turning to the other. She wasn't ready to join the rest. Her hands trembled as she tucked the pendant inside her coat, but it wasn't the cold.

Now we know. The sending was emotionless; Naryn's hair lay flat, like ribbons of blood. *The Oud killed the Tuana Om'ray because you wanted to stay here. They will let the rest of us live because you've promised we'll stay.*

Aryl accepted the guilt, drew it deep inside. *Yes.*

When the others know, they'll hate you more than Enris hates me. Are you prepared for that? Are you prepared for his hate?

"My people will understand—" she whispered. As for Enris . . .

"Understand what? Your ability to *push* yourself and others through space? How you've included that—that *thing* in dealings between Speakers? Why you took it on yourself to set the terms for all our lives?" The words were harsh, but Naryn's eyes swam with compassion. "I understand, Aryl. I do. We're the same. I know what it is to be set apart by my Power, by what I've done. And you've done what's right. I believe in you. Those of greater Power must care for those of less. We must use our abilities to lead. But there's a price."

"I don't want to lead—I never have."

I have always been drawn to Power. An undertone of deep *affection. I've always known who possessed strength. You are the most powerful Om'ray I have ever sensed, Aryl Sarc, heart-kin. Let me help with your burden. With your Choice. Only the most powerful Candidate is fit for your Choice. Enris must be yours.*

"No!" To what, Aryl didn't know. Confusion warred with desire. She had to think, to know what was right, to know what to say to her people. Enris . . . his family had just died. How could she feel . . . how could she want . . . "No," this more calmly. "There's time—time for any of that. We have to meet. Explain. Help."

"It won't be an easy Choice. He could refuse you."

Something Naryn knew from experience. His refusal had cost her everything, including her life and that of her unborn, if they couldn't find a way to sever that link.

"No."

"He's the only one you want. The one you trust." Soft. Implacable. "The one who knows you. Who better?"

This wasn't how it was supposed to be. How she was supposed to be. Cold. Alone. Afraid.

Her people loved her. They wouldn't hate her. They couldn't. They'd understand.

Enris was her friend. He couldn't hurt her. When he was healed, happy again, he'd . . .

She could wait . . . she had to wait . . .

A wisp of hair slipped across her forehead, every strand a separate sensation. The chill of her toes and fingertips burned with sudden fire. Her next breath carved a channel through her throat and body, intricate and deep.

Not here. Not now. Aryl, wait! The dark centers of Naryn's eyes reflected the snow. *He won't accept you now. We have to prepare, be ready. You could both fail. Hold on.*

"I'm trying . . ." A hoarse, futile whisper. Aryl dropped to her knees, her hands buried in the cold, cold unable to stop the heat rising inside her. The *DESIRE!*

"Aryl?"

His voice.

NO! She threw herself away from him, from everything, launching herself into the M'hir, seeking safety, seeking control. Aryl *pushed* . . .

. . . and found herself on a wide branch, gazing out over the canopy.

Chapter 18

THE CANOPY'S GREEN AND BROWN made a living carpet, flowing to the mighty rastis of the Sarc grove. Flocks of flitters wheeled below; lingering clouds covered the sun. Slapping a biter, Aryl drew a deep breath of air that was as air should be: moist and warm and full of fragrance. The last time she'd been here, it had been with young Joyn, sailing fiches. Before running from the strangers.

She'd removed her Sona outercoat, willing to sweat in the inner. The rains might be over for the day, but that only made the biters worse. Her knife was free and in her hand, having just dealt with an overly bold stinger. Home, she thought, taking another deep breath.

Daughter. Taisal's greeting held an undertone of *threat.*

Home, indeed. *Mother,* Aryl acknowledged, her reply through the M'hir holding them together. *Are you well?*

You shouldn't be here.

I'll leave soon. Before firstnight. She had no interest in feeding the canopy's hunters. Until then . . . Aryl feasted her eyes on what was, beyond doubt, the most beautiful part of Cersi.

There are none for your Choice in Yena.

Which wasn't true. Aryl's inner sense had found two, from

their direction both inside the Yena Cloisters, but she didn't argue. *Haven't the Tikitik rebuilt the village?*

We are patient.

They were prisoners. Aryl kept in her pity. Taisal and the others had picked their path. Still . . .

Tuana. Sona. Do you know what's happened?

I know what you've done. Fury mixed with fear. *All of it. Did you think you could change the face of the world and no one would die?*

How old was the grove? Aryl wondered for the first time. How many times had it been destroyed and regrown? How many times had Yena been Oud, then Tikitik, then Oud . . . with Om'ray lives the cost?

Do you think we can leave the world as it is, Mother, she sent, *and live?*

Taisal listened. She knew it. And heard. The M'hir eased between them, if only slightly. *We do what we must for our people.*

Yes. Her people. Aryl thought of them all, pictured each of the Yena exiles for her mother. *They've done well.*

Too well, she realized suddenly. There couldn't have been a better group to bring Sona back to life. Beyond their Talent and Power, they had all the knowledge they needed, the strength and courage and drive to take any challenge, even a Birth Watcher. Given a chance, nothing would stop them, if they were together.

Her sense of Taisal faded, as if her mother had followed that thought and tried now to slip away. Aryl sent Power through their link to hold it.

How did you pick us, Mother? It wasn't just those with Forbidden Talent. How did you decide who to exile?

Taisal fought free, began to vanish. But then, ever-so-faint, came her answer.

We dreamed.

The branch on which she sat was larger and stronger than any of the stalks grown at Sona, the nekis itself a mountain by comparison. A frond from the neighboring rastis crossed over her head, seeking light. As for light . . . it was time. Standing on her toes, Aryl ran her fingers along the soft gray down of its underside. A farewell.

The branch swayed and she staggered to regain her balance. The thick Sona boots.

She bent to take them off.

"Won't you need those?"

Enris. Suddenly *there,* in front of her. Like turning on a glow in the dark.

He glanced down and sat quickly, hands grabbing hold of the branch. "Why did I think cliffs were bad?"

Aryl frowned at him. "Why are you here?"

"You Called me."

She hadn't. She'd quenched the slightest urge. Which had been, she realized desperately, much easier before he arrived. "I didn't. Go away."

The annoying Tuana merely made himself comfortable. "I came to bring you home. It's getting dark."

"This is home," Aryl told him. "This is what I am—nothing else. Not their leader. Not a Speaker. Just me, here. Nothing else."

He made a noncommittal sound, and shooed a biter interested in his bare arm.

No coat. Clean clothes. Mended scratches. His hair shone. Aryl narrowed her eyes. "You used the 'fresher." She felt itchy under her damp coat.

"Worin needs to stay with Marcus. Yuhas took the rest back to Sona. To meet those coming from Sona," he corrected. "My guess is Haxel wants to know about the new arrivals."

"What will they say about—about how you—Enris, we can't let them tell the others about moving through the M'hir, not until they understand the dangers!"

"Oh, I'd say they all know what we can do now. Stop worrying. Marcus warned us until his face turned blue, and no one else knows how until we show them." The big Tuana shifted and frowned. "You could have run somewhere with padding."

"I didn't," Aryl said stiffly, "run."

" 'Port, then." His lips quirked. "In order to run. From me."

"Go away." She walked out to the tip of the branch, feeling it dip under her weight, riding the motion.

Then it dipped a great deal more.

Aryl whirled around. "Stay where you are."

Enris stopped, knees partially bent, arms out and tipping from side to side. He looked ridiculous. And anxious.

And oddly determined. "Come here, then."

"No."

He took another step, almost losing his balance, seriously risking hers.

"Do you want me to fall?" she complained. "Stop!"

An eyebrow lifted. "Thought Yena don't fall."

"They do if a clumsy oversized Om'ray fool shakes the branch! Stop!" Quickly, when he raised his foot.

He was impossible. Aryl took three quick steps. "There."

"Closer."

"Move back."

Enris looked over his shoulder, teetered alarmingly, then eased toward the trunk, where the branch was wider and stronger. One step. Two. A slip and Aryl's heart pounded. "Be careful!"

Another two steps put him on better footing. "Your turn," he challenged. "If you can."

"I live here, remember?" Aryl began to walk easily along the branch, Sona boots or not.

Without warning, Enris stepped forward again, meeting her where the branch was not wide enough to pass.

She'd forgotten how tall he was.

"This is no place for games, Tuana," Aryl warned him. "You'll fall."

"Then you'll have to catch me." He held out his hand. "You will, won't you, Aryl Sarc?"

This wasn't about falling or catching.

She couldn't move. Could hardly breathe. "Don't." The urge within her was rising, nameless and wild.

Enris didn't smile, didn't laugh. His face was weary with grief, his eyes unutterably sad. "Don't what, Chooser of my heart?" he asked softly. "Don't reach for the only joy I can feel in this world? Don't hope, in case I fail? Some risks are worth—"

Aryl stopped his mouth with hers, his *taste* ending all thought. Her right hand found his arm, trailed the rise of muscle and bone, reveled in the fine hair and warmth of his skin, until their fingers met and intertwined, until their palms met and . . .

. . . Power sought Power, mind sought mind.

Found!

Fire struck metal and took away its shape. Water found slope and carved its own channel. The M'hir Wind screamed through chasms and split rock, reached the canopy and tore limbs, found the rastis and freed its wings to soar in a sky . . .

. . . a sky of heartbreaking color and movement and life, as if every moment of happiness had been tossed too high to reach, waiting until they could lift each other there . . . until two . . .

. . . became one.

Interlude

A ND fell.

Not fair, Enris complained as he tried in vain to grab one of the thousands of branches whipping by his face. Just when . . .

. . . the M'hir took him, spun him about, and left him . . .

. . . standing. He was standing. That was good.

And being held. He looked down, bemused to find Aryl clinging to him. That was better.

Cautiously, he probed at the new *something* inside. Definitely not the kind of link he'd shared with his mother.

This was—this was—

"You made me fall." Aryl pulled back to glare at him. "I don't believe it. You knocked us off the branch and made me fall."

"I was falling, too," Enris pointed out, trying not to smile. He also tried not to dwell on the indignant swell of her lower lip. Briefly. Then he leaned down to explore it more thoroughly with his own.

Which found her fingers. "We're in Sona," she told him. Her fingers traced his mouth then followed his jaw. "And this, my dear Chosen, is not allowed." The lightest imaginable slap. "Yet."

Chosen. The word sang along his nerves. The reality was like having her nestled by his side, instead of walking to a makeshift door to look out. The ache and need he'd managed to ignore might have never existed, save for how wonderful he felt right now. And how much more wonderful he planned to feel as soon as possible.

Aryl went out the door.

That wasn't right.

Enris followed. "What do you mean . . . yet?"

✳ ✳ ✳

"You two stay with me. That's the way it is."

There were more Tuana here, including his uncle's family, a discovery that at any other time would have occupied his every thought.

Today? Enris looked at his cousin Ezgi, who shrugged, then back at Yuhas. "But we're Joined." He liked saying it. Loved feeling it. Every breath contained his awareness of Aryl, her joy to be aware of him. It drove the pain and grief to the shadows of his mind, like the rising of the sun.

He didn't like being told he couldn't go any closer than that feeling until Husni and the others said so.

His friend laughed. "We all go through it." A fleeting *sadness*. "Your father endured me while I wanted for Caynen. It's the least I can do for you."

"How long?" It had been, to his mind, too long already.

"Until both are ready. I'm told Sarcs are—" Yuhas looked embarrassed. "They're unpredictable."

"Giving you trouble, Yuhas?" asked Galen sud Serona as he entered and put down a tray of steaming cups.

"I'm not," his son said pointedly. "And I've waited longer." This with a sigh.

His father's older brother. The resemblance was there if he looked for it, Enris thought. The kindness of the eyes, the careful strength of the hands, the patience. He'd gone to Galen for the wood of his bench. He'd gone to him when Kiric slipped from his mind, unable to share that burden with his parents.

"I—" What could he say now? Their Clan had been destroyed.

How dare he be so ridiculously happy? Enris fought for words to explain, to apologize, and failed.

Galen's hand pressed his shoulder. *It's all they ever wanted for you.* Aloud, "Find joy, Enris sud Sarc."

"Just not yet," Yuhas added hastily.

Chapter 19

ODD.

    Aryl didn't open her eyes, unwilling to lose the scent. Though how could there be dresel cake in Sona?

. . . because it's the best day of your life, Daughter . . .

Mother?

Silence . . . she must have imagined the voice.

Though when did the pile of blankets the Sona called a bed become one, so comfortable her body was unwilling to move?

And that sound. A wysp, its three voices trilling an end to truenight. Nothing sang in Sona but the wind.

Wait . . . that was a giggle.

Her hair *moved* across her face.

Aryl brushed it away. A breeze.

Her hair *moved* again, this time slapping her cheek.

Not a breeze.

Another giggle.

Aryl sat up suddenly.

"I thought you'd never open your eyes." Seru's sparkled like fresh leaves in a sunbeam; her smile dimpled both cheeks. "Honestly, Cousin. I know Sarcs are different but two days?" She was sitting cross-legged on the end of Aryl's bed. Her black hair, thicker, shinier, peeked over one shoulder, then spilled forward in a flood. "I think poor Enris is going to burst."

Enris . . . ?

Here! with a rush of *joy* and *longing* and *impatience* and . . .

Hush! she replied, trying to catch her breath.

I've been hushed all this time . . . along with images of years passing, harvests being harvested, children growing to adulthood, rocks weathering . . . *I've suffered!* with distinct *glee*.

"Ezgi pesters me, too," Seru said matter-of-factly. "Just tell him Husni's on her way."

Husni . . .

I heard!!! Wild *excitement*.

He heard? Aryl frowned, very slightly. *We're going to have to talk about privacy, my dear Chosen.*

I'm all for privacy . . . images of frankly incredible beds, fields of fragrant grass, even a brief glimpse of a wide branch, quickly dismissed for a simple blanket on snow. *Can we be private now?*

Hair caressed her cheeks and slipped around her neck. Opinionated stuff.

Seru giggled and bounced closer. "How do you feel? I feel—I feel wonderful."

Feel. About to say she felt rested, if a little confused, Aryl stopped. "I feel—I've never felt like this." It was true. Her body was aglow with strength. The accustomed aches, including the one in her left elbow, were gone. She wasn't hungry, or tired, or cold. But she was, she discovered, looking down, different. "I'm lumpy."

Seru pressed her hands against her own new breasts. "Aren't they wonderful? And we've hips, too!"

"So long as they don't interfere," Aryl muttered to herself.

Show me and I'll tell you . . .

HUSH! she sent, feeling heat suffuse her face from eyebrows to throat. And elsewhere.

Enris, wisely, didn't comment. Aryl smiled to herself.

"Is it wrong?" Seru leaned forward, her smile gone. "To be

so happy? All those Om'ray, dead. Naryn and the rest—they're being brave. Most of them. But I feel—" another giggle burst out, rekindling the smile, "—I just can't feel guilty or sad."

"Don't try." Myris stepped through the door, followed by Husni. "Your happiness is a gift to all of us. If there's a future, it's here, with you four."

"There's a future," Aryl said, making it a promise.

How you glow, her aunt sent softly.

"I will have bathing!" Husni declared. "It's bad enough you, young Sarc, had to go off and Join away from everyone else. At least you had the sense to come home to commence! Now. There will be respect for tradition if I have to hold the both of you down myself!"

Seru peeled herself off the bed. "Yes, Husni."

Aryl's hair twitched with annoyance. It didn't help that she could *feel* Enris laughing. "There isn't water to waste—" the words died in her throat as Ziba came through the door with her mother, Taen. Both held a cup in one hand, a cloth in the other.

Then Veca and Juo. Morla and Weth. Oswa and little Yao hovered in the doorway until Haxel swept them both through with her.

Naryn and Caynen.

Oran.

The rest of the Tuana: Menasel and Beko, Cien and Lymin, the sisters and their mother, Stryn.

All wore their best, or what they could find to be their best. All held a cup and cloth. They formed a generally solemn semicircle before the beds, though Yao giggled and Ziba couldn't stand still.

"Bathing." Husni ordered. Her face wrinkled in a smile. "Now, show us yourselves."

Some rituals, Aryl grumbled to herself, she'd have gladly left behind. But they looked so expectant . . . she stood, dropping the blanket as Seru did the same.

Nods. More giggles. Smiles of approval. Weth squinted but managed a smile, too.

"He'll be happy." This from Naryn.

Aryl's hair picked that moment to express its own opinion, lifting into the air, sliding over her shoulders, generally misbehaving. She would, she vowed as she tried in vain to hold it back, be using a metal net.

Still, her hands lingered on it. There was something about the stuff. No longer hair, really. From pale brown, it had lightened to a red gold. Thicker, longer.

A tendril wrapped around her wrist.

Annoying.

"Get on with it, Husni," Haxel said. "Or those lovesick oafs will break their way out of the meeting hall." There was an unusually broad smile on her face. The others, even Oran, laughed.

Aryl picked up the wristband she'd taken off before going to sleep. Before becoming what she was and would be. She slipped it over her wrist and ran her fingers over its smooth lovely design. *Enris . . .*

Here. Always.

She smiled to herself. *There's to be a bath . . .*

Not entirely mock dismay. *How long will that take?*

It doesn't matter, Chosen of my heart, she sent, with all the *love* and *excitement* and *joy* she felt. *We have the rest of our lives.*

With a roar of laughter, the Om'ray of Sona soaked washcloths in cups of melted snow and rushed forward to scrub their newest Chosen.

I could help with that . . .

Soon.

Chapter 20

ARYL PRESSED HER HANDS against the door. "I don't know about this."

Enris squinted through a dirty window. "Ziba dreamed it."

"That's not to say she's right. The Adepts already tried, you know."

She felt his *encouragement*, along with the nip of *dare you* that hadn't been affected one bit by their Joining.

The Cloisters was the last piece of Sona's puzzle. Water flowed down the river, if so far a mere trickle easily jumped. Spring might bring more. They'd learned how to open the mound doors and rebuilt snug homes for every family, including the Tuana.

The nightmares came less often.

It helped that the Oud collapsed their tunnel without fuss. In fact, it might never have been there at all. They might be alone . . .

Marcus knocked on the metal. "What kind of lock?"

. . . Or not. She glanced at their friend, persistently curious. So far, he'd kept his kind away. They'd been, he said, disturbed by what had happened at Tuana. They'd wanted to remove him from the Oud. He'd refused.

"If we knew, it wouldn't be a problem."

Though Enris was right. Ziba had given them a clue of sorts. She'd dreamed only those of Sona could work the door mechanism.

Aryl caressed the round firmness below her breasts. *Little one, it's up to you.*

She leaned against the door, and applied the *twist* of thought Naryn had taught her.

And with no more fuss than that, the great doors of the Cloisters turned open in welcome.

And Sona was once more a Clan.

Epilogue

T HE ONLY LIGHT SHONE above a beige desk. There were other beige desks, rows upon rows of desks, but only this one was in use tonight.

On this desk, on all the desks, were stacks of glittering cubes and disks. Records from hundreds of worlds, data from thousands of research teams. Expectations, ramifications, explanations, excuses, pleas.

Centered under the only light, on this desk, lay something else.

A solitary sheet of plas, covered in handwriting, entitled: "Hoveny Concentrix Prospect 893ZE28L (Cersi: Site Four) Upgrade Request."

Hands entered the light, thin, scaled, delicate of finger and touch. They bent the sheet exactly in half, creased the fold neatly, then in half again, creased. One last time.

Then turned out the light.

The Om'ray of Cersi

(Note: Names shown as first encountered in the story.)

YENA CLAN:
 Adrius sud Parth (Member of Yena Council)
 Ael sud Sarc (Chosen of Myris)
 Alejo Parth (Seru's brother)
 Andace Vendan
 Aryl Sarc
 Barit sud Teerac (Bern's father, Chosen of Evra)
 Cader Sarc
 Cetto sud Teerac (Member of Yena Council, Chosen of Husni, Bern's great-grandfather)
 Chaun sud Teerac (Chosen of Weth)
 Costa sud Teerac (Aryl's brother, Chosen of Leri)
 Dalris sud Sarc (Taisal's grandfather, Unnel's father, Chosen of Nela)
 Ele Sarc (Nela's great-grandmother)
 Evra Teerac (Bern's mother)
 Ferna Parth (Seru's mother)
 Fon Kessa'at (Son of Veca)
 Ghoch sud Sarc (Chosen of Oryl)

Gijs sud Vendan (Chosen of Juo)
Haxel Vendan (First Scout)
Husni Teerac (Bern's great-grandmother)
Joyn Uruus (Son of Rimis)
Juo Vendan
Kayd Uruus (Son of Taen)
Kiric Mendolar
Lendin sud Kessa'at (Chosen of Morla)
Leri Teerac
Mele sud Sarc (Aryl's father, Chosen of Taisal)
Morla Kessa'at (Council Member, Veca's grandmother)
Myris Sarc (Taisal's sister)
Nela Sarc (Taisal's grandmother)
Oryl Sarc
Pio di Kessa'at (Adept)
Rimis Uruus (Joyn's mother)
Rorn sud Vendan (Chosen of Haxel)
Seru Parth (Aryl's cousin)
Sian d'sud Vendan (Adept, Member of Yena Council)
Syb sud Uruus (Kayd and Ziba's father, Chosen of Taen)
Taen Uruus (Kayd and Ziba's mother)
Taisal di Sarc (Aryl's mother, Adept, Speaker for Yena)
Tikva di Uruus (Adept, Member of Yena Council)
Tilip sud Kessa'at (Fon's father, Chosen of Veca, née Sarc)
Till sud Parth (Seru's father, Scout, Chosen of Ferna)
Troa sud Uruus (Joyn's father, Chosen of Rimis)
Unnel Sarc (Taisal's mother)
Veca Kessa'at (Fon's mother)
Weth Teerac
Yorl sud Sarc (Taisal's great-uncle, Member of Yena Council)
Ziba Uruus (Daughter of Taen)

TUANA CLAN:

Beko Serona

Caynen S'udlaat

Cien Serona (Ezgi's mother, Runner)

Clor sud Mendolar (Ridersel's uncle, once of Amna, née Prendolat)

Dama Mendolar (Ridersel's mother, Member of Tuana Council)

Deran Edut

Enris Mendolar

Eran Serona

Eryel S'udlaat

Ezgi Serona (Runner)

Galen sud Serona (Chosen of Cien, Runner, Jorg's brother)

Gelle Licor

Geter Licor

Irm Lorimar (Mauro's brother)

Jorg sud Mendolar (Enris' father, Chosen of Ridersel)

Josel Licor (Netta's sister, Runner)

Kor sud Lorimar (Chosen of Menasel, née Edut)

Lymin Annk (Runner)

Mauro Lorimar (Irm's brother)

Menasel Lorimar (Mauro's cousin)

Mirs sud S'udlaat (Chosen of Eryel)

Naryn S'udlaat

Netta Licor (Josel's sister, Runner)

Olalla Mendolar (Enris' cousin)

Ral Serona (Enris' cousin)

Ridersel Mendolar (Enris' mother)

Sive sud Lorimar

Sole sud Serona (Speaker for Tuana)

Stryn Licor (Josel and Netta's mother, Runner)

Suen sud Annk (Chosen of Lymin, née S'udlaat, Runner)

Tai sud Licor (Chosen of Stryn, Runner, once of Amna)

Traud Licor

Tyko Uruus

Worin Mendolar (Enris' brother)
Yuhas sud S'udlaat (Chosen of Caynen, née Parth)

GRONA CLAN:

Bern sud Caraat (Chosen of Oran, née Teerac)
Cyor sud Kaar (Member of Grona Council)
Efris Ducan (Member of Grona Council, Grona Speaker)
Emyam sud Caraat (Member of Grona Council)
Gura Azar (Member of Grona Council)
Hoyon d'sud Gethen (Grona Adept, Chosen of Oswa)
Kran Caraat (brother of Oran)
Lier Haon (Member of Grona Council)
Mysk Gethen (Member of Grona Council)
Oswa Gethen (Yao's mother)
Oran di Caraat
Yao Gethen

VYNA CLAN:

Etleka Vyna
Daryouch Vyna
Fikryya Vyna
Jenemir Vyna
Nabrialan Vyna
Tarerea Vyna (High Councillor)